P9-CCS-641

SEAPUIT SEAWOLVES

CAPE MARLIN BASEBALL LEAGUE

"Patrick Robinson is a marvelous writer
and he really loves baseball. *Slider* will make you laugh
and touch your heart. I loved it.
GO SEAWOLVES!"

—LOU MERLONI,
Boston Red Sox

SLIDER

ALSO BY PATRICK ROBINSON

One Hundred Days
(with Admiral Sir John "Sandy" Woodward)

True Blue

Nimitz Class

Kilo Class

H.M.S. Unseen

U.S.S. Seawolf

The Shark Mutiny

PATRICK ROBINSON

HarperCollins*Publishers*

SLIDER. Copyright © 2002 by Patrick Robinson. All rights reserved. Printed in the United States of America. No part of this book may be used or reproduced in any manner whatsoever without written permission except in the case of brief quotations embodied in critical articles and reviews. For information, address HarperCollins Publishers Inc., 10 East 53rd Street, New York, NY 10022.

HarperCollins books may be purchased for educational, business, or sales promotional use. For information, please write: Special Markets Department, HarperCollins Publishers Inc., 10 East 53rd Street, New York, NY 10022.

FIRST EDITION

Designed by Elliott Beard

Library of Congress Cataloging-in-Publication Data is available upon request.

ISBN 0-06-051026-9

02 03 04 05 06 ❖/RRD 10 9 8 7 6 5 4 3 2 1

*This book is respectfully dedicated to
the Three Amigos—Arnold, Mo, and Art—who
kept our little corner of the Cape League
flourishing, down all the years . . .
just for the love of the game.*

SLIDER

1

June 3

At 5 A.M. the sun had not yet risen over the long winding Bayou Lafourche. But it was light, and two hundred yards from the house Jack could see the two great Southern oaks, draped in Spanish moss, guarding the western bank. The sun came up right between them at this time of year, and the square of sky, framed by the giant trees, was turning a deep ocher in color. It was already hot, and very still, here in the sullen morning twilight of the Louisiana marshes. Jack Faber was not altogether unhappy about his forthcoming journey to the cooler North. He had never left Louisiana before. Except to a half-dozen neighboring ballfields in Texas and Mississipi.

In the distance, across the undulating land, he could hear a big flock of snow geese preparing for flight, and closer to home, there was the endless throb of the drilling rigs of the Louisiana Oil and Gas Corporation, driving deep below the brackish water, with its teeming wildlife, in search of natural gas. Modern man had not yet found the time to make a serious mess of the vast natural sweep of the silent marshes in this part of the Mississippi Delta, but right now, here in the sugarcane fields owned by the Fabers, he was doing his level best.

Jack stood on the screened porch of the wooden farmhouse, drinking coffee, staring out toward the bayou. At his feet was the big white sports bag of St. Charles College, with its emblem of crossed baseball bats beneath a royal crown, set in dark red. Jack Faber was extremely proud of that bag. And in turn, St. Charles College was proud of him. He was the best right-handed pitcher they'd ever had.

Which was a considerable achievement. There was a superb baseball program in place at St. Charles that, for a small, remote university of only six thousand students, punched out an annual record well beyond its weight. To baseball in the far South, St. Charles College was like Notre Dame to football in the Midwest—ferociously competitive and nationally renowned. Jack Faber had been touted by all the good schools in the area, Louisiana State, Tulane, Southwest Louisiana, but in the end he had settled for the feisty, 180-year-old university, set just eight miles along the bayou from his home near Lockport.

They awarded him a baseball scholarship, which saved the family a lot of money they did not have. And the short distance from Lockport meant he could get home often to help his dad out with the farm. Also his dad could come and watch him play. A distance much farther was always questionable for Ben Faber, because his battered blue 1981 Chevrolet might not make it.

Despite his powerful build, on a six-foot two-inch frame, Jack Faber was a shy, introspective boy of twenty. He was deeply intimidated by people he did not know well, and it had taken him weeks to become accustomed to the grandeur of the stone-built halls of St. Charles. But no one who was at the Chevaliers field for the opening game against their arch rivals, ever forgot the first few minutes of his debut. Jack Faber sent down the first three Southwestern hitters with eleven pitches. A couple of foul-backs for an 0-and-2 count was the closest the Ragin' Cajuns came to sniffing the ball in the first inning.

In seven two-hit innings that day, Jack Faber produced a flamethrower of a fastball, a curve that drove the Cajuns mad with frustration, a change-up of baffling pace, and an occasional slider which was just about unhittable. Jack Faber walked to the mound that day as a soft-talking unknown freshman in a university founded on heroes. When he came off after seven he was greeted with a standing ovation.

St. Charles College was built in 1824 by the French General Hugo de Fontainebleau, who had been wounded at the battle at the crossroads of Quatre Bras, then trampled in the final cavalry charge of the Scots Greys at Waterloo the following day. The general, recovered from his wounds, but unable to face living in a France dominated by England, had packed his worldly goods and sailed for the Gulf of Mexico and the French-speaking part of south Louisiana.

Those goods included a trunkload of gold ransacked from a Belgian duke, via his wife, whom the general had also ransacked. It was this plundered wealth which had purchased the land and built the school. A mark of the general's self-esteem was located right outside the main building of St. Charles College, where there was a life-size bronze statue of the great man on his battle charger, the two of them mounted on a massive granite plinth which bore the words GENERAL HUGO DE FONTAINEBLEAU, SOLDIER AND SCHOLAR, FOUNDER OF ST. CHARLES COLLEGE, CAST IN BRONZE AND ERECTED HERE 1821. The university itself was not completed until three years later. General Hugo had his priorities.

One of the great traditions of the school, aside from its baseball, was an annual black-tie dinner, by invitation only, held on May 5 to honor the anniversary of the death of Napoleon in 1821. The new strikeout king from the bayous made the dinner in his first year, and they invited his father as well.

Jack's first two seasons at St. Charles were of such impact he had been scouted by no fewer than six coaches from America's leading College Baseball League, the one on Cape Marlin off the coast of New England, where the best young ballplayers in the United States have spent their summers for more than fifty years.

Which was why, broadly, the sophomore Jack Faber was now standing around drinking coffee in the dark green dawn of this hot, muggy June morning waiting for his father to fire up the Chevy and hit the road, 1,600 miles to New England, and the best baseball of his life. Reputations were won and lost on Cape Marlin, which, for nine weeks in the high summer of the year, is besieged by Major League scouts. There was a lot riding on the performance of the 1981 Chevy during the next three days, but Ben Faber had been working on it all week. He had changed the tires, changed the oil, put in a new battery, and checked all the levels. "She'll get us up there," he had pronounced on the previous evening. "No trouble."

And now Jack could see the familiar hickory-strong figure of his father striding around the outside of the little house. He wore a plaid shirt and jeans, with an Atlanta Braves baseball cap and high, quilted leather cowboy boots. Ben always wore boots, as did Jack, just in case he stepped on one of those black king snakes that sometimes lurked around the backyard. You had to be careful of the wildlife around here. There were a lot of Southern water snakes, and Jack had seen a big old alligator cruising out in the swamp, on the edge of the bayou just a few days ago.

"Hey, Jack," called his dad. "Bags in? All set? I just closed up the barn . . . Charlie's here in the morning . . . slam the door locked, willya . . . we're on the road."

He was a big man, an inch taller than Jack, and built like a fire truck. They had the same mop of dark hair, and the same slightly freckled complexion, cornflower blue eyes, and wide smile. But father and son did not look in any way alike. Jack's face was altogether more refined. He could have been a bank clerk or even a law student. Ben Faber was an unmistakable, deeply tanned Louisiana farmer, the years of work in the cane fields precluding his body from carrying one ounce of fat. He was a cheerful man, but there was a sadness about him since the loss of his wife five years previously.

Nonetheless, he still worked physically hard at the age of forty-three, and he lived with a deep yearning that Jack should make it as a Major League pitcher, hopefully with the Braves. The boy was, he knew, a tough kid, with no airs about him. He had, as yet, no concept of the world beyond the pitcher's mound, but Jack carried with him a thoughtful quality, and he harbored no malice about the country poverty of his childhood and youth. He was patient both on and off the mound. In many ways he was every ex-pitcher's son, every father's rookie.

Jack climbed into the front seat of the car. Ben slid the keys into the ignition and kicked over the engine, which coughed, recovered, coughed some more, then died. They were both used to this. And they shouted in unison, "STRIKE ONE!" Then Ben spun the engine over one more time, and this time it coughed, backfired loudly, coughed again, and died. "STRIKE TWO!" they yelled. Once more Ben stepped up to the plate and hit the starter, and the ancient Chevy fired, roaring, belching fumes from the exhaust. "BASE HIT!"

Jack tuned into band 1490, KEUN, country music, news, and sports. Ben slipped the Chevy into gear, and they rolled over the light sandy soil, across the first few yards of their long journey to the Northeast of the United States. They drove out along the track around the house and then past the big barn. Right in front of the long, straight planks of the wall, Jack could see the tractor front tire hanging down from the tree, sixty feet and six inches from the center of the dirt mound his father had built eleven years previously.

They both glanced over at the old practice ground as they passed. But the memories were different. Ben saw a little boy with the oil-smooth action of a major leaguer at the age of twelve. Jack saw a pile of dirt on which he had nearly killed himself, throwing long into the night, in terrible summer heat, beneath a big light, which his father had fixed up on the barn wall. He remembered hating it all when he was younger, but he also knew he had never asked his father if he could quit. Because, like all real pitchers, deep down he *wanted* to do it. He wanted to do it so much nothing else mattered.

"That's it, son, go for the corners . . . now let me have one higher, right up close to the batter's head . . . hit the tire top right . . . that's good. Now lemme have the slider . . . I want it to drop right through the hole."

Those baseball phrases, that inimitable inflection of the bayous. The sounds would be with Jack Faber for all of his life, though he did not speak with the same accent himself. School and university had ironed that out. Even Ben seemed to speak with less accent these days, as if preparing himself for a big outside world, beyond south Louisiana, where the whipcord right arm of his only son was surely going to take him.

They ran down toward Louisiana's Route 1, the long state highway which meanders south along the Lafourche Bayou to the Gulf shores of Caminada Bay, where Jack's uncle René operated a shrimp boat. Going north, the road headed right out of Lafourche Parish, but before that it hooked up with Route 90 after the Blue Bayou. That was the route to glory for the new Cape Marlin pitcher, and Ben Faber gunned the old Chevy eastward, driving fast along the southern approaches to New Orleans, and then hitting their main east-running highway, Route 10, along the shores of the vast salt-water Lake Pontchartrain, eighty miles from home.

"It's about a hundred miles to the Alabama border," said Ben. "We ought to knock that off in a couple of hours, then we'll stop for some breakfast. How about that?"

"Sounds awful reasonable to me. Ol' Chevy's running good."

"This is a great automobile, Jack. Little old. But classy. She's takin' us there, no worries about her. Just a few worries about you, though. You sure you really understand what this summer's gonna be about?"

"Sure as you are, Dad. You ain't been up there neither."

"No. But I know about it. Lotta top guys came outta that league."

"Well, that's good, right? That's where I'm going."

"Jack. What I'm trying to tell you is, going there is not enough."

"Well, I know one thing. Each team gets twenty-three guys from all over the country. That's two hundred and thirty of us. Ten teams, right? Well, there's about two hundred and thirty guys *in my school* who wanted to go. That probably means there's about two hundred and thirty million guys in the whole country wanna go. And I'm one of the two hundred and thirty who are going."

"I know. But it's still not enough."

"Maybe not. But it ain't bad."

They drove on in silence for a while, running through the narrow stretch of Mississipi which borders the Gulf Coast. Ben stayed north of the water on Route 10 rather than take the coastal Route 90, which runs past the permanently moored gambling riverboats, casinos, bars, and restaurants, a lot of them open round-the-clock. There's some ideas in the outside world I don't need Jack to get distracted by, he told himself. Things that won't improve that slider any, rolling dice and playing on slot machines. That's the road to hell.

They hit traffic on the approaches to Mobile, Alabama, but the first moment they saw the sign for the great tree-lined Southern shipping port, Ben Faber muttered, "You see that name Mobile, son? Well, whenever you see it, just remember that's the birthplace of one of the greatest hitters of all time, Mr. Hank Aaron, and one of the greatest pitchers of all time, Mr. Satchel Paige. Both of them came from right here. Satchel played in the old Negro Leagues."

"You think those ol' guys could still cut it today, Dad?"

"Well, Hank banged the ball out of the park seven hundred and fifty-five times, so I guess he knew something. Ol' Satchel's record was thirty-one–four in 1933, so I guess he could throw a bit. He once struck out twenty-one major leaguers in an exhibition game. Hitters were still scared to death of him when he was forty-two years old. Think you could do that?"

"Maybe. I'm working on it."

Ben smiled at the confidence of youth. Then he pulled off the highway into a service area, gassed up the Chevy, parked, and took

Jack for breakfast. "Looks pretty good. I'm going for the sausage, bacon, and ham with eggs."

"Uh-uh, not right here you're not."

"I'm not? Why not?"

"That was one of Satchel's main rules for long life as a pitcher. No fried meats. They anger up the blood. I can't let you sit here, defyin' the rules of the greatest pitcher who ever came out of this state or anywhere else. Not five miles from his birthplace. That'd be kind a sacrilegious, right? Tempting providence. You get yourself an omelette and toast. No fried meat."

Jack laughed. "You think the ghost of ol' Satchel might come all the way to the Cape to haunt me?"

"I dunno, boy. But I'm not taking chances. Those rules of Satchel's are well known, about clean living. Not gettin' involved in vices. But I've always remembered the one about fried meat, and you can't have it, not right here in his home territory."

"Okay. I'll just get a bacon omelette."

"Mushroom and cheese. No bacon."

"Screw Satchel. But I guess you're paying."

They both laughed. When they hit the road again they were laughing at another of Satchel's famous laws, solemnly announced by Ben: "Don't look back. Something might be gaining on you."

They didn't look back much either. The Chevy raced around Mobile and passed the main junction with Route 65, the highway that leads up to the Alabama cities of Montgomery and Birmingham. "When you see that name, Jack—Birmingham—I want you always to think Birmingham Barons, home ball club of the great Willie Mays."

Jack shook his head, smiling. He was finding out his dad did not have a road map of the United States. He had a baseball map. They crossed the long, wide road bridge that straddles Mobile Bay and headed on east into Florida along Route 10. They passed the big U.S. naval air base at Pensacola and then drove all the way along the north of the state, as far as Tallahassee. Right there they swung north, up a smaller highway signed to Thomasville and Moultrie, and they crossed the state border into Georgia right before a small township called Moncrief.

As they did so, Ben nudged the sleeping pitcher next to him and spoke for the first time for a couple of hours. "See that sign coming up, Jack? That says Cairo. That's Cairo, Georgia. Ever heard of it?"

"Not me, Dad. Never heard nothing of it. I thought Cairo was in Egypt. Tutankhamen and all that bullshit."

"No, son. This one's different. Just as famous. Or it ought to be. It's the birthplace of Jackie Robinson. Cairo, Georgia, 1919. Every baseball man ought to have that written on his heart."

"Jeez. Did you drive off the highway, up all these country roads, just to show me that road sign?"

"Not really. But I knew we'd pass it. You know about Jackie Robinson?"

"Guess so. First black man ever to play in the Majors, right? Brooklyn Dodgers."

"You got it. But can you imagine how long the road was he traveled? From that little place at the back end of south Georgia right to New York City and then into history."

"Guess that applies to most great men."

"To some. But I always thought Jackie's was the longest road."

In the evening, they were on the outskirts of the city of Macon, running north up Highway 75. Ben turned off and drove slowly into the town. He drove as if he knew where he was going, and Jack looked up as they came to a halt outside a small ballpark with a tin roof over the bleachers. LUTHER WILLIAMS FIELD was written above the entrance.

"See this place, Jack? Come on, let's get out. I wanna show you something." The park was empty of spectators, but the main gate was open and Ben led the way through to the field. And there he stood, silent for a moment, recalling far-lost days when he too lived on the dirt infields of the sweltering South, when he too followed the sultry rhythms of the baseball summer. Then he pointed to the mound and said quietly, "That's the spot, Jack. That's where I pitched the only no-hitter I ever pitched. Right out there for the ol' Kraemer Crawdaddies 1983. Got a half of them with my knuckleball, the rest with the slider."

Jack had been hearing about that day for as long as he could remember, and he smiled at his dad, and nodded an unspoken word of admiration and respect. One pitcher to another. "Who plays here now?" he asked.

"Oh, this is a Single-A team in the Braves farm system. They're always good. Lotta top guys have pitched on this field. I remember my day here like it was yesterday . . ."

"Well, come on then, Pop. Get back out on the mound. We've come this far, you may as well go stand on the sacred spot."

"Yeah. Guess I better." And Ben Faber slipped through the gateway next to the home dugout, and he walked across the third-base line, into the infield, and he climbed the slope. And in his mind he heard the echo of a distant announcer . . . *and starting for the Crawdads tonight—Ben Faber.*

And he stared down toward home plate, and he held his hands high to his chest as if feeling again the baseball in his glove, and he nodded once, imperceptibly, toward a far-lost catcher, and he felt again the thrill of the game.

Jack watched him in silent understanding. He already knew the feeling. But suddenly the spell was broken, and he saw his dad shake his head, and then walk quickly back toward him.

"Come on, Jack. Let's go get some dinner. No fried meat, mind, not till we cross the Mason-Dixon Line."

"Jeez. D'you think it would really piss off Satchel's ghost if I had something grilled?"

"Nossir. Grilled would be just fine."

They found a diner around the corner from the ballpark, and ate hamburgers, cheesecake, and coffee. Ben was tired, so Jack took the wheel for the drive north toward Atlanta, then followed Route 85 up toward the South Carolina border. By 10:30 they were in a motel sleeping.

The next morning, before they had gone not more than two miles, Ben instructed his son to stay on alert, to watch for the sign down to the little town of Royston, which sits roughly ten miles off the main highway.

"Okay, who lived there? Lay it on me."

"Royston was the childhood home of Ty Cobb, the Georgia Peach. His dad was mayor of Royston, ran the local newspaper."

"Ty's pretty early for me. But everyone says he was great. Guess I don't know that much about him, 'cept he played for Detroit and was a pretty nasty kind of a guy."

"There's only one thing you need to know about him, aside from his *twelve* batting championships."

"Uh-huh?"

"Yep. He batted .300 or better from 1906 to 1928 *every goddamned year.*"

"Jesus . . . hey! There's the sign: Royston ten miles. We going down there to see his house?"

"Hell, no. Ty's had his time. I'm working on your career right now."

The Chevy kept going, heading up the last ten miles to the South Carolina border, directly into the rising sun, which had now fought its way out of the Atlantic, above the Outer Banks, 320 miles away. It was like driving toward a fireball, and the light made Route 85 shimmer in the glaring dawn. Ben reached for his sunglasses, Jack went briefly back to sleep, but only for a half hour.

Running through the loneliest part of the smallest southern state, they saw a big sign up ahead announcing the city of Greenville.

"Okay, Dad. Lay it on me. Who was born there?"

"Can't help there," said Ben. "But I sure can tell you who died there. Shoeless Joe Jackson, 1951."

"Shoeless Joe? Christ, I thought he was a ghost who lived in the cornfield."

Ben could see his son laughing. And he knew this display of profound ignorance was intended merely to wind him up. And he was not going to bite. But he couldn't help himself replying, "Yeah. Right. A ghost who *never* hit less than .300."

Jack shook his head. "How'd he die?"

"Oh, a heart attack. Happened the night before he was gonna be on *The Ed Sullivan Show* . . . must have been some kind of a heart, though. Took thirty years to give out . . . after they broke it."

"You mean the Black Sox Scandal and all that? Throwing the World Series?"

"Uh-huh . . . vicious goddamned people they were. I never thought Joe knew what he was doing . . . he couldn't even read or write. But they never let him play again . . . I always thought it was the cruelest sentence ever passed . . . Life—and they meant it."

"You think he really helped to throw the World Series?"

"Not really. The White Sox guys were charged and acquitted. No one went to jail. Joe Jackson batted .375, he drove in six runs, set a series record with twelve hits. Never was charged with an official error. If someone fixed the series, I don't believe it was Joe . . . you know, both Ty Cobb and Babe Ruth said he was the best hitter they ever saw."

"Jesus. Can you imagine what it must have been like never to be allowed to play ball again? The gap in his life? For a guy like that?"

"There weren't any guys like that. 'Cept him."

"Was he born right around here?"

"I'm not sure. But he was from South Carolina. And he came back here to die."

They crossed the border into North Carolina and stopped for breakfast just beyond Charlotte. The fried meat rule was still in force, but Jack Faber worked his way around that with fried eggs and grilled ham with home fries. They drank coffee and read the newspapers, checked the baseball scores, and hit Route 85 again, armed with a bag of sandwiches and orange juice.

The Chevy chugged along, no trouble, speeding past Greensboro, Burlington, and Durham, then turning hard to the northeast through beautiful country, with long lakes and endless woodland.

"We far from the ocean?" asked Jack.

"Hell, yes. Coupla hundred miles. Way down there to the right. That goes down to the the Outer Banks right on the Atlantic. There's a lot of swampland on the way, a lot like home. Lotta water, lotta fishing, lotta boats. Went there one time when I was about your age."

"Any ballplayers? Or are they just fishermen, like René?"

"One of them fishermen could pitch some. Used to play for Oakland. Won twenty-five games one year. Won twenty or more five years in a row. Wicked fastball. Catfish Hunter. Died too young, just a little while back."

"Yeah, I heard of him, right? Big name back in the seventies. Fantastic action. I saw him one time on a video. Christ, I wish I could ever throw a fastball like that."

"You gonna throw one like it, Jack. Just stay focused."

Ben handed over the wheel at a gas station inside the Virginia border, and Jack ran on up to Petersburg, where Route 85 converges with Interstate 95 North. As they circled around Washington, D.C., and approached Baltimore, Ben said, "Don't tell me—birthplace of Babe Ruth, right? I saw the movie . . . the orphanage and everything."

"That's right, son. Birthplace of the Babe. But we're not stopping, we're going straight by, hanging right in there on 95 North."

"What time do we stop? The sandwiches are history."

"I wanna get through Delaware, cross the river and onto the Jersey Turnpike. Then we stop for dinner and find a motel. There's plenty of 'em. One thing about the northeast . . . they got a lot of food and a lot of beds. Not many ballplayers, though. Ballplayers come from the South and the Southwest, where the sun always shines."

"Okay. Meanwhile I'm going for another coupla hours, right?"

"Yep."

Jack wound the old Chevy up to 70 mph and kept driving north while his father slept in the passenger seat. They reached the Jersey Turnpike right after 9:30 P.M. and Jack turned off the highway immediately and gassed up. Then he drove into a diner right next door to a motel. Ben booked them in, and told Jack to go and order a couple of steaks with fries and salad "before we both die of exhaustion and hunger."

They hit the road again at dawn for the last leg of the journey to Cape Marlin, via Boston's Logan Airport, where Ben had agreed to meet another incoming ballplayer, with his mother. Then they would drive down to the picturesque little coastal town of Seapuit, home of the Seawolves, for whom they would both play this summer. Ben already had a white rectangle of cardboard in the car, on which was written, *Natalie and Tony Garcia—Seapuit.* Jack would hold it in front of him like a chauffeur when passengers from the American Airlines flight from Chicago emerged into the arrivals area. It was due at 2 P.M.

They journeyed straight up to New York on the turnpike, over the Hudson River on the George Washington Bridge, and then up the New England Thruway. They deserted the coastal Interstate 95 at New Haven, and split inland for Hartford, Connecticut, then Springfield and the Massachusetts Pike, which runs almost straight into Boston airport.

They entered the Callaghan Tunnel at midday exactly, ran under the Charles River and into Logan's sprawling parking lot areas. Twenty minutes later they were inside the airport, eating hamburgers and drinking milk, reading the *Boston Globe*, laughing like hell at the fact that the Red Sox just got wiped out four straight on a road trip to Texas.

At 2:10 P.M. sharp they were on duty outside the arrivals gate, awaiting Tony Garcia and his mother from the Midwest. Ben's identification card proved utterly unnecessary. Tony Garcia was hard to miss; a broad, heavily muscled Hispanic kid, with a wide, smiling face, showing a lot of teeth, and carrying a long black sports bag with two wooden baseball bat handles jutting out, and the words NORTHWESTERN UNIVERSITY BASEBALL engraved on the outside.

His mother, Mrs. Natalie Garcia, was also hard to miss. A slender, dark-haired beauty, surely under the age of forty, she pushed a baggage trolley, and wore no smile. In fact she looked rather aloof. Ben thought her disposition was the price a lot of women pay for their beauty. Wasn't true of his own wife, though.

He offered his hand in greeting to Mrs. Garcia, "Hi, I'm Ben Faber. This is my son Jack. We're your ride down to the Cape."

"I'm very glad to meet you, Mr. Faber. I'm Natalie Garcia and this is my son Tony."

Ben appraised her white summer suit and dark blue blouse, and he shook hands politely. But Tony stepped forward and slapped Jack on the shoulder, offering a beaming smile, and said, "Pitcher, right? From Louisiana. I just been reading the team lists. That's some kind of record you got this year. I'm looking forward to catching you."

Jack grinned back. Only Ben noticed the shudder of disapproval from Natalie Garcia as she turned away, back to the baggage trolley.

"Okay, you guys, lemme take the luggage," said Tony, "And we'll follow you out to the wagon. What are we driving? Something big and powerful?"

"Yeah, right," said Jack. "It's got a couple decades on her and I'll count it as some kinda miracle if we get there—sorry, kids. Pop and me ain't got much bread . . . it's a tough game raising sugarcane down in the bayous."

"Join the club." Tony laughed. "Me and my mom ain't got any bread either. It's even tougher playing the harp."

"Christ, are we back to Shoeless Joe Jackson?" said Jack.

Tony Garcia laughed, as any self-respecting White Sox fan would. But he said, "Hell, no. This is for real. My mom's a part-time music teacher at the university. She plays the harp, and the piano, and the violin. She sat in with the Chicago Symphony . . . coulda stayed on with 'em, but for me. You know, gone on tour and everything. But it doesn't pay much, teaching kids music. Not like the big leagues, right, Jack? BAM! BAM! Strike one! Million bucks a year. That's the game."

Mrs. Garcia grimaced.

"Sorry, Mom, just joking. Winding you up a little. You know I'm all-out for my law degree . . . I'm not gonna let you down."

"If I believed that, Tony, I guess I wouldn't be quite so horrified every time you mention this ridiculous game."

By now they were on their way across the parking lot, to the spot where the blue Chevy was still cooling its wheels after the long journey north. The heat was pleasant, around eighty-eight degrees with a light westerly breeze drifting in off Massachusetts Bay. It was a lot better than the bayous.

Ben put the luggage in the trunk and invited Mrs. Garcia to sit with him in the front. The two boys sat in the back. And the start of the journey to Cape Marlin was tinged with awkwardness because the baseball-loving sugarcane farmer had not the slightest idea what to say to the beautiful musician who sat beside him.

He would have liked to ask her about Chicago, and her husband, and where they lived. But he did not really know how to start such a conversation. And so they rode out of the airport in silence, and Ben paid the toll at the tunnel and used the roar of the traffic to avoid saying anything. Mrs. Garcia too seemed glad to remain out of communication. She sat staring straight ahead, ignoring the howls of laughter from the backseat, and wearing an expression which stated with irrevocable clarity that she wished right now to be anywhere on this earth except in this terrible car with these two baseball people who were beguiling her only son.

Ben Faber found his way up onto the south-running lanes of the raised freeway that runs down to Cape Marlin. Just as he felt compelled to open up a conversation with his passenger, they swooped down into another long, noisy underpass in which talk was almost impossible. But then they climbed a short gradient and the late spring light once more flooded the car, and Ben took the bull by the horns and ventured, "Looking forward to the new season, Mrs. Garcia?"

"Please," she replied. "Do call me Natalie. And no. I'm not looking forward to anything about Cape Marlin. In fact, I'm dreading the new season. Dreading the fact that Tony will emerge as some kind of star."

A yell of pure delight erupted from the back. "THAT'S IT, MOM! You got it . . . and tonight, ladies and gentlemen . . . catching for the White Sox we have the great Northwestern University star of the Cape Marlin League . . . the one and only, the incredible TONY 'IRON GLOVE' GARCIA!"

"YES! GAR-CIA! GAR-CIA! GAR-CIA!"

"Shut up, Jack," said Ben, trying to stop laughing.

But even Natalie saw the funny side of it, and she did chuckle at the new double act that was so clearly evolving in the rear seat. But then she became very serious again, and when she spoke it was with a strained dignity.

"I'm going to call you Ben," she said. "But that does not mean we have now, or ever will have, anything in common. However, we seemed to be unavoidably thrown together for the next couple of hours, so I will try to make a few things plain to you, the first being that I was married very young and that my husband left me in Detroit with a three-month-old baby before my twentieth birthday.

"Since then I have spent my time trying to build a life for Tony and me. I have never married again. I worked as a waitress to pay for my tuition at the Chicago College of Music. And I have worked all the hours God made. But still, most times I struggle to pay the rent for the cheap tenement in which we live. And I struggle to put food on the table for us, and pay for my car. You may not have noticed—yet. But Tony has a first-class brain. And I believe the way out of the poverty trap is for him to use it, to get through law school, and then make things maybe a little easier for us."

She paused, as if unwilling to reveal more. But then she closed her huge brown eyes for a moment, took a deep breath, and continued.

"Ben, he earned a scholarship to Northwestern. He could be as good as he wants to be. But all he wants is to play baseball. And I know he'll end up on some team bus, at the age of twenty-seven, moving around the Double-A Leagues in Wyoming or somewhere for one thousand dollars a month. And everything I have tried to do will have been for nothing." She shook her head, and added, somewhat dramatically, "I'll probably die in a Chicago tenement someday, still trying to send him handouts."

"How about if he makes it? I mean as a ballplayer."

"Yeah, Mom. How about that? How about if I make it big?"

"Almost no one makes it big, Tony. As I've told you a thousand times. Out of every twenty thousand hopefuls, only about three make it big. How about you, Ben? What do you want for Jack? You want him on a team bus, earning next to nothing, not quite making it? Knowing he's good, but not that good. Watching this loathsome game slowly break his heart, like it breaks the hearts of most poor kids who grow up worshipping it."

"Natalie, I guess it never once occurred to me that Jack Faber wasn't going to be one of the greatest pitchers who ever lived."

2

*B*en Faber's old blue Chevy faced up to the long, hot drive down to the Cape with commendable resolution. She was burning oil, but she never faltered. At the first gas stop, way down in the woodlands that border Massachusetts Route 3 South, her oil light was just flicking on, and Ben had them pour two quarts into the engine. The boys checked the water level and the new tires, and with renewed faith they set sail down the final twenty miles to the great bridge that spans the canal joining the mainland to Cape Marlin.

"For an automobile worth about five bucks," said Jack, "this baby's doing a big job. You confident, Tony? We're gonna make it?"

"Absolutely. No doubt in my mind. Mom, don't touch anything. We can't afford hotels if it stops."

Ben laughed, and said, "C'mon, guys. Natalie wants us to get there, even if she doesn't approve of what we're doing."

"Don't count on that," she replied. Smiling, but only just.

"Anyway," said Ben. "You guys, just remember you're going to play in a league which has seen some of the best ballplayers of modern times. Coupla years ago the entire Red Sox infield had played in the Cape Marlin League. Just take the Seawolves alone . . . Will Clark played for them, and Terry Steinbach, Ed Sprague, Tim Naehring . . . even Thurman Munson, the great Yankee catcher. This isn't any old ballpark, this is one of the goddamned temples of the game, a place where the dreams begin.

"Natalie, lemme tell you something. A few years back, in the All-Star Game, I checked through some records of the professional players who took part. I found seventeen of 'em had played in the Cape League. There are folks who say that one player in three, of all the major leaguers, has played right down here over the big bridge we're about to see. Isn't that something? Even if you don't want Tony to do it, you gotta be proud of the fact that he's got here, right?"

"Ben. I am not proud. Tony is at university to try to earn a top law degree. Baseball may actually prevent him from doing that. Don't ask me to applaud it. Because for me, this game is the road to oblivion. And I seem to be able to do nothing about it. I love my son, Ben. I do not want to see him ruin his career for a game which belongs in a schoolyard."

Ben was silent for a moment. And then he said, "Why did you come here with him, Natalie . . . when you knew how it would upset you?"

"I came only because Tony has never been away before, not by himself, out of the university. I just wanted to make sure he was settled. Not for any love of watching him play, I assure you."

"But you're gonna stay and watch the first game, right, Mom?"

"Well, I promised to do that. But then I have to leave."

"So do I," said Ben. "Have to get back to the farm. But I'd give anything to stay."

"Christ, Ben . . . you driving this baby all the way back to Louisiana?" asked Tony.

"Sure am, son. I couldn't get here without it. Airfares and car hire's a little steep for me right now. I can make it up here and back in this car on a hundred and seventy bucks' worth of gas. We cashed Jack's air ticket and used the rest of the money for the motels and food. Two for the price of one, right?"

The hostility of Mrs. Garcia cast a slight shadow over the next few miles. But it failed to subdue the high good humor in the backseat. "Hit him right in the head . . . Jesus Christ, I thought he was dead! . . . then he hit the next one over the fence . . . I wished he hadda been!"

Each recollection was accompanied by howls of laughter. "And you know that ol' bastard from Oklahoma . . . we had the whole team lined up to shake hands afterward, and he came out and said his men didn't shake. Ever. Because to him the game was war!"

"That ol' guy did the same to us. Left us standing in a line, all on our own. That was the only time we went there, and our coach was furious even though we beat 'em five–four . . . wouldn't play 'em again . . . we all left the field dancing and singing, 'Shake, baby, shake . . .' "

At that, both front-seat passengers were laughing, and up ahead they could see the high bridge spanning the swirling currents of the wide, deep Cape Marlin Canal two hundred feet below. Ben gunned the old Chevy straight up the outside lane, passing a busload of schoolgirls, waving at the young ballplayers in the back.

"I just know I'm gonna love it here," said Tony.

Three miles later, Ben Faber left the main highway and drove into narrow country roads for the first time since they left Jackie Robinson's rural birthplace more than a thousand miles ago in Georgia. And again Ben became very serious, and he said to both boys, "Try to remember that just getting here is not enough. Getting here is just having the door opened for you. It's up to you both to walk through it. And that's going to require you to stay real fit throughout this season.

"I happen to know an old baseball guy from Atlanta who scouts this league. And what matters to him is the last three weeks, when they're looking to see which guys have the stamina for this game. They're looking for the guys who can pitch, or catch or hit, night after night, in the highest class of the college game. Which this is. We're on Cape Marlin now, and right now is the time to stop congratulating yourselves on your selection to come here. Right now's the time to start thinking about the mountain in front of you, and to work out how determined you both are, to climb, not just halfway up it, but all the way to the top."

"Is it true, Ben, that guys come here and get whipped straight off to the pros?" asked Tony.

"It sure is. Few years back there was a kid playing for the Henley Mets beating the hell out of the pitchers for five weeks. And the Yankees swooped right in the middle of the season. Paid him a million bucks right off the bat. There was a hell of a funny picture of him in one of the baseball weeklies, working at his job here on the Cape. He was doing twenty-three hours a week as a janitor at the local police station . . . picture showed him with a bucket and a mop, and a check for a million in his back pocket."

"Jesus," said the catcher from Northwestern. "Hey, Mom. How

'bout that. Gotta win a lotta legal cases to get a mill in one hop, right?"

Mrs. Garcia sighed the sigh of the profoundly misunderstood.

By now they were running down toward the southern coastline of the Cape, and they'd seen their first road sign to Seapuit. Ben had the address up in the visor, but they missed it first time, driving right through the quiet village, beneath tall leafy oaks already making a late spring canopy over the main street. They drove past beautiful summer homes, guarding the views to the bay, but soon they petered out, and the old Chevy ran downhill to a deserted public beach where the tranquil waters of Nantucket Sound washed onto Seapuit's long, picturesque shoreline.

"Is this paradise, or what?" said Jack. "Think we'll be able to go fishing out here?"

"I expect so, but you may not have the time if you're concentrating on your career," replied his father.

"Ain't this something?" said Jack. "Here we are, me and Tony, on one of the greatest days of our lives. And we're stuck in this car with a couple of professional party poopers . . . Natalie wishes the place wasn't even on the map . . . and my own father hopes like hell I never have one moment of fun. Jeez. I hope I never get old. At least not like you two."

"RIGHT! *That's exactly what I was thinking*!" yelled Tony Garcia. "Come on, you guys, give us a break. This is great. We're all here safely, and Jack and me are gonna play great ball. Jeez. This might be one of life's turning points. It's an adventure, right? And we're ready for it. Turn this car around. Get me to my leader . . . er, coach. I'm moving forward. Hold me back. I could do anything."

By this time Jack was laughing at this cheerful comedian from Chicago's South Side. Even Natalie had lightened up. Ben was so amused, he stalled the car and Jack observed that this could be catastrophic "since the son of a bitch may never fire again."

But it did, and five minutes later they pulled into the drive of a big New England Colonial house one street in from the ocean. And before they even opened the door, a slim bespectacled man, well dressed in a suit and tie, came out of the house to greet them. "Come on in, everyone," he said. "Welcome to Seapuit . . . I'm Dick Topolski, general manager . . . you must be Jack Faber and Tony Garcia, just in from Logan?"

"Correct, sir . . . and this is my dad, Ben . . . and this is Tony's mom, Natalie."

Inside the house they met the Seawolves chief coach, Russell Maddox, from the University of Maine. Also in the house was his pitching coach, Ted Sando, from the same school. Jane Topolski poured them all lemonade and welcomed them, offering coffee cake, and, without asking, serving the boys two serious slices with a major scoop of coffee ice cream on the top. Both of them charged into this feast as if might be their last meal on this earth.

Her husband then brought in two complete uniforms and told them to go into the den downstairs and get suited up. Ten minutes later they emerged wearing the white pinstripes of the Seapuit Sea-wolves, complete with dark maroon socks, cap, and jacket.

"Everything fit okay?" asked Jane, who was, after seven years, a world expert on fitting college ballplayers into the exact-right-size uniform.

"Perfect for me, ma'am," said Jack.

"And me," replied the catcher.

"Hey, you guys clean up pretty good," said Ben. "At least you look like ballplayers, and I guess right now Coach Maddox is just waiting for you to get out there and prove that's what you are."

"Right on, Ben. That's what I'm waiting for."

"Mrs. Tolpolski, there's just one thing," added Tony Garcia. "I think I could play even better on one more half slice of that cake."

Jane laughed. "Two?"

"Yes please, ma'am," said Jack.

"Okay, guys. Now I would like to just mention the basics here," said her husband cheerfully. "Beyond the coffee cake, that is. Now, you all know about the boys' amateur status, as collegiate players, right? And, as you also know, that means they gotta do some work, twenty-three hours a week, for the exact same pay a normal person would get. Now, we have some jobs right here at the ball club, either working on the field, or helping at the summer baseball clinics for the local kids, some years about three hundred of 'em. We operate three fields, every morning, for several weeks. Brings us in a lot of income."

Dick read down his list. "Okay, Jack, farmer's son. I've got you down to drive the tractor and look after the field. Mowing, spraying, and taking care of the infield. Tony . . . you can either teach at the clinics—the kids are all under twelve—or you can join Jack's ground crew. There'll be three of you working under the supervision of Coach Maddox. Every morning."

"Okay, I'll go with Jack. But I don't know how to drive the tractor."

"That's all right, I'm an ace," said Jack.

Dick Topolski shuffled his papers. "Right. Houseparents. You will each live with a local family right here in Seapuit. There will be house rules, you'll be treated like one of the family, and you will hand over two-thirds of your weekly pay to cover your room, board, and laundry. 'Specially to cover food, and judging by your perform-ance with the coffee cake, your houseparents are not looking at a bargain situation."

Ben and Natalie chuckled.

"Jack, you're staying with Ward and Ann Fallon right here in town . . . you can walk to the ballpark. Tony, you're in with Dr. Paul and Nancy McLure right around the corner from Jack. Both families are heavily involved with the ball club, I've known them for years. And you'll like the houses. Specially Jack."

Jane stepped in here with the hospitality list and confirmed that everyone knew that Ben and Natalie were bringing their boys in, and both would be staying with the houseparents for a few days before returning home. It would be up to them to make whatever arrange-ments were agreeable for future visits.

They left in two cars, and Russ Maddox said he'd meet the two sophomores at the field in the morning at 9 A.M. They'd work until 1 P.M., break for lunch, and report for practice at 2:30.

Jack Faber and his father thus moved into the two spare rooms at the Fallons' sprawling white Cape-styled house, with its wide screened porch and distant view of Seapuit Bay. Ward Fallon, an American Air-lines pilot, was not due home until the following day, but his wife and teenage children—Greg, seventeen, and Jessica, eighteen—were in res-idence. They spent a couple of hours sitting outside drinking coffee in the late afternoon, and Jack listened wide-eyed as Ann recounted the exploits of the previous ballplayers who had stayed there: a pitcher now with the Yankees AAA; a hitter from Vanderbilt now with the White Sox; a third baseman from Chicago, now with the Pittsburgh Pirates; a shortstop who went to the Brewers.

"This is a lucky house, Jack," she said. "We expect big things of you."

"Ma'am, I'd just like to say one thing," said Ben. "It really is awful good of you to open up your house all summer for these kids. I mean, that's a huge sacrifice."

"Well, my husband's a senior vice-president of the ball club, and around here we all pitch in. Some summer residents can't go to meetings and arrive too late to be houseparents. So they give money, and whatever else we need. Some local craftsmen can't give money, so they work on things for us for nothing. The Seapuit community keeps the ball club running. It works pretty well."

"But's what's really in it for you?"

"Oh, it just becomes a way of life. Helping out, going to meetings, looking after one of the kids all summer, making lifelong friendships, following their careers when they leave here. Staying in touch with families is fun. When one of our boys makes the Majors . . . well . . . it's like one of our own children. They always call."

"How about if these guys get out of hand?"

"They don't. They refer to my husband and me as Mr. and Mrs. Fallon at all times. They have a curfew that they must observe. If they break it and start staying out late, they get one warning. Then they're on the next flight home. They're not here to stay out late and goof around. They're here to play baseball, make a career for themselves, and win for us. We hate losing, and the scouts are here from the Majors every night. Any kid has his mind on other things, he's history. We won't put up with it. Sure, there's nights when a boy comes in a bit late and there's a lot of 'Please, Mrs. Fallon, please don't report me. I just couldn't get back.'

"Most times we laugh it off. But if it starts happening again, that's trouble. Remember, Jack, you will be treated here as if you were our own son. If we think you are abusing that privilege, you could find yourself back in Louisiana, real fast."

"Yes, ma'am," said Jack, smiling. "But I'm not here to goof off. I'm here to play ball. So's that catcher we brought down, Tony Garcia. Now, there's one ambitious guy. Like me."

At 8:45 sharp, the following morning, Ben Faber drove Tony Garcia and Jack to Cabot Field, home of the Seapuit Seawolves. Russ Maddox was not yet there, but the third member of the ground crew was, a strapping 220-pound first baseman from Oklahoma State. He stood about the same height as Jack, but he was built more on the lines of Ben Faber, big all around, wide shoulders, tree-trunk legs.

"Hey, guys," he said. "I'm Zac Colbert, from Spavinaw, Oklahoma, birthplace of Mickey Mantle."

Ben Faber's eyes lit up. "Jesus, never thought I'd meet anyone in New England who knew where the Mick was born."

"It's hard to forget it back home. Not a whole hell of a lot ever happened to Spavinaw, 'cept for Mantle."

Jack moved in and made the introductions and announced himself as head tractor driver and chief of the field crew. Zac Colbert said he lived right out on the edge of the Spavinaw State Park, close to the Arkansas border, and he was pretty good at raking leaves. Tony Garcia said he'd hardly ever seen a leaf until he went to college. "Guess I'm stuck with a coupla real country boys," he said, smiling his wide smile. "I'll probably have to wise you up some—on the big city, that is."

At this point Ben Faber made his exit, explaining that he was taking Mrs. Garcia and Mrs. McLure out for the morning, probably for a walk along the sand dunes. And he drove out of the parking lot, just as Coach Maddox drove in.

Russ said for now he was planning just to concentrate on getting the infield cut and watered. He showed the boys the pavilion, behind the Seawolves kitchen, showed them where the gasoline for the big mower was kept, and the shed where they stored the rakes, shovels, spanners, and machine tools.

He and Zac spent most of the morning trying to fix a fault on the watering system while Jack carefully mowed the grass. All three boys were enthralled by the picturesque ballpark, surrounded by trees, from the end of the left-field bleachers all the way around to the smaller visitors bleachers on the right-field line. Zac noted it was four hundred feet to the centerfield fence, took a couple of practice swings, gazing out over the treetops as if watching the flight of a thunderous home run, right off the middle of his bat.

"Looks like a long way," he muttered. "How far to the left-field fence, Tony?"

"Three-thirty—same as right."

"Better go for the corners, right?"

"First coupla games anyway. Till we get used to the wood."

When they regrouped for practice, suited up and ready, Russell Maddox called an immediate team meeting in the dugout. The players were almost all in Seapuit now. At least eighteen of the twenty-three were there, and the following two days of training would decide which eleven players, including a starting pitcher, a reliever, and a DH, would face the Henley Mets at Cabot Field three days from now.

Coach Maddox made the introductions, announcing each player and his school to his teammates. He then gave a short, lighthearted, career-highlight rundown, just so everyone knew how good a group this was. Then he grew serious, and he said, quite suddenly, "Just remember one thing always. This summer, you're not playing for yourself. You're playing for every person who ever wore a Seapuit uniform. And that's a serious group of ballplayers.

"And before I go on, I want to tell you one thing . . . you see that deep green infield right out there in front of your eyes? Well, three years ago this ballpark needed complete new turf and a watering system. And it was going to cost thousands of dollars . . . more than ten, less than twenty. You know what they did? They decided to write and ask for a donation from every current major leaguer who had ever played for Seapuit. You know how long it took to raise that sum of money? One week. That's what it meant to those guys . . . to have played here . . . and that's what it has to mean to you."

The dugout was silent. "You will not yet understand the pride, and the work ethic, and the years of baseball tradition here. But you will learn very quickly. If you give one hundred percent, these people will rise up to you . . . you will hear thunderous applause right here in this little ballpark. They will give you a standing ovation when you *lose* . . . just so long as you have given it everything.

"But if you should dog it, when things are going bad, if they should sense you as an outsider, without due care for this team . . . you'll know by the silence in this ballpark. You will walk back to the dugout and it will be as if you're in a graveyard. They'll forgive you anything . . . except not caring . . . as they themselves care, as everyone associated with this place cares.

"Just so long as you remember, that when you pull on that shirt, you're pulling on the shirt of Will Clark, Terry Steinbach, Ed Sprague, and Tim Naehring. They also walked up these same dugout steps, and out to that same plate to face the pitchers from Wellfleet, Lancaster, Nauset, and Rock Harbor. It mattered to them, as it matters to me and to Ted right here. As it has to matter to you."

He paused, just for a moment, to let his words hit home. And he looked at the young, earnest faces that surrounded him. And then he reminded them: "You're going to be playing six days a week. This is the first time you've ever had a chance to prove you can withstand a long season. These nine weeks, right here, will show who has the will, the stamina for a professional career. I know we're all excited right now, in a new place, at the start of a new season. But what I want to know is who's still gonna be excited when it's mid-July, and we just lost two in a row, and we're three–nothing down in the sixth, in someone else's ballpark, and every damn thing that can go wrong is going wrong? Who's with us then? Ready to get out and hurl the big strikeouts, bang that ball into the gaps when we got men on. Which of you guys has the real stuff?

"Well, I hope all of you. That's why we're here. And right now I want the pitchers to line up with Coach Sando and get ready for your first practice . . . and let me warn you . . . he's a tough and diffi-cult taskmaster . . . but he's always on your side."

Big Ted Sando, six and a half feet of baseball passion, made his way out of the dugout and signaled for Tony Garcia to bring his mask and armor. The pitchers who had arrived followed them, first Jack, then a tall, bespectacled six-foot four-inch junior from Stan-ford, Kyle Davidson. Behind him came a lanky Georgia Bulldog, Doughnut Davis, named, according to Ted, because his father once proclaimed, "That boy o' mine's so damned accurate with his fast-ball he could throw it through the hole in a doughnut."

Anyway, Linus Davis, at the age of twenty, had never again been called by his given Christian name. Not in six years. Doughnut, he became, and Doughnut he stayed. In terms of pure velocity, Dough-nut was undeniably very fast. Russ Maddox had recruited him per-sonally, and readily admitted the Bulldog needed some rough edges to be smoothed away. But did he ever have a fastball.

Kyle Davidson was the most senior. He had played on the Stan-ford team in the College World Series and everyone knew how good he was. And how rich he was. Buck Davidson, his attorney father, had come to the White House as an adviser to the Reagans, and then in 1989 accepted a senior partnership in one of the biggest law firms in Washington. Kyle thus commuted between his parents' palatial home in Chevy Chase and his school in the foothills of the San Fran-cisco peninsula. He had flown business class to Boston, where a member of his father's staff had delivered Kyle's own dark blue Ford Thunderbird, freighted by road from Stanford.

Right now the automobile stood in solitary glory beneath the trees in Cabot Field, right there in the players' parking area. Its owner was running through his stretching exercises, limbering up, working his huge shoulders and upper arms, a look of deadly seriousness on his wide, handsome face. Kyle Davidson was a thoughtful, crafty pitcher with a blazing, tailing fastball which was almost impossible to hit. In the College World Series he struck out thirteen batters in one game, nine of them in the first six innings.

The fourth pitcher was Aaron Smith, a doleful six-foot 3-inch black economics student from LSU. He had a rocket for an arm and was a distant cousin of the great former Red Sox reliever Lee Smith. They were both out of Shreveport, Louisiana, and while Aaron wanted to emulate his cousin as a Major League player, he lacked the focused ambition that requires, and saw himself also as a hitter and a right fielder. In time, he considered it not impossible that he might become president of the Louisiana National Bank.

Ted Sando stared at his charges, watching them warm up. Then he called them together and said there were a few points he wanted to make clear. "The first thing is that we have only a very short time to establish those very special pitcher-catcher relationships. Tony Garcia, who has a superb record at Northwestern, is almost certain to start, and I expect him to claim that spot right through the season. Therefore I want you guys to throw to him today.

"But first I want to explain something to you . . . it is not in your interest to go out there and pitch just for yourselves. Because this is simply not about you becoming an all-star. I want you to think of yourselves as a pitching team. I want to see you helping each other to achieve team goals . . . that way you're gonna get us high in the league, and that's when the Major League scouts start showing up big time, to see the pitchers who are holding Seapuit on top. Remember my words . . . you will help each other whenever you can. By that I mean with technique and fitness, but also mentally, just being there when things are going wrong for your teammate. It is in none of our interests for *anyone* to pitch badly, and then to feel isolated. Right here we need each other.

"And that brings me to technique, and I want to say right away that I am not going to try and change you. I have no wish to alter whatever it is that has made you successful. I am here to keep you sharp and fit, and to advise, help you if I can to improve. The one thing I will insist on, however, is communication. You must tell me how you feel about your game, physically and mentally. It is your responsibility.

"And remember things are pretty tight up here. The players have to do everything. We do, of course, keep a highly detailed pitching chart, logging every ball thrown, every out, every hit, every foul-back. I expect you do that in college anyway, but here that chart is *really* important, because it tells us everything, if we read it carefully. Usually I have a rota naming which player will keep the chart on given nights. But I understand there may be someone who has a natural inclination for it, and I have no objection to anyone who wants to do it whenever possible . . . is there anyone?"

"Yes, Coach," said Kyle Davidson. "I do it a lot at Stanford, and I'm real happy to do it here any night I'm not playing."

"Great. Also you will have seen my notice board in the dugout. That's where the sheet goes up for each game, detailing the groups of four hitters, and which of you is throwing practice to which group. It will name the guy who's got the bucket, who's collecting the baseballs in the outfield during practice, who's raking, the starting pitcher, the first long reliever, then the short reliever. Remember we are responsible for everything. Coach Maddox does the white line machine. Jack Faber, as you know, is in charge of the field, assisted by Tony and Zac Colbert.

"We always say the grass gets a bit long sometimes when you have a pitcher in charge of the mowing, because he's apt to spend two hours on the grass and three on the mound. Raking and watering, tamping it down, getting it firm and compact, smoothing it to a nice gradual landing area . . . all that stuff which seems like nothing to most people, but represents life and death to us.

"Anyway, guys, let's get into it . . . right now I want to see Jack first, then Kyle, throw a couple of innings each . . . Tony, you catch Jack . . . Aaron, you take Kyle . . . Doughnut . . . just keep warm."

The big pitching coach from Maine watched as Jack Faber and Tony jogged into left field, each of them pulling on a glove. At first they stayed quite close, just throwing the baseball back and forth. But after five minutes they began to move farther apart, to thirty feet. Ted moved closer to Jack, watching the action of the pitcher from the bayous. Now Jack and Tony were forty feet apart, Jack was lengthening his muscles, and his body was becoming looser. A light sweat was forming on his brow.

After six minutes they stopped, and began to walk toward the bull pen, talking intently, discussing the pitches Jack was about to throw and Tony Garcia's signals. And now the catcher pulled on his chest protector, then his helmet and mask, and took up a crouching position in the bull pen, a short fifty feet from the mound.

Jack Faber stepped up and faced him, nodded, and threw a three-quarter-speed pitch straight into Garcia's motionless left glove, held just below and outside his right eye. Garcia nodded, threw the ball back, and again went into his crouch. Six more times Jack threw the ball right into the glove, wherever Garcia placed it. The pitcher was focused on his target, he felt balanced, and he motioned for Garcia to move back six more feet.

Ted Sando, standing quietly on the edge of the bull pen, watched carefully, and Jack Faber sent down another ten pitches, all at three-quarter speed, all into Garcia's glove. Only once did the catcher have to move significantly to collect the pitch, and Ted noticed Jack shake his head, betraying irritation.

And now Garcia moved back full-length, pulled down his mask, and went into his crouch, watching for the signal. Ted saw Jack flip his glove forward, indicating to the catcher, that the fastball was coming in, hard.

He watched the lazy windup motion, and then WHAM! Faber's 90 mph dead-straight pitch, right over the plate, smacked into Tony Garcia's glove. Then he did it again. And again. *"Attababy!"* yelled Ted. This cat from south Louisiana really could throw it.

Ted Sando never took his eyes off the pitcher. And now he saw him flip the glove again, with a rolling movement, forward—the signal, he knew, for a curve. Tony Garcia nodded, and Jack sent in a high dipping slower ball which the catcher only just grabbed. Jack tested him with three more variations on that pitch. Then he went back to his fastball for three more pitches, each one interspersed with a deceptive change-up.

Jesus, he thought. I've only ever caught one pitcher this good. And right here we have Faber, who's as good, if not better than Kyle Davidson, *plus* this fastball wizard Doughnut, *and* Lee Smith's cousin.

Now Jack signaled another fastball, as he continued to run through his repertoire, pitching sometimes inside, sometimes out on the corners, sometimes right over the plate. Garcia counted twenty-two pitches thrown, but the next one was the hardest yet. The catcher from Northwestern thought it would have clocked in the low nineties.

He watched Jack standing still on the mound. And then he saw the new signal, the pitcher's glove moving gently, *sideways.*

Christ. Don't tell me he can throw a slider as well? This is unbelievable. He never even mentioned it to me.

Jack went into his windup, looking for all the world as if a fastball was guaranteed. But Garcia could not see the change in the grip, although he caught the hard twist in the pitcher's wrist as Jack put a spin on that ball like a buzz saw. It screamed in toward the inner third at 84 mph and then *dived down* right before the plate, swerving out at the last second. Garcia moved like lightning, caught it just below his right knee on the outside corner.

"HOLY SHIT!" said the catcher.

Ted Sando, still positioned right behind Jack, just shook his head and very slowly clapped. There were, he knew, only about ten college pitchers in the entire country who could throw a slider like that.

"Could you do that for me one more time," said Ted. "Just wanna check I'm not dreaming."

"Coach, would you just give me a minute? I'm never quite sure of it. And I have to psych myself up. I sometimes can't throw it to order."

"Whatever you say," said Ted. "But that was beautiful."

One more fastball. One more curve. And then he did it again. The ball came whipping in, once more at more than 80 mph and then it made this sudden, mind-bending dive toward the plate. A top college hitter could miss that ball by a foot.

"Oh, my God," said Ted. "Are we gonna have fun with that . . . whaddya say, Tony . . . you like?"

"Like? I'm fucking in love," yelled Garcia. "How 'bout that *slider?*"

"Tell me about it. I've seen Clemens throw one like that, and Curt Schilling down at the Diamondbacks. But Jesus, Jack, where'd you learn it?"

"My dad taught me," said Jack. "He was an old knuckleballer down in the bayous. Pretty good in his day."

"Okay, guys . . . that'll do, Jack . . . Tony, will you warm up

Doughnut? He's sitting over there like a spare prick at a wedding. Then we'll see what he can do. Kyle we know about. Zac Colbert's getting him ready right now . . . they can take over the bull pen."

And Ted Sando walked over and put his arm around Jack's shoulders, and walked him back to the dugout, thrilled beyond words at the young pitcher's command, his natural fluid motion, his variety, and, oh boy, that slider. And he thanked God for Ben Faber.

3

Doughnut Davis was a lefty. He was the son of a rich used-car dealer from Savannah, Georgia, and he stood tall on the mound. He was six foot five-inches, slim and rangy in build, with a lugubrious expression on a face like the Tin Man in the Wizard of Oz. But beneath the somewhat gloomy exterior, there was a pure-bred wild man trying to get out. He had an ego the size of Atlanta's Olympic Stadium, and if he'd ever demonstrated his pitching action to a purist like Nolan Ryan, he'd probably have advised him to take up tennis.

Doughnut's left arm was a baseball phenomenon, in a windup action that was not much short of amazing. As he broke his hands from the middle, the right arm shot straight up into the air, completely obscuring his vision, denying him any possibility of actually seeing the target. Various school and college coaches had mentioned this to him over the years, but Doughnut would always shrug it off.

Ted Sando unknowingly faced just such a confrontation. And now, watching the lefty from Georgia winging random balls at Garcia, he was puzzled by the lack of a progressive schedule, something that normally sees the pitcher starting short, getting longer, getting loose, getting into harmony with the catcher, before taking to the mound.

Doughnut had no time for any of that. He hurled fifteen balls at Garcia, and then wheeled away like a halfback coming out of the huddle, and said, "Okay, boy. That's it. I'm ready." And he broke off and jogged into the bull pen, limbering up as he went, while Tony Garcia got into his chest protector and helmet.

Two minutes later, mask down, glove ready, the catcher from Chicago squared up to take Doughnut's fastball, from the full distance, sixty feet and six inches. Ted Sando, in company with Jack and Kyle, stood behind the bull pen netting, watching.

Doughnut pulled himself up to his full height, cradling the ball in his right glove against his chest. Then his hands broke, the left moving back behind his head, the right shooting skyward. Right after that it happened. Doughnut lunged forward, his left arm coming through like a whiplash, the ball howling in at 94 mph WHAM! Straight down the pipe, straight into Garcia's glove. Nearly knocked it off. "*Jesus!*" said the catcher. It was a fabulous fastball.

The pitcher wheeled around on his left heel, staring straight at Ted Sando, his arms now rigid out in front of him, palms upward.

"How 'bout that, Coach?" he demanded. "How 'bout that?"

"Outstanding," said Sando, nodding.

"What about that fucking right arm?" whispered Jack. "He can't see a thing."

"Screw his right arm," replied the coach. "I don't care if he sticks it up his ass, not if he can throw like that."

Jack and Kyle were both falling about laughing as Doughnut rewound himself for the next pitch. Leaning back, his right knee high across his body, his right arm pointing up into the afternoon sun, he let fly with another screamer, 94 mph. Except that this time it flew four feet above the catcher's head, still rising, hit the wire fence eight feet above the ground, and jammed.

"How 'bout that?" said Ted.

Doughnut shrugged. "Just a little off," he muttered. "I'm gettin' there. I'm gettin' there."

Ten pitches later it was apparent that Doughnut Davis had absolutely no idea whatsoever where the ball was going. He fired two into the ground, another two high into the fence, one went six feet wide, and the other five looked like they'd been thrown by Roger Clemens at his peak.

Jack Faber shook his head. "Coach, he's either gonna win us a championship, or he's gonna set the Cape Marlin League back fifteen years!"

Doughnut himself was unbowed. "Just a little practice, Coach.

That's all I need. Get a few of those kinks ironed out. I'll be okay. How d'you like my fastball, eh? Not too bad, right?"

"Got a little work here, Doughnut," replied Ted. "I think we might have to do something about the precise position of that right arm."

"Hell, don't worry about that, Coach. Koufax had a similar style. Same minor problem."

Ted Sando looked incredulous. He stared at the lanky lefty from Georgia, as if grasping for words, knowing this required unusual, drastic correction. And then he spoke carefully. "Doughnut, whatever your problem is, it bears no relation to any problem Sandy Koufax ever had in his entire life. We'll start off tomorrow by tying your right arm down. Let's do a little work, see if we can steady your aim down a bit."

"Tie it down? Jesus, Coach. You wanna disrupt my natural rhythm?" Doughnut was outraged. The son of a slick-talking father who had been telling him he was the next Roger Clemens since he was twelve years old, he found criticism abhorrent. Any criticism, that is. Gentle, constructive, well intentioned, abusive, ridiculing. It was all the same to Davis Junior . . . uncalled for. That simple.

"Doughnut," continued Ted. "There ain't one thing I can see that's natural about your rhythm. In fact, you don't have a rhythm. And I'd like to start off by enabling you to see, for a change, precisely where you're aiming the goddamned baseball. That is, if you want to become a starting pitcher for us."

Doughnut opened his mouth to protest, but Kyle was too quick for him. "Shut up, Doughnut," said the big right-hander from San Francisco, putting his arm around his shoulder and walking him away from the situation. "Just thank the coach for trying to help you and then get down to it. I expect you know Ted Sando was in Yankee AAA, a couple of curveballs from the Bronx, when he injured his shoulder."

"Ain't no coach never spoken to me like that before," said Doughnut, agreeably enough.

"I bet a hell of a lot of 'em wanted to," replied Ted. "Wait up here by the bull pen with Tony, will you? I want Russ to take a look at that action . . . see what he thinks."

The pitching coach walked toward the infield, where Russ was concluding his talk about the wooden bats, explaining how different they were from the regular, virtually unbreakable college aluminum.

He pointed out that with wood, the baseball would travel a few miles per hour slower in a line drive, and that fly balls would drop a few feet shorter. The wood was altogether more difficult, heavier, and the hitters would need to be especially careful taking inside pitches close to their fists.

Not only was it almost impossible to get the ball away, and into play, but swinging at such tight pitches would probably shatter the bat. All of the hitters had been used to the aluminum and its forgiving nature. Russ Maddox told them the high college batting averages, and long games, were the direct result of using aluminum. "You're gonna find it very different up here," he said. "Remember, we're your first step toward the Majors. In the end you're gonna have to master the wooden bats. And the quicker you can do that the better."

Right now Russ was moving in behind a pitcher's L-screen placed about fifty feet in front of the batter's box. Kyle Davidson and Aaron Smith had taken up position in the outfield, and Jack Faber took the bucket for the balls.

The outfielders were lining up to hit, and first up was Gino Rossi, leadoff hitter from Seton Hall, New Jersey. He was a lithe, athletic-looking Italian kid from New York City, where his father owned restaurants. Gino had built a big reputation at his university. He was only just nineteen and a bit cocky, the kind of kid who would quickly develop a fan club on Cape Marlin. All girls.

He stepped up to the plate, took a few practice swings, and nodded to the coach, who began sending in easy pitches for the young Italian right-hander to hit. He missed the first two, but he connected with the next eight, banging the baseballs way out into left field, where Aaron scooped them up and send them back in to Jack Faber with the bucket. It was clear to Russ Maddox that Gino had an excellent eye, and yet Gino seemed irritated, unable to find the precise sweet spot on the bat. Which did not surprise the coaches. It's smaller on the wooden bats, considerably smaller than on the aluminum. They were well used to seeing the young college hitters struggling early on with their new weapons.

Russ threw Gino a lot of balls, and then he called time and walked over to talk to him. The others could hear snatches of the conversation . . . "Gotta start that swing with your hips just a fraction earlier than you're used to . . . keep your head well down . . . remember you need a little more time . . . this bat's heavier than you're used to."

Next up came Ray Sweeney, a junior center fielder from the University of Maine, well-known to both Russ and Ted, who had witnessed his meteoric rise to prominence with the Black Bears. Ray was a walk-on. He had been neither scouted nor recruited, nor had he been awarded a scholarship. But his grades were good and he applied to the university, and was accepted. He went in search of the coaches and told them he'd played some baseball in high school and would like to try out.

No one had ever heard of him, but Russ Maddox had taken one look at the strapping 6 foot one-inch 220-pounder from Vinalhaven Island and given him a trial. In addition to a throw from the outfield like a howitzer shell, Sweeney had a brilliant eye and quick hands. When he caught the ball right, he could slam it a country mile. Russ jokingly assessed at least half of his body weight was in his shoulders and arms. Ray's strength, for one so young, was astonishing, and he made a striking figure. With his jet-black straight hair, tanned face, and dark blue eyes, he looked like a Spanish pop star with muscles.

He was the son of a working lobsterman out of Carver's Harbor, a busy commercial fishing center, which lies in the southern lee of the island, facing the Atlantic Ocean. Vinalhaven itself is located way down east, in Penobscot Bay, which is probably the finest cruising ground in the state of Maine. Forty miles long, fifteen miles wide, and scattered with more than two hundred other deep-pinewooded islands, Penobscot is the preferred summer water of some of America's most elegant yachts and wealthiest people.

Vinalhaven lies south of the picturesque seaway of Fox Island Thoroughfare, which divides it from the welcoming shore of North Haven. But Ray Sweeney's home port of Carver's Harbor has nothing to do with the rich and famous. It is a working place, full of lobster boats and draggers. It scarcely has facilities for cruising yachts. There's no sign of guest moorings and yacht clubs, the bottom is soft mud and only reluctantly holds an anchor.

All day long, and for much of the night, lobster boats run in and out of Carver's. Fred Sweeney was a third-generation fisherman, and his son Ray had honed his great strength hauling traps since he was a boy of eleven. In his later teenage years, Ray Sweeney sometimes worked twelve hours a day, in all weathers, way out in the bay above the granite ridges, pulling inboard the big, heavy wooden traps, running the boat between the brightly painted lobster buoys, watching for his dad's colors of purple and orange.

Ray was an excellent seaman, a first-class navigator, and a qualified master of a fishing boat. But his life's goal was a source of confusion. Whether to roam the misty, lonely acres of his beloved Penobscot Bay, privately earning a good living, and answering to no one, or to roam the outfield of Fenway Park, where his lifelong heroes, the Boston Red Sox, might one day position him.

Right now he faced up once more to an easy pitch coming in from Russ Maddox, and he swung the new wooden bat, taking an almighty cut at the ball, and missed it badly. "Steady, Ray," called the coach. "Nice and easy now."

He caught the next one low, and sent the baseball a hundred feet into the air, high over the infield. But the next one was different. Ray Sweeney found the sweet spot and slammed the ball high and far, right over the left-field fence, deep into the trees. Everyone heard the unmistakable sound of a perfectly struck baseball, the solid whack of the wood. And everyone automatically stared into the light blue summer sky searching for the soaring ball.

Kyle heard it hit a tree and tumble through the branches. "Christ," he murmured. "He gave that a ride. We got a real bat-breaker right here."

Ted Sando watched a few more shots, three of them just as well hit, and then he relieved Russ Maddox behind the L-screen, while the chief coach went to examine the problem of their number three pitcher, Doughnut Davis.

Next up was the right fielder Andy Crosby, a local twenty-year-old from Camborne, a small town with a large marina way down the Cape, where the long narrow peninsula curves 'round in a great sandy hook-shaped bay with westerly views of the sunset, toward the shores of New England. Andy's family owned the marina; had done so for more than a hundred years, though in the early part of the twentieth century it had been much more of a fishing port, a trading center for striped bass.

Andy had been recruited to the University of Connecticut by their nationally renowned veteran coach Andy Bayloch. Young Crosby was not a power hitter. He was slim in build, just less than six feet tall, but he had the strong, muscle-heavy legs of a deep-sea sport fisherman, and he was fast between the bases. He hardly ever hit a home run, but he hit the ball often, aiming for the gaps, driving it down the lines. He was Connecticut's best bunter, and he came to Seapuit with a batting average of close to .400.

He was easily the first of the new players to master the wooden bat. And as Ted sent in the easy pitches, Andy kept banging them out into left field, then right field, then to the center. He seemed to be able to hit anywhere, and Aaron Smith was all over the place, scooping them up, and Jack kept filling the bucket.

"BALLS!" yelled Ted. And Jack came loping in with his load of baseballs, emptied the bucket, and returned to his position infield of Aaron and Kyle.

Ted summoned Tony Garcia in from the bull pen, where Doughnut was still trying to steady down his fastball under the watchful gaze of Russ Maddox. Progress was slow. Doughnut's right arm was not in control. It shot skyward when he pitched because of habit, not by design. Doughnut did not know why he did it. Neither did he know, yet, in which precise direction the ball would travel when he let go. But they were working on it.

Tony Garcia jogged toward the dugout and took off his chest protector. Then he too made his way to home plate and took a few practice swings with the strange wooden bat. It felt heavy. Tony ran his hands down its smooth length, felt the weight in the head. Then he pulled on his gloves a little tighter and swung hard at Ted's first pitch. Missed.

Tony was feeling a little tired, and having caught a hundred hard pitches, he was feeling his left wrist. He cocked the bat high and took his regular stand, and again Ted sent in a simple pitch and again the catcher swung too late, clipping the baseball on the bottom half and hitting it straight into the top of the batting cage.

Then he popped three up in quick succession. Ted told him to steady down, to swing nice and easy, not too hard, get the head of the bat through. But young Garcia was getting rattled, and when the next pitch came in, he really concentrated, swung with all of his strength, and caught the sweet spot. The ball rocketed off the bat, flying high and straight, hit the fence in center field.

"That's good you got that out of your system," said Ted. "Now could we practice the swing? Nice and steady, concentrate on the timing, get the feel of the bat. You got the next two and a half months with the wood, so let's get into it."

Tony nodded. And Ted Sando kept him at the plate for a long time. The kid could hit, no doubt of that. But for the first few games at least he was going to need patience. Ted guessed correctly that Garcia was a player to whom the game had come very easy. This might be the first time he'd ever had to think hard about what he was doing. And he was finding that a bit of a struggle. But Tony was very ambitious, and he was a lot more of a hitter when he returned to the dugout than he was when he had left it twenty minutes before.

Russ Maddox came in to join Sando. The Oklahoma State first baseman Zac Colbert came up to the plate and proceeded to hit all three of the first pitches, long and easy, two of them out close to the center-field fence.

Russ Maddox looked at him sideways. "You used a wooden bat before, Zac?"

"Yessir." He had been practicing with the wood for several days before the trip.

"I thought so. And I like what I'm seeing. You like the wood?"

"Sure do, Coach. Matter of fact, I prefer it. It has a nice weighty feel, once you get used to it."

Zac was one of this team's two straight-up power hitters. No frills, not much of a bunter, nor even an accurate placer of the ball. Zac's game centered around a great eye, fast hands, and terrific strength. He was probably not quite so strong as Ray Sweeney, or so fast as Crosby, but he had Major League potential, and there would be a lot of scouts to see him in this, the summer that divided his junior and senior college years.

He was a typical product of the intense Oklahoma State system, the "Bedlam Baseball," which operates out of the newly renovated Allie P. Reynolds Stadium, right on the Stillwater campus. As a kid, he'd been taken to a lot of the OSU games by his father. In fact, he saw the game against Kansas when the great Oklahoma State pitcher Jason Bell threw fifteen strikeouts. And now he had followed Jason's footprints to Seapuit, and hopefully on to the Majors.

Totally focused, tough mentally and physically, and determined to hit and win, Zac *hated* to lose. Even his mother had been heard to observe that in defeat he was just an everyday, thoroughly unattractive person; bad-tempered and without charm. He had been brought up never to shake hands with the opposition, an unusual trait which would be broken here on Cape Marlin. Meanwhile he was whacking

Russ Maddox's pitches all over the field. And the Coach thought he was going to be a big asset to the squad, a natural-born number three hitter.

Next Maddox called in the second baseman, a highly intelligent five foot nine inch black athlete named Bobby Madison from The Citadel, the great military college in Charleston, South Carolina. Bobby was the son of a Pittsburgh steelworker, and the grandson of another. Since the age of twelve he had been ruthlessly determined not to join them at the blast furnaces.

Bobby had worked relentlessly to win an ROTC scholarship in The Citadel's elite South Carolina Corps of Cadets. This, he knew, would require him to seek and accept a commission in the armed forces, but he was one of those team-spirit guys to whom the military is a natural home. Many people thought he would probably graduate first in his class, and it was most unlikely that he would follow a career in professional baseball. Bobby's watchwords were the watchwords of The Citadel—honor, integrity, loyalty, and patriotism.

He had a lot of military written work he wanted to complete this summer, and he had been difficult to recruit. But Coach Maddox had desperately wanted to bring a working partnership to Seapuit of shortstop and second baseman. And he had watched Bobby and his teammate Rick Adams several times last autumn.

Rick Adams badly wanted to play, but it was not a done deal without Madison. Finally the second baseman agreed, but it meant he spent the entire Easter break working eighteen hours a day on his studies.

But what mattered to Russ was that Madison was here right now. And he tossed in the first pitch, which The Citadel star slammed way out into the gap between center and left. It did not escape the coach's attention that it landed in that no-man's-land which is almost unreachable to the fielders; too far back for the shortstop, too far forward for the center fielder. "He's put the ball there a few times in his life," murmured Russ.

Madison stepped back to readjust his batting gloves. He had a straight, erect posture, and his uniform was immaculate, bright white against his dark skin. He looked like an army officer to the tips of his polished black cleats, and he took the next six pitches in succession: line drive left; line drive right; screamer over Russ's head; hard bang center and left; hard bang center and right; towering fly ball which failed by thirty feet to reach the empty flagstaff at center.

"You used a wooden bat before?" asked the coach.

"Yessir. Been practicing on and off."

"Hope you can use it like that when we start playing for real."

"I'll be trying, sir."

"Good job, Bobby . . . let's take a few more before I take a look at your teammate."

Coach Maddox assessed the Citadel second baseman as a smart hitter, lacking real power but likely to get a lot of base hits. He already liked him immensely, as any coach would. Madison was extremely organized, punctual, and gung ho about the team. He had been selected to work in the junior baseball clinics, coaching batting and infielding.

The second Citadel player, shortstop Rick Adams, came to the plate next. He was from a South Carolina military family with deep Civil War roots. He was the fifth member of the Adams clan to attend the military college, but the first to make a name for himself at the ballfield—the excellent College Park, which seats four thousand for Citadel home games.

Rick had been a high school star in South Carolina and he went to his father's old alma mater with one eye on the outstanding baseball program. The Citadel has won the Southern Conference Tournament Championship several times and has been ranked in the nation's top ten. Rick Adams was clean-cut, well mannered, and nothing short of an acrobat in the field. At only five feet eight inches, he had a lot of leaping, jumping, and diving to do, but he had an uncanny ability to focus, and a fine baseball brain. If Seapuit had ever fielded a captain, which they hadn't, Rick Adams would have been Coach Maddox's first choice.

Like Bobby Madison, he was not a power hitter. He was an organized hitter. He made base hits when they really counted. He had an extremely high RBI count, and he could pull the ball hard, down the left-field line, over the third baseman's head. He was very sharp between the bases, fit and athletic.

But Rick was expected to become a career officer in the United States Army. He was, he knew, a little small for the Majors, where power hitting was becoming an increasing requirement, even for the most effective infielders. And, if he was honest with himself, the U.S. Army was probably the correct place for him. He had been brought up with its history, its traditions, and its creeds. The Citadel's tough regime of barracks life, training, drills, formations, parades, inspections, and studies were second nature to him. And he believed in The Citadel's assertion that "every cadet enters this place on the basis of absolute equality with all others."

Rick was the son of a major general and the grandson of a lieutenant general, but Bobby Madison, steelworker's son, was his closest friend. Best second baseman he'd ever played with, "and a guy who'll make general before I do."

Facing the easy pitches from the coach, Rick demonstrated a fast but deliberate swing. He and Madison had plainly been practicing with wooden bats over the previous few weeks, and Seapuit's new shortstop hit a lot of baseballs deep into the outfield. In the first dozen pitches he took, he popped up only two. He almost hit one over, and Russ turned around to watch it bounce and hit the left field fence.

Like most of the other hitters, Rick was instructed to make three bunts, and he executed them stylishly. Russ had coached guys from the military before and he knew that potential officers from The Citadel would "sacrifice" in the interest of the team anytime it was required. He thus resolved to put Rick Adams at number two in the order, right behind Gino Rossi. Zac Colbert would come in at three, followed by a couple of power men.

He called out, "Good job, Rick," and summoned one of those power men, the third basemen from the University of Texas, Scott Maloney, who had been making practice swings, with the weights on the wooden bat, for the better part of a half hour. And now he took off the weights and moved up to the plate. A big, beefy junior with short-cut blond hair, Scott affected a hard, gruff manner and his conversation was studded with *uh-huh*s, and *yup*s, and *Is that right*s. He offered little in the way of personal revelation except that he was from West Texas, Amarillo, where his dad worked at the Livestock Auction Corporation.

His reputation as a big hitter had, however, preceded him. The Longhorns had recently made the College World Series and everyone had seen Scott slam two three-run homers in the early games, one against LSU, one against Stanford, off a weary Kyle Davidson in the eighth, when the Cardinals were out in front 8–0.

However, Scott had little or no feel for the wooden bat, and when he failed to find the sweet spot once in Russ's first eight pitches, he stepped back and shook his head. "Coach, I'm doing something wrong right here."

Maddox came forward, dispensing advice, slowing down the swing of the frustrated Longhorn, telling him he must start to hit a split second earlier because of the extra weight. It almost worked immediately, but not quite. Scott hit the next two a hundred feet in the air, still striking the ball a fraction late and low. He got ahold of the next one, though, and slammed it way into center field. If it hadn't gone so high it might have gone out. The one after that screamed into the loose netting of the L-screen right above Russ Maddox's head.

"Yup, Scott. I'd say you were getting the hang of it right about now," he said.

The big Texan laughed for the first time since he arrived, clenched his right fist, and pumped it. "Makes a great sound, don't it, Coach? When you hit it right."

"No sound like it, son. Not in all the world."

At the end of practice, Russ was putting together a lineup in his mind. "Rossi, Adams, Colbert . . . then Scott Maloney . . . then Ray Sweeney right behind him . . . that gives us three big bangers in a row and a couple of fast leadoff men who might get on. After that I need a smart hitter . . . Bobby Madison . . . seven, eight, and nine aren't clear . . . but Tony Garcia's in there somewhere . . . so's Crosby."

He called over to the bull pen to Ted, who was watching Aaron Smith throw to Tony Garcia. "Lemme see Aaron hit in a half hour," he called. "He's supposed to be good, and he can operate in the outfield as well."

Ted signaled he had the message and continued to watch the silk-smooth action of the pitcher from Shreveport, hurling in fastballs to Garcia. They were, he noted, as fast as Faber's, but young Smith did not yet have the variety to be a top starting pitcher. Not in this league. Not yet.

The afternoon sun was high over the two-mile sweep of white sandy beach that makes up Cape Marlin's Outer Bank, the stretch that faces the North Atlantic, where the offshore breeze whips the crests from the incoming rollers.

There are few perfectly calm days out here. The long, blue-green

waves, plowing into the vast shallows, begin their journey hundreds of miles out, building and building before crashing upon this
unprotected shore—occasionally bringing a hapless cargo ship with
them.

In bad weather, the Outer Bank is, historically, a graveyard. With
a wind coming in from the northeast and the tide running inshore,
the elements can simply overwhelm the marine engines of unwary
captains. Today the wind was from the southwest, mild inland, but
out here it was gusting out to sea, across the incoming waves. Ben
Faber and Natalie Garcia had rarely seen such spectacular water, certainly not Natalie, who could not remember seeing the ocean before
at all. Ben told her the Great Lakes didn't count.

Nancy McLure had given directions to the two visitors up to this
wild stretch of the Cape, where she knew there would be few tourists
this early in the season. Ben's Chevy had made the journey without a
hitch, and now he and Mrs. Garcia were taking a long walk by the
water, trying to find a common subject to discuss, which was not
easy, since baseball was not going to do it.

"Were you originally from Detroit?" he asked her finally.

"I was. My mother died when I was very young, and my father
worked on one of the car assembly lines. He was from Puerto Rico,
but Mom was American."

"How come you married so young?"

"Well, I was trying to go to college, to study music. But there was
no money. I had this boyfriend, Tony's father. And then I got preg-
nant and we married. His family were Puerto Rican, friends of my
father, and I thought we might make it work. At least I assumed it
would have to work since we were both the same age and both
Catholic. He worked in the car factory too, and we had some money.

"But one day he just left, saying he could not take it anymore. I
think it was the small apartment in a bad part of the city that did it.
The new baby was just too much for him. He couldn't stand the
noise and the mess, and the nights awake. So he went back to Puerto
Rico. I divorced him about ten years ago."

"How did you cope? I mean, when he first left you and the baby?"

"Badly. But my father helped. And then later it was very hard to
get into a music school in Detroit, so I tried to get into one in
Chicago. And finally I made it on a scholarship. I had to work half
the night as a waitress in order to pay for a sitter. But I got through

it, and I got an honors degree . . . I studied both the harp and the piano, and I also played the violin."

"Did that all get you a job?"

"Yes, it did. The Chicago School of Music was wonderful. They placed me with the Chicago Symphony, but I still had to waitress, and of course I could never go on tour, where I might have made some money."

"What did you do when they went on tour?"

"The school helped me find work at the university. I taught there for several years, and sometimes, when the symphony was in the city, I was able to make reasonable money. One time I was making eight hundred dollars a week, but I needed two hundred dollars of it for the child minders. I couldn't just leave him."

"How about his school?"

"Well, he went to the local high school, and he did very well. He actually won a full scholarship to Northwestern. And then he was quickly on the road to law school. But the more successsful he was academically, the more he seemed to want time off from his studies for baseball."

"I understand, Natalie. That must have been an awful disappointment for you."

"It was just terrible. And it got worse. He went to the College World Series, and that seemed to take weeks off from his schoolwork. Then, just when everything seemed better. Tony was working again at university, and I was sitting in with the symphony, *and* teaching on a regular basis in the day. Then he announced he had been recruited by this dreadful baseball club on Cape Marlin and was putting everything on hold with his studies until after the summer."

"Oh, Jesus, I see now why it was so bad."

"Ben. All I could see was that this bright, clever boy, for whom I had given up everything, all those years—and he was throwing it all away. I put down the phone after he called me, and I literally wept for an entire day—and you want me to like this horrible place?"

"Well, not exactly. But it ain't too bad right here, eh?"

Natalie Garcia smiled despite herself. "Not right here, Ben. It's that damned ballfield I mean."

They walked on past the slow, pounding rollers, silent for another few minutes, before Ben Faber ventured: "Natalie, you want me to tell you some things about baseball . . . what makes it so great . . .

and why it's an honorable profession for any young man who's that good at it?"

"No, thanks. I don't. And in return for your avoiding the subject, I won't bother you with the finer points of Bach's Sonata in E-flat for Harp and Flute."

"Now, you listen to me, Miss Natalie . . . I'm not nearly the uncultured redneck you think I am. Let's face it, you don't even know . . . for all you know, I might be a virtuoso flute player."

"Flautist, actually. And anyway, are you?"

Ben Faber threw back his head and laughed. "No, actually, but I used to throw a hell of a knuckleball one time."

Natalie Garcia suppressed a smile. She just shook her head, and punched the big sugar farmer playfully on his massive right arm.

4

Natalie Garcia and Dr. Paul McLure did not attend the annual barbecue for the players, the houseparents, and the team committee on the following evening. Dr. McLure, because he had a late surgery. Natalie, because she could not bear the thought of it.

Ben Faber noticed her absence with just a twinge of sadness, feeling, unaccountably, that he had been personally slighted. He knew he had no reason to think such thoughts, and he told himself firmly, *The lady hates baseball. I guess that's that. She doesn't even notice me. Unless she has to. Probably she's got more important things on her mind.*

Anyway, the barbecue was a huge success. All the players were now arrived in Seapuit, and they gathered around the pool at the Fallons' house, eating hamburgers and hot dogs with potato salad, chips, and five different kinds of desserts. They were permitted to drink only soda and fruit juice, and they listened politely through speeches made by the coaches, the general manager, and finally the president of the Seapuit Seawolves.

Then each player was required to step forward and announce his name, his school, his position on the ballfield, and anything else that seemed significant. Five of them admitted it had been a longtime ambition just to get to the Cape Marlin League, but now that they were here, they realized their task had only just begun. "And I'll be trying my best out there tomorrow night, yessir."

The party broke up before 10 P.M. Coach Maddox informed each player they all had work to do in the morning. There was a light training session scheduled after lunch, then batting practice at 3 P.M. At five o'clock they would face the Henley Mets in the opening game of the season at Cabot Field. Jack Faber would be the starting pitcher for the Seawolves. Kyle Davidson would start on the following evening, under lights, down the Cape at Bart Bradley Stadium, home of the St. Ives Red Sox, runners-up in last year's league championship.

Russ Maddox had already explained to the two pitchers the order they would work. "We know much less about Jack," he had said. "I'm very anxious to see him out there. Kyle, you're world famous. I know what you can do. That's why I'm holding you in reserve . . . I don't want to lose two in a row . . . and this unknown Louisianan might screw it up!"

He had his arm around Jack's shoulders as he spoke, and Ted Sando laughed at the joke. But the unknown Louisianan took it very seriously, and the responsibility he bore was uppermost in his mind. He did not sleep very well after the barbecue, and he reported to the field for work forty-five minutes early. He had the shed doors open, the mower filled with gas, the line marker ready, and the rakes in the infield before the others arrived.

He spent the last twenty minutes before Ted and Tony Garcia showed up running between the foul poles, right across the outfield and back, working up a sweat, driving himself, preparing himself for this evening's battle.

When they finally got down to preparing the field—Zac Colbert was late—Jack mowed the area immediately outside the bases, then he cut the infield, driving the tractor back and forth, making neat, professional lines in the grass. But by 11 A.M. he was at work on the mound, raking it, shaping it, tamping it down, walking endlessly across it, preparing his private domain. Sometimes he glanced across to the newly painted empty home bleachers, and he tried to imagine them filled with a thousand people as it would be this evening.

They broke for lunch at 12:30 and the three players walked down to the beach. It was a warm June morning and they sat at the edge of the water eating sandwiches and drinking fruit juice, watching a ferry moving across the horizon.

"There's an Oklahoma State guy catching for Henley tonight," said Zac. "Read it in the paper this morning."

"That why you were late?" asked Tony, grinning.

"Kind of. It'll be real strange having ol' Pete Higgins as the enemy. He's a buddy of mine back home."

"I suppose you could get him to tip you off what pitches are coming," said Garcia. "But Coach Sando says we'll all run into guys we know back at school while we're here. Better not to speak to them under the circumstances, 'cept for a quick chat before batting practice."

"Yeah. Guess so . . . still, it'll seem pretty strange, ol' Pete right behind me, not speaking."

At 2:45 the team assembled at Cabot Field, suited up and ready for one hour's batting practice from 3 P.M. to 4. The visitors would have the field from 4 to 4:30. Russ Maddox had posted the lineup, formally, that morning and there were no surprises:

1. Gino Rossi (Seton Hall). Left field.
2. Ricky Adams (The Citadel). Shortstop.
3. Zac Colbert (Oklahoma). First baseman.
4. Scott Maloney (Texas). Third baseman.
5. Ray Sweeney (Maine). Center field.
6. Bobby Madison (The Citadel). Second baseman.
7. Andy Crosby (Connecticut). Right field.
8. Tony Garcia (Northwestern). Catcher.
Starting pitcher: Jack Faber (St. Charles College, La.).
Reliever: Doughnut Davis (Georgia).

Kyle Davidson was down to keep the pitching sheet.

On the mound for the Henley Mets would be the six-foot six-inch Arkansas Razorback Ned Taylor, a lanky right-hander out of Little Rock. Zac Colbert had played against him, said he never had much left after four. "But he can throw the sonofabitch when he's fresh."

Russ Maddox took batting practice himself while Jack and Kyle fielded balls in the outfield and threw them to Doughnut, who had the bucket. At four o'clock sharp the Seapuit hitters vacated the infield, and the Henley players came streaming out of their dugout. Spectators were already arriving at the ballpark, the kitchen was open, yearbooks were going on sale along with the new T-shirts, hats, and sweatshirts.

Kyle and Jack sat quietly in the corner of the Seapuit dugout watching the visiting hitters, making notes, speaking quietly. Tony Garcia joined them for the final twenty minutes of the Henley practice.

With fifteen minutes to go before game time, Ted Sando called for Jack to start getting warmed up, and the pitcher from the bayous and his battery mate, Tony Garcia, jogged into the bull pen.

"Hey, Jack. Butterflies?" asked Sando.

"Yup. Got a few."

"I'd be concerned if you didn't."

Tony Garcia now went into his crouch, standing a little short, around fifty feet, and Jack Faber began to pitch, conscious that his coach was standing right behind him, aware of his father watching discreetly from a far corner.

He threw eight, before Garcia moved back to the full distance of sixty feet and six inches. Jack threw four half-speed fastballs, then signaled he was stepping up the pace. Garcia nodded, deadly serious now, and he took four in succession right over the plate. The catcher from Northwestern had come to Seapuit with a towering college reputation, and Jack was beginning to find out why.

"Attaboy, Jack . . . keep it up . . . let's work the ball inside and out . . . come on, baby . . . let's find that groove . . . that's good . . . that's a real good pitch . . . now let me have one for the lefty . . . great . . . now the curve for the righty . . . and another . . . we got another lefty . . . watch my signal . . . beautiful . . ."

Tony nodded to Ted Sando, a nod of confirmation. Sando thought, This kid really can put the ball where he wants it. And now Jack signaled, ready to throw ten hard pitches, just as if he were facing three batters.

Garcia nodded, went back into his crouch. Ted called softly, "Steady, Jack. Don't rush it. Keep your arm up on the breaking ball . . . stride's just a little long . . . cut it down a tad . . . elbow up . . . that's real good, Jack."

The tenth hard pitch smacked into Garcia's glove, and Jack Faber pulled off his glove. "Okay, Coach," he said. "All set."

"Okay. Now get your coat on . . . get a drink of water . . . and take a few deep breaths."

They walked back to the dugout and watched the opening ceremony performed by Dick Topolski, welcoming the big opening-night crowd of over one thousand in the home bleachers. Then the Seapuit Seawolves came running out of the dugout, together for the first time, each of them shocked by the thunderous burst of applause and cheering that accompanied their appearance—nine young men from hundreds of miles away, strangers in this leafy New England village, welcomed onto the ballfield as if they had lived here all of their lives.

In the outfield, beyond second base, facing the long wall of pine and oak trees and the lightly fluttering Stars and Stripes, Gino Rossi, Ray Sweeney, and Andy Crosby stood shoulder to shoulder, caps off in readiness for the National Anthem.

The infielders, Rick Adams, Bobby Madison, Zac Colbert, and Scott Maloney, stood in line just behind second base facing the outfield. The two Citadel men, standing rigid, one on each end, made it look like a honor guard.

Jack Faber and Tony Garcia stood to attention by the mound, and as Seapuit's superb resident singer sent the sacred words echoing into the cornflower-blue sky, each player placed his hat over his heart, respecting the timeless traditions of the game. As the long-drawn-out *Home of the brave . . . "* finally died away, the nine players broke from the lines and ran into position. Jack Faber spoke briefly to Tony Garcia, and then he moved up and quietly paced the mound, clutching in his right hand the little silver Saint Christopher medal which had belonged to his mother.

He tucked it into his back pocket, pulled on his glove, nodded to Tony, and threw his last four warm-up pitches. Then he prepared to pitch to the opening Henley batter, a big guy called Masters from the University of Arizona. Jack flexed his shoulders. He could smell the damp, just-watered infield grass, and the drying red mud of the mound, the mystical odors of baseball. The rays of the late afternoon sun rested lightly on his shoulders, and his shadow grew longer, and the field seemed to sit breathless as Garcia signaled for a fastball. Jack went into his windup and fired in a smoking 90 mph pitch, arrow straight, over the plate. Masters hit it hard and badly, on the upside of the bat, and the ball rocketed about two hundred feet into the air, almost vertical. Zac Colbert had to run in to catch it.

The crowd cheered, though not as loudly as they would three minutes later when Jack Faber whipped three fastballs in a row straight over the plate, and sent down the second Henley hitter without a swing.

The third man lasted, if anything, even less time. Knox was his name, from Vanderbilt, Tennessee, and he immediately fouled back two fastballs. He was a good hitter and he set himself up carefully, ready for the next. But Jack Faber, for the first time, hurled in a hard breaking curve. Knox swung himself off his feet, missed by an embarrassing distance, and that was the end of the Henley first inning.

Jack could barely believe the reception he received, hundreds of total strangers, people who had never even heard his name five days ago, were standing up in the bleachers clapping and shouting . . . "ATTABOY, JACK!" . . . "WAY TO GO, JACK!" Jeez, was this place something, or what?

And now the Razorback Ned Taylor took to the mound and he was almost as effective; sent down the first two with eight pitches, walked Zac Colbert before Scott Maloney was caught in center field. The entire second inning was over in fourteen minutes. Jack retired three in a row, and Ned Taylor walked Ray Sweeney before sending down Madison, Garcia, and Crosby in succession.

Jack came up for the third and sent down three more without a hit, two strikeouts. The opening game at Cabot Field was shaping into a pitching duel, but deep in the home dugout, Zac Colbert was still saying, "This pitcher gets tired. Trust me . . . we just need to stay patient and he'll fade."

The Seapuit leadoff hitter Gino Rossi now made his way to the plate, and laid off the first two pitches—2–0. The third was closer, breaking away to the outside, but Rossi still refused to swing and the umpire called 3–0. Ned Taylor, angry now, went back to his fastball, but it came in too high, and Gino walked to first base.

Rick Adams, the future army officer from The Citadel, stepped up next, and Ned Taylor hit him right in the backside with a wayward change-up. Adams never flinched, tossed his bat, and trotted to first base. Which brought up Zac Colbert.

The power hitter from Oklahoma took his stance, and allowed the first pitch to go right by. It was a good hard fastball. Strike one. Taylor stared down at Zac. The two were old enemies. The pitcher went into his windup and unleashed a deadly-straight fastball right over the plate. Zac didn't let this one go by. He swung hard, slammed a line drive just in front of the Henley left fielder, who dived, twisted, and hurled the ball into third base. Too late. Rossi got there first, sliding in like a torpedo in the dust, hands outstretched. Bases loaded.

Ned Taylor did not like what he was seeing. He fired a fastball past Scott Maloney, then tried his change-up, which the big Texan misjudged. He took a terrific cut at the ball, popped it high over the catcher's head and was neatly caught when it came down. One away. Bases still loaded.

Big Ray Sweeney stepped up next and slammed into the first pitch, a scorching line drive straight over the head of the second baseman. At least that's what it looked like, but the Henley second baseman rose and caught the ball spectacularly high above his head, then flipped it to the shortstop, who doubled off Adams as he tried frantically to get back to second. Every one of the five third-inning Seapuit hitters sensed they had squandered a huge opportunity, and a sense of frustration was creeping over the dugout.

But Russ Maddox was cheerful. "Hey, that's all right. Keep your heads up. This is just a matter of time. We're on 'em."

Ray Sweeney growled, "Taylor's already losing it."

And once more Jack Faber headed for the mound, feeling confident. No hits so far. The first Henley hitter whacked the opening pitch, a bouncing drive straight back to Jack, who fired him out at first base.

The second Henley batter was a brawny power hitter named Lee from Florida State, and to the delight of Tony Garcia, his natural batting stance put him a foot and a half off the plate.

Garcia called for Jack's slider. And the Seapuit pitcher threw it, the ball breaking hard and downward right over the outer third of the plate. Lee left it alone, and Garcia called for another.

This time Jack threw it two inches farther outside. Lee swung and connected all wrong, fouled it off, 0–2. Garcia knew this was a dangerous game, but he signaled, "Slider again."

Jack nodded, standing stock-still on the mound as Tony set himself up on the outside corner, moving over, his right hand in the red dust. He set his glove directly on the corner, and he watched Jack wind up, and he knew Lee was looking for a fastball. He also knew he was not going to get one.

Tony saw Jack's right wrist twist on the release, spinning the ball in. For a split second the catcher's heart stopped as Lee swung, but then the ball broke viciously down and away. The batter wasn't even close, and Garcia caught it neatly, pumping his right arm up and down with pure joy.

The Seapuit crowd, fired up by the obvious elation of the catcher, was on its feet, cheering the right-hander from Louisiana, yelling his name, in readiness for the appearance at the plate of Henley's top hitter, Ray Pulaski, a big brawny outfielder from Nebraska, one of the stars of the Big Twelve Conference.

Tony Garcia went into his crouch and signaled for a fastball. Pulaski swung hard, caught it wrong, and fouled it off his foot, hopping up and down with the pain. Jack heard him yell, and he stared down at Tony, who was asking for another fastball, this time high and tight. He threw the pitch as instructed, right in front of Pulaski's chin. Garcia heard him mutter, "Tell him to bring that shit inside, one more time."

Tony chuckled, and signaled for another slider. Jack nodded and hurled a fierce downward-breaking ball, right across the outside corner. Pulaski swung hard, and missed, 1–2.

Garcia knew the batter was anxious, wound up, angry with the pitcher. He signaled for a high fastball, not in the zone, because he was certain Pulaski would now swing at anything. And he was right. Jack wound up, reaching far back for a little more power, and ripped a 93 mph tailing fastball like a swerving bullet. The Nebraskan's eyes lit up, but he was too anxious. He swung ferociously, missed by three inches, and fell to the ground, cursing under his breath with rage and frustration.

Jack Faber never even looked up for the call. He just wheeled away and walked off the mound, heading for the dugout, head down. The Seapuit crowd went berserk, and out of the corner of his eye, Jack could see his dad, standing up on his seat, waving his old red baseball cap, and above the roar he could still hear that voice, the voice of his childhood, *"Attaboy, Jackie! That's the one . . . that's the one!"*

As Jack reached the top of the steps, Russ Maddox came out to shake his hand, Kyle Davidson alongside him.

"Good job. You okay, Jack?"

"Never felt better."

And now they prepared to go out for the bottom of the fourth. No score yet. Everything to play for. Ned Taylor was back on the mound and Bobby Madison was getting ready.

"Be patient, Bobby. Gimme a good leadoff. Let's get on base, right? Get things started."

To himself, the Citadel cadet whispered, *It's gotta be a good pitch to drive, or I'm leaving it.* To the coach, he snapped, *"Sir."*

Up at the plate, he got himself focused, wary of the words Kyle Davidson had murmured to him as he left. "This guy's just a bit rattled, watch for his best pitch . . . the fastball on the outside corner. He goes away with it more often than he comes inside."

Like clockwork it came in, and just missed the outside corner. Bobby Madison left it, and the umpire called a ball. The next pitch was identical and Bobby left that too. The umpire called it 2–0. Then the tall Razorback pitcher made a real mistake. He decided to send in an inside fastball, try to back Madison off, set him up for the big sweeping curve.

But the pitch was never tight enough. It came in fast, too close to the middle of the plate. And Madison picked it up early. He turned, hips wide open, threw his hands forward, very fast, and landed the barrel of the bat right on the ball—banged it hard down the left-field line, the ball bouncing past the third baseman's outstretched glove.

The plate umpire whipped off his mask in his right hand and silently held it out, rigid, pointing in toward the field. *"FAIR BALL!"* bellowed the crowd as Bobby Madison came hurtling into second in a cloud of dust and commotion.

And up came Andy Crosby, the Connecticut outfielder, thoughtful, determined, and deceptively smart. Taylor immediately sent in that sweeping curve, and Andy swung away, recklessly. *Here's a guy trying to make a name for himself,* thought Taylor, and next he hurled down a heat-seeking fastball, straight and true. But in that split second, Andy suddenly slid his back foot four inches away and slipped his top hand down to the LOUISVILLE SLUGGER label on the bat, the soft grip for the classic drag bunt. Andy killed that fastball at birth, dropped it stone dead, and everyone saw it trickle down the grass toward third base. But it never got there, and Taylor charged off his mound to field it. Too late. The runners were gone, Madison on third, Crosby on first, and Tony Garcia on his way to the plate. No one out.

Again Ned Taylor opened with his curve, but this one was too low, and Tony left it alone. The second pitch was a fastball, and the Seapuit catcher fouled it back, 1–1.

And now Taylor had firm plans to fool the hitter completely. He decided to go to his change-up, making his windup suggest all the signs of the fastball but holding the baseball well back in the palm of his right hand, cutting down its speed, tempting the batter to swing too early.

Tony Garcia was not an ideal man on whom to try this experiment. He had been watching Jack Faber's delivery for almost an hour, and he spotted the deception by Taylor right when the ball left his hand. It came in at 80 mph and Tony Garcia kept his hands and weight well back. He never even started to move forward, just waited, and then he absolutely exploded on that fat, slow ball. Slammed it high and far, out into the soft, billowing offshore breeze, clean over the left-field fence, just left of the scoreboard, straight into the trees, for a three-run homer. Seapuit 3, Henley 0. Fourth inning. No one out.

Tony ran around the bases to rapturous applause. The crowd rose for the team's first home run of the new season. Garcia ran back to the dugout, and Russ Maddox met him at the top of the steps, shook his hand. "How to pick 'em up, kid."

Garcia smiled as he high-fived his teammates. "The key to this guy is his fastball. Watch him . . . he gives his change-up away—his arm slows up."

High in the bleachers Ben Faber was searching for Natalie Garcia, hoping she was enjoying the moment of her son's triumph. His eyes scanned the packed rows of seats, but it took him a full minute to spot her, sitting quietly with Mrs. McLure, talking but not animated, smiling but not applauding, cold to the feats of her own son. Cold to the beauty of the game. Ben Faber could have wept for her.

Next up, DH Aaron Smith, the gap-hitter from Shreveport. But he had little to do. Ned Taylor, uncertain, unable to settle back into his rhythm, couldn't find the plate, and four pitches later Aaron jogged to first. The Seapuit crowd was loving it. There was still no one out, and now Gino Rossi ran to the plate as he always did, and a loud, steady chant began, emanating from the back of the bleachers. And it would not be silenced all season . . . "*GEE-NO . . . GEE-NO . . . GEE-NO!*"

The Henley pitching coach called "*TIME!*" and walked out to the mound. Everyone could see him out there, trying to steady down the big Razorback. Finally he left, and Ned Taylor began to work again. Right away he threw a fastball, a pitch with a lot of zip. But he left it right in the middle, and Gino Rossi, who had grown up playing stickball in the streets of New York's Little Italy, was waiting. He swung hard, drove the ball over the second baseman's head and into right field. Aaron Smith started to round second but third-base coach

Brad Colton stopped him right there, respecting the Henley right fielder's arm.

Then Rick Adams arrived at the plate and immediately hit a sharp ground ball straight to the shortstop. But what seemed a certain double play turned into an error as the Mets fielder bobbled it, and the ball hit the heel of his glove, ran right up his arm. By the time he was back in control, all the runners were safe and the bases were loaded. Again. And the mighty Zac Colbert was on his way to the plate.

There was real concern in the Henley dugout, where the pitching coach was sending three men scrambling to the visitors' bull pen way down at the end of the right-field line, a sure sign of an imminent change.

The Henley catcher ran to the mound to speak to the now distraught Ned Taylor, and a form of quiet settled over the field. The Razorback hurled in a fastball. Zac fouled it off hard, and then did the same with the next pitch, 0–2.

Taylor knew he had to finish off Colbert right now, and he sent in a sweeping, hanging curveball. Zac had seen it before, and he read it right, never took his eye off the baseball. He unleashed a full swing, a vicious cut which sent the ball into orbit, high and straight. No one moved. They just stood and gazed upward as the ball flew way over the fence, over the scoreboard, into the center-field woods. Grand slam. Seapuit 7–0. Bottom of the fourth. Still no one out. The home crowd stood and cheered Zac Colbert all the way to the dugout.

Scott Maloney took an almighty cut at the first pitch to come over the plate and was caught at the base of the fence. Ray Sweeney did precisely the same, thirty feet to the right, and Bobby Madison just failed to beat out a ground ball to the shortstop and was thrown out at first.

Which brought Jack Faber back to the mound, still pitching immaculately. He got rid of the next hitters, three straight in the next three innings, after which he was scheduled to come out, and the crowd gave him a standing ovation for the seven-inning two-hitter. Jack touched his cap to them politely and left the field with Seapuit holding a 9–0 lead. Sweeney had drilled in two runs with a double in the sixth. Way down at the bottom of the seventh Andy Crosby repeated the exercise, leaving the 'Wolves out in front by 11–0.

The eighth inning was fraught with peril, as the gangling, erratic figure of Doughnut Davis headed for the mound. But to the surprise of Ted Sando and his two starting pitchers, Doughnut retired three of the first four Henley batters, his fastball working exceptionally well, in full control at last.

At the bottom of the inning Seapuit struck again, loaded the bases with the power hitters, Colbert, Maloney, and Sweeney. And Bobby Madison hammered them all home with a triple to right center. 14–0.

Seapuit was done. Three more outs required, and the opening ball game was over. Doughnut moved back to the mound, cheered all the way by the home crowd. Everyone anticipated victory, and there was a humorous gasp as the Georgian whipped the first pitch four feet above Tony Garcia's head.

The trouble was he did it again with his second pitch. The next one was wide, and the next one hit the dirt three feet in front of the plate. Even Masters, the leadoff Henley batter, was laughing as he trotted between home plate and first.

With his very next ball Doughnut slammed the next hitter hard in the upper arm, sending him to first and Masters to second. Two on, no outs. Ted Sando came to the mound. "C'mon, Doughnut . . . steady it up . . . you can get these guys . . . but we don't need mid nineties. We need strikes. C'mon now. Settle down. Let's end the ball game right here . . ."

Doughnut nodded. Ted left the field, and the Seawolves reliever prepared once more for action, leaning back and sending in two ex- cellent fastballs, each of which was fouled back hard. Doughnut worked his way to 3–2, and then fired another diabolically high fast- ball straight over Garcia's high outstretched glove. Jesus," shouted the catcher. Then to himself, Just where the hell did they get this guy?

With the bases loaded, Doughnut threw to the next hitter, who popped up and was caught by Rick Adams. "*Infield fly,*" yelled the umpire. "*The batter is out.*" Then the next Henley Met went down chasing a fastball. Two out. Bases still full. Russ Maddox covered his eyes. Which was just as well because Doughnut's next pitch screamed over Garcia's head and hit the wire fence ten feet above the ground. The runners advanced one base apiece; the shutout was gone on Doughnut's wild pitch

"Jesus Christ, Russ," said Sando softly. "Where'd you get this guy?"

Russ shook his head. And Doughbut pitched again; another high, wild throw, and Tony Garcia, tired after catching for two and a half hours, somehow leaped three feet into the air and came down with the ball. *"Ball Two!"* yelled the umpire, an edge of sarcasm in his voice.

"Jesus," hissed Ted. "This lunatic could walk in all fourteen runs for them."

"Don't," muttered Russ. "Not now."

Garcia, shaking his head, signaled for a fastball low and wide. Doughnut shook his head. Garcia signaled again and snarled, "Throw it, you crazy prick."

The umpire laughed quietly, and Doughnut sent in a fastball, straight down the pipe, where the Vanderbilt man, Knox, was waiting. He leaned back and slammed it hard, out toward the fence. Helplessly the Seapuit faithful watched it fly into the dying breeze.

Ray Sweeney, running fast from center, could never get there, but Gino Rossi was racing across the grass, flying toward the fence with every ounce of strength he had. And the ball was falling . . . falling . . . right up against the wire. The crowd was on its feet as Gino dived at full stride. His glove was outstretched, both feet were almost three feet off the ground, and in the loneliest part of the field, only he heard the sharp smack of the ball hitting the leather. Gino hit the turf hard and fast, rolled the last four feet into the wire fence, which bulged and stopped him going into the woods.

As he climbed to his feet, deep grass stains on his knees and, down the center of his shirt, blood trickling off both elbows, the ball could be seen, held triumphantly above his head, still in his glove. And from the exultant home bleachers there rose the new Seapuit anthem of victory: *"GEE-NO . . . GEE-NO . . . GEE-NO!"*

Doughnut stood on the mound, his right arm raised, his left pumping up and down, shouting over and over . . . *"YESSSS! . . . YESSSS! . . . YESSSS!"* Jack Faber walked over and shook his hand, and as he did so, the crowd burst into loud spontaneous applause for the sudden appearance of the winning pitcher. Jack watched deadpan as Doughnut acknowledged it with grace, touching the peak of his cap.

"How 'bout that, Jack?" he said proudly.

Back in the bleachers Ben Faber went over to visit Natalie, who smiled a warmer welcome than he thought he would receive.

"Natalie," he said. "You gotta be proud of him. Do you have any idea what kind of a job that kid of yours did out there tonight?"

"Well, Ben. I know he caught the ball, and I know he threw the ball, and I know he hit the ball two or three times. But I'd rather he passed his pre-law finals."

"You're a hard lady," he replied, grinning. "But I just want you to know that I'm damned proud to know Tony Garcia tonight. And I really wish you felt the same."

"I'm proud of him in a different way," said Natalie, still smiling. "As a mother with a son in a top school, not as the mother of a base-ball player."

"Okay. Just tell him you're glad he played well, will you? For me. It'd mean a lot to him."

"I might," she said. "What time are we leaving tomorrow?"

"Well, I'll pick you up at about ten in the morning. That way you'll be in the airport by midday, plenty of time for your flight. And I'll be way down into Maryland by dark."

"Thanks, Ben. I really appreciate it, you know. I'm not as awful as I pretend to be."

"I know. You sure you don't want to take a later flight? The Red Sox are at Fenway tomorrow afternoon."

Natalie laughed for the first time. "Why do you like teasing me, Ben Faber?"

"I guess because I'm good at it."

Just then Jack and Tony came through the ballfield gate, clutching their bags, chuckling at some private joke. They stopped to sign au-tographs for the kids, then they made their way up the steps to the seats where Ben and Natalie were still talking.

"Hello, parents," said Tony jauntily. "May I assume, for the ben-efit of the court, that you both enjoyed the near-flawless baseball played tonight by your respective sons? Ben? Mother? Speak up . . ."

Jack laughed as he did most every time the Midwesterner spoke. But Ben was very serious. "Tony, I thought you did just a super job out there tonight. Jack, I was proud of you. Got the ol' slider really humming in there, right?"

"Yup. Hey, what about that Doughnut? You ever see anything like that?"

"Christ, you should try catching the son of a bitch," said Tony. "He could throw the fucker anywhere . . . ooops . . . sorry, Mom."

"Yes, it would be nice if you could hold back on the locker-room language just for the remaining few hours I'm here." But then she softened, and kissed him on the cheek, and she said, "You played very well, darling. Ben is proud of you."

"How about you? Aren't you proud of me?"

"Yes, but for different reasons," she replied.

"How 'bout when I dragged down those two pitches that lunatic Doughnut threw over my head? Were you proud of me then?"

"More relieved, I think. It's such a damned dangerous game."

"Well, Mom. Doughnut is a reliever. So I guess you got that right. But how '*bout* that son of a bitch? Is that a wild man, or what?"

"He is that, Tony," said Ben. "But he's all you guys got. You just gotta steady him down. Somehow get the best out of him. He's your number three pitcher, and it's no good laughing at him. Doughnut's a real proud guy. And he thinks he's great. And don't you guys try to knock that outta him. You need him. The better he is, the better the team is. Don't try to shake his confidence."

"In the absence of a nuclear warhead, that'd be just about impossible," said Jack. "In my view, Doughnut is probably insane. You realize when the crowd gave me that round of applause tonight, he actually thought they were cheering for him?"

"No, son," said Ben gravely. "They weren't cheering for him—or you. They were cheering for eleven guys wearing pinstripes with SEA-WOLVES written across their jerseys."

The four of them walked out through the parking lot in the gathering gloom of evening. For Natalie it was just a walk to the car, like any other. But for Ben, and Jack and Tony, there were other sights and sounds and smells. Defeated players on the other side, walking slowly, eyes down, bags made to look heavy, the slow gait of those whose star had not yet shone. The hollow thump of the bins being emptied, the dying odors of the hotdog kitchen, the subtle hint of sweat on the air as he and Tony dumped their stuff in the back of the car.

Before they climbed in, Tony turned and took one more look out across the desolate field, to the place where he had slammed the home run. And the light breeze still rippled over the grass as the sprinklers hissed in the outfield. Jack stared again at the mound where he had fought it out for more than two hours. And he gloried quietly in the pain of his aching right arm. Natalie Garcia would never know what they knew: the thrill of the ballfield. Just to have played this game.

Tony and Jack and Ben left Cabot Field, each of them comfortable in all the rituals of the place, and their first game within it. Each of them was smiling inward, remote smiles. Some things would never be said, because some private glory is just too private. There were things they would not even say to one another. And there were memories of this night, for each of them, which would remain forever unspoken. And the ballfield would still be there tomorrow, and their secrets were safe.

5

Ben Faber's old Chevy turned out of the McLures' driveway and headed through the village toward the highway to the mainland. Natalie Garcia was neatly dressed for her flight back to Chicago; white blouse, and the same suit she had worn on her outward journey. Her short New England vacation had made her feel much better, and if she had been honest, which she wasn't going to be, she had almost enjoyed the game last night.

Ben had gassed the car up early in the morning and now they were driving fast, north to Boston airport. Conversation was hovering awkwardly around the zero mark. Ben did not dare to bring up the subject of baseball, and Mrs. Garcia was not yet ready to test him on Mozart's Serenade in B-flat Major. As things happened, a new subject elbowed its way into the old car without either of them really trying. That of poverty, the breadline hand-to-mouth existence to which they were both accustomed.

"You hope to get down here again this summer?" asked the sugar farmer.

"Oh, no. I can't afford it. The air fare is too expensive, and anyway I can't manage Tony's expenses unless I work real hard from now until September."

"Hmm. When do you start?"

"This evening. I have two private harp lessons, and I'm sitting in with the Chicago Symphony all day tomorrow. It's much harder for me when the university is out. I only get paid for what I do, and I have to go out and find work. Sometimes I advertise private music lessons, but if I don't get work, I just can't pay the rent, never mind my car payments and Tony's living expenses."

"You ever worked out what it costs you, exactly, each month, to live?"

"I do that just about every other day. And I always come up with the same figure. I must have nineteen hundred dollars after taxes, each month, or I can't make it. If the orchestra's in town it's fairly easy. But if they're not, it's very tough, charging twenty-five dollars an hour for private lessons in harp, piano, and violin. There's just not enough people. After I pay my bills, I usually end up with about two hundred and ten dollars a week to live on. And I have to pay for Tony's rent and meals out of that.

"Airfares," she added, "to watch my son play baseball do not figure in my budget."

"Christ. That's worse than being a farmer."

"Yes. It is. At least you have the farm. A house, some land, and a crop. If all fails, you and Jack are still sitting under your own roof. If I fail, I'm in the street. With my son, and presumably his catcher's mask. But possibly not his law degree."

Ben was silent. "Yeah. But there's another side to it. A downside. And you don't have one of those."

"How do you mean?"

"Well. You and Tony might be out in the street. But you're both young; he's twenty and you're not even forty. You're both educated, attractive people, and you're gonna make a comeback."

"So?"

"And it doesn't sound like you're carrying a lot of debt. That's what farmers have to cope with . . . you know, I have a bad crop . . . borrow from the bank for replanting . . . world sugar prices fall and I end up owing thirty thousand dollars I don't have, and have no way of getting, for maybe a year. If I'm lucky."

"Has that ever happened?"

"It's happening right now. You check the commodities market, you'll see sugar real low. That's my crop we're talking. If things turn up a bit, I might break even on the year. If they don't, I'll lose maybe twenty thousand on the crop, on top of the twelve thousand I already owe."

"But what happens if things go right, and sugar prices go up?"

"Well, then I might make fifty thousand for my year's work. And if I owe thirty thousand, that leaves me with twenty thousand, for me and Jack to live on. Plus I have to go back to the bank for more finance for next year."

"But what if there are two good years in a row?"

"Well, then I'm in Fat City. And I need a new tractor and machinery needs replacing. Always seems to end up in the same place, owning a working farm, without any money. I lose the farm, I'm destitute. And anyway, there haven't been two good years in a row for the past decade."

"Which explains why you cashed Jack's ticket to fund your trip."

"How did you manage it?"

"I got a bank loan for three hundred dollars, which I'm not sure I can pay back."

"Better start hitting those E-flat sonatas for flute and harp." He chuckled.

"How d'you remember that?"

"I told you. I'm not that much of a redneck. Jack's mother was a teacher. Taught painting and American history at the local high school."

"Yes, but how did you remember the E-flat sonatas?"

"I remember what people say."

"All people?"

"No. Just some people."

They crossed the high bridge to the mainland shortly after 10:30 A.M. and set off along the highway to Boston. They rode in silence for almost a half hour, and then Natalie asked, quite suddenly, "Ben, is there *any* light at the end of your tunnel? I mean, is there any hope for you ever to be better off?"

"Not so far as I can see."

"Well, how about if you sold the whole farm for building, or something like that? How big is it?"

"Probably around four thousand acres of land. But a lot of it's swamp, and some of it's river. I just have maybe a thousand and a half acres for raising sugar. Not much of it would be any good for building. That's why most of it's not worth much. Not unless they strike oil."

"Is that likely?"

"Not hardly. They been looking for natural gas in our area. There's some drilling on my land right now. But they never seem to find anything. State o' Louisiana's big in natural gas, though . . . they pump billions of cubic feet every year. Never found much in my area, though, so I'm not anticipating a damn thing."

By now they could see the skyline of Boston, the Prudential Tower jutting up over the distant tree line. And their financial meanderings went into a lull. Then Ben said, "How 'bout you, Natalie? Any hope down the road for a better life?"

"Two chances. First, my ex-husband strikes it rich and returns to Tony and me and begs my forgiveness in return for a huge settlement. Or second, Tony gives up baseball, gets down to his studies, and is offered a partnership in a big Chicago law firm."

Curiously Ben found himself not very keen on either of these possibilities. But he just nodded, in a noncommittal manner, and pressed on toward the underpass and Logan Airport.

They drove in just before midday, and as Ben pulled up outside the terminal, he handed Natalie a small piece of white card on which he had written his name and address and phone number. "Maybe I could take your number, just in case we ever find ourselves going to the Cape on the same weekend . . . save you a little if I can give you a ride down there."

Natalie looked at him, and smiled. Then she took a pen from her handbag and wrote down her phone number in Chicago. Then she leaned over and kissed the big farmer on the cheek, and said, "Ben, you have been really nice to me and Tony, and I do appreciate it. I hope we meet again sometime, but I don't know when . . . drive safely."

And with that, she was gone, clutching her small, worn suitcase, lost in the airport crowd. Ben Faber felt the kind of sadness all good-byes induced. And he pulled away from the terminal building, resolved to drive as far as Richmond, Virginia, for his first overnight stop.

He drove all day, pondering intermittently his two overriding concerns: that Jack might not be so good without him on the Cape, and that he might never see Mrs. Garcia again.

The latter problem was easily the worse, since neither of them could ever afford the airfare, and anyway he suspected she might not want to see him again. For what? He had nothing to offer. And she was a very beautiful woman. Frankly, he was amazed she was still single, and what good could it possibly do either of them conducting a relationship separated by a thousand miles, minimum. *Anyway,* he told himself. *We don't have a damn thing in common . . . she's just pretty, that's all. And I haven't spoken to a real pretty lady for too long.*

Ben Faber crossed the Potomac and ran into Virginia just before 9 P.M. But he never made Richmond. He pulled over right before the little township of Doswell, sixteen miles short. He picked a motel next to a diner, bought himself a hamburger and fries, plus a couple of Cokes, and made a long-distance call from his room.

"Hello, this is Bart Bradley Stadium—St. Ives Red Sox."

"Oh, hi, my name's Ben Faber . . . my son plays for the Seawolves. Could you tell me the result of the game tonight?"

"Yeah. Bad one for us. Seapuit won it six–nothing. That big Californian kid Davidson pitched a shutout."

"Thanks. Sorry to trouble you."

The next evening he was well into Georgia and he stopped for a hamburger and called Cabot Field to find out the result.

"Oh, hi, Mr. Faber. We won it seven–four. Aaron Smith pitched eight, then Davis came in and that's when we dropped the four runs. We were lucky. Coulda dropped ten! Doughnut was kinda . . . well . . . erratic."

Ben Faber grinned as he put the phone down and decided to drive another couple of hours. That way he'd be all the way around Atlanta for his second overnight stop. Tomorrow, with an early start, he'd be home before dark, running through Birmingham and Meridian, then dead straight down to Baton Rouge.

He made it too, driving into the little sugar farm in the swamps just before 8 P.M. No phone call tonight. The 'Wolves had the day off. Jack, Tony, Zack, and Andy Crosby were going fishing with Andy's father. Tomorrow night a newly arrived pitcher was starting against the Nauset Rollers, out on the east coast at Monomoy Stadium, under lights. Ben had the phone number.

Jack would start the following day, in game five, a long ride down the Cape for the inevitable struggle with the champions, Wellfleet Athletics, at Big Rock Point, a wonderful natural baseball arena with high grassy hills on two sides which held huge summer crowds in deck chairs. It was strange how the old traditions of Cape Marlin always seemed to hold true. Seapuit *always* had a struggle at Big Rock, whereas the other annually tough team, the Lancaster Sentries, *always* had trouble with Seapuit. All three teams had parks hard by the ocean.

Ben Faber would have given almost anything to have been back in New England, traveling down the long narrow land, past the spectacular beaches and seascapes. For him it was not so much the enthralling ocean views, but the knowledge that along these same highways and byways, some of the great ballplayers of modern times had traveled. When Ben looked at a baseball field, he saw only ghosts. His vast knowledge of the game, and its supreme practioners, made him able at a glance to pull up names and even faces of those who had played there before. When he looked out at Cabot Field, he had imagined big Mo Vaughn out there, swinging his bat with his lightning-fast hands on behalf of the Sentries. He could see the great Oakland catcher Terry Steinbach behind the plate, Will Clark in the infield, Tim Naehring on third.

To Ben a ballpark was sacred, the sight of it, the smell of it, the sound of it. He could stand in a deserted Turner Field in Atlanta, or beneath the tin roof of a bush-league stadium in Macon—and he could hear again the roar of the crowd or the crack of a bat.

He already had a copy of the Cape Marlin League handbook, and he already knew the names of the college stars who had passed the summer in the little ballparks by the sea. The Major Leagues were full of them. If Ben could have gotton to Wellfleet two nights hence, he would have been there early, before the players, and he would have sat on those grassy bleachers and checked the roster of the men who had played there, and he would have felt at home. More at home than he ever would feel in his desolate farmhouse in Louisiana. Ben Faber's soul was held together by 206 slightly raised red cotton stitches.

That night he went to bed, and in the distance he could still hear the throb of the drills searching for gas out in the wetlands beyond the main crop. Exhausted by the long drive, he slept like a rock, and in the morning he walked the plantation in the heat, checking the cane, under the sun, in the deep solitude of a man whose life had been almost bereft since his wife had died. Except for baseball. Except for Jack. Ben's boots might have been striding through the bayous, but tonight, while he sat alone, drinking a beer, eating a few fried shrimp, his heart was in the Seawolves dugout as they faced the Nauset Rollers.

He called the number at 10 P.M. It was over. Well over. Seapuit had rolled all over them 8–1, two home runs, one from Scott Maloney, one from Ray Sweeney. They had won their first four games. And tomorrow night Jack would start in the toughest game so far. Ben would have given his last dime to get there. But he did not have a last dime. The bank did—about $20,000 worth, actually.

Back in Seapuit the team was home late. Their record of 4–0 placed them top of the first published League Tables—the Western Division, which contained the Lancaster Sentries, the Exeter Braves, the Cardiff Commodores, and the Henley Mets. The eastern group saw the unbeaten Wellfleet Athletics on top of the Truro Cardinals, the Rock Harbor Mariners, the Nauset Rollers, and the St. Ives Red Sox.

Seapuit's record was superior because of the few runs, only five, against them, with thirty-five scored. The Friday-night game at Wellfleet, against the reigning champions, would sort out the early pecking order in the league. Every member of the team was ordered to bed immediately when they arrived home. Ted Sando wanted to see the pitchers at Cabot Field one hour before departure, at 2:30 P.M.

Everyone could feel the screws beginning to tighten, not least because tonight the hitters would face the acknowledged best pitcher in the league—Wellfleet's Brett Fisher, a six-foot four-inch farm boy from Laramie, Wyoming, the star hurler from the University of Michigan. The right-handed Wolverine was expected to be a number one draft pick.

Jack Faber felt good. His arm was completely rested, and he was ready to go. Ted Sando had a long talk with Doughnut Davis on the journey down the Cape, because the lefty from Georgia was scheduled to relieve again tonight if Jack tired. They arrived at Big Rock Stadium together just before 5 P.M. Russ Maddox gave them a short talk about commitment, about the dangers of complacency, and warned them that the scouts would be here tonight, from the Boston Red Sox, the Baltimore Orioles, the Kansas City Royals, and the Yankees. That was to his certain knowledge. There might be others.

By game time, 7 P.M., there were 2,500 spectators on the hillside. And the battle was everything it had been built up to be. Jack Faber held Wellfleet hitless for four innings, and Brett Fisher held the

'Wolves to one ground-ball base hit. It was a grim struggle between two top pitchers, under the lights, with a gentle sea breeze just taking the edge off the mugginess of the evening.

In the sixth, Wellfleet went ahead. Jack Faber walked their leadoff man, and the next hitter sacrificed him to third. Right after that, Seapuit had only their second fielder's error of the season, when the Wellfleet catcher Freddy Baron got hold of a fastball and slammed it past Bobby Madison, straight through his legs, which brought in the run.

In the seventh, Wellfleet managed successive base hits, and a sacrifice bunt put the runners on second and third, with one out. A hard base-hit single up the middle brought both runners in, and Seapuit was seriously behind for the first time this season, 3–0.

The eighth inning was their most frustrating. They squandered a chance with the bases loaded, Brett Fisher striking out both Gino Rossi and Rick Adams. Zac Colbert came to the plate and took a huge cut at the first pitch, sending it a hundred feet into the sky with Wellfleet's second baseman underneath.

As the seafret began to roll in, a tired Jack Faber went back out to the mound, and with a superhuman effort blitzed out the next three Wellfleet hitters in order, with fifteen pitches, nine strikes.

A solemn, serious Seapuit batting lineup prepared for the ninth, Russ Maddox exhorting them, telling them there was nothing to lose . . . "C'mon guys, stay aggressive . . . let's get out there and win this thing right now."

Scott Maloney, pumped up for the battle, came straight out and whacked a double off Fisher's second fastball, straight into the left-center gap. Ray Sweeney came up and took the first pitch, an inside fastball he banged right between the first and second basemen. This put runners on first and second.

Bobby Madison was next, and with iron discipline, he took Brett Fisher's first two fastballs without moving: 2–0. Then he fouled one back, then he left a tailing fastball high and tight. It was 3–1, and Fisher threw another fastball low and away. Madison left it. Ball four. The black officer cadet was on first, the bases loaded. No one out.

Wellfleet's coach called, "TIME!" and headed for the mound, talking earnestly to Fisher, trying to stop it getting out of hand. Coach Maddox was telling Aaron Smith to take his time, wait for the pitch. But Fisher had recovered, and he sent down a looping curveball, which broke in. Smith fouled off the next pitch and it was 0–2.

Fisher went back to the curve. But he got it just wrong. The ball came in, but it was not far enough outside, and Aaron got ahold of it, hitting a soft drive over the second baseman's head. Maloney and Sweeney both scored and Wellfleet failed to get Madison at third, the Citadel man racing in with a left-footed hook slide to the bag. Smith, not hesitating, took second base on the throw from right, and Seapuit, down 3–2, now had runners at second and third. The Wellfleet coach was scrambling three pitchers in the bullpen.

Tony Garcia stepped up to the plate, but the Athletics were desperately trying to buy time, praying the fog would roll in from the sea quicker. Catcher Baron went to the mound and started to talk to Fisher. The umpire yelled for him to get back, which he did, slowly.

Garcia took his stance, but the Wellfleet coach called "Time" again, and made a very slow progression to the mound, buying critical seconds for his closer to get ready.

This was his second trip, so Fisher was coming out. The umpire, plainly irritated, stepped forward and snapped, "Which one, Coach?" And the coach did not answer.

The umpire had plainly had enough of this, and he yelled, *"WHICH ONE, COACH?"*

"The right-hander," he replied, signaling, pointing to his right hand.

"OKAY, LET'S GO! RIGHT-HANDER!"

Fisher dropped the ball into the coach's hand and walked in. Out to the mound came Bobby Perez, a big, surly-looking guy from the University of Miami Hurricanes. He took eight warm-ups, five fastballs. Tony Garcia never took his eyes off him.

Garcia went into his stance again, and went after the first pitch, whacking a high sacrifice fly to left center. Bobby Madison tagged up, and bolted for home, thundering into the dirt headfirst, arms out for the tying run. Both he and Tony were given heroes' welcomes as they jogged back to the Seawolves dugout, with the game all tied up 3–3.

Andy Crosby was up next, and he hit a hard line drive off the first pitch. For a split second a shout went up from the Seapuit faithful, about forty of them behind the dugout, *"THAT'S IN THERE!"* But it wasn't. The Wellfleet left fielder made a spectacular shoelace catch, and Andy was gone. Aaron Smith was trapped on second with two outs.

But the 'Wolves sensed there was still a chance, even though the fog was getting visibly worse. And as the leadoff hitter Rossi ran to the plate in his customary action-man style, a muted chant from far-distant Cabot Field filled the fog-shrouded air above Big Rock Point . . . *"GEE-NO . . . GEE-NO . . . GEE-NO!"*

Perez sent down a curve, low and away, which Gino left for a strike. Gino stepped back, adjusted his batting gloves, and moved back into his stance. Perez, accustomed to intimidating hitters, sent in a fastball, riding in on the hitter's hands, trying to back him off. But Gino was not backing anywhere.

He dug in deeper, tapped the bottom of his bat twice with his left hand. Perez knew he should try again to back the hitter up. But he was impatient, and he went into his windup too quickly, fired a screaming fastball straight down the plate across the outer third. As he released the baseball, Perez knew he had made the most terrible mistake.

Gino slammed it back, dead straight, 100 mph right at the pitcher's head. It missed by about a half inch, rocketed way out into center field, and Aaron Smith came racing in for the run. Seapuit led 4–3.

Perez threw again, and Rick Adams banged a one-hopper into his glove, and the Wellfleet reliever threw out the officer cadet at first. Bobby Perez stormed off the mound, disgusted with his performance. And as he made his way to the dugout, he could still hear them chanting, . . . *"GEE-NO . . . GEE-NO . . . GEE-NO!"*

By now Jack's arm was too painful to continue. He had one bag of ice on his shoulder, and another on his arm. Doughnut Davis jogged out to the mound, and to everyone's utter astonishment threw out the final three Wellfleet batters, with fourteen pitches, twelve of them fastballs, all of them on target and delivered with a more orthodox motion than usual. Took him all of four and a half minutes. Win number five for the Seawolves. The first time they had come from behind.

The dugout was an outburst of noise, and the big crowd stood and applauded as the players shook hands. No one heard the phone ringing in the little Wellfleet field office, long distance from south Louisiana.

"Yessir. Oh, yes. They just finished. Well, we led all the way and Seapuit won it four–three in the ninth . . . they came up with a pitcher as good as our best. We'd never heard of him . . . but, boy, could he throw a baseball."

Ben Faber went to bed that night, as lonely as ever. But he was smiling as he lay listening to the thudding of the gas drills.

The last Seapuit pitcher was now in residence. Brent Thomas, a heavily built, bespectacled Orange County player, a starter for UCLA. Brent did not have the power of Jack or Kyle, or even Doughnut. He was a precision pitcher, with a lot of control and a good repertoire. Maddox was starting him in the next game, against the weakest team, the Cardiff Commodores. Kyle would start in the next game at Cabot Field, against the Exeter Braves.

Neither Cardiff nor Exeter had a chance against this very classy Seapuit team, and they were beaten 6–0 and 9–2, respectively, which gave the Seawolves a 7–0 start to the season, their best ever.

Game eight was away, at Oceanside Field, home of the Rock Harbor Mariners. And this, in the opinion of Ted Sando, was liable to prove a problem for two looming reasons. One, the Mariners had a formidable track record of beating the best teams in the gusting sea breezes of Oceanside. And two, in response to days of pleading, Russ Maddox had finally given in and named Doughnut Davis as the Seawolves starting pitcher. Mr. and Mrs. Bo Davis had flown up from Savannah to watch their son in his moment of triumph. Privately Ted thought Doughnut might be too wound up to pitch his best game. And he was not wrong.

There was trouble immediately. The Seapuit leadoff men went in order. Then, in a stiff onshore evening breeze, Doughnut walked the first two Mariner hitters with eight straight pitches, all fastballs, all low and away, all at least a foot and a half off the plate.

And now there were runners on first and second, and even the umpire shook his head as Garcia yelled, *"For fuck's sake, Doughnut, pull yourself together, man!"* Tony was so worried, he ran to the mound, asked him again, *"What the fuck are you doing?"*

Doughnut was a little distraught, but more or less in control. "I'm all right . . . I'm all right . . . just a little off . . . we're gonna get right back . . . just a little off, that's all . . . fastball, right?"

Garcia nodded, jogged back. He went into his crouch and signaled for the fastball on the outer third, low. He believed the Mariner hitter would go right after it. Doughnut fired it fast, straight at last. Tony moved his glove to catch a ball that was going to bisect the plate, thigh-high. The Mariner hitter was waiting, slammed it high, right over the four-hundred-foot marker. The ball landed on the beach.

"*FUCK ME!*" roared Garcia.

Seapuit was 3–0 down and they'd only been playing for five minutes.

Sando was on his way out of the dugout, calling "*TIME!*"

"Come on, Doughnut, forget what's happened. We'll get those runs back. Just start focusing on the hitter. And for Christ's sake, watch Tony's mitt. That's your target."

Doughnut nodded, faced the next hitter, and hurled in an absolutely deadly tailing fastball, a perfect strike. And deep in the dugout, a relieved Russ Maddox said, "There you go . . . he's all right."

With his very next pitch Doughnut hit the batter in the middle of his back, sending him to first base.

Garcia glanced at the umpire and muttered out of the side of his mouth, "Jesus. We could be here awhile tonight."

Ted Sando could not believe what was happening. He looked at Russ helplessly. "You want me to get someone ready?"

"No. He wanted this start. He's got it. Let's all find out what he's made of."

Doughnut slowed up a bit. Sent in a steadier fastball, which the batter hit, a one-hopper straight to the shortstop, Rick Adams, standing fifteen feet from second base. Adams caught it instinctively, low and left, spun, and fired it straight into Bobby Madison's glove. He never even had to look up. He winged in a bullet to first base, where Zac Colbert stretched as far toward the ball as possible. The entire stadium heard that ball smack into the leather of Zack's glove, for the classic double play. And the burst of applause from the home crowd, and the Seapuit visitors, seemed to inspire Doughnut, who promptly threw three screamers, straight past the last Mariner batter. Each pitch was pinpoint accurate, tailing away over the outside corner, 90 mph plus. Picture perfect.

Garcia ran in shaking his head. "Beats the shit outta me, Coach. I can't figure this guy out."

Doughnut jogged in off the mound, elated, totally disregarding the chaos of his first twelve pitches. "How 'bout that, Coach? I told you I'm all right . . . *BAM! BAM! BAM!* Right? They can't touch those fastballs, right?"

Ted Sando rolled his eyes heavenward. Jack Faber, sitting quietly in the corner with Kyle, helping with the pitching chart, murmured,

"How 'bout that Patriot missile . . . the one on the beach?" But he grinned, and said, "Doughnut, get over here!"

The lanky Georgian walked down the line and sat next to Jack. "Now listen, Doughnut, I know this is your first start. But you gotta relax. You're just too tense. Nobody gives a shit whether you throw at ninty-four mph or eighty-eight. It's *where* you put it. That's what counts. You gotta get into control of your pitches. Steady up a bit. Think."

Doughnut, more worried than he was letting on, toughed it out. "C'mon, Jack. Gimme a break. I got the fastball working now. I'm all right."

"Doughnut, shut up. I know you have a great fastball. Faster than mine, faster than Kyle's. Probably more difficult to hit. I haven't seen one better in this league. But that's not the issue, is it? Right here we're talking how often it works. It's no good having the world's best fastball if you can't throw it when and where you want it. I'm not talking quality. You might be a pitching genius . . . I'm just trying to get you to throw two or three times as many of them, maybe a little slower. You're trying to fool the hitter, not break his fucking bat with every pitch. Remember the words of the great Branch Rickey, 'Control is not putting the ball over the outside or the inside. Or pitching it high or low. To me, control is throwing a strike when you have to.' My daddy told me that when I was about nine years old."

Doughnut nodded, and the three pitchers sat together and watched the hitters struggle. The Mariners had a very crafty guy on the mound, and he kept the batters off balance, varying his pitches and speeds. He had three different speeds on his curve. One of them was extremely hard, one looping and soft, another completely deceptive.

By the sixth inning it was 5–0 Mariners. By the bottom of the seventh, Doughnut was starting to feel the pressure of losing this game. He knew it was on the verge of slipping away entirely. The hitters could not get a key hit, and he could not be sure of getting them out. He decided therefore to blitz them out in the next inning, the bottom half of the eighth.

And he walked to the mound with the score still 5–0, a look of grim determination on his face. The first pitch went in like a rocket, up and away, one-hopping the backstop.

The second was even faster, may have hit 94 mph. Flew four feet over Garcia's head. The catcher was just too tired to leap for it, and he shouted, *"For Christ's sake, what's going on?"*

Doughnut had his reply ready. Another smoking fastball howled in, right down the same trajectory, four feet above Garcia's head. The catcher turned to the Seawolves dugout. There was no response, and Doughnut was into his windup. The fourth pitch screamed in six feet above his head.

"What the fuck is going on?" yelled Garcia. *"I never even gave you a signal!"*

"Easy, baby," called Doughnut. "I'm getting there."

Inside the dugout Ted Sando said, finally, "Russ, now do you want me to get someone ready?"

"No. This kid's gotta learn to keep his composure, all by himself. Let him get out of it."

But Doughnut could not get out of it. He managed to walk the first three batters, with a barrage of pitches, three of them wild, several over Garcia's head. There were only three strikes thrown, all foulbacks.

Garcia again went to the mound. "Doughnut, come on, pull it together. You gotta hold the score right here or we'll never get it back."

Doughnut resolved to go to his curve, a pitch he rarely practiced, or threw. And to the plate came the Mariners' beefy first baseman, Spike Miller from Clemson.

Garcia signaled the curve as agreed and placed his glove low on the outside edge of the plate. Doughnut wound up and hurled a great looping curve, which unhappily came in right over the middle.

Miller just crushed it. A full swing, terrific impact, and the ball soared clean over the left-field fence for a grand slam. Mariners 9, Seapuit 0.

And now sheer frustration began to permeate the Seawolves dugout. Everyone was out there trying to land the big hit. Everyone was trying to hit the ball into the ocean. As a result, nothing happened in the eighth.

Doughnut somehow got rid of three Mariner hitters at the bottom of the inning, thanks to a high fly ball to second base and a sharp double play between Garcia, Adams, and Colbert. But the ninth was a familiar Seapuit pattern. Colbert, Maloney, and Sweeney all showed signs of irritation and went down swinging, in order. And that was the first loss, nine–zip at Oceanside Field. They were still top of the league, but there was a bad taste in everyone's mouth, the kind of bad taste that comes when a lot of players know they have not done themselves justice.

The stadium was still as the players began to throw their kit into the cars. Beneath a pale quarter moon, a low mist hung in streamers along the beach, where the incoming tide would soon flow over the home-run ball banged out there in the first five minutes of the game. Beyond that, the lights of four local trawlers could be seen, running hard toward the fishing grounds, leaving wide silver wakes. A few of the boys stood looking out to sea, full of concern at their performance.

Ted Sando stood quietly talking to Doughnut, architect of the shattering defeat. The coach's task was made doubly awkward by the presence of Doughnut's father, Bo Davis, who was equally anxious to get his son back on the right track but was apt to be rougher with him than Ted would have recommended.

The fact was, Doughnut was a critical part of the 'Wolves pitching staff. And right now he was so inclined to lose his cool it was almost impossible to imagine him filling even the role of closer. In Doughnut's mind, the only pitches worth remembering were the big ones, the strikeouts. *That's what I'm all about, Coach, right?*"

It was late now, after 10 P.M., and Mr. and Mrs. Davis were planning to take their son out for a late supper. They were leaving in the morning. Russ Maddox told everyone not to stay awake worrying, but to get something to eat, then get some rest. Most houseparents would leave late-night sandwiches and milk. Tomorrow night was, after all, Seapuit's biggest game of the season; playing away, at the home field of the Lancaster Sentries, Kyle Davidson starting.

But there was an air of melancholy about it all, as the 'Wolves, tasting defeat for the first time, swung their little armada of automobiles away from Oceanside and headed back down the Cape, to the little waterfront village.

6

*D*oughnut's new automobile arrived in Seapuit just before lunch, delivered by one of his father's accountants. He met the wayward pitcher at the field and had him sign the insurance forms. Then he boarded an accompanying taxi for Henley Airport, leaving Doughnut now in sole command of a gleaming custom-made 1975 Cadillac convertible.

It was a racing scarlet in color, Georgia Bulldog red, with black lines. On each of the front doors was painted a huge, pure-white, wrinkly English bulldog wearing a red jersey. Another, even grander version of the dog was painted right on the hood. Below his massive paws were written the words HOW 'BOUT THEM DAWGS!

The license plate was UGA 5432, UGA being the traditional name for the University's canine mascot. They all have personally inscribed gravestones inside the field . . . UGA II (1968–1972), FIVE BOWL TEAMS— NOT TOO BAD FOR A DAWG. Doughnut's new car represented deep, sacred UGA folklore. "Right here we're talking heritage, boy"—as his father, Mr. Bo Davis, had explained, when he arranged the delivery of the automobile.

Doughnut loved it. The powerful wraparound stereo was blaring away right now, with the top down, Jack, Tony, and Zac, aboard, and Don Henley urging them to *"Take it . . . to the limit one more time."*

"YEEEEEH-HAH!" yelled Doughnut, stepping on the gas so the needle hovered to seventy-five. "Hey, Jack . . . how 'bout when I nailed that Mariner hitter last night, right there in the first, eh? How 'bout that, Jack? *BAM! BAM! BAM!* You liked that, right, Jack? You really liked that, right? Fastball. *Yessir.*"

"There were a few I wasn't absolutely so fucking crazy about," said Tony.

"Yeah, but that's bullshit. I'm getting there. Coach Sando knows I'm getting there. And I'll tell you something else, boy. I got the range now. He knows it. Kyle gets into trouble tonight, he'll wish I was ready to come in and close it."

"Doughnut, has anyone ever mentioned to you that you could be some kind of a nutcase?" asked Tony.

"Yeah. Few times. But they ain't *never* been right. Nossir. Where am I? Right here is where I am. Starting pitcher for the best college team in the country. *W-a-a-a-a-y* up there at the top of the league. And I'm telling you, boy, I ain't even got going yet."

Jack Faber shook his head, attempting to bring an element of sense to these ramblings from the Bulldog hurler. "Doughnut, like I've told you before. You just got to steady it down. All of us want you to do well. But you gotta stop losing your cool, like last night.

"That kid should never have hit that grand slam off you. But in the heat of the moment you threw a pitch you were not sure of. You should have just slowed it down, thrown a nice tailing fastball, around eighty-eight mph, low and away. He'd never have hit it. Instead of that, you ripped a big fat curve right over the plate for him to whack. Didn't make any sense . . . you, old buddy, have to stop geting rattled, and stop trying to blitz your way out of trouble."

"I'm working on it, Jack. Believe me. I wanna take this team all the way."

"Jesus Christ," groaned Tony Garcia, and then, brightening, he asked, "Doughnut, lemme into one of the big mysteries of this season, will you? When you throw a fastball four feet over my head, at which point do you know that right there you have thrown a lunatic pitch? Before you let go the ball? When it leaves your hand? Or when it starts on a crazy trajectory?"

"Well, that all depends."

"On what?"

"On everything. Atmospherics, my aim, the windup. There's a lot to it."

"Tell me about it. I'm usually at the other end. But let me ask again. Do you know that ball's outta control before you throw it? Or at the moment of release? Or even later?"

"C'mon, Tony. It all happens kinda fast. Usually I'm not real happy at the moment of release. But sometimes I can't tell what's happening."

"Those are the times I'm mainly concerned with," replied Garcia. "Shit, man, you're gonna end up killing someone. Hopefully not me."

"No. I'm getting better all the time. Next time I start, you're gonna see a lot of real control. I wanna promise that."

Control on the mound was one thing. However, control on the big traffic rotary at the mainland end of the canal bridge was entirely another. Doughnut slowed, no doubt of that, but then he completely ignored the rule about giving way to traffic moving in from the left. He glanced up, at an oncoming eighteen-wheeler, assessed the gap in front of him, and went for it, his right foot hitting the accelerator like a jackhammer.

The truck killed its speed with a frenzied hissing of air brakes, and the driver let rip a blast on his horn like an ocean liner. Jack Faber covered his eyes, and Tony Garcia shouted a now familiar phrase at the loose cannon from Georgia, *"FUCK ME! DOUGH-NUT!"*

The Cadillac shot forward, missed the truck by about four inches, almost gave an elderly lady driver a heart attack as it crossed her bows, and then the white bulldog thundered forward, hard west along the north side of the Cape Marlin canal.

"YEEEEH-HAH!" whooped Doughnut. *"Power, boy, power. That's what it's all about. Goddammit! That's what I'M all about. Yessir."*

"Holy shit," groaned Garcia, shaking his head.

Jack Faber, who by now had opened his eyes and confirmed that everyone was still alive, just said quietly, "I'm not sure winning tonight matters. Just getting there would be some kind of a goddamned triumph."

Anyhow, UGA 5432 was now clocking 70 mph, aimed directly at Lancaster, the only park in the league not on the Cape. The little town was situated on the northwest corner of Hawke's Bay and once clear of the commercial sprawl which surrounded the waterfront, the route wandered through some surprisingly rural lands.

UGA raced along a two-lane highway, which bisected several cranberry bogs, now beginning to turn dark red after spending the winter and late spring underwater, away from the frost.

Drained now, and forming a unique Massachusetts landscape, the bogs glinted in the afternoon sun, and one or two elderly farmers looked up from their hoeing, shaking their heads at the sheer speed of the scarlet Caddy belting along the highway, transporting the ballplayers to Andy McKillop Field.

High above them, a long V-shaped flight of Canada geese made a slow path down to the marshes on the left. The roar of the big V-8 engine drowned out the calls of the newly arrived, diving arctic terns, along the shore, just a couple of hundred yards across the maroon-tinted bogs.

"This is kinda peaceful country, hah?" said Zac Colbert, the first words spoken by the big Oklahoma country boy since they'd left Seapuit.

"Would be if the fucking chauffeur wasn't chasing the world land-speed record," replied Tony Garcia. "Jesus, Doughnut, I swear to God, if you put this thing in a cranberry bog . . ."

"Easy, Tony baby. This a beautiful trip . . . the Georgia Bulldog rides again . . . *HERE WE COME . . . YEEEEEH-HAH!*"

"Tell me I'm just dreaming," muttered Garcia as the Cadillac squealed around a bend with the needle still hovering around 70 mph along the deserted road.

The speed sign signaling forty was just a blur, and the 30 mph sign on the bridge didn't even exist as Doughnut gunned UGA straight over and onto Lancaster's main street, making a hard right and coming to a complete halt at the traffic light. All four seat belts took the sudden forward strain as the brakes gripped.

"The mark of a great driver and a great pitcher," said Doughnut. "Gotta know just when to take the ol' foot off the throttle."

Garcia groaned.

They crawled through the town looking for the left turn up the hill to the ballpark. In big letters Andy McKillop Field proclaimed its presence, right behind the high school, a deep amphitheater surrounded on all sides by bleachers. The place could seat seven thousand, but no one ever called it charming.

In any event, Lancaster Sentries coaches did not do charm. The team was backed financially by Walter Farrell, a short, pugnacious multimillionaire, retired banker, and the only thing that counted here was victory, with a Big V. Year after year the Sentries made the play-offs, but year after year there were unproven rumblings of basic Cape Marlin League rules being broken—young college players being given the use of cars, players offered inducements to sign on for the summer.

And, at the other end of of the season, there were mysterious disappearances of certain players at Lancaster, even more mysterious appearances of new players for the final games, in total contravention of the spirit of the league laws. No player had ever been sent home from Seapuit just because the coaches thought he could be replaced by a better one.

Coach Maddox said it succinctly. "I'm not in the business of breaking kids' hearts. We name our squad right up front, and that's the twenty-three players we go with till the last pitch is thrown. Except for serious injury."

Jack Faber climbed out of the passenger seat and stared down at the hard, pragmatic-looking ballpark. He turned his head sideways to the light wind, just picking up off Hawke's Bay, and he muttered to anyone who was listening. "That sea breeze is gonna build, if I'm any judge. Don't even think of hitting for the left-field fence because you won't get there. Go for the gaps."

Tony Garcia nodded. "You can just feel it, eh? Just a little too cool off the ocean. You get it off the lake back home. You're right . . . it's gotta be more than three hundred and fifty feet to that fence down there, into a building headwind. There's gonna be a few big catches out there tonight. Gino will need his running shoes."

Unsurprisingly Doughnut's group were early at the field. And it was another eight minutes before the next Seapuit car arrived, Andy Crosby's big four-wheel-drive jet-black Cherokee, bearing the two Citadel cadets, Bobby Madison and Rick Adams, plus the power hitter from Maine, Ray Sweeney. The coaches were next in Ted Sando's aging Chevrolet, at which point the players began hauling their big bags out of the vehicles.

They zipped up their jackets against the breeze, pulled on their Seawolves hats, and began the walk down the steep incline to the visitors' dugout along the right-field line. It was almost 5:15 P.M., forty-five minutes before they had the field for practice. The Sentries were already out there hitting.

Doughnut, who always had a bit more cash than the rest, insisted on buying hot dogs as they passed the Lancaster field kitchen, and he also treated everyone to big bottles of ice-cold fizzy water.

"Goddamned small reward for risking our lives in that fucking dawgmobile," said Tony.

Doughnut ignored him, as he ignored all insults and criticism. "Just don't wanna be drinking no water supplied by the Sentries," he said. "They'd drug us if they thought it would help 'em win."

"I'd drug you if I thought it would help you throw straight," said Tony. And even Doughnut laughed.

By the time they had all wandered down to the dugout, everyone was there. It was still a warm evening away from the sea breeze, and the bleachers were more or less empty. But the place was surrounded by large redbrick buildings, and there was already a forbidding atmosphere. The Sentries out on the field looked all business, and the relative silence of the empty stadium was interrupted only by the shouts of the coaches and the crack of the baseball off the wooden bats.

The Seapuit boys could see the long-serving veteran Lancaster coach Dick Frazier out there watching his hitters warm up. The former Dodgers manager had been coaxed here by Walter Farrell, and now had a summer home on Cape Marlin. He'd taken the Sentries to the play-offs and then the final in eight of the last ten years.

Seapuit was 7–1 so far, but the Sentries were not far behind, 6–2. It was rare to have two such distinct and bitter rivals squaring up so early at the top of the Cape Marlin Western Section, but there was no mistaking the high stakes of tonight's game. Defeat for the 'Wolves meant they would be sharing the top spot with Lancaster. And no one wanted that. Every single houseparent of every single player had already made the situation clear in various phrases, jokes, and innuendos. But it all meant the same: *You guys do anything you like . . . but BEAT the Sentries.*

The 'Wolves took the field at 6 P.M. sharp and spent a half hour running and hitting. Kyle Davidson worked for fifteen minutes in the bull pen, watched by Ted Sando and Jack Faber and caught by Tony Garcia. The big Californian was smooth and quickly into a groove. The curve was good and there was real heat in the fastball.

Back in the dugout, Coach Maddox was in a very serious mood. He sat on the stone steps facing the players, and he told them, "We lost last night for the first time, and it wasn't all Doughnut's fault.

We also lost because you guys couldn't get one single run between you—and the Rock Harbor pitching wasn't all that tough.

"At the heart of that defeat there was something other than a pitcher who temporarily lost his cool. There was something I really don't like—I was seeing arrogance. And that ain't good." Russ paused and let his words sink in.

"For the first few games we came out like lions. I saw real desire. Real commitment. But last night I was seeing players who thought they just had to throw their gloves on the field to win. And in this league you cannot do that. Because every night you face a top pitcher, and it's a hell of a long season.

"No good thinking those first seven wins were everything. We still got another thirty-five games to play after tonight. It's gonna be a long haul, and you can't start swinging at everything, like you did last night. You gotta be patient, wait for the right pitch, then pounce on it. I wanna see those lions, hear me?"

Everyone nodded. "Okay," said Russ. "Tonight we're playing our greatest rivals. And I don't need to tell you the importance of this game. You will have heard it all from the fans, houseparents, and everyone else in Seapuit. This is huge for us. And we've won more games in Lancaster's park in the past ten years than any other team. They know it, like we know it. And there's gonna be intensity tonight, real hard baseball.

"But I expect victory. And just remember who we are. We're the Seawolves, and we represent a very important Cape village, full of influential people. A lot of 'em are counting on us. A lot of 'em are already here tonight. So play the game with pride, no arguing, no signs of temper. Just dig deep, stay focused, and pounce on your chances. Like lions."

By now the bleachers were filling up fast. By game time there'd be three thousand Sentries fans in the park. Behind the dugout there were three hundred of the Seapuit faithful who'd made identical, but slower, journeys to the mainland than the Dawgmobile. Their Seawolf hats formed a maroon square behind the dugout.

Soon there was a roll of drums echoing from the field loudspeaker system, and then the Lancaster battle anthem—"Sweet Georgia Brown"—rang out through the stadium. And the Sentries trotted out onto the field, dead slick, their cleats in strict time to the rhythm. A great roar erupted from the bleachers as the home team moved into field position. And then there was another roar, almost as loud, as the Seawolves, led by Tony Garcia, stepped out of the dugout for the National Anthem.

On the mound for the Sentries was the short, stocky, gum-chewing, Texas A&M Aggie Split Candlewood from Big Spring, West Texas. He had a formidable college record, a smoking fastball, and the first three Seapuit hitters went down in order. Split fanned Rossi, struck out Adams with two foul-backs and a tailing fastball low and inside. Colbert came up next and hammered the first pitch 150 feet into the air with the Sentries center fielder waiting underneath.

"Christ," said Coach Sando, "he can't keep that up, can he?"

"Hope not," said Russ. "Or this could be a tough night."

But however good Split was, Kyle Davidson matched him, sending down the first three Sentries in short order. And so it continued, a grim uncompromising pitching duel, through five innings, at which point Lancaster had it by 1–0. Kyle was pitching a strong game and he was greeted by a burst of applause every time he returned to the dugout. The one run he gave up came in the fourth, on a walk, and a triple through the gap, which just eluded the diving right fielder from the University of Connecticut, Andy Crosby.

The stalemate continued through seven, with the Sentries hanging on to their narrow lead. By now the sea breeze was just beginning to die. And in the opinion of Garcia, the left-field fence was no longer unreachable, and at the top of the eighth, Scott Maloney, Seapuit's slugger from Texas A&M, stepped up to face once more his regular-season college teammate, Split Candlewood.

Both pitcher and hitter were from West Texas, and there was no great love lost between them at the best of times. Scott, who was twice the size of Candlewood, was essentially a humorist, but he worked at disguising this with a gruff, aw-shucks cowhand manner. The trouble was he almost died laughing every time Garcia spoke. On the other hand, Split's grim, unsmiling manner perfectly displayed his personality. And on this night he wanted nothing more than to strike out Seapuit's big, beefy hitter from Amarillo.

Scott took his stance, staring down at the pitcher. The ball came in at 92 mph, belt-high, tailing away. Scott swung at it, caught it low, and fouled it back.

The second pitch was straighter, same height, and again Scott swung and caught it wrong, sending it into the backstop wire net, where it jammed: 0–2.

Split went to the curve, hurling it in, taking a little off it, outside. Scott declined, 1–2, and the pitcher silently cursed. Everyone was sure he'd go back to the fastball, including Scott, but everyone was wrong. Split threw the same outside curve, tempting the Seawolves' Aggie to swing again. But once more Scott declined to chase it. The umpire signaled 2–2.

Then Split fired in a smoking 92 mph pitch over the inside of the plate. Scott picked it up early, turned fractionally, and swung hard and true, straight through the wheelhouse. He caught the ball a savage smack, driving it high, into the place no one had reached all night, the misty, but now still, cool air out over the left-field fence.

The outfielder never even moved. He just watched the white ball curving down into the bleachers, and the crowd heard it rattle around in the loneliest part of Andy McKillop Field. Three hundred Seapuit fans leaped to their feet as Scott made his stately progress around the bases, with the game all tied up, 1–1, at the top of the eighth, no one out.

Ray Sweeney, the iron man from the coast of Maine, was next up. Candlewood, frustrated, angry at himself, immediately tried to fool the new hitter with his curve, but Ray left it. Split went back to his fastball, and hurled it in at 90 mph, dead straight over the plate.

Sweeney anticipated the pitch and he jumped right on it. Those steel forearms which had dragged a thousand lobster traps out of the ice-cold waters of the North Atlantic, flashed downward, and Ray's bat smashed the ball hard and high down the right-field line, over the fence, and into the bull pen, the complete opposite side of the field from Scott's home run five minutes earlier.

The Seapuit crowd was ecstatic and they clapped and cheered Ray all the way around, amid an unmistakably sullen silence from the Lancaster regulars. The 2–1 score held, but the next three Seawolves went in order, and once more a tired Kyle Davidson, who had already thrown 114 pitches, made his way to the mound to protect this hairbreadth lead at the bottom of the eighth, in this most hostile environment.

The pain in his right arm was a couple of ticks below a permanent throb, but his shoulder was getting stiff. Kyle pulled his cap peak down and prepared to pitch through the pain, and overcome it.

Both Ted Sando and Russ Maddox sensed their pitcher was in trouble, and the quiet sense of unease in the dugout was suddenly dragged into the open.

"FABER!" snapped Russ. "Get down to the bull pen and get yourself ready."

Sando stepped forward and said quietly, "Russ, he's starting tomorrow."

"The hell with tomorrow. We gotta win tonight. We can't drop two in a row."

Jack grabbed his glove and set out at a jog to the bull pen, and meantime Kyle hurled down a fastball, which the Sentries hitter fouled back on the end of a vicious cut with his bat.

"Jesus," breathed Russ, and without taking his eyes off the mound, "Teddy, get down there with Jack. I wanna know the second he's ready." But the big ex–University of Maine pitcher was already on his way.

Kyle Davidson pitched again, another fastball, which should have tailed low and away but failed to do so. The Sentry hitter swung and caught it hard but too low. The ball flew high and left, and Gino Rossi snagged it easily twenty feet in front of the fence.

Tony Garcia looked over to the dugout, concern written all over his face. Russ Maddox missed the glance, but whistled for Garcia to pay attention, indicating that the catcher should immediately go talk to Kyle, just to buy Jack some time in the bull pen.

Tony jogged out to the mound and asked the Californian if he was okay. Kyle shook his head and muttered, "My arm hurts like hell."

The catcher started back toward the plate and twirled his finger in a tight, fast circle toward the dugout, indicating to the coaches to have someone ready to pitch ASAP. He took his stance and signaled for the slider. But it came in soft, with no bite, and the new Sentry hitter slammed it over the shortstop's head for a base hit.

Russ Maddox stared helplessly out to the bull pen, where Jack was throwing hard, trying to get warm, trying to get loose. But it was cold now, and he was just not ready. Still stalling, Russ called time and made his way to the mound.

"Take it slow, Kyle old buddy. You got anything left?"

"I got another batter in me . . ."

Russ walked back to the dugout. And Kyle Davidson, grimacing at the now throbbing pain in his right shoulder, refused to give in, reared back, and hurled in his eighty-fifth fastball of the night. One time too many. The Sentries right fielder, Jake Quinn from Tennessee, swung hard and drilled a double into the gap. Lancaster had men on second and third, with one out.

Garcia, his face fraught with anxiety, again looked to Maddox. And the coach again turned to the bull pen, where Ted was waving his hat signaling that Jack Faber was ready. Maddox called time, again walked out to the mound, took the ball from Kyle, patted him on the rear end, and said, "Gutsy performance, kid."

And as Jack Faber came loping in from right field, the Seapuit crowd gave Kyle Davidson a standing ovation. Russ Maddox handed the baseball to the hurler from Louisiana and just said, "This is yours, kid. You know what to do."

Jack nodded, and steadily took his eight warm-up pitches. Tony Garcia came out to the mound, punched his fist into the glove, and said, "Okay, Jack. This is it." Again the pitcher just nodded, without a word.

He was totally focused. He couldn't hear the crowd. Garcia moved into his crouch and called for the fastball, signaling the outer third of the plate. Jack nodded, imperceptibly, leaned back, and sent in a 90 mph screamer. The hitter hesitated and took it on the shoulder, watching it go by. Strike one. Jack's next pitch was, if anything, a little harder, and the Sentry never even swung. Strike two.

Garcia called for the slider. And Jack, who had just thrown four of them in the bull pen, was ready. He went into his windup and let rip with a vicious downward-breaking pitch. The hitter saw the danger, and in the last split second tried to check his swing.

Ted Sando, unable to contain himself, yelled, "*YES, HE DID! HE WENT!*" The plate umpire, uncertain, swung around and appealed to the first-base umpire, who had no hesitation, held up his right fist, and punched the air downward. Out number two.

The next batter strode out to the plate, cocksure, knowing a base hit was all he needed. Frazier had already told him Faber would go back to his fastball, and in that he was correct. But it was right on the outside edge of the plate. The batter opened his hips and hit a sharp, hard ground ball, pulling it to third. Scott Maloney, ranging two feet to his left, snagged it as the lead Sentry runner broke for home.

Maloney swung around and released a bullet to Garcia, who had now moved to block the plate. Everyone heard the smack of the ball into his glove as the Sentry runner came racing in, a flurry of dust and fury.

The entire Seapuit team was up and out of the dugout cheering as Garcia swept in the tag, left-handed, raising his glove to show the ball. And the roar from the Seapuit crowd split the night air as the plate umpire lifted his left leg off the ground and punched the air downward with his right fist to end the eighth inning.

Still 2–1 in front, the Seawolves came to bat for the last time tonight, but got nothing out of the Sentries reliever. Which very quickly brought the home team up again, now to face a warmed-up, confident Jack Faber at his peerless best. It was as if Walter Farrell's men knew their chance had gone.

Jack threw six straight strikes, all of them absolute flamethrowers, to send down the first two. No one even touched the ball. The third hitter immediately fouled two back, and in rapt anticipation the big crowd watched the dying embers of the game.

Two outs, no one on, bottom of the ninth. An 0–2 count on the batter. Ted Sando signaled to Garcia, slider. And the Seawolves catcher instantly pointed three fingers down, his thumb aiming at his right leg—outside pitch.

Jack went into his windup and hurled in the most lethal ball in his armory, the wicked, breaking slider, which silently sounded the last post for the Sentries. The hitter saw it coming, watched it break down and outside, but he never even swung. And the night air was this time split by one solitary voice as the plate umpire pivoted, rammed his right arm outward and back, shouting theatrically, *"STRIKE THREE!"*

Russ Maddox and Ted Sando immediately walked across to shake hands with the Lancaster coaches while Tony Garcia ran to the mound and lifted Jack Faber off his feet. Twenty minutes later it was an ecstatic little Seapuit army that made its way through the dark silent streets of the town, heading back to the Cape, which already felt like home to them all. Near the canal bridge, they stopped and bought fried clams and Cokes at a late-night stand.

Meanwhile Walter Farrell and Dick Frazier were sitting with a couple of beers in the Lancaster field office when the phone went. A perfect stranger was on the line long distance from Louisiana.

"Not our night," the former Dodgers coach told him. "Thought we had 'em, but they beat us two–one with two swings of the bat, and a relief pitcher who was murder."

"Hey, you remember his name?"

"No. But I remember his arm. I think they said he came from St. Charles College, down in the South."

"Yeah, I think I know the kid," said Ben Faber. "He can throw. Good night."

Dick Frazier replaced the phone and delivered his verdict on the game to the team owner. "Good night's right. Good night for us. Screw the Seawolves, and screw that pitcher. Especially screw that goddamned slider. There's major leaguers couldn't hit that."

7

*T*he players and coaches were home late. No one was in bed until after midnight. But the weather gods who had kept an eye out for the boys in the cauldron of Andy McKillop Field were still on duty as the sun failed to rise out of the Atlantic in the morning.

Heavy gray cloud hung gloomily over the entire Cape and it was raining like hell, as it had been for the past several hours. By 10 A.M. the Exeter Braves, with a foot of water flooding their slightly sloping and badly drained outfield, called the game.

Their general manager admitted that even if the downpour stopped by midday there was no way they could mop up this kind of flooding by late afternoon. The following day had been a scheduled night off for both the Braves and the Seawolves, and so the league officials decreed a twenty-four-hour delay.

Which left the 'Wolves essentially on the beach. The sun came out before lunch and most of them decided to goof around swimming and "getting some rays" until the evening. Mysteriously, a group of local college fans, already fixtures at home games, materialized on the same beach. All girls.

Ted Sando, however, had a different plan. He was going fishing off the eastern end of the Cape, way down in the crook of the great curl of the sand dunes that surrounds the village of Cambourne, home of Andy Crosby. The right fielder had already left and was well on his way down to the commercial marina his family had owned for the biggest part of a hundred years. By the time Ted arrived at the Cambourne dock, the Crosbys' forty-foot, black-hulled, diesel-powered Albin sport fisher would be fired up and ready to head out to the fishing grounds along Horseshoe Reef, twelve miles offshore.

Ted had already invited the inseparable Jack Faber and Tony Garcia to come with him, declined their request to bring a couple of girls, and told them to round up Zac Colbert to join them on the trip. Tony had said, "He might not want to come with us." But Ted clarified the matter: "This is not an invitation. This is an order. Get him."

The four of them set off driving along the highway in Ted's Chevy, out along the narrow land. Inside a half hour they were clear of the little baseball towns and now made their way up through the dunes. Sometimes they could see the ocean to the left and to the right, and they all quietly marveled at the God-given splendor of this jewel of land, studded all the way along by broad, glistening sea ponds, some of them a mile wide.

They swung into Cambourne before one o'clock and swerved left down Harbor Drive. In big letters on a twelve-foot-wide piece of curved driftwood were the words CROSBY MARINE (FOUNDED 1896). Ted drove straight in and parked in the area marked private, as instructed by Andy.

Almost below them was a black-hulled sport fisher, named *Striper,* with Captain Crosby at the wheel. "Hey, guys . . . get in . . . we're outta here . . . Ted, get up for'ard and cast off . . . Jack, leggo that stern line, willya . . . Zac, come and sit by me . . . and hurry up before the tide turns . . . or we'll be beating our brains out through the rip."

"Just for the record, right-field asshole," said Zac, "I'm not sure I understood one word you said."

"What about me?" said Garcia.

"Siddown in the fighting chair and let me know if I'm gonna hit something while I'm reversing . . ."

"Aye aye, sir," replied Garcia, who had never been in a boat of any kind in his life. "And make it snappy. I'm planning to catch me a big-assed shark before this day is done. Yessir."

Expertly, Jack Faber uncoiled the stern line from the big dock cleat, leaving a single turn and holding it tight while he clambered aboard. When Andy called, "Cast off stern," he flicked it loose, hauled the line inboard, and absentmindedly made a perfect coil, running the line end through the loop and hanging it neatly on the cleat. Everyone can do that down in the bayous.

Ted Sando was equally expert up on the foredeck, like most young men who spend time fishing along the rocky shores of coastal Maine.

"Jesus," said Garcia. "I'm out here with a bunch of sea dogs . . . no wonder you can't throw worth a damn on land. You'd probably be better at water polo."

Like his buddy back on the Seapuit beach, Scott Maloney, Zac Colbert always laughed when Tony Garcia spoke. The two power hitters from West Texas and Oklahoma were both essentially country boys, and there was something likeable about the fast-talking Chicago-based city slicker behind the plate.

Ted, Jack, and Andy tried to ignore Tony's worst quips, among which the water-polo analogy was right up there, but Zac still laughed.

By now *Striper* was chugging out through the gap in the harbor wall and making headway to the northwest in a quartering sea. She aimed at the final point of land at the eastern end of the Cape, where the north-running tide up from Massachusetts Bay swirls into the south-running waters from the coast of Canada. It was always a little choppy out here where the tides converge, but *Striper* had been designed for deep-sea fishing and she made her right turn to the east, shouldering her way through the short bucking waves effortlessly, making an easy eighteen knots in the slashing salt spray.

"Nice boat," said Jack.

"Yeah, we just got it. First time my family's bought a fishing boat in a hundred years . . ."

"Yeah?"

"Yup. We always made our own. Most of the last century we made the best-known bass fisher on the East Coast—the Crosby Striper, beautiful wooden-hulled boat—you still see 'em around."

"Why'd you stop making 'em?" asked Zac.

"Oh, I guess the new glass-fiber hulls made by the competition were a lot cheaper and quicker to produce. These days people want a new boat right now, at the keenest price. The old skills, and boat-building craftsmanship, kinda went by the board. My grandpa didn't want to get into a rat race, and in the end we weren't making much money out of a custom-built boat, so we just converted the workshops for boat repair only. Kept all the guys on."

"Does the marina make money now?" asked Tony.

"Hell, yes. A ton of it. Costs for dock space in the summer are real high. We could close down all winter if we wanted. But there's a lot of commercial fishermen out of Cambourne and my dad has shares in a few of their boats. Crazy pricks work all winter. Right here we got a real good business."

"You thinking of pro ball?"

"No. I don't have the power. And that's the way the game's gone. They really only want power. Anyway I don't want to spend time in the Minors, I gotta come right back here and get ready to run the boatyard. I don't have any brothers and my dad's sixty-five. I'm probably finished with baseball at the end of college. Gotta get my marine engineering degree and get right back to the factory."

"Hmm. Well, all I can say is, the pros are losing a damn fast man," said Jack.

"They don't want damn fast men," replied Andy. "Unless they can whack the ball like Mickey Mantle."

By now the rolling eastern shoreline of Cap Marlin was low on the horizon. The swell was longer now and Andy had opened the throttles on the twin Yamaha 175s. *Striper* was making twenty-six knots east-nor'east through the water. The sun was out and the air was once again warm.

"Where the hell are you taking us, Crosby?" said Tony. "Portugal?"

"How'd you guess?" replied Andy. "Thought you'd like a few sardines for lunch."

"What do you mean, sardines?"

"That's what they eat, for chrissakes. Little fish. Grilled. On the beach. Taste great."

"How d'you know?"

"I been there, asshole. How d'you think I know?"

"Portugal?"

"Sure. My mom's got a Portuguese cousin by marriage. We went there two summers ago."

"Jeez. I'm playing ball with the fucking jet set," said Garcia. "Anyway, in the absence of fresh-grilled sardines, you got anything American to eat?"

"'Course we have. You don't come on fishing trips without food, stupid. Get into that cooler to your right—there's a stack of sandwiches in there, all wrapped. Ham, cheese, chicken, tuna—whatever you want. There's Cokes and water in the cooler right behind it."

"Crosby. You're a mighty man," said Garcia. "Call out your orders and I'll toss the sandwiches up to you . . . since I'm the only one who can throw straight."

"Straight but not quick," joked first baseman Colbert. "So hurry yourself up."

"QUICK!" yelled Garcia, staring up at his crewmates. "I've got a right arm like a thunderbolt. You may not know it, but there's a special kind of electric storm you get over Lake Michigan . . . they've named it after me . . . Garcia Lightning, fast and jagged, not to be fooled with."

"For chrissakes, throw me a tuna sandwich," called Ted, who was operating the depth finder in the small cabin under the cockpit, listening to the sonar pings, watching the screen . . .

"That's right, fire up a couple of chicken ones for me and Andy," said Zac. "Jack wants ham and cheese . . . and try to keep 'em low . . ."

Tony, laughing, finally threw the sandwiches. "Jesus," shouted Zac. "You call that low? You nearly hit me in the eye with the ham-and-cheese . . ."

"You're probably the only person in America who needs a baseball glove to catch a fucking sandwich," said Garcia. "It's a goddamned miracle we've ever won a game."

"HEY! THIS IS GETTING SHALLOW, ANDY." Ted had a note of surprise in his voice, as Striper came in fast over the reef. Andy eased back on the throttle, knowing that Horseshoe was much more of a shoal than a reef, and they came down to just seven knots as Ted Sando called out the depth . . . "Twenty-eight feet . . . twenty-three . . . nineteen . . . twelve . . ."

Outside the hull, the water chopped and boiled and turned light green as the sandbar rose up to meet the boat. A red warning buoy bearing the number eight cut a deep wedge into the incoming tide, and a long white wake made a trailing pattern on the water. The boys could all see the line where twelve feet of depth suddenly became four feet.

"Right out there," said Andy Crosby, turning his head sideways to the wind. "That's where we're gonna catch them babies." And he cut the throttle back to idle and turned the black bow into the tide.

"Hold the wheel, Jack, and keep steering zero-seven-zero on the compass." Andy Crosby was all business now. He came down from the pilothouse and grabbed three rods out of the holders, handed one each to Tony, Ted, and Zac, and dived into the lure box and came up with a couple of pink-and-white chuggers, and one bullet lure, which was shaped like the weakest bait in a shoal, the least likely to evade a determined predator.

"That flappy little bastard for me?" asked Tony, who was holding a big fishing rod for the first time in his life.

"Hell, no," said Andy. "You need a chugger. In case that big-assed shark you were going on about shows up."

"Doesn't look big enough to me," replied the catcher.

"Maybe not, but the all-tackle world record, a fourteen-hundred-pound Atlantic blue marlin, was caught with one of those. Same color, just a little bigger."

"Aha, that's what I mean . . . wanna get a little more size right here . . . shit, Andy. I'm an ambitious guy."

"You are also unlikely to be within twenty miles of a basking shark," said the captain. "You're looking for a big striped bass for your dinner. But you're not going to catch anything unless you listen to what I'm telling you."

"I'm not in the business of listening." Tony chuckled. "I'm about two ticks away from law school. I'm gonna be an advocate, not a goddamned shrink. I speak, I don't listen. Get that goddamned hook over the side."

At this point Zac Colbert, an excellent freshwater fisherman who wanted to learn but couldn't stop laughing at Garcia, put the catcher in a headlock.

"That's it," shouted Tony. "I'm suing. You've given me whiplash on the high seas."

"Will you shut up, Garcia?" said Zac, still laughing.

Meantime, Jack Faber had cast his lure over the side and could already feel a tremble on his line. Then he felt the steady jolt of a fish trying to break free of the hook in its mouth.

Expertly he flicked the rod back twice, then began to reel in, slowly, playing the fish, just as he had done a thousand times down in the bayous on his uncle's shrimp boat.

"Steady, Jack . . . you got him," called Andy. "Lemme get the net." And they all watched in rapt attention over the stern of the boat as the striped bass, its silver scales glinting in the afternoon sunlight, came writhing up from the cliff face of the shoal and landed in Andy Crosby's waiting net.

"Hey. That's just about the coolest thing I ever saw," said Tony. "A little small by my own standards. But still damn cool."

"He's a little small by all standards," said Andy. "Keepers have to be more than twenty-eight inches long out here—otherwise you have to throw 'em back . . . this guy's only two feet long . . . hand me those long pliers in that box there, Tony, and I'll get the hook out."

"Who the hell knows how long he is?" asked Garcia. "Except for us. That could be my dinner you're fooling with."

"We know the size of this fish, and we're Cape Marlin fishermen, residents, and we don't break any rules that interfere with the fish stocks. That way they'll always be here."

"Well, if that's the case, it's a lucky day for both you and Colbert."

"Whaddya mean?"

"I'm not going to proceed with either lawsuit—against Zac for causing me whiplash on the high seas, and you for causing me stress and aggravation while occupying my natural place on the food chain."

"Christ, Garcia," said Ted Sando. "I'm not sure whether you'll end up on television or attorney general. Either one would be bad."

Striper was now stationary in the tide, her engine just idling marginally forward against the flow of the water, the rudder locked in position, steering zero-seven-zero, fifty yards to the right of the rip. Tony Garcia had his lure in the water off the starboard stern, Ted sat in the chair next to him, fishing dead astern. Zac Colbert cast beautifully, out off the beam, toward the roiling waters of the rip, and Jack sat fishing off the bow. Andy Crosby moved between his teammates, offering help and advice. But they were in a quiet period right now, waiting for the shoals of stripers, and maybe even early bluefish to swarm along the underwater ridge.

So far the entire trip had been conducted in a jocular careless manner, a lot of joshing and razzing. But now, quite suddenly, Ted Sando introduced a serious note. "Guys," he said, still sitting in the fishing chair. "It is not a fluke that we are out here together away from interruptions. Andy, who is not planning a career in baseball, knows why we are here and what we're gonna be talking about. I want to talk to each of you—a kind of private Seawolf executive meeting.

"Anyway, you all know, we got twenty-three guys on the squad. Tony here, as the catcher, is the obvious on-field boss, and it's a long time since I had more faith in any catcher to demonstrate such a complete grasp of the game. For the duration of the season, Jack Faber is gonna be my right-hand man. He's in overall charge of the pitching chart, his opinions on all pitchers will be listened to, and he'll assist both Russ and me in every way he can.

"Now, Zac, I want you to come down to the chart area and have a talk while these fucking Ahabs carry on looking for the Great White Haddock."

Zac chuckled and climbed down the ladder from the cockpit, and Ted Sando went straight to business. "In any top baseball team," he said, "there's a special slot needs filling, and it's a vocal one, a guy who not only has the character to keep trying, but the energy to encourage the rest of his teammates to keep going, no matter how bad the situation. He's a kind of field general.

"Right here with the Seawolves, at first look, you'd probably go for Gino, who's a city boy with a lot of pizzazz and a heart like a lion. But I'm not sure guys would follow him, especially guys who are not as good as he is. Anyhow, for this task Russ and I have chosen you, young Zachary . . ."

For a moment the big quiet Oklahoman looked surprised. And he turned around to face Ted, a quizzical expression on his face.

"Zac," said the coach. "We think a power hitter of your quality has more to give the team. For a start, everyone likes you, and we often hear you out there encouraging other guys at the plate. Russ and I have both noticed you make very thoughtful observations about opposing pitchers. The kids all wanna hear what you think. We've noticed that too. And what we really think is this . . . if we get in a jam against any opponent, and the coaches sit down in the dugout with Jack, Tony, and Zac, there's a damn good chance we'll reach correct conclusions. We might not always be able to solve problems, but at least we won't fuck it up before we start to try."

"Coach, I'm not really a vocal guy, not like Gino or Tony."

"Thank Christ, or no one else would get a word in," replied Ted. "But what you say counts. I heard you the other night giving Andy tips when he came up to bat for the first time. Andy jumped all over the first pitch and banged it straight into the gap. Remember that?"

"Well, yeah, I guess so."

"That's what I mean. And we've all seen you up on the edge of the dugout talking with guys, talking about the pitchers and what to expect."

At this point there was an interruption from the incorrigible Garcia, yelling down from the helm, "Whatever the hell you want Zac to do, don't let him start putting guys in headlocks if they screw it up . . . he's got an arm like a fucking mechanical digger."

As ever, everyone laughed at Garcia, which served only to warm him to his task as resident comedian. And now he deepened his voice . . . "Okay, now you all know you're going to play for Seapuit this summer—we just need two measurements . . . bat? Thirty-four inches—fine. Neck brace? Sixteen inches—excellent . . ."

"Shut up, Tony, this is serious," growled Ted, turning quietly back to his first baseman. "Okay, Zac, ignore that fucking lunatic up there. You know what I'm saying, right? Russ and I have spotted you as the main man to keep the team going, to provide that extra vocal stuff—stuff the coaches can't really say."

"I got it, Coach. I can do that."

"And I don't suppose we're the first to notice a quality of leadership in you, are we?"

"Not really."

"Well, let's get back out there with the other guys."

The two big men climbed out into the stern area, and Ted called Jack and Tony down to join them. Ted was curious about Zac's background and asked about his hometown.

"Well, you already know I'm from Spavinaw, Oklahoma, birthplace of Mickey Mantle. My dad's foreman of a huge cattle ranch down there. It has oil out on the eastern boundary, owned by a very rich man called James P. Rollins. He lives in Europe, my daddy takes care of the whole place."

"You know Mr. Rollins?"

"Oh sure, known him all my life. His wife died years ago and he never remarried. Just has one daughter. She lives in Paris."

"Guess you worked some, on the ranch?"

"Hell, yes. I still ride with my dad. But not so much. Last year I was in a few rodeos, mostly broncos, but I rode bulls two or three times. Till I hurt my wrist. Dad doesn't want me to do it again, says it'll stop me breaking Mantle's records!" Zac chuckled.

"Matter of fact, Mr. Rollins expects me to take over the ranch in time. But he and my dad are still pretty young, 'round forty-four, forty-five. I'm telling you, Jim Rollins has been real good to me, paid all my expenses through high school and college. Treats me kinda like the son he never had. Gave me a brand-new Jeep Wrangler when I graduated. My mom and dad are driving it up here tomorrow . . ."

"No worries about your future, eh? That's where you get that leadership," said Ted. "It's all about confidence and calm. That's what you have, kid. And the guys can sense it."

"You gonna inherit this ranch, Zac?" asked Tony.

"I think so."

"Thank Christ. I can't play on a team with a goddamned bull rider on first. But a future billionaire? Hey, there's a big difference right there. If I don't make it to the Bigs, you'll give me a job?"

"You'll make it," said Zac quietly.

There was still no action on the lures, and Ted Sando was still very focused on the subject of baseball. "The question, guys," he said, "is do we have what it takes? What it *really* takes? I'll admit I thought so until the other night, the game up at Rock Harbor. But how about that? I never saw a real good team fold up that quick, lose all its composure, *that* quick . . ."

"Well, goddamned Doughnut . . ."

"Forget Doughnut," snapped Sando. "That was not our only problem, so let's not waste time jumping all over Doughnut. The score was nine–nothing. We never even scored a run. I know Doughnut dug us a very quick grave, but we didn't have to go jump into it. I wonder if you noticed the St. Ives Red Sox came back twice this week, once from six–nothing down, once from six–one down. They won both games."

"Well, we just couldn't hit against them," said Zac. "Didn't seem to matter what we tried."

"Jesus," said Ted. "You mean that's gonna happen all year, soon as we go down three or four runs? I'm telling you, we can't just hang our heads and pack our bags just because some team gets a jump on us."

"Yeah, I know."

"And Zac, I've told you what Russ and I expect of you. As from right now it's your job to keep the guys up—keep 'em focused—keep 'em believing we can win. Keep 'em believing we can always win, even when we're in trouble. I don't care if we're six or eight runs down after eight . . . we can still win. Because in the end the games always come down to character. They come down to courage under fire. Anyone can win when they're already winning. It's winning when you're losing . . . that's what matters. We gotta develop a mind-set . . . fighting for every game, every inning, every out, every pitch."

"Coach, you're right," murmured Zac. "I know you're right. I've played on a few teams at Oklahoma who seriously believed they would win *every* game. But it's never like that. You mostly end up in a battle. And that's when you need to dig deep."

Ted Sando looked stern. "I want to remind you of one famous baseball quotation. It was said by Mr. Branch Rickey of the Brooklyn Dodgers . . . 'The greatest single thing that makes a championship player is his desire to be one. The greatest single quality of a championship club is a collective, dominating urge to win.' "

That kept everyone quiet for a few moments. Until Tony Garcia miraculously caught a fish.

"Holy shit!" he yelled, "There's something pulling my line! *ANDY* . . . it's the big-assed shark and I'm gonna reel him in."

"*WAIT!*" Andy Crosby was right next to Tony now, touching the rod lightly with his fingers. "That's a good fish . . . now take it steady . . . jerk the rod, then let some line out . . . bit more . . . now haul him in a little . . . let some out . . . he's heading for the shoal . . . that's good . . . we don't want him to dive under the boat . . . that's good, Tony . . . I think you're gonna catch him . . ."

"I can catch anything," shouted Garcia, predictably. "Fastballs, bullets to home plate, striped bass, sandwiches. Shit! I can do it all . . ."

"*GOT ONE!*" Zac yelled.

"*SO'VE I,*" called Jack.

"We got a shoal of 'em right here," said Andy. "Jack, you and Colbert know what to do. But this monster on Tony's line is fighting. I think he's a big bluefish, and those suckers are tough . . ."

For a few minutes they all struggled. Ted wasn't paying attention and somehow lost his lure, the fish on Zac's line got away but left the lure behind, and Jack was still playing his. Tony, with a lot of help from the captain, had his fish under control, and they all again gravitated to the stern to watch the unforgettable sight of a big fish moving up to the surface from mysterious depths, twisting and turning, scales gleaming silver blue in the sunlit water.

"WOW!" said Andy. "That's a major bluefish, two and a half feet long, and heavy. We gotta be careful when we land him, the bastard will have your fingers off."

But they did land him. Right in the net. Andy killed it instantly with a sharp blow of the mallet. Then he shoved the fish into a locker full of ice. "That's dinner," he said. "I'll fix it back at the dock. You're gonna love it."

By now it was after 3 P.M., and with the bluefish shoal now moving northward along the underwater ridge, Andy decided to run back the other way, slowly, fishing as they went, leaving the shallow, roughish water to starboard. But again the seas seemed bereft of fish, no one landed anything more, and the talk, as it often did in the absence of high drama or excitement, turned to a subject of near-universal emotion. Doughnut Davis.

Zac Colbert wound in his reel carefully and said, suddenly, "You know, a pitcher like Doughnut puts the entire team on edge. Everyone's heart rate goes up as he walks to the mound. Don't matter if we're winning or losing, when he gets his hand on that baseball no one knows what the hell's gonna happen next."

"Tell me about it," said Tony Garcia. "He's such a loose cannon. I don't know what the hell we're gonna do about him. Trouble is— and I'm sure even Jack and Kyle will go with this—he throws the best smoking fastball we have."

"Sometimes," said Zac. "Sometimes. It's the other times that worry me."

"The kid has one fundamental problem," said Jack, interjecting. "He needs someone to kick him back a notch or two. He's going forward at a hundred miles per hour *all the time*. He's gotta learn to think. He never gives himself time. He *never* reads the situation. He's *always* trying to throw the fastest pitch in the history of the fucking world.

"And then he gets in a mess. And then he's trying to make up for two pitches he's just screwed up. And inside his mind there a voice telling him, 'Throw this right by him right now!'

"He has to step back at these moments . . . come right off the mound and take a deep breath, compose himself. Talk to Tony . . . try to understand it would be better to throw something that might be hit and caught in the outfield—anything, but don't walk him. We have to make this Calm Down Doughnut Week."

Ted Sando said, "I agree with that. But it's not that easy. You guys remember the other night? When he was relieving? It's a three–two count and I walk out, and I say, 'Doughnut, steady down. Throw him something he might hit, but please, please don't walk him . . . how 'bout that nice change-up, eighty miles per hour? You'll get him with that.'

"Doughnut nods. Agrees. Real earnest. And he says 'Coach, you got it. Change-up, right? Breaking to the outside. No problem.'

"I jog back to the dugout, turn around just in time to see him hurl in a screaming fastball. *WHAM!* Dead straight over the plate. Must have been ninety-four miles per hour. Hitter never even moved. And before the umpire even called the strike, Doughnut was turned toward the dugout, pumping his arm. 'How 'bout that, Coach? How 'bout that?'

"Now I ask you," said Ted. "What do you do about a guy like that?"

The boys were too busy laughing to reply. But the point was made. Somehow, between them, they had to get the Georgia Bulldog under control.

The sea was building now as they turned twenty degrees to the southwest, back toward the northern headland of Cape Marlin. Andy opened up the throttles and gunned *Striper* up to twenty knots. Her sharp seagoing bow cleaved through the short, choppy waves, and the Seawolves huddled in the cockpit, away from the new offshore breeze, which was bringing more rain before the night was over.

They swung around the great sandy hook of the Cape and cut across the calm waters of the natural bay above Cambourne. They reached the dock by 4:30, and Jack automatically jumped off holding the bowline and made it fast to the for'ard cleat. Then he took five quick steps to his left and caught the stern line expertly tossed by Ted Sando and took it once around the aft cleat, looking up at Andy for final instructions as to how the boat should lie on the falling tide.

"Little more, Jack . . . little more . . . right there. That's good."

And the pitcher from the bayous smoothly wrapped the line around, twisting in the loop and pulling it tight. "You want the waterline, Andy?"

"Yeah. Just do the hull, willya?"

Jack sprayed off the starboard side, washing away the salt. Then he passed the hose up to Ted, who washed the decks down, leaning out to clean off the portside hull. Tony and Zac carried the coolers off, handing them to Jack, while Andy clipped on the big plastic-and-Perspex cover for the aft end of the cockpit.

As soon as the boat was secure, Andy took a big knife and severed the head and tail of the bluefish right there on the dock. He had Jack busy with the pressure hose washing away the blood as he gutted and cleaned the fish. He split the skin away, sliced off all the superfluous parts which contain the little bones, then he cut big pristine fillets away from the main bone. It was a beautiful bluefish and yielded ten fillets. They washed all the remnants in the water and placed their dinner in a large white dish that just fitted the cooler.

Then they climbed the ladder up to the jetty and walked back to the main office of the marina. This was situated at the sheltered end of the harbor, with views due west out across the dunes. Outside, there was a private deck where generations of Crosbys had sat and watched the sunset during dinner, but remained on duty to visiting mariners and returning fisherman.

Andy's father, Bucky, came out to meet them and welcomed everyone to the marina. He took the dish of fillets and put them on the table, leaving immediately to bring out a little "marinade."

What he actually brought out was two bottles of London dry gin, which he opened and upended onto the fish, covering them completely. "Bluefish is a little more oily than anyone wants," he said. "And there's nothing better'n gin to suck that excess oil right out."

"You sure I'm gonna be able to walk straight after a plateful of that, Mr. Crosby?" Tony Garcia had never, personally, seen such extravagance.

"Hell, yes," replied the marina chief. "We take those fillets out coupla hours from now, dry 'em off, then pop 'em on the grill with a little butter, salt, and pepper. You can't get anything nicer than that. And you won't even taste the gin. Unhappily we're going out, so you guys'll have to rough it, cook your own dinner and guard the homestead."

"Jeez, I've had dinner in a lot worse places than this," said Tony, gazing out across the harbor. "This is some kind of setting."

"Kinda grows on you after a little bit," said Bucky Crosby. "Makes you glad to get back here when you been away."

"I could settle for this right now and never go away," said Tony thoughtfully. "Me and my mom only have a couple of rooms back in Chicago. No views of anything."

Bucky Crosby smiled. "Keep working, son. Keep trying your best. You'll get your views."

"He'll get 'em all right, probably of the bleachers at Wrigley Field," said Andy. "I'm telling you, Dad, he's the best godamned college catcher I ever saw."

"So I hear," said Crosby Senior. "So I hear."

They said their good-byes to Andy's dad and took a stroll around the harbor, looking at the big fishing boats, chatting to a few local captains, most of whom were staunch supporters of the nearby Truro Cardinals. But everyone, it seemed, knew all about the hot shots of the Seapuit Seawolves.

There was a lot of banter, a few cold fruit drinks, and then they wandered back, fired up the gas grill on the deck, and spread out the gin-soaked bluefish on the hot, well-oiled bars.

"This better be good," said Andy, brushing butter on the fillets. "We've only got potato salad and hot bread to go with it."

At which point he disappeared into the kitchen alongside the office and reappeared with a six-pack of Budweiser.

"They for us?" said Tony, amazed. "I thought you had to be twenty-one in this state to have a drink. Or is Coach Sando gonna drink the lot?"

"Hell, no," replied Andy. "Coach gets two, we get one each. This is private property, surrounded by private land, and right over there is the police chief's boat. He wants it still floating tomorrow, he better stay the hell away from us for the next hour!"

The bluefish was a triumph. Garcia naturally took full credit for the catch, and told Andy Crosby that he would be sure to thank him for the minor role he had played when the Great Garcia was voted Sports Fisherman of the Year at season's end.

They watched the sun sink in a fireball below the sand dunes, and an hour later they watched the moon rise out of the ocean beyond the harbor. As they walked back to Ted's car just before 9:30, the rays of the afternoon sun still felt warm on their skin.

A trawler chugged past them on the way out to the fishing grounds, and the skipper gave them a wave as he disappeared in a silvery wake out toward the harbor wall.

"You know," said Garcia, "I think I'd trade Comiskey Park for a life like that, with my own boat."

"Yeah, for about five months a year you might," said Andy. "But there's nights here in the winter when we watch 'em headed out into a freezing gale, and I've heard my dad just say, 'God help them.' See you tomorrow, guys. And take this crazy damn catcher home, willya?"

8

*J*ack Faber was first man at the field the following morning. The sun was bright and already hot in clear blue skies. By the time he wheeled out the mower, Coach Maddox had opened up the equipment shed, and just a few moments later Doughnut's car containing the pitcher plus Tony Garcia and Ray Sweeney came hurtling around the corner into the parking lot in a flurry and dust and bravado.

"*Yeeh-ha!*" cried Doughnut, announcing his presence in his normal, everyday understated fashion. And as Doughnut yelled, the telephone in the shed rang, and right away there was trouble.

Coach Maddox emerged three minutes later with a shout of "Goddammit!"

"What's up, Coach?" called Jack.

"You know that new pitcher from South Carolina who's due here in the next hour?"

"Sure. Remick, right? Starting tonight."

"Yeah. Except he's not coming. Signed for the Orioles about a half hour ago. That was his dad." This was a perennial Cape League problem in the early season—a sudden swoop by the pros on an incoming player.

"Jesus. You want me to pitch—my damn shoulder still aches a little, but I'll be okay."

"I don't really want to use you tonight, Jack. I'd prefer you started here against St. Ives tomorrow and get your proper rest. Anyway, the problem's permanent. We need another pitcher and I was counting on Remick."

Just then Coach Sando's Chevy drove into the parking lot and came to a halt right outside the equipment shed. Russ Maddox relayed the bad news before Ted was out of his seat.

"Teddy, we gotta find a new pitcher in a hurry. You got anyone local on the list?"

"Well, I've been thinking that Cronin kid—remember his dad's the maître d' at that club we went to with Geoff and Margaret last year?"

"Sure. The Flianno Club over at Oyster Hills."

"Remember his dad told us he really wanted to play this summer? He's a freshmen at Massasoit Community College, you know, the Warriors . . . small school, but a good baseball program. They won the Junior College National Championship coupla years back. I told his dad we'd certainly look at him if we had a vacancy."

"Well, we got one."

Ted retreated into the office, called the Flianno Club, and was connected with Mr. Cronin instantly. He explained the situation carefully, and added that the Seawolves needed a pitcher right now to start under lights against the Exeter Braves, departing Cabot Field at 4 P.M.

"Coach, the one thing I can tell you is that Chris is ready to pitch. He had a great freshman year at college, and he's in the gym every day. We have a miniature bull pen at home and he throws three times a week with an old high school buddy. They both work here lunchtimes. He'll be thrilled."

"Look, sir, can we come and pick him up? Give him a tryout at the field?"

"Sure—say a half hour?"

"Excellent. What size is he? Uniform, I mean."

"Chris's is six foot two inches, weighs one-ninety."

"Hat?"

"Not sure, but he's got a lot of hair."

"Okay. We'll be over there in thirty minutes. And, hey, thanks Mr. Cronin. I'm sure glad we had that talk last summer."

Ted came out of the office and called to Mike, "Chris Cronin's ready to pitch, if he's good enough. He's just nineteen. Excellent college ERA, very fit. We've got to pick him up in a half hour."

"Can you go get him?"

"Not really, I got Aaron and Kyle coming over to work in a minute. Then I want Doughnut an hour from now."

"Okay, maybe Doughnut will drive over and pick him up."

"DOUGHNUT!" yelled Ted. "Can you run an errand for us?"

"Sure. Where'm I going?"

Eleven minutes later the Dawgmobile, hood down, was cruising along toney Flianno Avenue, past the great white-and-gray summer homes that line this rarefied Nantucket Sound coastline. Almost every one of them built with old New England money.

Doughnut's general preference for bluegrass music played at full volume, an echoing din perhaps never before heard in the immediate precincts of the Flianno, a 120-year-old golf, country, and beach club (annual dues: private; ethnic membership: zero).

Ladies in white tennis dresses stared in astonishment as the painted Georgia bulldogs moved at a stately pace along the quiet road, Tammy Wynette beseeching them at the top of her voice to "stand by your man."

Up ahead, Doughnut spotted the club, the largest building on the street, a sprawling, gray-shingled traditional Cape mansion that housed a ballroom, two vast dining rooms, two impeccable summer lounges, and thirty bedrooms for guests. It stood guard over probably the most elite, roped, private bathing area north of Newport's Bailey's Beach.

Several ladies reclining on lounges below the terraced al fresco lunch bar could hear Tammy a hundred yards out. She could not have caused a more stupefied silence if she'd been singing in the Sistine Chapel.

Doughnut pressed on, swinging the Cadillac hard around into the valet parking area in front of the main door, where uniformed attendants stared uncertainly at the scarlet interloper cooling its wheels. The head doorman bounded down the steps and said sharply, "I'm sorry, sir. You cannot park there."

"Just gonna be a coupla ticks, buddy," said Doughnut in reply. Then he exited the car and slammed the door, leaving the engine running and Tammy essentially standing by her man, full blast.

"Sir? Sir? You have to move that car."

"Get lost," said Doughnut by way of clarification. "Right here I'm on business. I'm here to see the main man."

And with that, the lanky pitcher from Savannah bounded up the steps, his baseball cap on back to front, his scarlet training jacket reflecting, in huge white script letters, HOW 'BOUT THEM DAWGS?

He pushed his way into the hundred-foot-wide oak-floored foyer, which he thought was pretty swish for a ball club, and was confronted by an eighty-seven-year-old committee member wearing white pants, a straw boater, a Harvard tie, and a dazzling lime-green blazer.

The man stared at Doughnut in nothing less than absolute horror. In sixty-four years of unbroken Flianno membership, he had never seen a male person inside the club without a tailored jacket and tie . . . "Er, can I help you in any way?" he asked politely.

"I doubt it, pal, not unless you can throw some real heat."

Arthur M. Witterson III was dumbfounded.

"Nossir," added Doughnut. "Right here I'm looking for guys in the low nineties. You can't do much for us."

By this time the receptionist had summoned a waiter to deal with the intruder. "Excuse me, sir . . . I must insist you come outside with me and remove your car . . ."

"Keep quiet, boy," said Doughnut, towering over him. "Guess the guy I'm looking for's having lunch in there."

At which point he strode purposefully into the crowded air-conditioned, and reverently calm dining room, and there, beneath the disapproving portraits of former presidents dating back to 1880, he let out the shout which would pass into Flianno Club legend.

"CHRIS CRONIN IN HERE? SEAWOLVES CAR RIGHT OUTSIDE . . . MOVE IT . . . YOU'RE IN THE BULL PEN, RIGHT NOW."

The committee members' table was right next to him. Two elderly couples were sipping iced tea and eating grilled fish when Doughnut yelled within four feet of their plates. The more senior of the two men, an ex–club president, looked up irately and saw before him only the jacket bearing the emblem of the Georgia faithful.

It would not be an exaggeration to describe his expression as apoplectic. Forks were dropped, drinks spilled. Two waiters collided. All around the room astonished well-bred faces looked up irritably. Ladies shook their heads in disapproval as Doughnut yelled again, *"COME ON, CRONIN, GET YOUR ASS IN GEAR."*

At this point the maître d' himself came hurrying through the room and said quickly, "Hi, I'm Tom Cronin, Chris's father. Come on, we'll meet him in the foyer."

"What kind of a ball club is this?" said Doughnut. "Lot of old guys . . . this some kind of senior league?"

"This is not a ball club," replied Mr. Cronin, smiling. "This is one of the most revered country clubs in the United States. You just left a room in which two state-supreme-court judges were lunching, plus a Connecticut senator, plus the chairmen of two public corporations, all with their wives. The table for six to your left contained four du Ponts and two Mellons."

"Holy shit," said Doughnut. "That's not a whole lot to eat, right? Not for four. But I'm real confused about this place. When Coach Maddox said Flianno Club, I thought they meant baseball . . . Jeez, you come to the game, don't ever tell my daddy what I just did—he'd have a heart attack."

"If he'd been having lunch here today, he would not have been alone, I assure you of that. Meanwhile, turn that fucking music off, willya? Remember I'm not a member, and I played a lotta ball one time."

"Yessir, Mr. Cronin. I'm right there. Have Chris meet me outside. Yessir, no more music."

Thus Chris Cronin's first steps on the road to fame with the Seawolves were more a getaway than anything else. Doughnut introduced himself as the "'Wolves number one pitcher," and then hit the gas pedal, burning rubber as he howled out of the valet parking area, along the avenue and swiftly into the middle of Oyster Hills.

From there it was a quick drive to Cabot Field, and Chris was in the bull pen, throwing, watched by Ted Sando, Jack, Kyle, and Coach Maddox.

He was a powerfully built kid for nineteen. And he was in every way the complete antithesis of Doughnut. He was quietly spoken, and he threw with excellent control, nothing wild, and Sando had the feeling he would not give up walks with crucial pitches. He had a below-average fastball, around 88 mph, but he had two excellent curves, different speeds, one slow, one even slower, a combination that often makes a hitter swing much too early, keeping them off balance.

He also had a decent change-up, a "circle change" famously perfected by Frank Viola of the Minnesota Twins in the late

1980s. Ted watched in wry amusement as Chris held the ball between his index and middle fingers, snapping his wrist as he demonstrated the pitch. Three times he threw it, and every time it came in slowly, and then just tailed away. "Damn near impossible to hit," murmured Ted.

Chris finished the work as he had started, quiet, controlled, and thoughtful. And immediately Coach Maddox came up and shook his hand. "Very nice. You're hired. Doughnut will drive you home, get your stuff, and then the two of you head straight out to the Maritime Academy. Chris, you're starting . . . either Doughnut or Aaron Smith is relieving. You got all your gear?"

"I got it all right in the car."

"Okay, Doughnut, take Chris with you—and try not to drive like a lunatic. Chris's got enough on his mind already without worrying for his goddamned life."

"No problem, Coach."

Ninety minutes later the Dawgmobile was making roughly seventy knots down the narrow blacktop driveway of the Maritime Academy. A couple of passing navy lieutenant commanders might have mistaken it for a guided missile, except for the bulldogs and the music.

"Who the hell's that maniac?" asked one of them.

"Ballplayers, no doubt," replied his colleague. "Ain't got a lick of sense between 'em."

"Reminds me of that midshipman got hauled over at Annapolis for driving an old sports car flat out across the parade ground."

"Yeah. But at least I was in control."

Anyhow, Doughnut made it on time. And fifteen minutes before the game started, Tony Garcia led Chris down to the bull pen, where Coach Sando was waiting.

After he completed his warm-up with a series of fastballs, Chris Cronin pushed back his new Seawolves hat and said quietly, "Okay, Coach. I'm all set."

"Get your jacket on, Chris. Stay warm, and let's go see if the hitters can get us off to a start."

The answer to that was only ten minutes away. The 'Wolves' leadoff three, Rossi, Adams, and Colbert, all went down swinging—a little anxious, a little rushed, insufficient poise. Russ Maddox was talking quietly to them in the corner of the dugout as Chris Cronin made his way out to the mound, accompanied as far as the left-field line by Coach Sando.

It was not precisely a baptism of fire, but Exeter scrapped for a run in the first. Their second baseman whacked Chris for a stand-up double to right field, then stole third, before a sacrifice fly got him home, with two outs. Ted Sando was impressed with his pitcher's last out. Chris threw a devilish-slow hanging curve that caused the batter to get right under it and fire the ball into orbit, straight up, falling just behind Ricky Adams, who backstepped like a matador for an easy catch.

The 'Wolves got nothing out of the second, or the third, but then Exeter struck again. Their leadoff man laid a perfect bunt down the third base line and made it to first. Their next man banged a hard line drive to left, and suddenly there were Braves on two bases with no one out.

Chris Cronin kept his cool. He held his fastball in reserve and fired a succession of looping curves that drove the next hitter mad, and sent him down swinging. Then he worried his way to a 3–2 count before sending down Exeter's catcher with a tailing fastball that took him and everyone else by surprise.

The next man up was, however, Exeter's top hitter, a big burly farm boy from Iowa who was plainly on his way to the pros via Northwestern. Second pitch, he got ahold of young Cronin's best curve and slammed it straight over the infield. Ricky Adams made a fantastic high leap, but the ball was still rising and cleared his glove by about four inches, landing way out there, right in the deep gap between left and center field.

Ray Sweeney came pounding across the grass, hooked the ball on its first bounce, and hurled it back to Adams, from out near the fence. The lead runner was in, but the second Brave was still flying. Adams pivoted and rifled a screamer straight into Garcia's glove. Tony could see the runner charging in and he lunged forward, sweeping down the tag. But the Brave dived, and he dived right, the outstretched fingers of his left hand catching home plate as he torpedoed through the red dirt.

Tony missed him by about two centimeters, ripped off his mask, and yelled, "*DAMN!*" several decibels louder than the plate umpire's cry of "*SAFE!*"—3–0 Braves.

Right around here, a grimness set into the game. Exeter was

bound and determined to hang on to that lead. They hardened up their defense, brought in a long reliever after five. And he hurled smoke for two complete innings. No one hit anything.

Zac Colbert, mindful of the conversation which had galvanized the fishermen, was acting as a human pep rally, talking to the hitters, watching the pitching, encouraging everyone as they climbed the dugout steps. Ted Sando kept telling them they could win this. Hell, he would be amazed if they lost it . . . *Come on, guys, we're too damn good to lose to this crowd . . .*

And at the top of the eighth, the Seawolves struck back. Exeter's third pitcher sent in a dead straight outside fastball, and Bobby Madison leaned back and banged it hard down the right-field line. The ball kicked up chalk and rolled into the corner. Madison reached second, still on his feet.

Aaron Smith stepped up next and caught the first pitch a wicked crack, not quite hard enough, and was cleanly caught out in deep center field.

Tony Garcia came to the plate and took the first two pitches on the shoulder as they lasered in over the plate. The pitcher, full of confidence, elected to throw another identical fastball, and it came in at 92 mph on the Major League scouts' radar guns. But this time Garcia was waiting and he swung hard and true, driving a scorcher straight to third base.

And the luck that had eluded the 'Wolves all night now shone upon them. The ball smacked into the lip of the bag and ricocheted off the baseman's chest with a thud.

He scrambled for the ball, grabbed it with his right hand, and looked up at Bobby Madison, who was paralyzed at second. Instantly he swung around and hurled a frozen rope to first. But Garcia's powerful legs were churning, carrying him past the bag and still going when the throw came in. There were Seawolves on first and second. One out.

And Andy Crosby, shrewd, patient, and always determined, came up to the plate, with Gino Rossi now on deck, taking practice swings with the ring weight on the barrel of his bat.

Andy took his stance, the words of Zac Colbert clear in his mind . . . *This guy has a fastball and nothing else. That can fool you. And he always throws it first pitch . . . watch for it, then jump all over it.*

And Zac was right on the money. The fastball came in hard, 90 mph or better, cleaving a path down the middle of the plate. And the lightning bat of the Cape Marlin fisherman sent it back right where it came from. Straight up the middle. *BAM!* Over the pitcher's head into center field—and Bobby Madison wasn't paralyzed anymore.

With great raking strides the black officer cadet was away like a rocket for third base, where Coach Brad Colton was waving him on, arms flailing in a circle . . . *"GO, BOBBY! GO-GO-GO!"*

Gino Rossi had dropped his bat and raced into position twenty feet behind home to watch the throw. Madison made a Formula One turn around third and pounded toward home.

In came the throw. Gino was watching, signaling frantically, Down and away! He was beating his arms through the air as if putting out a fire with a rug, right to left, and he was shouting at the top of his lungs, *"GET DOWN! GET DOWN, BOBBY, GET DOWN!"*

Madison hurtling over the ground is bearing in on home plate. He sees Gino, and he sees the catcher blocking it with his left leg. With a spring that would have made a mountain lion gasp, he launched himself forward, headfirst, to the outside, three feet to the right of the plate, his left-hand fingers reaching for home.

His hand scraped the hard rubber, and simultaneously he heard the smack of the ball in the catcher's glove, a split second before the tag swept down over his back. Bobby peers up through the dust in time to see the umpire's outstretched arms. In time to hear him yell, *"SAFE!"*

Coach Maddox is up and out of the dugout to greet him . . . "Nice job, Bobby. Way to go."

"Thank you, sir," replied the Seawolves second baseman, always polite, even in moments of high emotion. "Two more, right?"

"You got it, kid," said Maddox.

"Nearly," snapped Ted Sando. "Three more. Now let's go!"

Gino Rossi had already run back to retrieve his bat and now he made his way up to the plate. The Seapuit faithful in the crowd were chanting, *"GEE-NO . . . GEE-NO . . . GEE-NO!"* as he took his stance. And the New Yorker was ready to deliver. He was pumped up, spoiling for this fight for supremacy on the shores of Hawke's Bay.

In comes the first pitch, another fastball, and Gino, like Andy Crosby, was waiting for it. He hit it hard, a screamer of a line drive straight up the middle.

Garcia thought it might punch a hole in the fence it was whacked so hard. But it never got there. Never got beyond the mound, because the pitcher, with the reflexes of a panther, stooped down and snagged it three inches from his right thigh.

Garcia was already on his way, and he slammed on the brakes, swung around, and headed back to second. But he was not in time. The pitcher swiveled, hurled the ball to his shortstop, who cut in behind Garcia and beat him to the bag by one stride. It was a perfect double play. The Wolves were gone for the eighth time, still 3–1 down.

Back in the dugout, Coach Maddox was in deep conversation with Ted. "We're gonna need a reliever in the ninth. Who do you like, for a game which might even be tied up?"

"We could go down the tenth here. I think I'd prefer Aaron. He's rested, he's got good control, and he's an experienced reliever."

"Guess it'll piss Doughnut off."

"Not as badly as it'll piss me off if we lose this," Sando said.

"I agree, and it might have a real side benefit. Tomorrow I'll have a long talk with Doughnut, explain that he's got huge potential, but right now he's too prone to mistakes to risk when a game's hanging in the balance. He's got to slow up if he wants to be our first-choice closer. Jack Faber will talk to him tonight—I'll tell him to ride home with Doughnut."

"Okay, boss," said Russ Maddox. "Now let's get our new man out there one more time. See if he can close 'em down."

And Chris Cronin, tired but still throwing steadily, did just that. He held the Braves hitless at the bottom of the inning. And in a cooling sea breeze, stark under the Academy's lights, the 'Wolves stepped up once more to try to bang home the required runs.

Rick Adams came to the plate, focused, disciplined. He knew the stakes were high, knew this was his last chance, and he worked his way carefully, leaving the first three pitches, all balls. He took a strike, then fouled one back.

The Braves reliever was Lars Svenson, a big blond son of a Detroit car worker, the star hurler for Michigan State. Garcia did not like what he was seeing. "Aside from the fact this guy looks like a fucking Viking—he's got a bitch of a fastball, even if he doesn't know how to mix 'em up."

Ricky Adams never flinched. And Svenson threw his next pitch straight at the Citadel cadet. Adams caught it early, sensed it was breaking toward the center of the plate. He kept his weight back because he'd seen the pitch before. And he summoned all of his courage and poise, throwing his hands down and through, triggering the barrel of the bat right through the heart of the strike zone.

The crack of the ball was a sweet sound in the Seapuit dugout, and they watched it fly past, straight over the third baseman's head, landing six feet inside the left-field line and scudding across the grass.

There were some fast men in the Seawolves lineup, but no one could explode out of the blocks like the ex-Citadel 200 meters champion, and Adams sprinted all the way to second for a stand-up double, his teammate Bobby Madison jumping up and down in the dugout yelling *"GO, RICKY, WAY TO GO, MAN!"*

And Zac Colbert stepped up, aware that he represented the tying run, aware that time was running out, aware that he must get on base. He cleared his mind and faced the pitcher, determined to hit only the right one. No chances. No risks.

But the Viking was tricky. He fired in a dead-straight fastball. Zac left it. Strike one. Svenson fired in another fastball. Zac left it. Strike two. Svenson, who was not precisely blessed with the imagination of Steven Spielberg, fired in a third, identical except it never got down, came in fast, but belt-high, right in the middle of the zone.

And Zac made him pay, with a short, protective swing slapping the ball out into right field, which left time for the Oklahoman bull rider to charge to first. Ricky broke for third, where Brad Colton held him up. Two on. No one out. But still 3–1 down.

Up to the plate came big Scott Maloney, the hard-swinging Aggie, who immediately cracked yet another straight fastball into the third-base–shortstop hole. Adams charged home like a bullet while the third baseman was snagging the ball on the first bounce.

Seeing Adams was long gone, he hurled the ball to second, attempting the five-four-three double play, but Colbert was bearing down on the base, and he came in hard and low, right against the baseman's feet in a cloud of dust. Zac was out, but the second baseman was off balance and fumbling the ball.

Recovering, he threw wide to first and the baseman had to come right off the bag just as Maloney came thundering in. *"SAFE!"*

Colbert, having systematically wrecked the double play, jogged back to the dugout, his job neatly done. Coach Maddox grinned across at him, then offered a terse, tight-lipped nod of respect, which the hitter returned.

The score was 3–2 Exeter. There was only one Seawolf out, Scott on first. Top of the ninth. And Ray Sweeney, the steel-armed lobster-man from Maine, came striding toward the batter's box, representing the potential winning run.

They had all decided the sea breeze was dying and that the head-wind off the water was nothing like so strong as it had been at the start of the game. No one had hit anything that dropped really close to the fence. But Coach Sando was absolutely certain someone could do it now.

Sweeney looked calm, but he was on the edge of his nerves. Everyone in the dugout was standing up. Svenson threw hard and straight just off the plate. Ray left it, 1 and 0. Svenson threw again. Ray swung hard, fouled it back, 1 and 1. Then again, third pitch, fastball, outside, and Ray took it, 2 and 1. Pitch four was clocked at over 92 mph, but again Ray left it outside: 3 and 1.

Svenson figured that if he could just get the ball over the plate, it's a strike for sure. And this time he gets it straight, and Ray Sweeney knew it was straight. He literally exploded onto that ball, catching it a murderous whack. The ball soared high toward center field, and Ray Sweeney never even watched it. He just took off, racing past first base, his arms pumping with a controlled fury all the way to second.

Maloney, out in front, came hurtling into third. Colton waved him on, yelling *"GO! GO! GO!"* He glanced up and saw Sweeney still coming, and waved him on to third on pure instinct. Just as well. The ball hit the fence and bounced back, but Maloney had scored to tie the game up at 3–3, and the 'Wolves still had only one man out with a man on third.

Bobby Madison returned to the plate, and caught a fast word with Aaron Smith, who was jogging back from the bull pen ready to pitch the ninth. "Lay it on 'em, man," said Aaron.

"Gonna try, yessir," replied the Citadel cadet. And he took his stance, the bat held high, his eyes on the pitcher's glove, watching for the grip that would betray Svenson's fastball.

But the Viking was not quite ready, and Russ Maddox suddenly rammed both fists forward and called out to his third-base coach, Brad Colton, *"LINE DRIVE, BRAD. UP THE MIDDLE!"*

Madison heard the command plain and clear. And he swiveled his eyes onto Coach Colton, who went into an array of signals. Instantly the infielders move in a step closer, ready to pounce on a hard-hit ground ball.

With Ray Sweeney still coiled at third, Bobby faced the pitcher again, sure now of his instructions. Svenson nods to his catcher and moves lazily into his windup. And in the split second he broke his hands, Sweeney was gone, driving down the runway to home plate.

Svenson knew he was gone, but he was too far into the pitch to change it now, and he stayed centered, drew his arm back, and hurled his best fastball straight at the plate.

Madison, disciplined as ever under fire, never moved till he saw the white of the ball. Then he rotated his cleats, scraping the dirt, squaring around for the bunt.

Svenson looks up in horror. Too late. Bobby's hand is sliding down the shaft of the bat like a cobra. Svenson opens his mouth to shout, but no sound came out.

Madison's grip is soft. His knees are bent and he's poised on the balls of his feet. And now he lays the bat out in front at eye level, at the last second angling it back thirty degrees off the horizontal. Everyone heard the dull thud as the very life was deadened out of the ball, and everyone saw it trickle down the first-base line between the pitcher and the first baseman.

Svenson bounds off the mound, furious at the deception, and grabs the ball just as Ray Sweeney came thundering onto home plate for the lead run. Disconsolately Lars tosses the ball to the first baseman to get Bobby Madison. But that's what a suicide squeeze is. Everyone knew he'd get Madison. But Madison wasn't the issue. Sweeney was.

The 'Wolves led 4–3 as Aaron Smith, with a lot on his mind, came to the plate. First pitch he popped the ball fifty feet high and vertical. It landed in the catcher's glove to end the inning for Seapuit. All Aaron had to do now was relieve the tired Chris Cronin, make three outs, and the ball game would be over.

When Aaron returned to the mound, he unleashed a broadside of fastballs, the likes of which would surely take him to the Majors. He blew three strikes in a row past the first Exeter hitter, fanned the second, and watched the third man pop straight up to the catcher on an

0–2 count. Ten pitches, it took him, and Aaron walked off the mound with his first save under his belt. Another five hundred like that he'd be right up there with Cousin Lee.

Chris Cronin, caught up in the mood, rushed out of the dugout to shake Aaron's hand. They'd never even met before, and they just stood there grinning at each other, while the hundred Seawolf supporters stood and offered them a standing ovation.

Back in the dugout, Coach Sando was saying, theatrically, "And that, ladies and gentlemen, is what this darned game is all about. It's about guts, grit, and character. We could have lost it. We all know that. They could have won it, and they all know that. But it came down to willpower. And when the chips were down, when it really mattered, we wanted it more than they did. I'm proud of you, every last one of you, because you showed me tonight, you guys can beat *anyone*. And you showed me a rare quality, not just talent and determination. You showed me you can get up off the floor, and *still* win."

And so, like Ray Sweeney fifteen minutes before, they broke for home, elected to travel in convoy, so long as Doughnut was in last position, straight to the fried clams at the late-night stall on the canal.

For a group of mostly landlubbers they had taken to fried seafood to a man. They were all hungry, but they also wanted to spend a bit more time together on this night, savoring the moment of their toughest victory; the one that made them 10–1, the best start of any team in the history of the Cape Marlin League.

And while the players' little convoy made 40 mph along the speed-restricted southern canal highway, another Seawolves automobile was traveling a lot faster. Ben Faber was determined to see Jack pitch tomorrow night against St. Ives at Cabot Field. It had been two weeks and he missed Jack, and so late that night the sugar farmer's blue Chevy was barrelling up Interstate 81, sixty-five miles southwest of Roanoke, heading up to the Shenandoah Valley.

Ben was tired, almost broke, and hungry. He had worked a full weekend in a local bar, washing glasses and waiting tables, to earn the $300 it would cost to drive to the Northeast, and he had not even phoned Jack to tell him he was arriving. He had made just one call on the evening before he left, to Natalie Garcia at the number she had given him in Chicago. There was no reply, just her voice on the answer machine; no name, just the voice, but Ben knew it was her.

At the sound of the beep, he just said, "Natalie. This is Ben Faber, Jack's father. I'm driving to the Cape tomorrow and I thought if you could make Boston . . . well, I'd be glad to meet you at the airport. But I guess not. I'm leaving at five A.M. tomorrow . . . I'd like to give you a ticket . . . but I just can't . . . sorry, I won't see you. So long, Natalie."

Ben was trying not to face it. The financial roadblock that separated them cast an unspoken sadness upon him. The fact was that they could not afford to meet. Perhaps never again. And expensive long-distance calls were out of the question. There wasn't any money and the sugar market was going to hell all over again.

Ben never knew it, but Natalie Garcia actually wept when she got the message a day later. The hopeless penury of her life, the modest possessions, every cheap air ticket she could never afford, and to top it off she had missed the call from Ben Faber, whom she had thought about, often. It was all too much.

Ben was moving fast. Beside him on the passenger seat was the critical equipment of the financially challenged, long-distance traveler: the map, the alarm clock, the thermos flask of hot coffee, big bottles of water, the box of sandwiches, the wallet containing $250 in cash, mostly for gas, and, for this car, oil.

But, if he could, he'd have traded his entire survival kit just to see the winsomely beautiful Natalie Garcia sitting, once more, beside him.

9

*H*ot, tired, but full of anticipation, Ben took his seat up in the crowded bleachers among a few familiar faces from his last visit. The trip was a long one, with few stops for rest or sleep. But none of that mattered as he watched Jack walk out for the National Anthem, and he saw him standing with Tony and the umpire, each of them holding his cap over his heart.

As the final notes drifted away over the deep green canopy of trees that surrounded the outfield, Ben pulled on his own cap, the scarlet headgear of the old Kraemer Crawdaddies.

"And on the mound for the 'Wolves tonight . . . Jack Faber of St. Charles College, Louisiana . . ."

And Ben straightened the Crawdaddies cap as a burst of applause from the crowd greeted the pitcher, now standing alone on the mound, facing Tony Garcia, who was already into his crouch for the final eight warm-up pitches.

Ben watched Jack throw four fastballs, three curves, and a change-up, and he wondered why the kid had not tried the slider, and he frowned briefly.

Jack stepped back and picked up the rosin bag, squeezing it with his right hand for the fine powder. He made a short signal over his shoulder with his glove and Garcia immediately threw to second—second to third, the ball winging fast around the infield—third straight back to Jack—"around the horn."

Jack felt good, strong and ready to throw. He pulled down his cap and patted the dirt in, directly in front of the rubber. The St. Ives Red Sox lead hitter, a left-hander, Frank Stoltz from Florida International, stepped up into the box.

Jack was focused just on Tony Garcia. He knew Stoltz could hit. He was the Red Sox shortstop, batting .310. Right now the pitcher is thinking *rhythm*. He flexes his shoulders, and Tony put down the sign, one finger, straight down. Jack nodded.

Then he reared back and fired a fastball right on that inside corner. The batter took it for strike one. The second pitch was another fastball. Stoltz swung and missed, and Garcia called for the curve. Jack threw it swerving to the outside. Stoltz, irritated, went for it and missed again. One down.

Next up: one of the two most dangerous hitters in the Red Sox lineup, Split Lowery, a big, ill-tempered right-hander from South Dakota, left fielder from the University of Iowa Hawkeyes. Garcia knew him from the Big Ten. He was a tough kid, but no tougher than Garcia, and about half as smart. Tony remembered him as a guy who could be easily needled.

"Hey, Split! How you been? What are you doing down here?"

The batter ignored this mock friendliness and took his stance.

"Guess they never saw your conference play-off stats," said Tony brightly. "Jeez, I thought you'd retired." And Garcia, full of concern, shook his head sadly.

"Fuck you, Garcia," grunted Split.

Tony went into his crouch and signaled for another curve. Jack flighted it perfectly, outside again. Split, already angry, swung wildly and missed.

"Hey! Not a bad swing," cried Garcia. "You got within a foot and a half of the ball. That's pretty good."

Lowery glared at the grinning catcher then at the pitcher. He kinda snarled, but he dug in, deeper into the box, and stared down the runway at Jack.

Garcia signaled for the fastball and left the final movement of his glove to the last second, ensuring the hitter could not see it. Jack was into his windup and he saw Tony calling for low and inside. Split swung hard and hit the ball foul, right off his left foot.

"*OUCH!*" roared Split.

"*JESUS!* I bet that hurt," said Garcia. "I hate it when that happens."

Split, hopping around, composes himself and steps forward again, down 0–2 in the count. "He brings that shit in again, I'll rip it right out of here," he gritted.

Tony put down two fingers, calling for the curve. And as Jack steadied himself for the windup, Garcia set his glove outside. Jack found his grip, his middle finger searching for the right side of the horseshoe. He pressured the seam, with his index finger in the middle, his thumb directly underneath the ball on the other seam, the grip now firm between the middle finger and thumb.

He shifted his left leg, then rock-stepped back, and pivoted his right foot in front of the pitching rubber. He swiveled, brought the left leg up high to balance, and motionless for a split second just on his right leg, rammed his left cleat down hard on the dirt in a fluid stride, breaking both hands out wide.

Jack's hips rotated forward as he turned his wrist over, snapping the curveball, only in the low seventies, but with a vicious tight spin. It flew toward the inside corner. From a hitter's point of view, it looked real meaty, and Split's eyes lit up. He took a full swing, but the ball broke, hard and sudden, swooping down and away. Split twisted like a corkscrew, his face full of fury as he watched it go right by. And he heard the fatal smack as the baseball hit Garcia's right glove for the strikeout.

Tony stood calmly while Split was still regaining his balance. He hurled the ball to third, exultantly around the horn again, and as he did so he said cheerfully, "Okay, Split. Why don't you go give that bat to someone who can use it?"

Lowery, inflamed at the entire world, trudged off amid the applauding Seapuit crowd, rising for Faber. Two out. Six pitches. And for the first time in three weeks, Jack heard the voice he'd been hearing all of his life, the one that had never, ever doubted him: *"Attaboy, Jack . . . attaboy, son . . . that's the way!"*

And up in the bleachers he caught a glimpse of the faded scarlet of the old Crawdaddies hat, and he shook his head. *Jesus, he's driven right across this continent, just to watch me.* And he thought again of the unending love he knew his father had for him.

And now, up to the plate came the one great college player on the St. Ives team, Butch O'Marra, the Arizona right fielder who topped the hitters' table in the PAC-10. He was batting .340 for the Sox, with ten RBIs, three home runs, and fifteen hits in forty-four at-bats.

Jack hurled in a fastball, and O'Marra only just missed it, skying an infield flyball, and Rick Adams came in fast, called everyone off, and caught it right behind the mound. The Sox were gone in the first inning, and Jack Faber had thrown only seven pitches. He was greeted by a burst of applause from the bleachers as the Seapuit hitters prepared to take this game by the scruff of the neck.

Full of confidence, the 'Wolves came out swinging. Gino Rossi stepped right up, and before the crowd had finished chanting his name, he had slammed the first pitch right out to the fence for a triple. Adams went down to an infield fly, but Zac Colbert banged a curveball into the right-field gap, which brought Rossi home: 1–0 Seawolves.

The Red Sox pitcher, Buzz Simpson, a tall, lean mountain man from White River Junction on the Vermont–New Hampshire border, only just held his cool, and he walked the next two Seapuit hitters, Ray Sweeney and Scott Maloney. Bobby Madison came up next and very nearly hammered a line drive up the middle to get the runners home . . . but an acrobatic catch by the Sox shortstop foiled him, and a sharp throw to second beat out the runner by inches, completing the double play and the inning.

So far as St. Ives was concerned, that was bad, but fourteen minutes later it was worse, because Faber sent them down again with only eleven pitches, by way of one strikeout, a ground ball to Madison, and an easy fly ball to Sweeney.

In the bottom of the second, the Seapuit hitters attacked again, and Sweeney, Madison, and Aaron loaded the bases. But Tony Garcia whacked a high soft ball straight to Sean Gallagher, the third baseman, who threw out Ray Sweeney at home. It was still only 1–0 but it felt like 10 to the Red Sox, who understood how lucky they were to be within one run. But Crosby and Rossi couldn't deliver the runs.

It was still only 1–0, and once again in the third, Jack Faber sent St. Ives down in order, which brought Seapuit back to the plate inside twelve minutes, Rick Adams to lead off. Adams crushed a 1–0 fastball, a howling line drive to right field, almost to the fence, and he made second base in what was for him a light canter.

Zac Colbert was next, and he smashed the ball in almost the same way Adams had, except that this one screamed away into the left-field corner.

Adams took off for third as the Sox outfielder reached the ball and hurled it in. Brad Colton held up both hands to stop him, but Rick's head was down and he was flying, charged straight through the stop sign, going for his life toward home.

"Jesus Christ!" yelled Brad. He watched the bullet from the outfield corner go clean into the third baseman's glove. He saw Ray "Clouds" Bryant wheel around the bag and make a perfect throw to his catcher, just as Adams came sliding into the plate.

The tag came down hard and accurate, but Rick's dusty momentum knocked the ball out of the catcher's glove, and Seapuit's luck held. It was 2–0, and in the St. Ives dugout their coach Biff Flanagan was furious; furious his hitters had hit nothing, furious his catcher had dropped the ball, furious at his pitcher.

Biff was prone to unnecessary tirades in moments of perceived stress. He was, in truth, a lousy sport, a big, gritty, barrel-chested, red-haired Irishman, built like Mark McGwire. He had spent four years in the minors with the AAA Toledo (Ohio) Mudhens. But he never made it to the Detroit Tigers, mainly because he broke his right wrist in a bench-clearing brawl at Columbus.

He returned as assistant coach to his alma mater, Wichita State, and he'd been in his Red Sox summer job for six years, always feared as a coach who could get his guys up to win from impossible situations. And on the subject of the impossible, it was nearly thus, trying to beat St. Ives at Bart Bradley Stadium.

Here at Cabot Field, Biff was less sure of himself, and he was working himself up, pacing up and down, cursing. He knew his men were tired because of the late trip home after last night's tight eleventh-inning loss to the Sentries. And he knew they were likely to be a bit sluggish. *"But not this sluggish!"* he railed at anyone who was listening. *"Can't hit, can't catch, and can't throw."*

It didn't matter that the Red Sox ended Seapuit's third in short order with a double play and a well-caught shot into the right-field gap by Ray Sweeney, Biff was deeply unhappy, and he could scarcely wait for his men to return to the dugout.

"SPLIT! YOU'VE LET THAT LITTLE BASTARD GARCIA GET RIGHT INTO YOUR HEAD! HE'S GOT YOU TOTALLY UNFOCUSED—AND YOU MIGHT AS WELL BE UNFOCUSED ON THE BENCH FOR THE REST OF THE GAME!

"BUZZ! WHAT THE HELL DO YOU THINK YOU'RE

*DOING? DO YOU HAVE ANY CONCENTRATION WHATSO-
EVER OUT THERE? I COULD PUT THE GODDAMNED BAT-
BOY IN THERE TO THROW LIKE THAT!"*

Biff paced the length of the dugout and returned to his pitcher. And he spoke softer now. "Buzz, come on, son. You're all I got. You know I used four pitchers last night . . . come on, kid, get yourself together . . . *START COMPETING!"*

And then he rounded on the rest of the team. *"ALL RIGHT!* These Seapuit hitters are good. All of 'em. I know that. But they're not *that* damned good. We should never be two runs down. Jesus . . . giving up goddamned runs like that. *WHAT THE HELL IS GOING ON OUT THERE?"*

In the next three innings, St. Ives never got a run; in fact, they never got a hit. But they did start to get after Jack Faber. They got the measure of that searing fastball of his. And only desperate, diving saves by Madison, Rossi, and Maloney kept them at bay.

Jack, sensing the tide might be turning, or at least ebbing, did what he always did when he came under pressure. He went to the slider, the unhittable disguised fastball that dives toward the ground, right in front of the batter. It was, by a long way, the pitch he had practiced most, but it was still the most unreliable. That is not to say sporadic, or even erratic. Jack's slider either worked or it didn't work. If it was right, he could throw the pitch intermittently throughout a game, driving hitters crazy. But if it went wrong early, it would keep going wrong all night. And tonight he could *not* make it work—it wouldn't even work in his warm-up earlier that afternoon.

Both Stoltz and Gallgher hit the pitch hard—one straight into Madison's glove, another right out to Andy Crosby, who snagged it on a forty-foot run toward the right-field line.

Jack returned to the mound for the sixth inning having more or less decided to abandon the slider altogether. He knew he was armed with essentially only two pitches, the fastball and the curve, and he felt vulnerable.

Which he was. And his second pitch, a tailing fastball, was hit hard by Clouds Bryant, so nicknamed because he was studying meteorology at Vanderbilt. It was a one-hopper and Rick Adams made a fast decision to take one pace back. As the ball ripped off the dirt, he flashed his glove down and left, like a gunfighter, and came up with it. One short stutter step and Rick winged it straight to first base, where Zac Colbert, foot on the bag, sent Clouds sharply back over the horizon.

"Goddamned lucky son of a bitch," he growled.

Tony Garcia was concerned about Jack. He glanced back at the umpire and called time out, before jogging to the mound.

"You all right, Jack?"

"Yeah . . . yeah . . . I'm okay." But there was uneasiness in his voice as he kicked in the dirt.

Garcia, not convinced, jogged back, went into his crouch, and called for the slider, three fingers down. And for the first time all season, Jack shook him off.

Garcia, worried, put down one finger, with his glove outside.

Jack nodded, went into his windup, and threw a cut fastball, away from the left-handed Rob Barrett, another gruff Midwesterner who'd played against Garcia. Barrett fouled it straight back for strike one.

Again Garcia signaled for the slider, hoping Jack would send it in with a deep, diving, final trajectory, right by the kid's knees. But Jack shook him off again, and Garcia now knew there was something seriously wrong.

And once more he asked for the fastball, and Jack delivered an identical pitch. But this time Barrett connected, blasted a line drive straight over second base, only for Bobby Madison, standing well back, to leap three feet into the air and catch it clean.

Frank Stoltz hit the next pitch even harder, a sloping curveball which ended two feet from the fence but in Ray Sweeney's glove.

Jack shook his head. For a pitcher who had not yet given up a hit, he was being knocked all over the ballpark, three times in five pitches.

Somehow the 2–0 score held, but Jack walked in from the mound, almost beside himself with concern. Garcia angled in from the plate, and Ted Sando was on his way up the dugout steps. The three of them met in the no-man's-land between the third-base coaching box and the dugout.

Ted looked at both of them. "Now, what the hell was that all about?" he said. "Right here we got Patriot missiles coming off Red Sox bats . . . are they hitting good pitches, or is it a location problem?"

Garcia shrugged, looked at Jack and then at Sando. "Coach," he said, "he doesn't want to throw the slider. It's not a location problem. It's a variety problem."

Sando says, "Jack, I know you don't like your change-up. That's why you gotta throw that other pitch. You gotta throw the slider."

"Coach, I don't have it. I can't make it work. It doesn't have the bite."

"But you can't just give up on it. You gotta get it back. Christ! You been throwing it all your life. At least according to your dad, you have. I expect you know he's here, right? I saw him a little while ago."

"Yeah, I saw him."

"Don't let him down, hear me? You gotta get out there and find that goddamned slider, the pitch he taught you. Unless you're tired?"

"No, I'm not tired. I just can't throw it."

Up in the bleachers, Ben Faber could see the earnest faces as Ted Sando tried to rescue the missing pitch. Thoughts cascaded through his mind. *What words could I say to him? Why isn't he throwing it? It has to be the slider in a game like this . . . Jesus, I remember this happened once before in college . . . he lost it for a month . . . oh, hell, could it be me? Am I making him nervous?*

The three Seawolves moved into the dugout and Kyle Davidson came over to sit with Jack. He could see how upset he was. "What's going on, old buddy?" says the big bespectacled junior from Stanford. "You all right?"

And Jack says quietly, "Kyle . . . I can't find my slider . . . I've just lost the feel. You ever lost one of your pitches?"

"Hell, yes. We were in the regional championship last year and I lost my curve. Damn nearly cost us the whole thing to UCLA."

"Christ. What did you do?"

"I didn't give up on it. But thank God my change-up was okay."

"Right now I don't have a third pitch. I hate my change-up."

"Jack, I know you don't wanna hear this. But you must get out there and throw the slider; otherwise you'll *never* get it back."

The seventh inning came and went, much like the sixth. Jack threw two dipping sliders, tentatively, as if afraid to throw either one of them anywhere near the strike zone. They both hung in the air, and they were both slammed hard down the right-field line.

Somehow first baseman Zac Colbert got to them, one in the dirt, and one narrowly over his head for two outs. Only Jack knew how unbelievably lucky he had been.

At the top of the eighth he was on his way out to the mound again when he heard Russ Maddox say to Sando, "We want to get Dough-nut ready?"

Jack was gone before Ted smiled and said, "Russ, I know it doesn't seem like it, and I know I shouldn't say it . . ." Then he whispered, "But Jack's throwing a no-hitter!"

"Christ!" said Russ, surprised. "Is he?"

Up in the bleachers, Ben Faber was literally trembling, his hands clenched tight as Jack stepped up onto the mound, with the game still in the balance. And all his worst fears crowded in as his only son threw two fastballs, and two sliders outside. Frank Stoltz left them all, and walked.

Split Lowery was up next, and Jack threw him a curve that was hit almost 350 feet left of center, where Gino Rossi, moving like a bat out of hell, dived and made a snowcone catch four inches above the grass. One on, and one out, and the Seapuit crowd was on its feet to a man, chanting his name over and over: *"GEE-NO . . . GEE-NO . . . GEE-NO!"*

With his next pitch Jack hit Butch O'Marra in the thigh with an inside fastball, and the right fielder from Arizona State limped to first. Then Jack walked Sean Gallagher, the third baseman from Notre Dame, another power hitter, with twenty-six home runs in college and four for St. Ives.

The new man was J. T. Healey, a pinch hitter from South Car-olina. And Jack sent in two fastballs. Healey swung at both of them, missed both of them. This was the moment for the slider. Tony Gar-cia called for it. Jack nodded. He knew he *must* try, and he wound up and hurled his arm forward, snapping his wrist clockwise, but not quite hard enough. The ball floated in, nothing like sharp enough.

Healey took one quick jab step with his front foot and smashed the bat into it. The ball screamed across the infield two feet above the grass at 110 mph. Up in the bleachers, Ben Faber jolted back in his seat as if he'd been shot. For a split second everyone could see the no-hitter was gone.

Everyone, that is, except officer cadet Rick Adams, who raced across the dirt, and still traveling flat out, launched himself from his right foot, headlong, left arm outstretched, and turned to the back-hand. He crashed into the ground, with the ball miraculously in his glove. He rolled, bounced up onto his knees, and in a cloud of dust arrowed the ball straight at Bobby Madison.

In one movement The Citadel's second baseman winged it straight at the outstretched glove of Zac Colbert for the double play. And Butch O'Marra jogged back to the Red Sox dugout, shaking his head, unable to believe what he had just seen.

Jack Faber walked off the mound, straight to the shortstop, and shook his hand. "Saved my life, Ricky."

In the dugout Russ Maddox called for Ted to "have Doughnut ready for the ninth." And Jack watched the lanky Bulldog loping out to the bullpen in company with Davis Green, a young utility player who had just arrived from Penn State.

Jack went to sit with Kyle and muttered, "For a guy who's left them with a two–zip lead after eight, I'm sure getting a lot of grief."

Kyle smiled and said, "For a team that's two–zip down, the Red Sox have hit a lot of baseballs."

Jack grinned, but he said loudly enough for anyone to hear, "I'm finishing this one."

The 'Wolves scored nothing at the bottom of the eighth, and once more Jack headed out to the mound, tired now, but steely determined to finish the no-hitter. He did not hear Coach Maddox tell Ted, "Only because he might get it, he's going back out there. But if the no-hitter goes, Jack goes."

They both stared out to the bull pen, where young Green was trying to get a baseball out of the wire backstop six feet above his head. Even Russ had to smile.

And Jack got the first two Red Sox hitters, both with high fly balls. But then it went south. He walked the next two, number seven and eight, before Frank Stoltz returned to the plate, representing the go-ahead run.

Jack took off his cap and pushed back his mop of dark hair. He willed himself to concentrate, and the cool of the June night seemed now to affect him. He felt the stiffening across his shoulders, fatigue in his legs, and the dread of the slider that would not work.

He stood alone on the mound and wished to God his father had picked any other night to come and watch him. The ball floated in from Tony, and Jack looked hard at the two runners on first and second. His hesitation must have been obvious because he suddenly heard the deep baritone shout of Coach Sando, *"MY TIME!"* And the umpire's arm shot theatrically into the air as he in turn bellowed, *"TIME!"*

Tony was on his way to the mound, and Ted was on his way out.

Jesus Christ! thought Jack. He's taking me out, right in front of my dad.

But Sando had complete respect for any pitcher's potential no-hitter, and he was full of encouragement, punched Jack lightly on the arm, and told him to stay focused. "You got this guy, now let's go right after him. He's a pull hitter . . . likes 'em inside . . . next pitch throw him a fastball straight over the plate . . . make him play our game, right?"

"Okay," said Jack.

"Then, once we get ahead, watch the runners, delay a little, make the hitter think about it, then fire a fastball right under his chin . . . high and tight, like we've practiced. He's not going to like that . . . and he's gonna sway back off it . . . watch for him to buckle his knees . . . and when he does that, you got him, right . . . because he'll expect you to do it again."

"And am I?"

"Bullshit you are. You're gonna make that slider work right now. Thigh-high with a big drop-off . . . he'll swing and miss because he's not expecting it . . ."

"Then what?"

"The exact same pitch again—the slider . . . at the outside third of the plate. No one can hit that when you throw it right, and you're gonna throw it right . . .

"Come on, guys, let's finish this thing . . . you all know the sequence, so let's get 'em outta here . . ."

And as he left the mound, the towering Italian-American pitching coach looked back at the catcher. "Don't let him baby that pitch again, Tony . . . or I'll blame you!"

And now Jack was alone on the mound again. He pulled his cap down hard, leaned forward, and stared down at the hitter. Stoltz stared back and Tony went into his crouch, immediately signaling for the fastball. Jack nodded, reared back, and with all his force let the pitch rip.

He looked up just in time to see Frank Stoltz cock the bat higher, but this ball was rifling in at more than 90 mph, straight over the plate, and the St. Ives man never even attempted a swing. The umpire called the strike as he had called all night—pulling his right fist out of his left palm: *"HEE-EEEE!"*

The ball came back slowly, but Jack made the next pitch quickly. The moment Stoltz was ready, he hurled it in hard, high, and tight, straight at the batter's chin. Stoltz swayed back, and Jack saw his knees buckle, and when next he took his stance, Stoltz was standing fractionally farther away from the plate.

And now he had to throw the pitch that right now terrified him, because if he misjudged the snap—again—the ball would float in nice and easy, more or less straight, at maybe 80 mph, and a hitter like Stoltz would knock it straight out of the park, maybe win the whole damn game. "Jesus Christ," breathed Jack.

He dreaded throwing it even voluntarily, because he had somehow mislaid the snap. Being *told* to throw not one, but two sliders in succession was his personal definition of hell.

He'd already changed his mind about his dad's presence, and right now he would have given almost anything just for a quick word with him. But that was not possible, and right behind home plate, aiming their speed guns, were scouts from the Yankees, the Royals, the Bombers, and the Boston Red Sox, all focused on the no-hitter by the home-field pitcher.

He held the ball lightly in his left hand, and he heard the quick yell from Biff Flanagan, out of the St. Ives dugout: "*Come on, Frank, babe . . . let's go . . . you can hit this guy . . .*"

Instantly there was another shout, louder, rasping, Deep South in its inflection: "*Okay, Jack . . . real steady now . . . he can't hit you tonight . . . no way.*" That was the voice he'd been hearing all of his life.

And now he tightened his grip on the ball. His index and middle fingers locked hard onto the horseshoe, right up against the seam. His thumb sought out the other horseshoe, directly underneath, and he kept it there, lightly.

His windup was slow, and lazy, exactly the same as for the fast-ball. But the hitter knew nothing of the change in his grip. Jack's left knee came high across his body again, and now his right arm wound way back. This was it. His lips were drawn back from his teeth with the effort, and his left eye was glued to the spot above the plate this pitch must penetrate.

And now he turned his body again, and he hurled his right arm forward. One-hundredth of a second later he converted that fastball into the slider, snapping his wrist around clockwise, harder than he had dared all night, as if he were twisting a stubborn doorknob, inches in front of his right eye. The violence of the motion sent him forward, and his left foot crashed into the precise same print on the downside of the mound for the 118th time this night.

He almost fell forward with the force of the pitch. He could feel the red dust on his fingers, and he looked up into the death zone where the baseball is flying in at only 80 mph, twelve feet from the bat.

Stoltz can see the ball. And he can see a big red dot bang in the middle of it, like a spot of blood in the vortex of the spin. He knew it was a curve of some kind, but he was standing too far back. In another hundredth of a second he knew his fate. For the first time tonight Jack Faber's slider dropped out of the sky as if it were falling off a table.

Frank swung in some kind of a reflex desperation. He almost swung himself off his feet, and he missed by all of a foot, and he heard the loud *"HEE-EEEEEE!"* as the crucial strike was called.

And long after the burst of applause had died away, Jack could still see one solitary figure in the bleachers, still standing, still clapping, calling out over and over, *"That's it, Jack, that's the one . . . that's it, Jackie, that's the one."* The old Kraemer Crawdads cap was now set at a positively rakish angle.

Stoltz recovered his poise and stepped back into the box, muttering to himself, "He'll throw smoke now. He's trying to end the game. Right over the plate. And I'll be waiting. This game ain't over. I catch this one good, that's three runs, and this pitcher's tired."

There was pressure on Frank. But nothing like the pressure on Jack. His wrist had hurt since the last pitch. He flexed it and felt the pain again. The very last thing in this world he wanted to do was to throw the slider.

Garcia signaled, three fingers, low and hard against his right thigh. No doubt about the signal. And Stoltz was ready. Jack wanted to shake Tony off, but he could not do that. He felt the expectant gaze of his father upon him. And he felt the gaze of Ted Sando. Jack turned helplessly to the dugout, hoping for a last-minute reprieve.

But Ted was standing up on the step, pumping his right arm, and Jack heard him bellow, *"THROW IT, JACK. FOR CHRIST'S SAKE, THROW IT!"*

He nodded curtly at his catcher, who moved his glove to a position four inches outside the plate. He now knew he was aiming for the edge, and he adjusted his grip, leaned back, and catapulted forward, snapping his wrist clockwise so hard the pain almost made him cry out.

He crashed forward onto his left foot, and looked up in time to see the slider dive viciously off its trajectory, straight down, right against the outside corner of the diamond. He saw Stoltz try to get forward, watched the terrific downward swing of the bat. And he turned away wincing in anticipation of the oncoming sharp crack of a well-hit baseball.

But there was no sound. Just the echoing

"*HEE-EEEEE!*" as the plate umpire bellowed the final out, followed by a collective howl of "*YESSSS!*" from the home crowd as Frank Stoltz trudged back to the dugout, offering a tight, formal nod of respect to the pitcher from Louisiana.

The no-hitter was complete. The grim 2–0 victory was somehow sealed against one of the best teams in the league. And up in the bleachers, Ben Faber was standing, his huge fists raised high, a faraway smile on his face. Jack could see him. But he could not see the tears streaming down his father's weather-beaten cheeks.

Later both Fabers, plus Tony Garcia, were on their way out for supper, just steak and fries and Coke in a local restaurant over at Oyster Hills. Ben told them about his own solitary no-hitter at Luther Williams Field, Macon, Georgia, all those years ago. When the check came it seemed too high, but Ben paid it anyway, wondering if he had enough cash left for the gas to take him home.

He told them he was staying in a small hotel, and he had to leave early tomorrow. He hugged Jack before they parted, and he told him how much it had meant to him to see the no-hitter.

Jack knew what that long journey and the expenditure had meant to his father, and as Ben drove away from the elegant Fallon house, in light rain, he just said into the night, "I love you, Dad."

He had no idea, of course, that Ben Faber was going back to Cabot Field, to stretch out and sleep for four hours in the dugout, out of the rain. And there, later, he would watch the moon rise out to the east, and cast its pale light upon the green covers draped across the mound.

The night had grown cool, and Ben did not sleep much, but he felt utterly at home on the dugout bench, in tune with the world and with the beloved game. He was wide-awake at 3 A.M. and he pulled out of the parking lot right on schedule, heading back down the dark, lonely New England highway, 1,600 miles to Lockport, South Louisiana, almost to the Gulf of Mexico, in the old blue Chevy.

1 0

*B*y Independence Day the Seawolves were charging, with a
15–3 record. By July 10, the halfway point in the season,
they were 18–4. But Ben Faber was unable to make it to another
game. He was so strapped for cash he was unable to pay his phone
bill, and they disconnected the phone before the holiday weekend.
His buddy Tom Thibodaux down at the Lockport gas station was a
big fan of Jack's, and he made the call to New England most nights
to check every Seapuit game result. Sometimes he and Ben sat in the
air-cooled office and sipped a couple of beers talking about the old
times when Ben had been the star pitcher for Kraemer.

The sugar market stayed low, so even if the crop was fine, there
would be no money made this year. Ben had a $30,000 debt to the
bank, and he needed more for replanting. The question of a long-
distance phone call to Natalie in Chicago was not even worthy of
thought. The situation was dire, and Ben was losing weight with
worry and hunger. The fact was, if the bank came down on him, the
game, financially, was up. He'd have to sell.

And this was not the perfect time to be selling a sugar farm set in
the heat of the Louisiana swamps. And there was nothing Ben Faber
could do about any of it. Except sit and brood, and worry about
himself, and about Jack, and what would happen if the bank said no.

By the evening of July 22, the 'Wolves were slowing down some.
With three parts of the season gone, they were 24–9. They had a few

injuries, and a few times they had lost concentration, but they were building an exceptional record and were six points clear at the top of the Western Section. In this league, a team earned two points for every win, one for each tie, and none for a loss.

On the night of the twenty-second, they were delivering a crowd-pleasing shellacking to the hapless Exeter Braves, winning 8–0 at Cabot, Doughnut closing the game out for Kyle with two sensational final innings. He sent six Braves down in order with only 22 pitches. Only two of which lodged ten feet up in the backstop wire, and caused howls of laughter from the bleachers, where Doughnut was becoming some kind of a folk hero.

The game finished at 7:30, which was 6:30 in Lockport. Ben had just finished changing the plugs and cleaning the carburetor on his big tractor and was on his way to the gas station. At least he was with any luck. But the blue Chevy was tired after its long-distance transcontinental exertions, and Ben called two strikes against that 240,000-mile engine, praying for a base hit next time he hit the starter.

But right then he had a sudden visitor, Jerry Segal, the tall, raw-boned regional site boss of Louisiana Oil and Gas, driving through the gates in a big, distinctive white-and-blue corporate Cherokee. The two men knew each other well, mainly because they paid Ben $4,000 annually for permission to drill out in his wetlands. But they'd found nothing, and with a chill in his heart, Ben guessed Jerry Segal was calling the expensive search off.

"Hey, Ben," called Jerry, striding toward the farmer. "How you been?"

"Pretty good, Jerry. You?"

"Hell, I'm keeping the wolf from the door. How's that boy of yours? I keep reading about him in the local paper. He's burning 'em up, right?"

"Guess so. But he might not make the Majors in time to save me from the goddamned sugar market."

"Well, these things go in cycles. But I have to admit, I'm in an industry producing something everyone wants more and more of. You're in one which half the fucking country wants to give up!"

"Ain't that the truth. You got good news or bad news?"

"Ben, I don't want to say it's great news. Not yet. But my guys think we might be getting close. The geologists keep saying the same thing—'running high, and looking good.' That's a kinda driller's mantra. And we continue to think there may be substantial oil and gas all the way northwest of Caminada Bay way up through the swamps either side of the Lafourche River. The thing is we don't really know the size of whatever there is. Or how long it might last. If it's gas we might be talking one week, or maybe thirty years. But the guys think the shape of the gas reserves may be a little more west than we thought."

Ben's heart skipped a beat. They were drilling out on the eastern edge of his land. From there he owned everything, four thousand acres to the west. "Oh?" he said, in a noncommittal way.

"And we really want to go on, except we may have to drill maybe a dozen shafts, pretty close to the house. And that's gonna cost you some sleep."

"Won't cost me anything if you hit a zillion cubic feet of natural gas, right?"

"Ben, if we hit a zillion cubic feet of natural gas, we'll probably find oil, not too deep either. That way you're gonna be one of my major stockholders. Yessir."

"But I'm not counting on anything."

"You're right not to. In this game you just never know. Guy once told me trying to find the dimensions of a natural gas reserve was like seven guys blindfolded walking around an elephant trying to tell you the shape of what they were touching."

Ben chuckled. "Well, you've gone this far," he said. "Guess you may as well proceed. There's sure as hell nothing else going on around here."

"Well, there is something, Ben. We want to go ahead for another twelve months, and I've suggested a payment to you of ten thousand dollars to make up for the grief and aggravation of a gas-and-oil operation in your backyard. Cash tomorrow, if you agree."

"Done," said Ben. "Won't solve my problems, but it sure won't hurt."

The two men talked a little longer, but Jerry was headed immediately back to the big refinery in Baton Rouge, sixty miles northwest. He declined Ben's offer of a beer, which was as well, since Ben didn't have any. And he hit the trail in a cloud of dust. Jerry Segal never hung around, save to clinch a deal and agree on a price. Unless something big happened, Ben did not expect to see him again before the twelve-month drilling time ran out.

"Ten grand! Thank you, Jerry. There is a God," muttered Ben as he retreated back toward the Chevy, which he considered was still batting, but only just. He slipped into the driver's seat, turned the key, and hit the starter. The Chevy coughed, spluttered, and miraculously fired, roaring into life, as if somehow elated by the visit of Jerry Segal.

"Base hit, old buddy," murmured Ben, banging his foot down on the accelerator before the Chevy changed its mind. He drove out through the gates, on toward the end of the dusty track which joined his sugar operation to the road, and sped out toward Main Street. Well, almost. Right on the edge of the blacktop, the Chevy did change its mind and stopped dead, with what Ben considered was a long tired sigh.

"Shoulda come on the tractor," he muttered. "This old friend's on its last legs." He hit the starter again, and against all the odds, the ancient automobile fired again, and moved forward, rumbling down to the gas station with scarcely another protest.

"Just a warning, eh?" said Ben to himself. "Just a little ol' warning, let me know there ain't gonna be no more trans-America expeditions to see Jack, right?"

He didn't get a reply, but he didn't need one. If he could keep her going for a few months she'd still fetch $400 for scrap.

Ben parked at the gas station and let himself into the office where Tom was sitting in back reading the sports pages of the *St. Charles Herald Guide*, the local newspaper out of the nearby town of Boutte.

"Hey, Ben. We play tonight?"

"Yup. Home to the Exeter Braves. Jack wasn't pitching. His buddy Kyle started."

"Lemme call. Go get yourself a cold one."

"It's already ten of eight up there. Guys'll be long gone, but Martha's probably still in the field office."

Martha Jamieson, the president and chief financial officer, was up to her eyes, counting money from the hotdog kitchen, tallying the raffle, sales from the store, filling out the bank slips. But she was graceful as ever. "Hello, Mr. Thibodaux. You call on a good night. We won eight–nothing, and we're still way top of the table. Give Mr. Faber our best regards, and let him know Jack's starting tomorrow night—another tough one over at the Sentries."

"Thanks, Martha. He'll be glad to know that."

"And tell him we're confident. Jack's in terrific form, and he hasn't lost one yet, right?"

Tom put the phone down and relayed the distant news from Cabot Field. Ben came in with his beer and asked Tom if he could make one more phone call. He spoke as if the cost were ten bucks a minute, but Tom was on all kinds of cheap-call plans with the phone companies, and he could call all over the States, if he ever wanted to, for pennies a minute.

"Help yourself, old pal," he said, and never even noticed that Ben kept delaying until a truck pulled up to the gas pumps outside. At which point Tom left the office and Ben picked up the receiver and dialled a 312 number on the South Side of Chicago, 950 miles due north of Lockport.

It rang three times, and then a soft, slightly accented voice said, "Hello, this is the Garcia School of Music. Natalie speaking."

"Oh, hello," said Ben, just disguising his natural inflections of speech. "I was wondering if you could offer me lessons in trombone and tambourines?"

"I'm sorry," replied the voice. "But our advertisement said quite clearly we specialize in the harp, violin, and piano."

"Ma'am, I'm sorry. But I regard those particular instruments as kinda soft for my taste. Actually I'm in the process of converting Bach's Sonata in E-flat for Harp and Flute into a major symphony for trombone and drums."

For a few seconds there was silence. And then Mrs. Garcia, who now regarded the caller as some kind of lunatic, replied, "I am sorry. We cannot help you with that."

"Well, ma'am, I'm real disappointed. You see, I just got my arm fixed after an injury, and I'm playing especially well. Just need a little polish."

"Well, I am sorry. And we are very busy. I have to ring off."

"Hold it, ma'am. I'm playing that trombone with the same arm that threw a mean curveball for the Crawdaddies, way down there, by that big ol' river."

"*BEN!*" shrieked Natalie. "Did I ever mention that you are one of the worst people I ever met!"

"I think so."

"Is that why you've called me just once in six weeks?"

"You been counting?"

"Yes. Since you mention it."

Ben laughed, and then he told her, "It's nice to hear your voice again, and I was sorry you weren't able to come to the Cape one more time to see the boys. I caught just the one game, saw Jack pitch his first no-hitter. Tony was great. He's the big man on that team."

Natalie was silent, and then she said, "I haven't changed my mind, you know, Ben. About baseball, that is. I wish Tony would give it up."

"Things been tough financially?"

"Awful. At least as bad as ever. I couldn't even start to pay off the first loan from the bank. I've tried to work all the time, and I've had a few weeks with the symphony. But all I've done is save enough for Tony's living at school for the next year . . . and I'm still without a nickel for myself . . ."

"The sugar business is on its way to hell too," said Ben. "One of the main reasons I didn't call was because they cut off my phone . . ."

"Oh, Ben . . . how awful. Will it get better?"

"I don't know. Not for a while . . . but, hey, Natalie, I didn't call to gripe and moan about money . . ."

"Of course not . . . you called for lessons in the trombone and tambourine!"

Ben Faber chuckled. "No, really. I called to let you know I'm going back to the Cape at the end of the season, probably on or around August eighth. That's the night of the third play-off game, and since Seapuit has obviously won the Western Section, they are going to be in it. But it could be their final game, since it's best of five."

"Well, I'm glad you're going, Ben. I know Tony loves to see you. He told me about your last visit . . . his houseparents are very good about letting him call me every week . . . I wish I could come. I'd really like to see you again. But it's not possible."

"Yes, it is. I'm sending you a ticket. And I'm picking you up at Logan around lunchtime . . ."

"But, Ben . . . how? Neither of us can afford it?"

"Well, I just found a little money. Small oil-drilling lease on my land. It's not much, but it'll get the phone reconnected, it'll ease the pressure at the bank, and there's enough for a couple of inexpensive tickets to Boston, one from O'Hare, one from N'Orleans . . ."

"But what about the journey from the airport to Seapuit?"

"I got enough to rent us a car for a couple of days. We'll stay with the houseparents, like before. Remember they both said we were welcome . . ."

"Well, there's nothing I'd like more—except for the stupid base-ball. Can you really do this?"

"Natalie, I've been biding my time only to call you when I *could* do something like this. And now I can. Just tell me you'll do it."

"Ben. I think you know. I would love to . . . if you're sure you can manage . . ."

"Natalie, I'm on someone else's phone. Obviously. But I'll pull this together, firm up the date and times, and call you this time tomorrow with the details."

"Oh, that would be lovely. Something to look forward to. I haven't had that in a very long time."

"Nor me," said Ben. "Nor me."

At which point Tom finished gassing up the truck and began to walk back to the office. Ben and Natalie said a hasty good-bye, and the phone was replaced.

Ben put a twenty-dollar bill on the counter by the cash box and said, "Take that, Tommy, cover a few calls, plus another coupla beers I'm just getting out of the fridge."

He said it with the casual confidence of a twenty-five-year friend-ship.

"Jeez, you just won some kind of lottery?" said Tom. "Hey, there's another pickup outside . . . check what time the Braves are playing, willya? In the *Guide,* right behind you. We better turn on the TV."

Thirteen days later, on the evening of August 4, the Seapuit Sea-wolves were declared winners of the Western Division of the Cape Marlin League with a record of 32–12, the most dominant margin in the entire sixty-year history of the league.

When Russ Maddox gave a short speech of appreciation for the Western Divisional Trophy, he stood on the third-base line with a mi-crophone and he faced the packed bleachers, and he said something no one who was there would ever forget.

"We didn't win this thing because of pure talent. There were four other hitters in the league with better numbers than ours. We won be-cause this was a *team.* When we had a pitcher struggling, the defense saved him. When our best men at the plate struck out, lesser hitters some-how grew taller. When our opponents knocked us around, my kids were ready to charge through a brick wall to either stop, or catch, that ball.

"They practiced and practiced. They stayed at the top of their fit-ness. They listened to their coaches, and they listened to each other. And when they were down, they fought their way back. And when they had to hang on, and arms were tired, and shoulders ached, and legs were weary, they still dug deep. They never once lost two games in a row. And thanks to Bobby and Rick, our two cadets from The Citadel, the team had a military, disciplined edge to it. And in my view, that swung it, and it was my privilege to have coached every one of them."

A huge burst of applause greeted that little speech, and then the team came running up the dugout steps and raised their hats to the big local crowd which had supported them, night after night, and would continue to do so as the postseason play-offs unfolded.

There would be updated stats at the conclusion of the champi-onship, but for now, the end of the regular season, there were some impressive numbers for the 'Wolves.

Jack Faber had some tense moments, but he had been the top pitcher on Cape Marlin, all season, finishing 9–0, with a 1.68 ERA. He and Kyle both played in the All-Star Game, and the big Californ-ian finished 8–1 with an ERA of 2.28. Doughnut's erratic start held him back, but he finished 4–5 with an ERA of 4.97.

Aaron Smith settled down to become the 'Wolves regular closer with seven saves. He also served duty as designated hitter and fourth outfielder. He was a superb all-around ballplayer, and Ted Sando con-sidered him certain to sign professional in the next draft.

The hitters had been solid all season. Ray Sweeney batted .327 and topped the Seapuit averages. He also hit eight home runs. Zac Colbert was right behind him, hitting .316, with six home runs. Bobby Madison, who was not a power hitter, batted .301, with a great on-base percentage of .400.

Big Scott Maloney, the Texas Aggie, led the league in home runs with nine and batted .283. The speedball Rick Adams was right be-hind him with .281, no home runs, but with twenty-six stolen bases. Gino Rossi led the league in doubles—twelve of them—and a .290 average.

Tony Garcia was fabulous. He averaged .271 with the bat. He hit five home runs, with thirty-seven RBIs, and he threw out twenty-four stealing. The other fast man, Andy Crosby, averaged .274, with one home run, three triples, and twelve stolen bases. By any standards this was one of the finest all-around teams ever to play on Cape Marlin.

And now they had to face up to the postseason play-offs, the first series of five against the old enemy, the Sentries, who finished nine points behind the 'Wolves and thus surrendered home-field advantage.

This confrontation, which occurred every three or four years, signaled the basic philosophical difference between the two ball clubs. Seapuit, with their connections to the families of Boston Brahmins like Lowells, Cabots, and Rowlands, etc., would never even dream of obscuring the rules, far less bending or breaking them.

The Sentries however had a more ruthless, almost professional reputation, often flying in brand-new players for the final stages of the season, an infuriating habit—for everyone else—but one which had a distinct double edge to it. Because new players may be fresh, and they may be excellent, but team spirit wins play-offs, rarely pure brilliance.

And sure enough, Lancaster turned up for the opening game with two players who had not played one single game for the team in the regular season, one of them a pitcher. And sure enough, the erosion of spirit that often follows when players are sent home was all too apparent. The Sentries seemed flat, and when their new pitcher began his night's work, the coach walked out for a short discussion, and a Seapuit fan stood up and yelled, *"KEEP QUIET, EVERYONE! HE'S GONE OUT TO INTRODUCE HIMSELF!"*

And from that moment it all went wrong for the Sentries. Jack Faber shut them out and the 'Wolves won it 2–0. The following night, Lancaster showed a little more pepper, but they still lost it 6–4 at Andy McKillop Field, and no one held out any hope for them in the cauldron of Cabot Field the following afternoon.

Meantime Ben Faber was on his way to Boston, arriving from New Orleans on an early morning Southwest flight. He went to the Hertz desk and, using a special dealers' courtesy card, thanks to Tom Thibodaux, rented a Ford Taurus for the rock-bottom price of $120 a week, rather than $40 a day.

He retired to the coffee shop to wait. He drank two cups of black coffee and read the *Boston Globe,* noting a small paragraph in the sports pages which stated the divisional play-offs in the Cape Marlin League could both be decided tonight—the 'Wolves favorites to beat

Lancaster at Cabot Field, and, in the East, the Rock Harbor Mariners looking for a similar 3–0 sweep against the St. Ives Red Sox at Bart Bradley Stadium.

At 1:25 the fifty-foot-long arrivals board announced that Flight 1179 from Chicago had landed. Fifteen minutes later Mrs. Natalie Garcia, wearing her white suit and a deep red silk blouse, came through the double doors where Ben Faber was waiting.

She carried a smart tan-colored shoulder bag, with her suitcase in her right hand, and she walked quickly toward him and kissed him on the cheek, and said, "Did you bring the tambourines?"

Ben slipped his arm around her waist and hugged her. Then he appraised her quite striking looks, the medium-length, jet-black hair, the wide eyes, perfect teeth, and slim figure. "As beautiful as I remember," he said. "Here, let me take that suitcase."

"Do we need a trolley?" she said.

"Guess we might if you had three of 'em," replied Ben, grinning. "Try to remember, I'm a farmer, not a violinist."

"Oh, yes. Of course. I had quite forgotten. You didn't play with the Lockport Philharmonic. That must have been somebody else."

"How d'you remember Lockport?"

"Oh, my head's not totally full of half notes and B-flats. I remember what people say."

"All people?"

"No. Some people."

They both smiled, remembering the reply was not original. Natalie linked her arm through his, and they walked out into the stultifying ninety-six-degree heat of Logan Airport in high summer. They made the most arresting couple, Ben Faber, six feet two inches, built like a running back, with deeply tanned arms and face, wearing chinos and a pure white polo shirt. Natalie, who could easily have been an actress or a model, Spanish in appearance, olive-skinned against the white of her suit.

Few would have guessed that the clothes they wore were the best either of them owned. And that they scarcely had a dollar between them.

But for now the sun shone on them as well as on everything else. They picked up the car and set off for the Cape.

Natalie asked, "Ben, have you lost weight?"

"Guess a little. And you can put it down to worry."

"Have things been very bad?"

"You know, Natalie, farming tends to be much the same all the time. It's the price you're going to get for your crop that matters. We all know what it costs us to raise, and so long as the price per ton stays above that, we're going to make something. But if it drops below that, you know you'll lose. Now, my costs are low, but there seems to be a glut of sugar around, and the market price I'm gonna get is way below what I need. So I'll lose. And if something does not improve, I'll lose big this year."

"What's big?"

"Fifteen thousand, instead of making maybe thirty-five thousand. And it could happen again next year, which would be a real worry."

"And how about the money you found for my ticket?"

"Well, that was from the drilling company who want to expand west over my land. But they're drilling all over the place, and they haven't made a big natural gas strike yet anywhere near my area."

"What if they do?"

"Then my worries would be over. I'd be a rich man, but there's small farmers all over south Louisiana who think that, have been for years, and they're still poor . . . anyway, how about you, Natalie, have things been any better?"

"A little, mainly because I was able to do a three-week summer tour with the symphony. With Tony away, I could go easily, and I made some good money. But he needs stuff for the new college year, and I had bills to pay, and at the end of it all I owed nothing, but I still had nothing. It's always just the same."

"Would it make much difference if you had a permanent position with the symphony?"

"Perhaps a little. But then your life is not your own. You have to be ready to play, night after night, month after month. And for me, with no other income, that would just stretch in front of me forever. And I'm almost forty years old. To be playing the harp until my fingers wore out, just to stay alive . . . Ben, my only chance of a reasonable existence is for Tony to make it young in a major law firm. And you know he has the brain to do that."

"What would you say if some Major League club came along with a half million for him to turn pro?"

"I'd know he was going to the Minor Leagues for maybe five

years. And all that time, the money would be growing less. And then he may not quite make it, and he'd have to go back to school, to get his degree, and the money would shrink some more. And then he'd be twenty-seven or twenty-eight, which is old to be without experience in the law, and the big firms would no longer want him, and he'd end up scratching a living chasing ambulances. All because of this lousy game."

"Natalie, I do see. I do understand. I hate to say it, but I think Tony really could make it big in baseball. He's a terrific catcher, with a great right arm, and he can power-hit. There's not many of them around, believe me."

"His tutor told me he has the brain to be in the first three in his class at law school. And there's not many of them around, believe *me*."

Ben laughed. And before he could reply, Natalie added, "Just remember, the law is about a hundred times more certain than baseball. Just ask yourself, where would you rather be, facing the world at twenty-two-near top in your class at Northwestern law school, heading for a starting salary of a hundred and twenty thousand with a Chicago law firm, or drafted into Single-A ball with the White Sox with a signing fee of three hundred thousand and a salary of two hundred and fifty dollars a week?"

"Me?"

"No, not you. A normal person."

Ben Faber chuckled. "Gotta say the law. You're right. It *is* more certain. Any damn thing can happen in baseball. And like you say, most of 'em never make it."

"That, Ben, is the correct answer. And it tells you something, doesn't it?"

"What's that, Miss Natalie?"

"I wouldn't be here for the baseball. So I think I must be here to see you." And she leaned over, and kissed him on the cheek, for the second time.

Not too long after, they were in the driveway of the McLure's house, and Nancy McLure came running out and hugged Natalie while Ben pulled her suitcase off the rear seat and carried it into the hallway.

He shook hands with Mrs. McLure and told Natalie he'd be back for her shortly. Then he drove around to the Fallons' big white Colonial.

No one was home, and on his bed was a short note, "Welcome back, Dad. See you at the field. Mr. and Mrs. Fallon are coming tonight. Save them places. It'll be a big crowd—Jack."

He was right about that. The Cabot Field bleachers were packed before the game started. Jack and Tony came out of the dugout and waved, but there was no way they could make it through the crowd to greet their parents.

The atmosphere was relaxed because everyone sensed the fight had somehow gone out of the Sentries. Doughnut was steady, throwing fastball after fastball all around the plate. And in the third inning the Seawolves exploded. They loaded the bases and Ray Sweeney slammed the first pitch he faced clean over the fence, just left of the scoreboard: 4–0.

And two innings later the 'Wolves did it again. This time Andy Crosby, Gino Rossi, and Rick Adams loaded 'em up, and Zac Colbert crushed a soft curveball, sent it a hundred feet into the air, and 390 feet deep, straight into the woods beyond right center for 8–0.

By the bottom of the eighth, the Sentries had fallen apart. With Crosby again on base, Rick Adams popped up, but the two Lancaster infielders collided trying to catch the ball. Now there were two on, and Colbert was on his way to the plate. He banged the second pitch hard, right out toward the fence, where the outfielder lost it in the sun, picked it up, and in desperation completely overthrew the cutoff man.

The ball one-hopped and smacked into the dugout back wall, where it ricocheted around but injured no one. The Sentries coach, Dick Frazier, was livid, and he charged up the steps of the dugout and hurled the ball into the woods in sheer temper. The crowd howled with joy, and in their own dugout the 'Wolves were rocking with laughter, trying to keep their heads down, trying not to show public disrespect to the visiting coach.

In the next fifteen minutes, the Sentries made four errors while the 'Wolves banged and hustled their way to five runs in the inning. Doughnut closed it out in the ninth, for the first time all season pitching a whole game, and landing his first-ever shutout.

It was more like a carnival than a serious game, but the Seawolves had won 13–0. To the Sentries' fans the series was a disappointment because it was so clearly a mismatch. But for Seawolves fans, they were in the championship final and nothing else mattered. Best of three games, starting tomorrow, against the Rock Harbor Mariners, who had beaten St. Ives 4–0.

And this would not be a carnival. Rock Harbor had the Indian sign on the 'Wolves, having beaten them four times in the regular season.

Cape Marlin League play-offs happen with almost frenzied speed, every night, no breaks, because so many of the players have to travel home and prepare for the new college semester. The officials have to get it done, and there is hardly time to draw breath between games. There have been times when the last two games that decide the championship have been played as a morning-afternoon double-header. The wear and tear on pitchers is unavoidable.

In Seapuit's dugout, Coaches Maddox and Sando were assessing their options against the Mariners—the trick being to save your best pitcher for the third and potentially last game. However, if the Seawolves should lose the first game, they would have a major problem: to bring in Jack Faber to pitch the second game and perhaps save the championship; or to risk someone else for game two, and then play the final with Jack Faber starting, after a proper rest.

Russ said, "Let's take it one step at a time, Ted. Let's give it everything to get a one–nothing lead tomorrow. Kyle's in good shape and we have a big chance of winning the first one."

"I just wish it wasn't the goddamned Mariners," replied Sando. "Trouble is they've got two outstanding pitchers, and you know we're gonna face one of 'em right here tomorrow, and one of 'em up there at Bradley Stadium the night after."

"I know. And every time I think we're gonna beat 'em, we lose."

Ten minutes later Russ dismissed the team for the night, but told them to get plenty of sleep and report to the field early tomorrow. "Everyone here by midday for extra batting practice, then lunch at the beach, which I'm having delivered—pizza and salad—then back to the field for a team talk and more practice."

Tony and Jack went off in search of Ben and Natalie and found them talking with both sets of houseparents, the McLures and the Fallons. It was a kind of reunion, though it was only seven weeks since they had last been together.

There was a difference now; the atmosphere was much more serious. The Cape Marlin League Championship was on the line. If the games went to the third and final game, there would be a major "take" of possibly an extra $7,000 for the Seawolves. And all four of the Fallons and the McLures served on various field committees. That extra revenue would set them well on their way to the new scoreboard they desperately needed.

The boys slung their big bags into the houseparents' cars and climbed into the backseat of the Taurus. It was a replica of the formation they had made on their first-ever journey together from Boston airport.

"Killed 'em, right, Mom?" Young Garcia was in a buoyant mood, as usual after a victory. "What did you think, Mr. Faber? Ain't lost my touch any, right? Still whipping 'em right out of the air. The ol' glove hovering there like a bird of prey!"

Jack and Ben both laughed, but Natalie looked less than enthusiastic. "Could you two try not to encourage him," she said, with mock seriousness. "Remember, I have to live with that brand of sophomoric humor."

"Mom, it just so happens I'm not the only one impressed with my lethal left glove."

"Meaning?"

"One of the scouts came over to talk to me the other night. Seems the Royals have a check for two hundred thousand dollars should I decide to sign."

"When?"

"End of the season here."

"You mean end of the week?"

"Well, yes. I guess so."

"Well, you may tell the Royals that there is no way you will be giving up your law studies, no way you will be leaving Northwestern until you have your degree, and no way, if I have anything to say about it, you will be playing professional baseball in the Minor Leagues."

"Goddammit, Mom. You have to sugarcoat everything? Can't you, just for once, tell it like it is?"

This, predictably, was too much for Jack, who was laughing. Ben saved the moment by announcing, "That's nothing like enough money, Tony. You play it very calmly, turn down all offers, stay with your law books, and wait for at least another year."

"Does that mean I could come back here again next year? Because that's what me and Jack are planning. 'Specially if we win the whole thing this week . . ."

"I don't know about that, Tony. Depends what your mom thinks about your exam results."

"Unless they are excellent, I shall think very little about them," said Natalie. "And I am sure they'd be a whole lot better if he spent a lot less time dressed in that ridiculous uniform, prancing around like the Man in the Iron Mask."

Ben thought he could discern where young Garcia inherited his spiky turn of phrase. But he elected to lighten up the conversation, and he chuckled. "Okay, Natalie. Where did you have in mind for dinner . . . Dexter's, Dexter's, or Dexter's?"

He referred to the waterfront restaurant overlooking the harbor in Henley—cheap and cheerful, fresh fish only, plenty of clams, scrod, flounder, tons of fries, served on upmarket plastic plates, very quickly. In the corner was a piano bar, and local yachtsmen pulled right up to the restaurant dock. A few of them, with some regularity, fell straight into the harbor on the way out.

The boys loved it there and Natalie, wearing her faded blue cutoff jeans, a white T-shirt, and denim jacket, was perfectly dressed for Dexter's. Jack and Tony, still suited up, would be greeted as heroes in their Seawolves kit. The Cape Marlin League is always big news in downtown Henley.

"Sounds a lot like Dexter's to me," said Natalie.

They pulled into the wide waterfront parking lot and made their way inside, ordered at the counter a large plate of fried clams to start with, with fried scrod to follow. They were escorted by the waitress to a table on the open side of the room, which was protected by a screen but still picked up the light southwester off the harbor.

Ben ordered a pint of ice-cold beer, a glass of white wine for Natalie, and diet Cokes for the boys—beer being illegal in Massachussetts until they were twenty-one.

"It's damned good beer in here," said Jack.

"How do you know?" asked his father.

"I got my ways . . . but they're awful secret."

Ben shook his head, smiling. "Be careful," he said. "Both of you. And remember what you're here for."

"I'm here for the scrod," said Tony.

"I meant, remember why you're on the Cape," replied Ben.

"Oh, yeah, that," said Tony. "Well, of course I'm only here for the beer."

Even Natalie laughed at this. And so did Jack and Ben. It was interesting how the incorrigible Tony Garcia shielded his iron will to win ball games and compete in every game, right to the death, with this casual banter.

"Ignore him, Dad," said Jack. "He can't get through any hour in any day without sharpening his teeth on some subject or other. The only time he's quiet is in the dugout, when we're losing. Which is not all that often."

"Better not be this week either," said Tony. And he raised his cardboard diet Coke cup on high, and announced he expected *"VICTORY!"* However, he said it just a little too loudly, and a big table of twelve local yachtsman right next to him gave him a standing ovation. Only then did Ben notice the blackboard on the wall next to the chalked menu. It read: CAPE LEAGUE: SEAWOLVES 13 SENTRIES 0; MARINERS 4 RED SOX 0.

One of the yachtsman leaned over and offered a handshake to Jack. "Great arm, kid. I've watched you twice this year."

"This is unbelievable," said Tony. "He didn't even play tonight. And I'm out there working myself to death, for him to get the glory."

"Try not to value easy fame too highly," replied Jack. "Let's face it, you *are* the Man in the Iron Mask."

"He's the Seawolves catcher, right?" called someone

"That's him," said Jack.

"Great job, kid."

"Hear that," said Tony, grinning. "Recognition at last." And he tipped his cap in the direction of the voice.

"Will you kindly take that hat off?" said his mother. "You look like some kid from the Chicago tenements."

Ben, who was caught trying not to laugh in midswallow, leaned over and put his arm around her, and she caught his hand over her shoulder. It was the first time Jack and Tony had ever seen a display of affection between them, and it registered. Big.

However, when they arrived back at the McLures' just before 10 P.M., Ben and Natalie were both very formal. Ben opened the door for her, and she thanked him for dinner, said good night to Jack, and followed Tony into the house. However, she did turn around at the door, and said quietly, "I'm really looking forward to our trip to the beach tomorrow, Ben. See you nice and early."

With that, she was gone. And again it registered with both boys. Big.

*I*t was a beautiful day on the majestic, oceanic sweep of Cape Marlin's Outer Bank. And Ben and Natalie had a light lunch in a village diner overlooking the Atlantic and then walked for miles along the shore, watching the giant rollers thumping onto the hard-packed tidal sand.

This was the beach they had visited back in June, when it had been Natalie's first sight of the ocean, any ocean. And this was the beach where Ben had first felt a quickening of his heartbeat whenever he looked at the coolly beautiful harpist from Chicago.

He considered it some kind of a miracle that they could find conversation, but they did have the shared experience of poverty, and the shared objective of trying to raise talented late-teenage sons, each of them alone.

And they found a common ground in their hopes and ambitions, and a kind of sureness, now, that the other would understand. And they talked all afternoon, not about *them*, but about each other separately.

Their afternoon could not be described in any way as romantic, but it was close, and kind and considerate. And it made them twenty-five minutes late for the first game of the play-off finals. The tree-lined country roads all around Cabot Field were packed with parked cars on both verges by the time they arrived. And the field parking spaces for players, officials, and guests were long occupied.

"We're never going to get in here," said Natalie. "Probably have to park a half mile away."

"You just leave that to me, young lady," said Ben, and he pulled the Taurus into the prime area of the parking lot, where there was no space, turned hard left into the shady trees, and presented his car a hairbreadth away from the bumpers of a black four-wheel-drive Cherokee and an adjacent red Chevy, thus trapping them for the duration.

"You can't do that," said Natalie.

"Cherokee's Andy Crosby's, Chevy belongs to Ted Sando. Neither one of 'em's going anyplace till we do. It's known as tactical parking . . . come on, let's go find some seats."

The more Natalie Garcia saw of her hard-muscled, take-charge sugar farmer, the better she liked him, and she allowed herself to be steered toward the home-team bleachers, catching a glimpse of Tony trotting out to the mound in his battle armor.

"He doesn't look happy, does he?" said Ben. "Hmm. We're two–zip down in the second, and Kyle's shaking his head. Whatever's wrong, it's worried Tony. Neither of 'em looks very sure of the situation."

What was wrong was Kyle's shoulder? It had been a long and intensive season, and he drastically needed to rest his pitching arm. The last two games it had begun to ache around the fifth; tonight it started in the first. He was already pitching through a dull and nagging pain, which became acute on the release of his fastball.

He'd given up the runs on a stand-up double by the first Rock Harbor batter in the top of the first, followed by two successive line drives to the left-field gap. Right now he was holding the Mariners at bay, but there were two men on and Kyle was grateful for a deep catch in center field by Ray Sweeney, which sent the visitors down for the second time.

He and Tony walked in together, frowning.

And now on the mound was the Seawolves' old nemesis, the six-foot five-inch, 205-pound hurler from Notre Dame, Trevor Boyd, who had shut them out 9–0 in their first loss. And tonight Boyd was as tough as ever, mixing up his pitches, an accurate fastball, an unexpected change-up, and a deceptive curve. Two speeds.

Boyd cruised through the game. He looked strong and determined and the pro scouts had radar guns on him every step of the way. Kyle

Davidson was white-faced by the fourth, wincing with the pain every time he threw. But the boys rallied, chased and caught, threw and fielded, no errors. And Kyle denied any pain to the coaches and to his catcher.

By the eighth it was still 2–0 Mariners, and they quickly put a man on second with one out. At which point their left-handed second hitter caught ahold of an outside tailing fastball from Kyle and sent a bullet screaming between first and second, a copper-plated double, no doubt. But somehow Zac Colbert got there, diving forward full-length and coming up with the ball. He hurled it off his knees, right at Bobby Madison, who now had the runner trapped between second and third. The runner froze, unable to get back, and Bobby threw him out at third to end the inning.

Ted Sando could see Kyle holding his shoulder, doubled up with pain, and he walked out to bring the pitcher in. Joe Roberts, a crafty left-hander from Salt Lake City, Utah, would pitch the ninth, and the 'Wolves scored their only run when Scott Maloney hit Boyd's hanging curveball over the right-field fence in the corner.

The game was essentially a stalemate, although the 'Wolves lost it 2–1, in front of a strangely subdued home crowd. And twenty-four hours from now they had to face the gusting sea breezes of Oceanside Field and the Mariners again, in order to save the entire season. Defeat would make them runners-up in a league they had absolutely dominated for more than two months. Defeat was unthinkable.

Everyone was ordered to bed early after the loss at Cabot. The McLures invited Natalie and the inseparable Tony and Jack to dinner at home, and Coach Maddox invited Ted Sando and Ben Faber to join him at Dexter's. Needless to say, in the screened dining room above Henley Harbor, the subject was pitching.

"Well, I guess I have his coach and his father right here with me," said Russ. "So I'll ask you guys what to do—shall I start Jack tomorrow? Or save him for game three?"

"If he's not still hurting, he'll go out there and give it everything. You know that," said Ben.

"That's the point," replied Russ. "Jack won't tell us if he's in pain. The kid's got so much damn pride. And if he thinks we need him to save this championship, he'll go out there and march into hell before he'll give in to it."

"I don't think he's a hundred percent," said Ted. "I had him throwing half speed in the bullpen this morning for ten minutes, and I asked him if he was ready to pitch. You know what he said?"

"Lay it on me."

"He said, 'I'm getting there.' And that's not Jack. If he wasn't hurting, he'da said, 'I'm all set, Coach.' Anyway, I could see he wasn't real comfortable."

"Trouble with Jack is, he'll just go out and do his best," said Ben. "But that's when he's vulnerable. Because when he's not a hundred percent, the first thing he loses is his slider. And without it, he's just a damned good pitcher. With it, he's a goddamned champion."

"And that's how we want him against the Mariners," said Russ. "But if he doesn't pitch tomorrow, there may not be another tomorrow."

"I know. It's a real problem," said Sando. "If we start Chris Cronin tomorrow, and have Jack standing by as a long reliever, we blow 'em both out. Kyle's finished for the year, which means we'd have to start either Doughnut or Aaron Smith in the final. And it'd have to be Doughnut because Aaron doesn't have more than three innings' endurance.

"I know he's improved," added Ted. "But if you had to name your first ten choices to start on the mound of the final game of the Cape League Championship in front of maybe four thousand at Cabot Field against the goddamned Mariners . . . well, Doughnut would not be among them. We need Jack for game three. That's all there is to it."

"And we need him for game two. That's all there is to that," said Russ. "I don't know what the hell to do."

"Well, it would be perfect if we could win tomorrow without him," said Ben. "How about starting Chris, and using Doughnut and Aaron only if things go awry? Then we got Jack for game three. And you know he'll go all nine for you. 'Specially if he's got the slider working."

"That'd be my instinct," said Ted. "I just feel Jack needs another day to get back to his best. And it's worth taking a chance going without him tomorrow. We'll give the kids a pep talk in the morning. Let the hitters know we need big things from them. Anyone puts a missile on the beach tomorrow, he's gonna be wearing a Seawolves shirt."

"I agree. Well, nearly," said Russ. "I'd just hate to see us get down in game two, not use Jack, and then lose it. I'd always feel we hadn't given it our best shot."

"It'd be almost worse to blow out our pitchers tomorrow, and lose the final because we'd no one left," said Ben. "But you know, I really like this team. And I think they'll get the game sewn up at Oceanside, and then we'll count on Jack to mow down the Mariners in game three."

"I think that's right," said Russ. "Anyway, it's a damned good note to start our dinner on. So let's get into these fried clams, drink some beer, and relax for a coupla hours . . . and a little toast from me . . . I've wanted to make it for several weeks . . . To Ben Faber, and that terrific kid of his . . ."

Both coaches raised their glasses to the farmer from the bayous. During their dinner, he imparted a piece of wisdom, for which both coaches were grateful. In a sense it confirmed something they had both thought, but rarely stated. And they were glad to have it clarified by a much older former player.

"Guys," he said. "Back when I was pitching with the ol' Craw-dads, we had an ex-Cardinals manager-coach. And he taught me something I never forgot. When you get yourself into a must-win sit-uation, never, ever, try to bang your way out of trouble, because it hardly ever works."

"I know exactly what he meant," said Russ. "The guys start get-ting overanxious, trying to swing at anything and everything. They lose their judgment and their patience real quick, and it all goes to hell more often than not."

"Correct, Coach. That's correct," said Ben. "That's what he meant. And he swore to God those kind of games—the ones you just cannot lose—get won by pure hustle, base hits, base stealing, run-ning like hell, and hitting for the gaps."

"He was right," said Russ. "And that's gonna be our plan to-morrow."

Neither of the Seapuit coaches realized that Ben Faber was not going to watch Jack pitch the final game, if there was one. His ticket speci-fied a return to New Orleans on the morning after game two. Natalie would leave at the same time, not just because her ticket was also un-changeable, but because she was playing with the Chicago Sym-phony that night.

It was thus doubly impressive that Ben had been in favor of Jack missing game two in order to try to win it all. And here there was a problem, because Jack did not have a ticket home, his father having cashed it to pay for road travel. Right now Jack had no way to get home.

Thus Ben, who had, after all, cashed the ticket, had some arrangements to make, and he decided to make them with Ted Sando, to whom he explained the predicament at the ballfield in the morning.

"So we're light a one-way ticket to New Orleans for Jack?" he said, moving to the heart of the matter. "Okay, lemme call someone and find out the cost."

A half hour later Ted had rustled up a cheap single ticket for $145, which the Seawolves organization could pay for with bonus mileage points totted up from their thirty-odd trans-America tickets per year.

"Tell you what, Ted," said Ben. "Jack loses game three, I'll find the hundred forty-five dollars and repay it."

"Spoken like a sportsman," said Ted. "He won't lose."

But first there was game two. And the Seawolves arrived at Oceanside along with five hundred supporters on a bright sunlit August afternoon. Chris Cronin held the Mariners hitless through four, and by the middle of the seventh they still had nothing on the scoreboard.

Alternately, the 'Wolves had twice loaded the bases and still come away with nothing, but in the seventh inning they struck. With two out, and Rick Adams and Gino Rossi on, Zac Colbert banged a standup double into the left-field gap. And both the Seapuit fliers got home for 2–0.

The Mariners pitcher walked Scott Maloney, and then Ray Sweeney hit a low flare up the middle just past the outstretched glove of the shortstop. The ball dropped into no-man's-land, and by the time the shortstop grabbed it, Colbert was 'round third and heading for home. The shortstop hurled the ball in, but it one-hop-bounced right off the lip in front of the catcher, skipped upward all the way to the backstop. Not only was Colbert in easily, Maloney made it as well, and the 'Wolves had it 4–0.

Doughnut Davis came in the for the last two innings and pitched brilliantly, sending down six hitters in a row to tie up the play-off finals 1–1.

But there was no air of celebration. The 'Wolves were, if anything, subdued. There was one more battle to fight in this particular war, and everyone wanted to win it. They were tired, and hungry, and it was almost eight o'clock and the light was fading and they were twenty-eight miles from home.

One or two of them were of course finished for the season—the pitchers Doughnut, Kyle, and a weary Chris Cronin. Aaron Smith was on standby to close tomorrow tonight if necessary. Though it might require a shot of cortisone to put him on the mound without pain. And significantly, before they left the dugout, Ted had asked Jack, "How you feelin', buddy?"

And the face of the giant lefty from Maine positively lit up when Jack replied, "Never better, Coach. I'm ready."

There were several parents at the game, most of whom had traveled specifically to accompany the boys home after the final. Mr. and Mrs. Bo Davis had sat with Ben and Natalie, and the genial, plainly wealthy Savannah car dealer had offered to take both of them, plus Tony and Jack, out to dinner on the way back to Seapuit.

He chose one of the best restaurants on the Cape, Barolo's in Henley, a spot neither the Fabers nor the Garcias could ever have dreamed of patronizing. Barolo's had a beautifully paneled main room with a glass-fronted conservatory facing a small quiet town square, and its huge polished mahogany bar would not have been out of place in a New York grand hotel.

Jack and Tony thought it was probably the best place they had ever seen. And Bo Davis told them to order anything they wanted. And so they settled into their last dinner together. All four of the parents were leaving in the morning, but Doughnut was staying for the game even though he would not pitch.

There were bottles of chilled Italian white wine on the table, and with some skilled interplay between the water glasses, all three of the boys managed to have a few swallows during a sumptuous dinner comprising veal piccata for Natalie and Mrs. Davis, grilled sole for Ben and Bo, big sirloin steaks for the three 'Wolves, all accompanied by superb pasta, salad, and hot Italian bread.

Bo Davis was a terrific host, but he knew the stakes were high, and at 10:30 he said solemnly, "I'm recommending you get our catcher and pitcher home to bed, Ben. They got a big day tomorrow."

No one disagreed with that, and when the wine consumption was mentally added up, it was considered prudent that the mighty Jack Faber, who'd had probably one glass, plus a half gallon of water and about four tons of food, including apple cake and cream, should take the wheel home.

It had been a superb finale to the season for everyone, and Ben was somewhat surprised that all three of the players wanted to come back next year and suspend any pro offers that might come their way.

Natalie did not remind anyone that Tony's law-school results would have a major bearing on his appearance at the Cape. Everyone knew that. Especially Tony.

When they arrived at the McLures', both Natalie and her son had to be awakened by Ben, who escorted them to the front door, said good night, and left. Mrs. Garcia was too tired to speak, except to murmur, "See you in the morning, Ben." She was unused to such lavish dining in the evening, which Ben privately thought was probably just as well.

Everyone slept like rocks, and at 9:30 A.M. sharp Ben Faber pulled into the drive to collect Natalie and return her to Logan Airport. It was a journey of unmistakable sadness because neither of them knew if they would *ever* meet again. Ben was returning to Louisiana to plead with the bank for more financing. Natalie was returning to Chicago to face the weekly grind of music lessons, appearances with the symphony, and the endless struggle to make ends meet for her and Tony.

Her flight left for O'Hare at 12:30, and they were in good time. Ben drove direct to the terminal and pulled up right outside. There was no possibility of waiting around for more than a few minutes because the airport was busy and heavily patrolled by police cruisers.

He left the engine running and said to Natalie, "I hope you've had a great time. Just wish we could have stayed for the final."

She smiled and said, "You're probably not going to believe this, but so do I."

Ben chuckled. "I'm nearly going to believe it, because I just don't know when we can meet again. And I know you don't either."

"Ben, I cannot afford to meet you in the South. And you cannot for the moment find a way to meet me anywhere. Which is why it is better we say good-bye now, and thank God for the fun we had, and try not to think of the future. I'm not being remote or anything, but we can't have any other relationship, except just friends."

Ben smiled, and told her not to worry. "Something might turn up," he said, and then he opened the door and walked around to the passenger side to let her out. He grabbed a nearby trolley and put his arm around her.

Natalie just said, "Perhaps," and kissed him on the cheek. And then she was gone, walking quickly, not looking back, tears trickling, unattended, down her cheeks.

Ben Faber climbed back into the Taurus for the last time and drove slowly over to the rental office beyond the terminals, ruminating on the 950 miles of U.S. soil that would soon separate him from Natalie. He was also ruminating on the goodwill of his pal Tommy Thibodaux, who was already driving to New Orleans this evening to pick him up, and would now be prevailed upon to make the journey again two days from now to pick up Jack.

He checked the car in and caught the bus back to his terminal, where he found a window facing the runway. And he stood watching the shiny metallic Boeings of American Airlines cleaving into the sultry skies above Logan, trying to figure out which one of them might contain Mrs. Natalie Garcia.

Ben Faber was twenty-five thousand feet above the Appalachians southwest of the Little Tennessee River when the Seawolves ran out onto Cabot Field to face the Rock Harbor Mariners for the last time, to play together for the last time. Later that evening they would say their good-byes and several of them would never see one another again.

It would have been simple to allow this game to be edged with a thousand regrets, but it was almost impossible for the players to realize the steel-trap finality of this encounter. Within twenty-four hours they would all scatter to the four corners of the United States, back to colleges in Florida, Georgia, the Carolinas, California, Maine, Connecticut, Chicago, Arizona, and Louisiana.

Most of them would want to come back next year, and some of them would intend to come back, but the world would move on during the winter. Pro contracts would be offered, players would sign, others would go off to play abroad for Team America, some would face the future without baseball, exams would be passed and failed, hitters would be frog-marched to summer school. And the halcyon days of summer in the little ballparks by the sea would soon become just a glowing memory, of a thousand smiles they left behind.

None of them would ever forget their summer on Cape Marlin,

but Russ Maddox and Ted Sando did not expect to see many of them again. And now both coaches tried to suppress the aching nostalgia of the evening, tried to get the boys up for one last battle, the battle for the championship, which would set them all apart, in a sense, for the rest of their lives.

Jack Faber jogged to the mound after the National Anthem was over. There was a light sea breeze off Nantucket Sound raising Old Glory on the flagstaff, and Tony Garcia was calling the warm-up pitches. Jack felt great; the air was just a little cooler than it had been for the past month, and he sent in two perfect sliders in his eight practice pitches.

He faced the incoming Mariner hitters with supreme confidence, and he sent them down inning after inning, throwing only sixty-five pitches in the first five. Seapuit led 2–0 in the second when Tony Garcia banged a line drive almost to the right-field fence, which brought Bobby Madison and Ray Sweeney home.

Nothing ruffled the poise of the 'Wolves until the seventh, when they were still holding that 2–0 lead. Rock Harbor got a man to second, with two out, when Garcia called for the slider, to break off the plate, on a 2–2 count. Jack debated the request, and debated shaking Tony off, mainly because his shoulder was just beginning to ache and he was unsure of the pitch at this point in the game.

He thought for a moment, and then nodded once. He reared back and snapped his wrist clockwise at the instant of delivery. Not quite sharp enough. The ball hung, but dipped bang in the middle of the wheelhouse, too far in, and the Mariner center fielder slammed it straight over the scoreboard for a two-run homer, tying up the game.

Jack, irate, stormed off the mound, picked up the resin bag, and hurled it down, sending a white cloud out toward second base.

Immediately there was a voice from the dugout, Ted Sando's voice . . . *"Easy, Jack. Take your time . . . stay centered."*

Jack glanced over, nodded acknowledgment, and slowly walked back up the slope to face the next hitter. He sent in two smoking fastballs, both of which were fouled back. Then Garcia signaled for another, and still fueled by his own anger, Jack sent in a 90 mph screamer, which tailed in on the batter's hands, hit the handle, and shattered the bat right below the Louisville Slugger label.

The barrel flew out, straight at the pitcher, like a navy shell, traveling twice as fast as the ball, low to the ground, full of jagged, splintered edges. Jack leaped high and it shot under his legs, kicking into the rust-colored dirt left of second base. Jack landed on his feet, and trotted forward, lobbed the ball to Zac Colbert at first for an easy final out: 2–2.

Back in the dugout Ted Sando came over and sat next to Jack and Tony. He looked the pitcher right in the eye and said, "Okay, Jack. You tell me honestly and truthfully, what d'you have left?"

"I've got enough to shut this damn team down," he replied. "Plenty for that."

Ted nodded, and did not raise the subject again. And true to his word, Jack Faber sent the Mariners down in order at the top of the eighth. And now the tension was mounting. Over four thousand people had crammed into the ground for the Cape League showdown, and all of them were still there after two hours and twenty minutes, packing the bleachers, lining the field in front of the pine trees all the way around the ground, as Scott Maloney stepped up to face the Mariners' reliever.

He took the first pitch, slammed the second way out to the fence, where it dropped neatly into the glove of the right fielder. Ray Sweeney was next and he caught a curveball with a hammer blow, driving it hard down the right-field-corner line.

Ray took off, charging to first, and just before he got there the ball kicked up plain and obvious chalk, before swerving into foul territory. It bounced to the fence, with the right fielder angling full speed across to retrieve it, trying somehow to stop the pounding cleats of Sweeney, trying to get his hand on the ball.

A fan had a similar idea, and leaned way over the fence trying to snag the "live" ball for a souvenir. But a Seapuit fan was right there and yanked him back, yelling loudly, *"LEAVE THAT BALL ALONE!"*

And the crowd roared as the throw finally went in to third, a full second after Ray Sweeney slid in for the triple.

The game had turned into a tense, knife-edge drama, both teams with everything to play for. Bobby Madison came to the plate, and immediately shaped up for a "suicide squeeze," the bunt that might just get Ray Sweeney home for the critical run. There was still only one out.

Everyone saw Bobby take his stance, and the Rock Harbor infield moved in. The first and third basemen each ran a few steps down the line toward home, ready to pounce and grab a near-dead baseball in awkward territory.

The pitcher began his windup and no one noticed Bobby harden his grip, even though his left hand was well down the bat. At the last split second he pulled the bat back, and he erupted on that pitch, slashing down, hard and high, the ball whipping toward third. It flew right past the incoming baseman's back.

It dropped into the empty field, and the baseman wheeled around, changing direction, trying to accelerate. Too late. Way too late. Ray Sweeney was in: 3–2 Seapuit.

And so they came to the top of the ninth, and the Mariners, desperate now for the tying run, immediately set about getting it. Bill Duncan from Arizona State was first up, and he laid down a near-perfect bunt on the first pitch he faced, sending the ball down to third, hugging the line.

Scott Maloney, standing off the base, came arrowing in, picked up the ball bare-handed, crouching. He swiveled, almost on his knees now, and hurled the ball right across his body, hard at the outstretched glove of Zac Colbert, who was leaning forward off the bag at first.

Scott fell flat on his face on the edge of the runway to third. But the ball smacked into Zac's glove, beating out the runner by less than a half stride, for the first out.

Matt Burke, a .300 hitter from Georgia Tech, was the next Mariner, and Jack sent in a slider, away. Burke hit it, right off the end of the bat, right under it, and the ball flaired behind third base. Rick Adams, racing in from left field, made a wonderful diving catch for the second out.

And now the Mariners' best late-season hitter, the left-handed Spike Miller from Clemson, stepped up, and Jack hurled in only his third pitch of the inning, a fastball straight at the plate, and Miller hit it, hard into the left-field–center gap, for a double.

Immediately in the dugout, Russ Maddox snapped, "Aaron Smith to get ready, right now."

"I need a few minutes, Coach."

"You got thirty seconds, unless you want these fucking beach bums to drive home with the goddamned trophy." Russ was on the edge of his nerves.

Aaron picked up his glove and ran up the steps, jogging down to the bull pen, a backup catcher sprinting after him. Ted Sando stood at the top of the steps on the corner of the dugout, and suddenly called, *"TIME!"*

He took a long, leisurely stroll to the mound, buying time for Aaron. Tony Garcia also moved to the mound, and the crowd was silent, staring almost in disbelief at the tying run at second, the go-ahead run at the plate, where Bobby Iliffe, the Mariners catcher, stood waiting.

Ted was about to speak, but before he uttered even one syllable, Jack Faber said, "I'm finishing this one, Coach."

"But, Jack, wait a . . ."

"Tell Aaron to siddown. I'm finishing this game."

Ted, anxious not to disturb the equilibrium of his pitcher, did not reply. He just nodded his head and left. Garcia said nothing.

And Iliffe, hitting .287, took his stance, and launched a monstrous cut at Jack's first fastball, fouling it off hard to the backstop.

Jack went to his curve, and Bobby Iliffe caught it a tremendous crack. And in the bleachers, more than two thousand Seapuit hearts stopped dead. In the dugout Coach Maddox jolted back like a condemned man in the electric chair.

The ball came off the bat like a missile, but it hooked high, towering out over the trees in the left-field corner. The call was close, but the umpire never hesitated, and the home crowd breathed again as his voice rang out, *"FOUL!"* The count was 0–2. One more strike.

Garcia signaled for a fastball, and he wanted it high, in the strike zone, because he thought Iliffe would go after anything right now. If the hitter even started to chase a high strike, Tony knew it would be damn near impossible to lay off at this stage of the game.

Russ Maddox, one out from the league championship, was pacing up and down. He could see Garcia's decision, and he could not improve on it. The boys were all up on the edge of the dugout. Ben Faber, clutching Tommy Thibodaux's phone card, was on a pay phone in New Orleans International Airport, on the line to the field office. Martha had told him to hold on, and all he could hear was Tommy saying over and over, "What's happening, Ben? What's happening, Ben?"

Jack nodded at Garcia. He took a deep breath and a long look at the runner at second, Spike Miller, hands on his knees, edging down the runway to third.

Jack leaned forward and nodded again. He put the ball in his glove, and again turned sideways, going into the stretch position, glancing at the runner. Then he stopped and gathered himself, feeling the ball deep in the leather. He stared down at Tony's mitt, which was edging up, just a little, over the plate. Tony kept easing the glove upward, like a snake charmer trying to hold the attention of cobra, and he was willing Jack to keep watching.

Out behind second, Rick Adams was making short stamping noises with his cleats, moving back, then forward, foot to foot, trying to unnerve Miller, keep him close to the base. Because everyone knew that if Bobby Iliffe landed wood on that ball, Miller would be *gone.*

Jack Faber had assessed the situation, and he zeroed back in, starting his delivery. He kicked his leg up high to his chest, and then glided forward, down into his stride. His right arm arched, and he hurled the fastball in, dead straight, at 86 mph on the scouts' speed guns.

And Iliffe chased it. He swung hard, but just too low, and the bat slashed into the underside of the ball, sending it 150 feet into the air, right over Jack's head, into the shallow center field.

The two Citadel cadets raced in tight formation, to camp beneath it, on the green grass of Cabot Field, which on this night had suddenly turned to plumes of pure emerald.

Everyone heard Bobby Madison issue his last command of the season: *"MINE! IT'S MINE!"* Rick Adams wheeled away to his left, disciplined to the end, and everyone heard the ball smack into the leather, for the final out.

No one who was there would ever forget that moment, but the lasting memory for most people was the sight of Jack Faber, falling to his knees, his arms above his head, a look of ecstasy on his upturned face, as the entire team, led by Garcia, swarmed to the mound to swamp him in hysterical congratulations.

In the field office, Martha just kept saying, "Oh, my God. Oh, my God," and at the New Orleans airport Ben and Tommy couldn't tell if Iliffe had hit a double or Jack had gotten him.

It was like waiting for the result of a photo finish at a classic horse race. And it took another couple of minutes before Martha remembered the phone, and informed Ben that Iliffe had flied out to center-left, having skied Jack's high fastball "about a mile into the air."

Meantime, Russ Maddox, always the gentleman, walked across to the visitors' dugout and shook hands with their coaches. On the field there was a scene of joyful chaos as houseparents and kids spilled onto the infield for the trophy presentation. There would be photographs that would be kept forever, and autographs that would never fade.

Nancy McLure, in company with Annie Morris, who had looked after Ray Sweeney, were both in tears at the departure of Tony Garcia and Ray, who were leaving for the airport right away, bound for Chicago and Maine. Most of the others were staying until the morning, but the Citadel infielders Rick and Bobby were taking off at 8 P.M. from Henley Airport, in a private plane chartered by Major General Adams and his wife, who were offering a free ride to South Carolina.

The remainder of the squad, in company with the coaches and houseparents, would attend a lavish barbecue overlooking the calm waters of the bay. Ward and Ann Fallon were as proud of Jack Faber as if he had been their own son.

And later that evening, as Ted and Russ strolled out onto the lawn, toward the ice-cold beer and the steaks, the head coach ventured two opinions: one, Jack Faber would go all the way in the Majors; two, "That's the best college team I've ever coached. And it's the best college team I ever will coach."

He was wrong on both counts.

12

*T*he Southwest Airlines Boeing 737 touched down at New Orleans International Airport at five o'clock in the afternoon. A reception committee of thirty teammates and supporters from St. Charles College, accompanied by Jack's coach, Joe Dwyer, had commandeered the team bus to drive out and meet him. Which was good news for Tommy Thibodaux, who was thus freed up to drink a couple of beers and pump gas in company with Ben, instead of making the fifty-mile round trip to the airport.

The Seapuit publicity director had done Jack proud, assiduously recounting his meteoric progress in the Cape Marlin League, sending regular press releases and photographs to the *St. Charles Herald Guide,* the *Houma Daily Courier,* and the New Orleans *Times-Picayune.* Copies of everything went to the athletics department of the college itself, and there was not a sports fan for miles around who was unaware of the LOCKPORT FLAMETHROWER HURLS SEAWOLVES TO CHAMPIONSHIP.

When they presented Jack with the coveted Senator Ted Kennedy Cup for the league's Most Valuable Player, the picture made the front pages of all three south Louisiana publications, Jack proudly shaking hands with the senator himself before the first game against Rock Harbor.

And now Jack found himself in the middle of a yelling backslapping mob of old friends, carrying his bags, holding up a banner that read WELCOME BACK TO THE FLAMETHROWER! They had brought him three pristine copies of the brand-new St. Charles College yearbook, which carried a picture of Jack Faber in full color right across the front cover.

Beneath it stretched a caption in large type, two decks, which stated simply, THE BEST PITCHER ST. CHARLES COLLEGE EVER HAD.

The bus ride back to the farm came about as close to hero worship as college kids ever get. Everyone wanted to hear about the Cape League, and how tough it was. The only down note on the entire journey was that Joe Dwyer, the coach who had carefully nurtured Jack since the day they met, was leaving the college just before the Christmas break. Joe, who was widely regarded as a near genius at producing classy young ballplayers from the rawest material, had accepted a superb offer from the St. Louis Cardinals to become director of player development.

Joe was on his way, and there was an air of foreboding deep in Jack's soul, because the St. Charles baseball coach was much like Ted Sando, always ready with the right words, always there for a pitcher in trouble, always encouraging, always on the side of his players. The entire St. Charles team would have done anything for Joe, and now he was leaving.

It wasn't betrayal, but Jack felt a gap that he knew instinctively would be hard to fill. Worse yet, no one had yet announced who Joe's replacement would be, and Joe himself said no one yet knew.

The bus ran southeast down Route 90, crossed the wide bridge over Lake Cataouatche, and picked up Route 1 south to Lockport. It pulled into the Fabers' farm and delivered the star pitcher home to his father. Jack disembarked with his Seawolves cap pushed back on his head, his big suitcase in his right hand, baseball bag in the other.

Ben came out onto the screened porch and waved to Joe Dwyer while the bus turned around and pulled away in a cloud of dust. It was Jack's first sight of the farm since he and Ben had left more than two months ago, back in early June, and it all looked different.

Lined up in front of the river were three pickup trucks, two belonging to Louisiana Oil and Gas, and the third to Southwestern Exploration, a subsidiary of the corporation that concentrated solely on the search for new energy supplies.

Bang in the middle of the field which stood between the house and the river was a major drilling rig, alongside a fifteen-foot-high pump that was on automatic, hauling out the water table and dumping it back into the river. It made a noise like a diesel engine. Well, fifty diesel engines.

"Hey, Dad, does that sucker ever turn off?" Jack asked, grinning.

"Not in living memory," said Ben. "Just keeps hauling ass."

"Hasn't improved the value of the house, I'd say."

"Only if they hit gas. Then it'll improve the value of Lafourche County . . . anyway, how you been, son? Heard you had a great final . . . went all nine, right?"

"Yup. I was tired as hell, and my shoulder hurt, but I just wanted to keep going. I wanted to throw the pitch that won it."

"And you did that, I guess."

"Yeah. I managed that. But Tony called it. Told me exactly where to put it. And he was right on the money. The Mariner took a wild cut at it, caught it wrong, and the ball flew off his bat, damn nearly straight up . . . well over hundred feet in the air. Bobby caught it, no sweat."

"That was some kind of a defensive team, right?"

"The best. All of 'em. Fast, safe gloves and terrific arms. Coach Maddox will be very pressed to get another one like it. What a group."

"Hey, c'mon. Gimme that big suitcase. I made some hamburgers . . . thought we'd grill 'em outside . . . maybe eat a baked potato . . . heat up a baguette . . . drink a couple of beers."

"Well, I guess so. I'm hungry as hell, and I was a bit worried you might want me on the practice mound before supper. I only went ten–oh on the Cape, and I was sure you'd want an improvement on that."

"Get outta here, willya? You're a big college star now. Probably as good as I was in my prime."

"Impossible, Pop."

"Get outta here. And go and snap the tops off a couple of cold ones."

Ben fired up the gas grill and put big Idaho potatoes wrapped in tinfoil toward the back. "We'll give these little guys a forty-minute start," he said. "Then unleash the burgers . . . make 'em play catch-up ball, right? That way we'll be all set in under an hour."

Jack grinned at his father's endless analogies involving the summer game, and he brought the beers out to the porch and recounted the plans he and several of the guys back at Seapuit had worked out.

"Dad," he said. "We just had so much fun, and everyone improved all season long. None of us has ever known anything like it. God, it was exciting. Well . . . I guess you know that already.

"Anyway, me and Tony are pretty well settled, we want to go back next year. And we told a few of the guys that's what we planned. And half the damn team wants to go back. I think seven of us asked Coach Maddox to protect us, make sure we didn't go to another team."

"Yeah? And what did Russ say?"

"Well, he seemed to think plans made in the heat of the play-offs may not be quite so relevant next spring. Said he'd heard it all before, but not many players turned up in the end."

"Well, I guess exams, pro offers, and Team America get in the way."

"I guess so, Dad. But I don't think it's gonna happen that way with this crowd. A lot of the guys really want that Cape League experience again. 'Specially after we won it all. The pro scouts were really great to us, and a bunch of 'em said we'd be a lot better on the Cape next season than anywhere else."

"Which of the other guys want to come back?"

"Zac Colbert for a start. If he doesn't he's probably gonna retire from the game, because he's got that damn great ranch to run. Ray Sweeney is definitely coming, and so are the Citadel guys. Ricky and Bobby will be giving up the game after next summer anyway because they have serious exams and then careers in the military."

"How 'bout Kyle and Doughnut?"

"Both wanna come back. Kyle because he has to finish his senior year, and he's not turning pro until he's done it. There was a scout who was real interested, I think from the Giants, and he told Kyle he should spend another summer at Seapuit."

"Doughnut?"

"I think his dad is going to insist he comes back. Says he never dreamed it was possible any pitcher could improve like Doughnut did . . . matter of fact, I agree with him."

"Hmm. That's a pretty good start to any college all-star team. Who else?"

"Not Andy Crosby—he's gotta go run the boatyard. And not Aaron, who's gonna turn pro at the first opportunity. But Gino Rossi's coming, because he'll get his degree in hotel management and then give up baseball . . . go take over his dad's restaurant in New York."

"How 'bout your big third baseman, slugger from Texas?"

"Scott Maloney really wants to come back. But I think his dad wants him to turn pro as soon as he can. He thinks the quicker a player like Scott gets into the Minors and starts on his way the better. Whatever Scotty wants, I have a feeling we won't see him again. He'll go in next year's draft. The Rangers scout came to see him specially, about four times."

"So Russ and Ted will be looking for backup pitchers, plus a couple of high-class hitters."

"If we can all get back there, you're right. But the hitters are going to be a problem, because we can afford maybe just one true but slow slugger. The other guy has got to be greased lightning between the bases . . . we're losing Andy, who stole twelve. And we're losing Aaron, who stole nine, and would have have stolen more if he hadn't been needed to pitch so often."

"Right there, on paper," said Ben, "you might be looking at a coupla dozen stolen bases . . . and in a league like the Cape, that's probably the reason you won it."

"Yeah. It is. 'Specially when you count twenty-six more SBs from Ricky Adams, and Bobby Madison's .400 on-base percentage . . . I'm telling you, Dad, those guys could fly."

Ben Faber was thoughtful. He sipped his beer and said slowly, "You know what set your team apart—and I'm only guessing?"

"What?"

"It's really unusual on a team like that, so many top college guys had their careers laid out for them without baseball—the Citadel guys, Zac, Gino, probably Ray Sweeney with the lobster boats, and probably Tony Garcia, if his mother gets her way."

"And how is your new sweetheart?"

"My *what*?"

"Mrs. Natalie Garcia, mother of the great, the one and on'y, Tony."

"*Natalie?* Hell, Jack, she's just a friend. A nice lady, who I may never see again."

Jack grinned in a conspiratorial way. He tapped his nose with his right index finger. "That's not what I hear, Pop. That's not what's on the ol' Chicago grapevine."

"Then the grapevine's kinda jumping the gun, that's all I can say."

"Is that the spray gun? Or perhaps"—he hesitated—*shotgun*!"

"Christ, Jack. You're getting too sophisticated for a tired ol' sugar farmer."

"Yeah, right. A handsome forty-three-year-old Southern landowner, unmarried, sitting on top of a goddamned oil well."

"Guess that sounds better. But it's a house of cards. Land ain't worth anything. I'm in debt to the bank, and I'm too rural for a city lady from the world of classical music."

"That ain't how Tony tells it."

"How does he tell it?"

"Well, the other day he said something pretty funny . . . 'How many of those fucking trumpet players in the symphony own four thousand acres and know how to pitch a slider?'"

"Not many, I don't guess. But most of 'em have four thousand dollars, which is a heck of a lot more'n I do right now."

"Doesn't change the fact Tony thinks you're a real dude, and I'm damn sure his mom agrees."

Ben was secretly pleased just to hear he was even talked about between Natalie and Tony. And he did not reply, just took another cool swallow of beer and looked out at the noisy pump in the field, and wondered, not for the first time, whether there was indeed, gold in them there swamps.

Back at St. Charles College, baseball training was in its usual sporadic mode of the fall. NCAA rules specified only twenty-four weeks for competitive baseball, and most schools preferred to use them in the late winter, spring, and early summer.

Coaches were permitted extremely limited time with the players, and they utilized this in late September and October. No one had more than an hour a week with Joe Dwyer, and that suited Jack Faber just fine, because he was tired after the intensive Cape Marlin season and he needed a break from the game.

He kept fit and, as a junior now, sometimes joined Joe assisting the new freshman players, assisting in giving advice, which was a huge help to the departing St. Charles baseball chief. Jack's reputation on campus was colossal. Everyone knew who he was, and half the school believed he was scheduled to turn professional before the next semester even started.

His picture was on all the notice boards, and the incoming freshmen were honored to have him watch them try out, especially the new pitchers. But like nearly all of his old Seawolf colleagues, Jack began to turn away from the game as the leaves began to turn to gold.

Serious examinations beckoned. Jack was majoring in business administration, and he had five courses to complete before the Christmas break. He was a good student, with a quick grasp of financial matters, and good antennae for a loss-making situation, but the work burden was heavy, and he scarcely touched a baseball through November, and then December.

Christmas came and went, and Tony Garcia and Natalie, alone in their apartment, called Ben and Jack from Chicago on Christmas Day.

The boys talked first for about ten minutes, mostly about exams, Tony telling Ben that he thought he had "made a few minor screwups in his prelaw courses."

Jack instantly sensed catastrophe, because any failures would surely end Tony's chances of returning to the Cape, since Natalie would be on him like Attila the Hun . . . *Summer school for you, kid, unless there's a drastic improvement before May.*

Tony was pretty subdued about it, and plainly had declined, at this stage anyway, to go to war with Natalie about his baseball career.

And then, 950 miles apart, the two ballplayers each retreated to another room while Ben and Natalie talked.

Ben told her about the harvest, a sharp rise in sugar prices which had at least fended off total ruin. And he listened carefully to her own story of her daily struggle to make ends meet. Her best news was of a ten-day tour with the Chicago Symphony that would bring her for two days to the new concert hall in Shreveport, Louisiana. "I hardly dare suggest it, but perhaps we could somehow meet," she said quietly.

Ben was even quieter. "I'm sorry, Natalie," he said. "I can't. I know it's the same state and all, but Shreveport's more'n three hundred and fifty miles northwest of here . . . my old car's not worth a damn anymore, couldn't even make it to N'Orleans, never mind Shreveport. So it'd be an airfare, or a bus, and then a hotel, and I'm just flat broke, trying to get cash together for new planting. It's what we always say, right now we're beaten by poverty."

"Oh, yes. I suppose so," she replied, plainly disappointed. "I had just hoped—"

"Listen, I think we better just buckle down, try to save some money, and make a proper plan for the summer, back down on Cape Marlin. We had some nice times there . . . and we could look forward to that."

"Ben, I'm almost certain Tony won't be going down there again . . . I was really disappointed in his exams . . . I know we don't have any results yet . . . but his professor called, worried that Tony had not put in sufficient work, and even Tony admits that . . . you know how hard prelaw is . . . and I probably have to send him to summer school—God knows how."

"Guess that hasn't endeared the game of baseball to you any, right?"

"Not entirely. I'm just sitting back here watching it systematically destroy Tony's life . . . not to mention mine."

"Well, I think you might want to give that some thought, Natalie. If you ban him from playing on the Cape, you're gonna have one resentful kid on your hands. I think it might be better to let him go, then see if he gets a big offer . . . honestly, Natalie, I wouldn't be surprised if some team had a million plus for a kid like him . . . he's a great catcher, with a great arm, a brilliant baseball brain, *and* he can hit . . . kids like that don't grow on trees . . . and if someone wants to give him a mil, or maybe even more . . . well, I think he's gotta take it."

"But what if he doesn't make it to the Majors?"

"Natalie, Tony's smart as hell. He'll know he's not going to make it a long time before anyone else. The moment he gets those doubts, we'll have him right out of there, and straight back to law school, where he might be a coupla years behind, but then he can give it his undivided attention, and still make it into a law firm . . . and there'll still be a ton of cash left to make life a lot easier for both of you."

"Ben . . . you just said *we'll* have him right out of there . . . is that a proposal?"

Ben Faber blushed. "Er . . . well . . . I think we better put that down to a minor slip of the tongue . . . given that I can't even make it over the Shreveport Bridge for a date with the most beautiful musician in America."

"I miss having a man in my life, Ben. What you just said was so

damned logical . . . about Tony, I mean. Do you think I'm too emotional about his career in the law?"

"Yes," said Ben simply. "Because he's gotta *want* it, and you don't
want him to end up *hating* the law, and blaming the whole process for
his failure even to get a shot at big-time baseball. Remember something about Tony, Natalie . . . all his life, he's been the very best at one
thing . . . better'n all the local kids, better than anyone at high school
. . . better'n anyone in college . . . maybe better'n anyone of his age in
the goddamned country . . . you have to think long and hard before
you try to snatch all that away from him, however superior your mo-
tives might be . . ."

"I would find it very easy to love you, Ben Faber. Do you know
that?"

"No. But I'm real happy to learn it. Merry Christmas, Natalie
Garcia."

The new baseball coach for the St. Charles College Chevaliers came
rumbling into the athletics department at 9 A.M. on the opening day
of term, right after the New Year. His name was Bruno Riazzi, a
hard-assed catcher, who had played a half-dozen games for the
Chicago White Sox. He owned a family tree full of Sicilians.

Bruno was recruited from a junior college in Miami County, where
he had won three consecutive NJCAA Championships. And if nothing
else, he looked the part of the consummate baseball taskmaster: permanently in need of a shave, six feet two inches tall, 250 pounds, reputedly hated during his limited days in the Major Leagues, even by
his own teammates.

Perhaps the best-known big-league incident involving Bruno was
the bench-clearing brawl he caused with the Cleveland Indians, when
his own team joined in just for the chance to pound him to the
ground and blame the Tribe.

He already owned a well-earned reputation as a coach who
would stand for no argument. He welded his teams together with
what he called "a commitment to the commitment." He swore to
God all great teams were so much greater than the sum of their
parts. He hated individuals who thought like individuals. His creed
was collective application—one for all, all for one. No big stars and
no prima donnas. 'Specially no prima donnas. And to the best of his
knowledge, there was only one of those among the St. Charles Col-

lege Chevaliers. His name was Jack Faber, *"hotshot pitcher from the bayous, struck out a few goddamned soft Northeastern college boys . . . we'll find out soon enough what he's really made of."*

The opening day of training for the "Chevvies" was scheduled in two days at 11 A.M., by which time the name Bruno was already sending a shudder through the college. He was gruff with secretaries, imperious with other sports coaches—even Cy "Brickwall" Brennan, the ex-Chargers defensive lineman who ruled the college football team, and who could cheerfully have thrown Bruno into the nearby Blue Bayou.

The players gathered early. It was a bright, cool January day, Jack's twenty-first birthday, as it happened. And the college clock, high above the mounted bronze figure of General Hugo de Fontainebleau, showed two minutes before eleven, when the last player came running in.

Riazzi never even looked at him, just snapped, *"Name?"*

"Who me? Faber. Jack Faber."

"Yes . . . I might have guessed. *You're late, Goddammit!*"

"Only if we're on Mountain Time, Coach. But right here in Louisiana, Central Time, it's *still* only ten-fifty-nine, and you called practice for eleven A.M. I am not late."

"If I say you're late, you're late. Is that clear?"

"Not to me, Coach. By the way, it's still not yet eleven A.M. But if we hang around we're gonna hear that big ol' clock start chiming real soon."

This was too much for the gathered ballplayers, several of whom started to laugh at the burgeoning confidence of the Birthday Boy.

Riazzi snapped back, "Shut up, all of you. Faber, let's just get one thing clear. You arrived after everyone else, and that's not good."

"Okay, you can accuse me of lack of interest, if you like. But not of being late, because I'm not . . . hey, listen, Coach Riazzi . . . hear the great bells of St. Charles chime, eleven o'clock, and everything's fine."

This, of course drew a howl of laughter from everyone, except Coach Riazzi, who said, superciliously, "I do believe you and I understand each other, Faber."

"I'm afraid we do, Coach."

And there was a moment of pure gloom which pervaded the St. Charles baseball squad, because it was clear that Riazzi was going to be all over their best player, and that he was determined to cut him down to size. And it was, for some of them, bewildering, because Jack Faber was not really the kind of guy who needed cutting down to size. Though ten weeks with the smart-talking Tony Garcia had certainly brought out a sardonic element no one had hitherto noticed.

However, the moment passed, and the pitchers began to train hard for the forthcoming game against the old enemy, the Ragin' Cajuns of the University of Southwestern Louisiana, which occupies 735 acres on the northwest side of the city of Lafayette, around 120 miles from the college. To the north, of course, because there's hardly anything to the south. Except for the wetlands of the Mississippi Delta. And that's a near wilderness of rivers, bayous, bays, and swamps, until you hit the hot, shallow islands, guarding the approaches to the mainland, for hundreds of miles, all along the coast of the Gulf of Mexico.

The Ragin' Cajuns. Now there's a name in college baseball to strike terror into the heart of almost any opponent. Only a limited amount of schools look forward to playing them, big powerful places like UCLA, Stanford, Northwestern, Arizona, Texas A&M, Oklahoma, LSU, maybe Tulane. And, of course, the mighty atoms of St. Charles College.

The Cajuns couldn't intimidate them, but their reputation for ruthless ball, towering, gum-chewing pitchers, and sluggers from the hot southwestern farmlands, had traditionally made the experience of facing them one of general trepidation, especially in the heat.

It was precisely the kind of battle a man like Bruno Riazzi might relish. And he employed a kind of single-minded nastiness in pursuit of his first major goal at the helm of the St. Charles Chevaliers.

Everyone had to work to get fit, running around the field, sprinting between the corner poles. The pitchers spent long hours in the bull pen, perfecting techniques, and it seemed there was a kind of permanent batting practice in progress.

Coach Riazzi kept after Jack much of the time, continually criticizing him and his relaxed manner. It took a man of this unique, bullying shortsightedness not to realize that in Jack Faber there was a baseball fanatic kept under control by a relaxed demeanor.

But despite his apparent dissatisfaction with the pitcher from Lockport, Coach Riazzi had no hesitation in starting him against

Southwestern. And right from the outset things started to go wrong.

In fact, they took a downturn a half hour before the game even started. One of the great New York Yankee pitchers, Ron Guidry, a local man from the town of Carencro, just north of the Lafayette campus, was at the game and he was escorted over to the St. Charles dugout for an introduction.

Bruno Riazzi started up the steps to welcome him, but the ex-Yankee star walked right past and just said, "Where's the Faber kid?" Then he went straight to Jack and shook his hand.

"Been reading a lot about you, kid," he said. "Guess you had a great summer up on the Cape?"

"Yessir. Sure did."

"Funny. I always check out that league," Guidry said. "My old captain in New York played for your team . . . Thurman Munson was a Seawolf . . . been some great ballplayers come out of that franchise . . . even my old 'enemy' Jeff Reardon—he was a Seawolf."

"Yessir. They still talk about both of 'em up there . . ."

"And they're gonna be be talking about you one day . . . least that's what I hear. Anyway, you're busy, Jack . . . I am looking forward to seeing you work today."

"Thanks for stopping by, Mr. Guidry. I really appreciate it."

The mighty ex-Yankee hurler took his leave, never even stopped to speak to anyone else, and Bruno Riazzi seethed; seethed at the perceived slight; seethed at the easy celebrity that somehow rested on the undeserving shoulders of his starting pitcher.

And once the game was under way, Bruno did a lot more seething. The Cajuns struck in the second, scoring a three-run homer off Jack Faber's tailing fastball. St. Charles got one back in the third, but the rest of the inning was a grim struggle in oppressive ninety-eight-degree heat.

And Riazzi, the complete control freak, was pacing the dugout, calling every pitch, his fingers flashing with Scott Joplin precision, all over his face, cheeks, nose, and forehead, trying to communicate with his catcher.

With two gone, no one on, and a 3–2 count, he signaled for a fastball, and the catcher relayed it to Jack, who shook him off. Then he sent in a superb change-up, which the hitter missed by about a foot. Jack was walking off the mound before the swing was even completed.

Back in the dugout Riazzi glared at the catcher and snapped, "Did I or did I not call a fastball?"

"Yeah. But he shook me off, Coach."

Riazzi turned to Jack. "Forget the strikeout, hear me? You throw what I call."

"I just thought the change-up was a better choice."

"Who coaches this team—me or you?"

"Well . . . but . . ."

"No buts. You throw what I tell you to throw." And he swung around to the pitching coach and growled, "Have Jerry warm up, right now."

But he did not take Jack out. At least he had not done so by the sixth. The Cajuns still led 3–1, but they had two men on, with two outs, and the count was 2–2.

Riazzi noticed that Jack was just beginning to tire, and he signaled for the slider. The catcher put three fingers down pointing to the outside knee.

Jack, as ever, was apprehensive about the slider. It had worked fine the few times he had used it today, but when he was tired it could be extremely susceptible to a hammering.

Jack stared down at the catcher, and imperceptibly shook his head. The catcher glanced toward the dugout and again put down three. And again Jack shook him off. Then he went into his windup and threw a fastball, which was summarily whacked, a hard, two-hop line drive into right field.

The fielder came in fast, picked up the ball, bobbled it, and then dropped it, by which time the first runner was in. He regained control and threw inaccurately to home plate, drawing the catcher off the plate. They failed to beat out the second runner, which made it 5–1 Cajuns.

Riazzi looked as if he was having a heart attack—but it was not the right fielder with whom he was angry. He rushed up the steps and yelled, "*TIME!*" And with a thunderous expression on his face, he stormed out to the mound, head down. He faced Jack, nose to nose, and gritted, "*Did I or did I not tell you to throw what I call?*"

"But, Coach, I'm never really comfortable—"

"*Don't give me your fucking life story . . . gimme the ball! And hit the showers . . . You're all done today.*"

Jack handed him the ball, put his head down, and walked off the mound, feeling, unaccountably, disgraced. There were three thousand to four thousand supporters of the Rajin' Cajuns at the game and Jack did not hear any one of them, all up hooping and hollering. This was a baseball stronghold, and they knew they'd just gotten rid of one of the best college pitchers in the game, who'd been hit hard for only the second time in one hour and forty minutes of play, just twice in eighty pitches.

"WAY TO GO, CHEVVIES . . . GET HIM OUTTA HERE!"

Riazzi tapped two fingers on his right arm. He was staring at the bull pen, indicating he wanted the right-hander. And when the new pitcher arrived he told him, "I want you to show that Faber kid how to get it done."

The sentiment was okay, as these matters go, but the Chevvies gave up eight runs in the last two innings, even though they scored four themselves. A lot of good judges of the game thought Faber might have saved it, rather than have his team lose 13–5.

Jack did not speak to Riazzi again that evening. But he did call home and speak to his father, admitting for the first time, "Dad, I've got a real bad feeling about this."

He explained some of his problems, but not all of them. And Ben was somewhat conciliatory. "C'mon, Jack. The guy's new. Don't worry about it. Get to know each other."

"Well, okay. But I just feel this guy really wants to humiliate me . . . I don't know why."

"Hell, Jack, forget it. You've done enough to earn a career in the Majors. Matter of fact, you got a registered letter today from New York . . . it'll be the first of many, now you're twenty-one. You want me to open it?"

"Oh, sure . . . what's it say?"

"Wait a minute . . . lemme get it . . ."

Two minutes later Ben was back on the line. "Well, son, this is your first pro offer. But don't get excited, you ain't going."

"I'm not?"

"Not to this outfit. It's from the Brooklyn Bombers, newest and most fundamentally useless outfit in the entire Major Leagues. Says here they're offering you a signing fee of three hundred thousand dollars, if you are ready to go now . . . forget it."

"*Forget it!* Christ, Dad, you can't even afford to phone Mrs. Garcia and you're telling me to walk away from three hundred grand?"

"I didn't say walk away. You're gonna *run* away. First of all, it's not enough money. Second of all, they have probably the worst farm system in the United States. The Bombers, for a kid like you, represent a one-way ticket to nowhere. You'll get better offers from better teams. The Brooklyn Bombers! What a joke."

Jack rang off, chuckling at his father's outrage. But the old man was probably right. The Bombers had put together a terrible record in their four short seasons in the American League, and it had all started with a wonderful idea, which was already turning to dust. Unless something big happened real soon.

The man behind the franchise was Donald P. Stargill II, who had replaced Bill Gates as reputedly the richest man in America. His corporation was Microlink, a worldwide conglomerate he had put together during the down years of the high-tech computer industry at the turn of the twentieth century.

Stargill had plundered some of the cleverest and cheapest corporations in California when they were inventory-rich and cash-poor. He then combined them into a formidable force, firing thousands of workers and keeping the best. When the market turned up again, he held a headlock on the entire high-tech global scene. He controlled four of the five critical programs which held the worldwide networks together. By the end of the year 2001, he was worth an estimated $90 billion.

It was a fortune to which there had never been anything even remotely comparable. There had been individuals allegedly worth $20 billion, maybe even $40 billion. But $90 billion! That was beyond imagination.

Donald Stargill was not only fabulously rich. He was also a romantic, and he decided to restore the Dodgers to Brooklyn. To the historic Flatbush area where his father had taken him as a boy.

Donald had taken a map and sketched out a diagram of where the old Ebbets Field had stood on four and a half acres beneath the cobblestones of Bedford Avenue and Sullivan Street. He added another six acres for a massive multistory parking area, added up all the houses inside his new boundaries, and offered everyone at least two and a half times their value. Cash.

There were three hundred houses and Donald was paying close to a million for most, and up to $2 million for some whose owners did not wish to leave. There were also two reluctant office buildings and he had to pay $30 million for each one. Which added up to $400 million for the land alone—or, more simply stated, the interest earned on his capital every thirty days (after tax).

He bulldozed the entire area in seven months, and built a sensational new park at a cost of $300 million. It was exactly the same on the outside as the old Ebbets Field, with its towering brick walls and great arched windows. But to the rear it was bigger, with much more fan capacity. On the inside it was the last word in modernity, a glittering tribute to one man's dream. And it would surely have astounded Donald P. Stargill Senior, whose ice-cream business had barely kept his family above the poverty line.

He would not, however have been quite so astounded at the team his son put together, full of top-quality free agents, who had made their money and were simply hired guns, a little past their peak, with no stomach for the battle. Semitough. Semidedicated.

Donald Stargill II was a man in a colossal hurry, and he wanted a team that would win right now. And he did not get it. He purchased at gigantic cost a lineup of all-star has-beens, full of talent, colossally overpaid, with about as much fight in them as a pack of frankfurters.

They had never played even .500 ball. They were always injured, and in one catastrophic season they had lost three in a row to the Yankees, by 12–0, 14–0, and 22–0.

The Bombers were rapidly becoming a national joke. And Donald P. Stargill II, brought up watching the immortals of the 1940s and 1950s Dodgers, Pee Wee Reese, Jackie Robinson, Duke Snider, Campanella, Hodges, Newcombe, and the rest, was absolutely baffled by the way things were going.

The current gag in baseball was that Stargill was selling the franchise to a group of Filipino businessmen who were moving it to the South Pacific and renaming it the Manila Folders.

Don Stargill was right now wondering about his own infallibility. He still thought he could buy *anything*. But he was finding out he could not buy a pennant team. At least, not quickly. And right now, his organization could not even buy the Lockport Flamethrower.

1 3

*A*n uneasy truce broke out between Coach Riazzi and Jack Faber during the next week of spring training. Big Bruno would surely resent any kid who was so strong, and so richly talented, but Riazzi was not self-destructive. His job hung on his ability to win major college ball games, and Jack Faber was the best pitcher he had. *Just so long as he understands, he does it my way, at all times. Goddamned smart-ass.*

And so they moved into their second week, preparing for the game against LSU at Baton Rouge on Saturday. And Tuesday afternoon found Jack in the bull pen with the new pitching coach, working on his slider, which today was adequate, but no more, lacking that last final snap which would send it diving to the ground bang in front of the hitter.

"Jack," said Coach Cody. "Right here I think we want to consider an adjustment to this pitch, maybe make it swerve a little, just outside, kinda slurve, halfway between a slider and a curve."

"Jesus, Coach, I really don't want to fool with technique. Not with this pitch. It's been great for me since I was a kid. I'm not ready to alter anything . . . I just need a little time."

"Jack, we can't wait. I wanna get this working on a more reliable basis. And that means you gotta get your wrist position down a little, on the side of the ball, right at the moment of release. That ought to make the ball bite across a little, not just straight down."

"But, Coach . . ."

Right then Bruno Riazzi came into the bull pen, and plainly over-heard the disagreement. "Look, Faber," he said. "The coach is trying to help you make an adjustment to the pitch. Now you go right ahead and make that adjustment."

"I hear you, but I'd appreciate it if you'd both lay off my slider," replied Jack. "It's been my bread and butter, carried me out of a lot of tight situations. And when I throw it right, no one hits it."

"THIS IS NOT THE FABER UNIVERSITY BASEBALL TEAM, MR. TED KENNEDY CUP WINNER," roared Riazzi. *"THIS IS ST. CHARLES COLLEGE. AND I'M THE HEAD COACH. REMEM-BER THAT! NOW MAKE THE GODDAMNED CHANGE."*

Jack turned to the pitching coach and said quietly, "My arm's a little sore right now. I'm gonna go ice it down." And he walked out of the bull pen.

Five days later the Chevaliers made their way to Baton Rouge, which was a little closer than Lafayette, along Route 90 and then up Interstate 10 for forty-five miles. Jack would again start against one of the hottest teams in the country, nurtured on a sprawling campus of almost two thousand acres, on the southern edge of the city, less than a half mile from the east bank of the wide Mississippi River.

They pulled into the precincts of LSU before noon and parked amid the grand tan-colored stucco buildings with their red-tiled roofs and Northern Italian flavor. Jack was suited up on arrival and immediately headed to the bull pen with Coach Cody and two other pitchers.

He felt good this afternoon, and when the game got under way he pitched as well as he had ever done, holding the sluggers of LSU hitless through five. However, it was hotter than hell, and he began to tire, and Coach Riazzi could see the signs. He immediately backed off the fastball and called instead for the slider, and he wanted it to rip across the front of the plate.

Jack took a grip and hurled it in, as always filled with the dread that he had not delivered it entirely correctly, and as always he waited that split second for the chilling sound of a hard whack on the ball. And this time he got it, and he jerked up in time to see it soaring over-head for a home run to deep center.

The next hitter came up, and Jack got ahead 0–2. Riazzi, smart-ing, and plainly embarrassed at the fate of the pitch he had helped to create, hunkered down and called it again, silently demanding Jack again follow the adjustments to the slider made by Coach Cody.

And Jack Faber did as he was told, though he would have traded the family farm, natural gas and all, if he could just have seen Ted Sando at the top of the dugout steps. But he did as he had been told, took the ball to the hitter again, and sent it swerving toward the outside, but again it did not have enough bite. And again he heard the resounding whack of aluminum on leather, echoing into the hot skies, as the hitter slammed it clean out of the park.

Coach Cody came hustling up the dugout steps, strode to the mound, and demanded, "Look, have you got it today, or what?"

Jack stared, and gritted, real slow, "Coach, I'm trying to throw your pitch—your slider, not mine. It might just be better all around if you came out and threw it yourself. It's not my style."

"Jack, you know Coach Riazzi wants it thrown like I told you— just stop feeling sorry for yourself, and for Christ's sake get into it."

Back in the dugout Riazzi told him, "There's no place for fucking prima donnas on this team."

Back on the mound, Jack threw three straight sliders in the old way, dead straight, dipping viciously, and the new hitter fanned each one of them, never got even close to contact. Jack walked back to the dugout, his face set defiantly.

"Your way, eh?" said Bruno.

Jack said nothing.

Riazzi turned to Cody. "We'll fucking see about that," he grunted. But he left Jack in for all nine, and the game ended with the LSU Tigers 2–1 winners.

Five days later they played their biggest local rivals, Tulane University, at the St. Charles field. This was a conference game and Jack again started, pitched well for eight in diabolical heat, but the Chevvies lost it 2–1 to the big, talented New Orleans college.

In their own locker room, right after the game, the head coach immediately began an attack on what he called prima donnas.

"You guys are almost there," he said. "But I'm seeing the kind of weakness that comes when certain players are playing for themselves rather than for the team. You're not quite the fighting unit, locked hard together, that I want to see. Big hearts win ball games, not big reputations. Right, Faber?"

Jack continued staring at his shoes, uncertain why he was being selected for criticism when all he'd done was stand out there in the heat for more than two hours, throw more than a hundred pitches, and hold one of the best teams in the country to two runs.

"I know it's heartbreaking to lose a two–one ball game," Bruno Riazzi rumbled on. "But we squandered too many opportunities. Although this did not disappoint me the most. It's the selfishness of certain players on this team. And quite frankly, I'm sick and tired of a certain pitcher working exclusively toward the scouts' radar guns behind the backstop. He'll know who I mean, won't he, Faber?"

Again Jack, who had not the slightest idea what Bruno was talking about, did not look up, refused to dignify this attack with his attention.

Riazzi glared around the locker room, his gaze coming to rest once more on the silent figure of Jack Faber. "Some of you guys need to decide who you're playing for—the name on the front of your jersey, or the name on the back."

And on that note, he walked out of the room. Instantly, Jack was on his feet, and he moved quickly after the coach. Out in the passage, he said loudly, "*MR. RIAZZI!* Will you kindly tell me what I've done to deserve all this. Is that really me you're talking about? Because if it is, I better tell you no one has ever said anything like that to me in all of my career."

Jack was as big as Bruno, four times as fit, and thirty years younger. And the coach's reply was measured. "Faber," he said, "let me tell you a few home truths that no one else is gonna tell you, okay?

"One, your slider is not good enough. Two, your fastball's too predictable. Three, you're too emotional, too petulant. Four, you're *never* gonna cut it in the Majors. Five, you might just be okay playing Northeastern college kids. Six, why don't you go pitch your goddamned trophies. Seven, you'll be all washed up by the time you graduate from here."

With that, he turned on his heel and strode off along the passage, leaving Jack Faber, aged twenty-one, absolutely devastated, wondering to himself, *Could he be right? . . . He must know something . . . he played in the Majors . . . am I really gonna face life without baseball a year from now?*

At that moment the most terrible change came over him. There was no one he could talk to, not even his father, because he could never properly explain the ache he felt inside. The ghastly disappointment of having prepared for something all his life, only to be told by a proven championship coach with a professional track record that he was not good enough.

The next time he went to the mound, just in a practice game, he felt cold fingers of fear grip him. And he was afraid to make a mistake, scared to death of doing something daring with the ball. And this cost him his aggression.

He was afraid to pitch inside. He was nervous about going for the outside corners. And he thus kept leaving the ball right over the heart of the plate. And he was afraid to tail them off, because he was afraid he might walk someone, which would surely cause Riazzi to come after him, publicly, all over again. And worst of all, he was afraid they'd hit his inside pitch because he no longer had sufficient velocity.

The problem with the slider was agonizing. They'd fooled with his action, and he could no longer get the old rhythm back. The ball was coming in too flat, and he always felt vulnerable when that happened. But now he was just afraid the slider was going to get hammered, and he was too afraid even to try it.

The speed gun showed his velocity was down from 92 mph to 84 mph. It was not that his rhythm was off. He *had* no rhythm, and his general mechanics on all of his most trusted pitches was terrible.

The next game was against another powerful college team, the Rice University Owls, and somewhat to Jack's amazement, Coach Riazzi chose him to start. And the result was shocking.

The Owls hammered him for eight runs in four innings. He gave up a three-run homer when the first baseman slammed a dead-straight fastball clean over the scoreboard in left-center. They banged nine hits off him, including three doubles, and four walks. All eight runs were earned, and Riazzi took Jack out with two outs in the fourth, the earliest exit of his entire career.

The slightly stunned St. Charles crowd observed this drama in appalled silence. And while they might have believed they were seeing some kind of aberration, they were actually watching the total mental breakdown of the finest pitcher ever to throw a baseball on the Chevaliers' field.

Bruno Riazzi walked in with Jack. And he was not done yet. "Faber," he growled. "You better decide. It's my way or your way. And your way won't get you to the end of the season."

The following day, the head coach demoted Jack to the bull pen, and he spent several days just going through the motions. When the team list went up for the next game, against Texas A&M, Coach Riazzi had penciled in young Joe Kubrik, a promising freshman, to start. Jack was listed with three relievers.

The Aggies home field stood more than 370 miles to the west. And the St. Charles team would arrive by bus, in time for dinner and an early hotel bed, smack in the heart of Texas, way down there in College Station, near the lush farmlands of the Brazos Valley, sixty-five miles northwest of Houston.

Jack had nothing to do but ponder his declining career in baseball throughout the seven-hour journey along the endless blacktop of Interstate 10, cleaving its path across the flatlands north of the long saltwater swamps of the Gulf Coast.

He sat alone, staring through the window, seeing nothing. He was filled with an unshakable melancholy, edged with a sense of betrayal, though he could not for the life of him fathom who precisely had betrayed him. Sometimes he found himself shivering even as the bus grew warm. Jack Faber was miserable to the tributaries of his soul. He was a demoted starting pitcher on the brink of a descent into the desperation that shadows every sportsman when the lifelong talent recedes, however briefly. There is no comparable misery to that which occasionally stalks the young would-be professional athlete.

The game was as tough as all games always are against the Aggies. It was tight and uncompromising, with hot pitching, and St. Charles held a 2–0 lead after three. By the eighth the score was unchanged, but Kubrik was very tired. Riazzi sent for Jack, who was warming up in the bull pen, and the result of this decision was another catastrophe.

With his father watching almost in disbelief, Jack immediately gave up a base hit off a weak fastball, and then walked the next two to load the bases. Jack wanted to take himself off, since he simply could not pitch. And he saw his old Seawolf buddy Scott Maloney coming to the plate for the Aggies.

Inside, he dreaded throwing to Scott. And he elected to try the slider, trying to concentrate, trying to remember how it used to be. But he hurled in a fat, slow, nothing kind of a pitch. Scott could not believe his luck. The ball came ballooning in, and to the big Aggie slugger, it looked like a beach ball. He leaned back and slammed it over the left-field fence for a grand-slam homer. *BAM!* 'Round the bases came Scott, and as he touched home, he was mobbed by his Texan teammates.

Riazzi yelled, *"TIME!"* and walked out to the mound. He offered his pitcher no respect. He did not look him in the eye, just held out his hand for the ball and said nothing. Jack gave it to him and walked off the mound.

When he reached the dugout, he just stood there, desolate, wondering what to say to his father. Riazzi arrived back and snapped, "That's it, Faber. You're all done." And Jack had no idea whether he meant for the game or for the season. Either way, it scarcely mattered.

Jack packed up his bag, and Riazzi went back outside to talk to the pitching coach, and he did not see Ben Faber leaning on the fence staring at him. In any event he had no idea who Ben Faber was. He just took the pitching coach aside and told him, "Faber's just played his last game. All that goddamned hype. He's never once pitched big for us. I knew it was all bullshit."

His words were like stilettos through the heart of Ben Faber, and he waited there in silence for Jack to exit the dugout. So that he could take him home.

Pat Olsen Field, home of the Aggies, stands precisely 370 miles west of Lockport, Louisiana, which added up to a real tall order for Ben's ancient dying Chevy. It was a long haul along the blisteringly hot highway even for a fit, modern automobile.

But Ben Faber was currently in possession of such a vehicle. Well, nearly. He had made the journey to watch Jack pitch in Tommy's reserve breakdown truck, a four-year-old black Dodge Ram pickup, with a crane bolted down in the back. It had only thirty-two thousand miles on it, since most of its work was local, and it ran sweet and fast. Tommy had lent it to Ben on the grounds that, "it's a whole lot cheaper to give you the son of a bitch than for me to have to come out and get you when th' ol' Chevy expires out there on the Texas border." There were times when Ben wondered what he would have done without Tommy Thibodaux.

He faced the journey home with a plainly devastated Jack, who quite suddenly seemed stripped bare of the talent that had set him apart for his entire life. He was also unrecognizable from the cheerful, brutally efficient pitcher who just a few months ago had wise-cracked his way all over Cape Marlin with his catching buddy Tony Garcia.

Ben slung the big baseball bag in behind the seats and prepared for the saddest ride home of his life. Jack, too deep in sorrow, never even looked up as they passed the George Bush Presidential Library Center. For him there was no beauty in architecture, no peace in the thousand acres of parks which glorify College Station.

There was just a stark immovable picture in his mind, of the hot, dusty mound at Pat Olsen Field, and it was etched into Jack Faber's fragile heart as surely as the one at Macon, Georgia, was engraved in the memory of his father.

They set off for the Louisiana border in silence, running hard cross-country through hot, sullen countryside. They drove under the Dallas-Galveston Highway 45, then skirted the spectacular Sam Houston National Forest and ran on toward Beaumont, where the southern swamps begin, guarding the coastal approaches to Interstate 10 all the way to Baton Rouge and New Orleans.

It took an hour for Jack to speak. "You think he meant I'm all through for the day, or for the rest of the season?"

His words hung in the cool air of the front seat, and Ben Faber made no reply. Slowly, with that old easy-living manner of his, Ben asked his own question. "You wanna tell me what's your problem with Bruno?" he said quietly.

"Dad, I don't even know how it started—but he's sure had it in for me, right from the start, from the first practice meeting."

"Jack, I know you. You sure you didn't do anything to piss this guy off? I mean *seriously* piss him off?"

"Dad, it's been like he hated me since before he even met me."

"Uh-huh."

"I've been no different since the first day I set foot on that campus till right now."

"Well, Jack, I guess I have to agree you ain't got no side to you. And that's unusual for a kid as . . . well . . . talented as you."

"Why don't you just say it? As talented as I used to be, right? Not anymore."

"Jack, I'm not trying to talk baseball technique here. I'm trying to solve a problem. And it's a people problem. And they're always the worst kind. Just try to think, free and clear, when did all this start?"

"Right from the get-go. He immediately accused me of being late when I wasn't."

"You sure?"

"'Course I'm sure. I'm positive. I can tell the goddamned time, can't I?"

"Guess you can. So what bugged him?"

"I think because I was the last to arrive."

"How soon before his deadline?"

"Maybe three or four minutes."

"I suppose he might have thought that as the best pitcher the school ever had, you should have set an example and been there first."

"Well, he could have. But that's not the same as being late. Practice was to start at eleven o'clock, and there we are standing beneath a clock that's nearly five feet wide and he's telling me I'm late when the sucker hasn't even chimed."

"Guess you didn't hesitate to remind him of that simple discrepancy, right?"

"Well, anyone would have, right? You can't have some fucking gorilla yelling you're late when the campus clock is right up there telling the whole world you're not."

"You give him a little lip, like I know you can?"

"Not really. I just reminded him to hang right there for a couple of minutes and he'd find out just how early I was. Since then, he's been muttering about prima donnas, always referring to me. Right in front of everyone . . . hey, Dad, you don't think I'm a prima donna, do you?"

"I don't think so, Jack. And if you are, hell, I ain't never seen that in you . . . Mind, you can have a pretty fast mouth—'specially since you met Tony Garcia."

"That damn Bruno should count himself lucky he wasn't dealing with Tony. Jesus, imagine what he'da said if someone had told him he was late when he wasn't."

Ben was thoughtful for a few minutes. Then he said, "You have to remember one thing, Jack. Around here we all know you, and we all know your ways. But there's other people who don't know you at all. And maybe this Bruno character just took you the wrong way, maybe expected you to apologize for being the last to arrive, what with your picture being all over the school and everything."

"Okay. Then he should have taken me aside and explained what he expected of me, and I would've agreed; not stand there yelling it's after eleven o'clock when the official campus clock of St. Charles College didn't even chime the goddamned hour yet. Stupid fucker."

Ben Faber grinned wryly.

"Jack, I just hate to see a misunderstanding turn out to be terminal. 'Specially if it affects you."

"Terminal!" gritted Jack. "He's been trying to terminate my best pitch, and I think he may have done it. I'm not even sure I could ever throw the slider again. He's been forcing me to change it, against my will, and against the fucking laws of physics, so far as I can see."

"Wouldn't want to see no change in that pitch, son."

"Well, Mr. Riazzi has been doing just that. And I've told him, and I've told the pitching coach, I wouldn't change it . . . Jesus, I know there's days when I can't make it work, but there's other days when no one can hit it. Thanks to those two assholes, I couldn't get a little leaguer out now. Not with that pitch."

Ben drove on, silently now, and they had traveled another ten miles before he said, finally, "Christ, Jack, You just shut down the best hitting talent in the country, up there at Cape Marlin. What the hell happened to the confidence I saw, every time you went to the mound?"

"Confidence! What the hell's that? Every time that god-awful coach gives me the ball, I get a hollow feeling inside—it's like I just know he *wants* me to fail. It's like he's only gonna be happy if I screw it up . . . that bastard . . . that bastard."

And he shook his head, and tried to hold back tears of rage, frustration, and sorrow, gripped as he was by a cruel, unearned unhappiness.

"Dad," he said. "When I throw the ball, the only thought I have is that, hopefully, it will stay in the ballpark. Nothing more. Bruno's right. I'm all through. I don't even *know* how to pitch anymore."

At which point Ben Faber understood the futility of the conversation. The hurt and the anger ran much deeper than he had imagined. Ben Faber knew as well as anyone the fragile nature of a pitcher's psyche and the career-threatening damage a total loss of confidence is likely to induce. Somewhere along the road to Lafayette, Jack Faber's dad realized the boy might never want to play baseball again.

The miles seemed to pass slowly, and they arrived home a little after midnight on a Saturday morning, amid a light summer rain swishing in the leaves of the old familiar trees of the Faber sugar farm.

Ben parked the truck in the yard close to the stoop, and Jack dragged himself out and pulled his huge white baseball bag out from behind the seat. He made his way up the steps, and flung it, low and away, under the backrest of a rocking chair. The proud coat of arms of St. Charles College, the crossed baseball bats set beneath a royal crown, sagged dolefully toward the damp boards of the deck, and Jack Faber did not look back.

Inside the house, Ben went to the fridge and pulled out a couple of cold beers. He handed one to Jack and suggested a roast-beef sandwich, since they'd had no dinner. But the former Chevaliers starter had no stomach for food, even after a sixteen-hour gap since breakfast. Concerned, Ben resolved not to discuss baseball once more this weekend before Jack went back to school.

Neither of them slept much. Ben, trying not to raise his hopes too high, could hear across the field the steady beat of the pump, out by the drilling rig. Jack went unconscious for an hour out of sheer exhaustion. But his sleep was haunted by the specter of a deserted pitching mound in the rain, running with dark rivulets.

He was trying to climb it, but the earth seemed to be sinking around him, and he stood helplessly clutching the ball under the weeping skies. In the far distance, he could hear his father's voice calling to him, but he could not make out the words. Somehow, he knew it was a dream, but he could not force himself to awaken. When finally he wrenched his way into conciousness, he was sweating, out of breath, and there was an ache inside him. He sat up in bed trying to get his bearings, and he could still hear the rain.

Jack stayed wide-awake for the rest of the night, and joined his father for breakfast. He only managed a cup of black coffee and a muffin, and they talked about anything other than baseball. Ben recounted the optimistic view Jerry Segal held about the prospect of finding natural gas on the land. And together they bemoaned the world sugar market, and the low forecasts for sugar futures. Jack's college workload also received an airing, and Ben was pleased with his exam results and good grades.

Deep inside, Ben had decided that he wanted Jack out of St. Charles College, and away from this Riazzi character. He thought that any of the big Southern schools would accept Jack, with some scholarship money, and that his best chance of making it back to the peerless stature he once held in college baseball would be under the auspices of another coach. *Any* other coach, since it was clear the relationship between Bruno and young Faber was essentially history.

They passed the weekend watching a few movies, and late Sunday afternoon Tommy Thibodaux came over to pick up the truck, take Jack back to school, and then drop Ben home. Again they talked about oil and gas rather than sports, and Ben felt unaccountably desolate as he waved good-bye, and watched his son trudge past the mighty mounted figure of General Hugo de Fontainebleau, soldier and scholar, set on its massive granite plinth.

Jack still carried the big baseball bag, the only difference being that the crest of the Chevaliers, embossed in dark red, no longer represented life and death for the right-handed flamethrower out of Lockport.

Four days later that crest represented death itself. Because when the list was posted, naming the team to face the University of Arkansas Razorbacks in Baum Stadium, Fayetteville, way up by the Oklahoma border, just south of the Missouri line, Jack Faber's name was missing.

He stood there, just staring at the other names. It was the first time in his life he had ever been omitted from any baseball team when he was fit and available. The fact was, he had been cut from the roster, and despite the chilling predictability of the event, he stood mournfully before the list, surveying this juncture of his career, the actual moment he parted from the game, to which he had devoted his life.

Was that a heartbeat he heard? Or merely the beating of a distant drum, sounding the retreat from all he once knew? Jack Faber steeled himself, nodded curtly, tight-lipped, at the notice board. Then he turned away and strode off, down the corridor, resolved to forget about the Chevaliers, and to hope to hell they lost, every time they played, and that the failure would end the ill-starred career of Bruno Riazzi.

And yet . . . and yet . . . he did not want them to lose. He wanted them to win. Every game. The spirit of this college still permeated his heart, and try as he might, the satanic presence of Bruno Riazzi did not erase the devotion he still felt for the ball club. And for the following twenty-four hours, while the team prepared to leave campus for the flight from New Orleans up to Fayetteville, Jack Faber lived and breathed the moments.

He was not in uniform now, but he hovered, a lonesome figure out on the edge of the outfield pretending to read, watching the bull pen, remembering, always remembering. He studied the Razorback lineup, counting the lefties, guessing the starting pitcher, trying to assess who was vulnerable at the plate, who caved in to the fastball, who couldn't judge the offspeed pitch.

For Jack it was just like always, except he wasn't going. And when the team bus pulled into the driveway to collect the players, Jack stood a distance away under the broad, heavy branches of twin hickories set to the right of the wrought-iron college gates. It was raining again now, and the trees deflected the warm sudden squalls.

He watched the guys board the bus, hauling their baseball bags, and he felt himself a stranger, slinking back behind the trees, unwilling to reveal either himself or his anguish to former teammates. He watched the bus coming toward him, bearing the guys who were going off to do battle on behalf of his little sports-mad college. And he hoped no one would pitch better than he once had done. But the oncoming bus produced a surge of adrenaline inside his competitive soul, and at the last minute Jack rushed out from behind the hickories, and he lifted up his right fist and yelled out loud, *"LET'S GO, CHEVVIES! GO GET 'EM, GUYS! COME ON, JOE, THEY'RE ALL YOURS . . . FASTBALL, RIGHT? THEY CAN'T HIT THAT!"*

Several of the players saw him on the left-hand side of the bus, and some waved to the former master of the mound at General Hugo Field. And they saw him cheering them, his great farm boy's right fist raised on high. After the bus pulled past, Jack slowly lowered his arm. It was a long way home.

There were four more weeks to the end of the semester, and the Chevvies followed up a 11–0 shellacking at the hands of the Razorbacks with five more losses in succession. Coach Riazzi was beside himself with fury and disappointment, but he never even considered recalling Jack to the squad. Instead he railed at his players, berated his pitchers, ordered extra batting practice, marched pitcher after pitcher to the bull pen, and threatened on a daily basis to cut players from the roster.

Behind his back a near revolution was brewing, and people were

demanding to know how this ape had managed to get rid of probably the best college pitcher in the country, and subsequently take the
team into the fray without its finest right arm.

"*What the hell else do you expect? Faber pitches, we win a lot of
games, like we always do. Throw him out, we lose a lot of games . . .*"

"*Jack Faber could match up with anyone in college ball . . . till
Riazzi came to town . . .*"

The heat was on for Bruno, no doubt about that. But Jack Faber
merely distanced himself from the team, taking no notice of baseball,
never throwing with anyone. Instead he embarked on a regime of
super fitness, driving himself forward in the gym, pumping iron, running around the sprawling campus in the sultry summer heat. As the
end of the semester approached, he was in probably the finest condition of his career. But he never touched a baseball.

And however understanding Ben Faber was, he could never quite
comprehend the demons that had gripped Jack's soul and turned him
away from the game. Sometimes he wrestled with the conundrum until
the small hours of the morning, and it took him several weeks to decide on a course of action. But then he had it, and he took hold of his
telephone and dialed the athletics department at St. Charles College,
asking to speak to Mr. Bruno Riazzi, who was unavailable. However,
the voice mail assured Ben the coach would return the call as soon as
he could.

And that voice mail was accurate. Coach Riazzi called back
within an hour. He was polite and quietly spoken, and there was no
malice in his voice. For the first time in a long while, Ben Faber felt
hopes rising again that Jack's pitching career could be resurrected.

"I'm not real sure there's a lot of point coming to see me, Mr.
Faber," said Bruno. "Young Jack has never asked me to talk to him. I
just got the feeling he was about finished with the game. Happens to
a lot of kids his age. I guess you know that already."

"Sure I do," said Ben. "But Jack's a very determined, special kid,
and I would not like to see him leave baseball if there was anything
we could still do to get him back on track."

"Okay, Mr. Faber. We can meet. But not till next week. Friday
night I'm headed to Cut Off, little place way down Route 1,
Lafourche County."

"Well, I don't guess this is gonna take long, and you'll be coming right through my town of Lockport. Why not pull right in there, little place on the main street called the Foxhole, and decide whether that boy o' mine's somehow worth saving?"

"I don't know why not. Say seven o'clock in the Foxhole, Lockport, Friday night?"

"You got it, Coach."

"Likewise, Mr. Faber."

14

*B*en Faber learned a very fast lesson at twelve minutes past seven o'clock on that Friday evening. Telephone voices can be as deceptive as a dipping slider. Bruno Riazzi came through the door of the Foxhole, accompanied by two friends, big, swarthy ex-baseball guys, neither of whom was much of an advertisement for Gillette.

"You Faber?" Riazzi said, striding across the dark, cool bar to the spot where Ben stood with a light beer. He was the only customer thus far in attendance.

Ben nodded and stuck out his hand, unsmiling. Bruno was not the kind of man at whom anyone would aim a smile. At least not voluntarily. And the agreeable, quiet telephone voice was entirely absent.

"Okay, I'm Bruno Riazzi," he said gruffly. "And these are my two fishing buddies, Carlos and Marco. We're headed down to Cut Off, so I don't have a whole lot of time to spare."

"Mr. Riazzi, I don't want to take a lot of your time. I just want you to tell me what has happened to Jack in the time since he was the best pitcher in the entire Cape Marlin League."

"Hey, lemme get some beers first," said Bruno, pushing his way into the bar. "You don't mind if the guys listen in on our talk, do you?"

"I'd prefer to discuss this one-on-one," replied Ben. "So maybe Carlos and Marco wouldn't mind sitting down over there for a while."

"No need. I trust these guys. Played a lot of ball with 'em in Triple A. They can listen in . . . yeah, three Budweisers . . . thanks."

Ben Faber sized up Bruno as well as he could. The coach was certainly ten years older than Ben. He was around the same height, six feet two inches, but he carried a beer belly and had lost the fitness he once had behind the plate for the White Sox. He was an obvious bully, impatient and used to pushing people around. Ben had rarely, if ever, disliked anyone so thoroughly at first sight. And he knew how *not* to deal with such people.

"I don't think you heard me, Coach," he answered quietly. "I said I'd prefer to speak to you alone about my son, his immediate past and his future. Please ask your friends to leave us for a while."

"Hey, you're kinda touchy, Faber."

"As the parent of the best pitcher St. Charles College ever had, I think I deserve perhaps *Mister* Faber, from a hired coach, don't you?"

Bruno glared back at the steady gaze of the hard-eyed, wide-shouldered sugar farmer leaning on the bar, and rasped, "Okay, guys, get over there. I'm just going to lay some home truths on this *Mister* Faber. And he ain't gonna like it. But that ain't gonna stop me getting it said."

Carlos and Marco backed away, taking their beers to a table across the bar, and Coach Riazzi turned back to Ben, nodded knowingly, and said, "First off, I want you to forget all about Cape Marlin. That damn league's full of Northeastern college boys. Your kid ran through 'em all right, but they ain't nothing. They're mostly rich kids who don't even want to play pro ball. You got that?"

"Well, I heard it," said Ben. "I think you're wrong. Jack's team, the Seawolves, had guys from Oklahoma, Chicago, Georgia, Texas, Alabama, California, and so did all the other teams. Are you sure you know anything about Cape Marlin?"

"*Mister* Faber, I played a damn lifetime in the Minor Leagues before I made Comiskey Park. I know every damn thing there is to know about baseball."

Ben said nothing. And Bruno took a deep swallow of beer and added, "I told you once, Mr. Faber, and I'll tell you again. That college league up there ain't worth a damn in the big scheme of things. That's why I made a study of its big star coming back to the South— your kid, that is. What's his name, Jim, no . . . Jack, right? Jack Faber."

"That's his name. Yes. Jack. Good of you to remember," said Ben, his hackles rising against the deliberate rudeness of the St. Charles College coach.

Bruno knew he had stung, and he pressed forward with his words and, in a sense, his luck. "Okay, lemme have another beer willya? . . . Now, as I was saying, your Jim has several major problems, right . . ."

"Don't say his name wrong again, Coach."

"Oh yeah—Jack, right? Keep forgettin' about him. Well, first of all, he's got a fastball that's too predictable. It just ain't good enough. He can't seem to hit the corners. When he gets that big curve going, that's not a half-bad pitch. But he's too timid with it. The slider—now there's his real problem. It only works for him when he throws it dead right. The rest of the time it's too suspect, and he's afraid of it. When he really needs it, he can't summon the guts to let it rip."

Ben nodded, hearing but not believing.

Bruno took another long swallow of beer. "You receiving my words, Mr. Faber? I ain't using 'em lightly, and I been around a lotta ballplayers. I know this game, right?"

Ben nodded again.

"And now lemme get to the heart of the problem. Your Jack is a natural-born smart-ass, doesn't like authority, doesn't react to coaching, doesn't want to listen, thinks he has all the answers. Well, he ain't got 'em. And just as soon as I started to ride him a little, I was getting resentment. He's too brittle to take that kind of criticism. And I can't put up with that."

"Not even from a pitcher with Jack's college record?"

"Not even from Pedro Martinez. Mr. Faber. You may not know it, but I coached a half-assed Florida junior-college team to three straight NJCAA Championships. I don't do stars. Or prima donnas. I do teams. Guys who knit together, play for each other. Jack just ain't that much of a team player. I see him out there on that mound, always looking at the pro scouts with the radar guns. Always thinking about himself . . . and there's one other thing—"

"Coach, you really don't like him, do you?"

"It ain't that. I can't afford not to like certain kids. It's just that I don't take to that *kind* of a kid. Just look at the words I been using to describe his pitching—the *safe, predictable* fastball, the *timid* curve, *afraid* to throw his slider. His *brittle* psyche. There's got to be

a pattern there, and I'm advising you to pay attention to that pattern
. . . Hey! Lemme have another beer, willya?"

Ben Faber's chin was trembling at the cruel attack on his only
son. He stood there, shocked at the coach's verdict, speechless at the
lies and the distortions. And somehow his farmer's strength could
not help him here.

"No one else has ever said those things about Jack before," he
said lamely. "I wonder if it ain't just possible that you're wrong . . .
you just rode him too hard . . . scared the courage and confidence
right out of him?"

"Mr. Faber," Bruno went on remorselessly. "I want to lay this
right on the line for you. Right now, as I see it, you're the father of a
second-class college pitcher, who ain't never going to the Majors,
cannot be coached anyway, and lacks guts. Face it, Faber. It's genetic,
and I seen it a lot of times. Country kids from easy-living farming
families. But I'm here to tell you Jack Faber ain't got the balls for it,
and I don't guess you've got the stuff to give him those balls."

They say a soldier never sees the bullet that kills him, and Bruno
sure as hell never saw the stupendous, lights-out right hook that
landed flush on his jaw, just right of center. The coach crashed unconscious to the floor, backward, Ben standing over him, both fists raised,
months of rage and frustration having exploded out of him like a vol-
canic eruption. It was a blow delivered by a man who suddenly had
the strength of ten.

Bruno never moved, but the entire bar was still shaking from the
impact of his landing. Glasses rattled. Bottles shook. Ben thought the
coach might be dead, but he had no time to ruminate about it. Carlos and Marco were out of their chairs and racing across the bar.
Marco got there first, and swung a vicious blow at Ben, missed and
overbalanced, still upright and still coming forward.

Ben Faber sidestepped and slammed a jolting right hand punch
into his rib cage, fracturing two on the left side. It was a blow that
would have knocked down a stud bull. Marco, gasping, hit the floor
right next to Bruno.

Ben now rounded on Carlos, who was more used to this kind of
fracas, and gazed at the iron fists of Ben Faber, and dropped his hands.

"Hey," he said. "I'm not fighting anyone."

"Not so long as you drag your two buddies right outta here, load
'em up, and get outta my town. Right now."

The barman, young Billy-Bob Shaw, who'd known Ben and Jack Faber all his life, looked at Carlos, and added, "Sure was a mistake for that ugly ol' bastard down there to have tried to hit Mr. Faber. Guess we all saw the second one try and do the same thing . . . but do like he says. Get your buddies outta my bar real quick, before I call the cops and have y'all put in jail. Goddammit. Who d'you guys think you are . . . comin' in here causing fights?"

Carlos bent over, grabbed the still-unconscious Bruno's wrists, and dragged him backward through the door. Then he came back for the moaning Marco and helped him out into the street the same way.

Billy-Bob poured Ben another beer. "That's sure some kind of a punch you got there," he said.

"Wouldn't know, really," replied Ben. "I never hit anyone before. But I couldn't have someone talk like that about Jackie. Nossir. That wasn't fair. I wasn't having it."

"Shit, old Bruno won't be pitching him no more for St. Charles games, I doubt."

"Guess not," said Ben. "Not unless they strike the natural gas out there on my land, and I buy the fucking college."

He finished his beer, paid for five more—three for Bruno, one each for the other two—and drove himself home. Jack was returning first thing in the morning for the weekend, since he certainly would not be required for the return home game against the Aggies. Matter of fact, Bruno Riazzi would just as soon have selected the school librarian, Mrs. Eula Herbert, to pitch relief. She was seventy-three.

Ben turned in early, tired from his physical exertions, and mentally exhausted from listening to the diatribe against Jack, criticism he knew could not be true. He went to sleep grateful to Billy-Bob, the only witness, who would swear the men had attacked Ben Faber. And worried that he now had to get Jack back on the mound, since he could not permit this subhuman baseball coach to destroy his son's career.

He understood that this might prove difficult. Jack did not want to pitch. But Ben had to give it a try, because in his view the whole subject was fraught with urgency. Jack had to get out there again, because to delay any longer might snuff out whatever flame might still be flickering.

When Jack arrived by bus the following morning, and walked

down the long, dusty drive, he found a tall glass of cold lemonade awaiting him on the stoop, and a father in very serious mode.

"Jack," he said. "I want you to do something for me."

"Yup," said Jack, leaning back in the rocker in the hot morning light, surveying the scene before him, contemplating a place he knew better than he knew his own heart: the gently sloping earth, the great sweep of the sky, the flow of the water along the creek, every crack in the decking.

"I want you to come back out to the mound by the barn with me and throw a few baseballs, maybe play a little catch with your dad, like we always did before."

Jack made no reply. He frowned, sipped a little lemonade, and weighed up the amount of hurt he would be leveling at his father if he said no.

He made no reply for a full minute. Then he spoke, slowly. "Okay, when you're ready."

Ben Faber refrained from mentioning any of the ten thousand reasons he had for forcing his son back into the game they had loved for so long. He just replied, "I'd really like that, Jack. Just like old times, right?"

"Nearly," said Jack.

Ben stood up and walked across to the barn, dug out the old gloves and a bucket of baseballs, and moved into the field behind the house and waited for Jack. He watched him pull on the glove and walk back, around fifty feet, turning, and nodding once, indicating he was ready. Ben leaned back and threw a soft easy ball at his son, and Jack caught it absently, changed hands, and tossed it back, lower and a little harder.

Ben snagged it and threw again. Jack, as ever, moved only at the last split second, moving the glove fast, twisting it face-out, and Ben heard the smack of the ball hitting the leather.

They each threw again, looking for the rhythm, and soon the throws and catches were snapping in, fast and regular, two professionals practicing a lifelong craft, concerned only with flawless execution. To watch Jack Faber and his dad winging the ball to each other was to watch poetry. Professional poetry.

They threw for several minutes, until Ben said carefully, "It's been a while now, son. I've missed watching you pitch—and I don't care what this asshole Riazzi says, it'll be a cold day in hell when he finds another kid who even looks like you do, never mind with your power."

"Hey, Pop. I'm retired now. We both know that."

"You just had a few weeks' break, because of a coaching problem. Let's get out back to the old tire. Lemme see you throw some, like we used to . . . you know, when Mom was here."

Jack had known this was coming. And the last thing in this world he wanted to do was hurl a baseball at the tire. He thought he'd miss, and more important, he had no desire anymore. Jack Faber did not care, one way or another, whether the ball went straight or not. Those concerns seemed long behind him, almost in another age. For his father, those concerns stood stark before him. They haunted his waking hours and his sleep. He tried to push the situation to the back of his mind, tried to ignore the profound disappointment he felt.

The picture Ben saw in his mind was the same, that of Jack rearing back, his left leg high, his gaze unyielding, as he scorched the ball through the air with that searing, perfect action of his. No sound disturbed Ben's dreams, save for the hammering thud of the water pump out by the drilling rig and the distant bellow of some far-lost umpire, calling out the very lifeblood of the big-time pitcher . . . *"STRIKE THREE!"*

"You're not expecting much from me, are you?" Jack's voice was firm, but there was a dead quality to it, none of the rising inflection Ben always heard when his son approached the battlefield.

"Some," he replied. "But not too much."

Jack caught the next ball, high and right, backhanded. And he did not throw it back. Instead he walked back to the gate, saying over his shoulder, "Okay. Let's go. For whatever the hell it's worth."

"I just want to see you throw, because I can't accept that the pitcher I have nurtured for an entire lifetime is somehow gone. I wanna convince myself this is all a goddamned nightmare."

"It's a nightmare all right. And a pretty bad one at that," said Jack. "Y'all go ask Coach Riazzi what he thinks. He'll tell you. And he's been to the Show, which is more'n we have."

"Screw him," snapped Ben. "I haven't been wrong about you yet."

They walked through the hot, still delta air, to a place Jack had deliberately cast from his thoughts since the troubles with Bruno. And when he turned the corner toward the back of the barn, there was a dull ache deep inside him. Possibly not so severe as the ache currently on the left-hand side of Coach Riazzi's jaw, but an ache just the same. And he pictured again his mom, standing where she always had, under the younger maple at the corner of the barn, just watching, sometimes clapping, always encouraging, usually ready with a tall jug of iced lemonade.

He looked at the mound, the same pile of dust-brown earth his father had constructed a dozen years ago, and he walked up to it, gazing down toward the tallest maple where the old black tractor tire hung mockingly, the very spot where he had learned to throw the baseball. The tire was motionless today in the deep still air, and Jack just stood there, the memories of a thousand curves and sliders crowding in on him, the memories of his parents in happier times. And he recalled especially the one time, when he was fifteen, when he hurled eight successive fastballs straight through the hole.

That was the day his father had told him, "Jackie, one day you're going to the Majors." It was the day upon which he had built his entire life, hopes, and dreams; now it was just the ghosts of summers past.

Jack gazed past the tire at the old shrimp net hanging behind, a nautical backstop. He made no attempt at a windup, but threw the ball in a desultory fashion at the tire, missing by a wide margin.

"Okay, Jack." Ben was standing next to the mound with the bucket of baseballs. "Gimme a dozen three-quarter-speed pitches at the hole."

Right from the first one, Ben could see that his son's heart simply was not in it. He was throwing, not pitching, not even trying to pitch. His concentration was terrible, his mechanics lethargic. Ben could see his balance was all wrong. He was dropping his elbow below shoulder height at the point of delivery. His stride was too far open, reducing the power drastically from his hips. More importantly his mental approach was horrific. To Jack Faber the entire exercise had become a chore, the precise opposite of the pure joy it once had been.

He sent in twenty pitches at the tire, and only two of them went though the hole. Most of them barely nicked the outside edge.

Ben knew the problem was bad. But not this bad. Unable to contain himself, he allowed his emotions to burst to the surface. *"STOP!"* he yelled. *"STOP! What the hell are you doing?"*

"I'm throwing—trying to pitch."

"BULLSHIT YOU ARE! I used to be able to tell you to hit a mosquito on the side of the tire, and you'd nail the little bastard

when you were fourteen years old. Right now you couldn't hit the barn wall."

Jack hurled the ball down into the dirt and walked, and he berated his father. *"YOU SOUND JUST LIKE RIAZZI . . . WHAT ARE YOU SAYING TO ME? DOESN'T ANYONE CARE WHAT THE HELL THEY SAY TO ME . . . ?"* And he strode back to the house, tears literally flooding down his cheeks. And Ben Faber's heart almost broke as he heard Jack's agonized final words.

"I CAN'T . . ." Jack sobbed without shame. *"I JUST CAN'T . . . WHY DON'T YOU UNDERSTAND . . . ? I CAN'T DO IT ANYMORE."*

Ben went after him, almost chasing him into the house, calling out his own devastation. "Jack," he shouted. *"What the hell has happened to you? What has this Riazzi done to you?"*

Jack stopped in his tracks, and he swung around to face his father. "Dad," he said. "I'm finished. And the quicker you get used to that, the easier it's gonna be on both of us."

Ben stared right back at him. "Listen!" he snapped. "A few months ago you were one of the premier pitchers in the country. Now you can't throw the ball through a tire—through a hole you've hit a thousand times. You used to be able to hit it blindfolded."

"But you don't know what Riazzi was like, the effect he had on me. He took me down, again and again. He humiliated me in front of everybody. I'll never pitch well again."

"Look, I know there isn't a coach alive who could get you back. But I think I probably could. If you'll just listen to what I tell you, take it real steady, take your time. Remember I got you to the pinnacle of the college game, and some other no-'count little bastard has knocked you down, which is a damned easy thing to do. But I'm still your best chance, and I want you to forget for a while how sorry you feel for yourself, turn around, and follow me back out to the mound. *Our* mound, right?"

"That little bastard. I could knock his head right off his fucking shoulders," gritted Jack.

"Too late," replied his dad, somewhat mysteriously. "Come on, let's get back out there. Give it another try. We can't let a little bastard like that beat us."

Ben walked back to their old pitching area, where a warm rising breeze was beginning to toss up the dust and make ripples in the gray silken ropes of Spanish moss that hung from the two huge live oaks. He stood on the mound with his bucket of balls and assessed the horsefly situation, debating whether to spray his arms and face. A gray lizard scuttled across the dirt, and Jack did not show up.

For a while Ben stood there, forlornly staring down at the old shrimp net behind the tire. He felt unaccountably alone, locked in a trap of past times, when Jack was on the rise, his right arm a human slingshot. Suddenly Ben leaned over and selected himself a baseball. He made no elaborate action, but wheeled around, and hurled it hard, straight through the hole in the gentle swaying tire sixty-feet away. It was the third time in twenty-four hours his own right arm had ripped into action. It felt pretty good. Three out of three—Bruno, Marco, Tire.

"Nice shot, Pop," said Jack as he walked around the corner of the barn. "For an old guy."

Ben laughed. It was the first time for many weeks he had heard that jaunty note in Jack's voice.

"Hey, get up here, willya, and let's see if we can't get some prac-tice—throw a few fastballs."

Jack walked onto the mound, and Ben moved into his old posi-tion right behind him, the same place he had occupied when Jack was ten and learning to throw the baseball. Ben stood there casually, trying to communicate through his easy body language that nothing had changed, rather than everything. He tossed the ball to Jack.

"Okay, son. Let's go. Lead off with some fastballs, nice and loose, nice and fluid, get into your rhythm. I just want to see your mechanics."

Jack wound back and hurled a low-velocity pitch straight at the hole, but it cannoned off the edge of the tire. He shook his head and caught the new ball tossed in by his father.

"That's okay, Jack. It's all right. Here we go. Let's try another . . ."

Again Jack wound up and unleashed another fastball at the hole. But it flew too high, straight over the top of the tire and into the shrimp net. Ben thought involuntarily, *Who the hell is this, Jack Faber or Doughnut Davis? Jesus, those halcyon days on Cape Mar-lin, just last summer, now seemed a lifetime away.*

"I'm a little concerned about your release point . . . let's go again . . . come on, Jack . . . you can nail down this pitch . . . but right now

I think your stride's a little long . . . makes it hard to get your release out front . . . just cut it down a little . . . you'll start to feel that release out front . . ."

Jack threw again, another fastball at maybe 85 mph. It tailed away, outside the tire by more than a foot, floated rather than zoomed.

"You absolutely sure you're really loose, Jack? C'mon. Lemme have another fastball . . . through the hole, Jack. *LET'S GO!* Zero right in on that spot . . . let's start getting our focus going . . ."

All the old familiar phrases of coach to pitcher seemed for a few moments to galvanize Jack. He stood tall on the mound, glaring down at the target of his boyhood. The tire swayed slightly in the breeze, and then Jack unleashed a fastball with a ton of velocity. For a split second Ben's heart soared, but the ball, pitched dead straight, flew clean over the tire, and the shrimp net, whacking hard against the barn siding. Jack Faber had not made a pitch that wild since he was in sixth grade.

It was a fact that Ben confirmed. "Jesus, son, I haven't seen you make a pitch like that since you were about twelve."

Jack turned back and shook his head. "I'm afraid of the ball, Dad," he said. "I kinda think I'm doing my best, but what I'm really doing is trying not to get it wrong. I've lost every bit of confidence. I can't throw hard *and* be sure of my aim. I can't do this anymore, Dad. I just can't."

"All right, c'mon, let's throw a pitch with less velocity. Let's go with the slider. Right here where you first learned it."

Jack caught the ball his father tossed to him, and his expression was pensive. He stood for a moment, as if his thoughts were far away, ruminating perhaps on the lost magic of the pitcher's art, the gifts which the gods of baseball had once bestowed upon him with such largess, now suddenly gone.

But inside, his head was whirring, trying to fathom the problem, not with his confidence, but with his mechanics, his action and balance, and the perfectly tuned cycles that are built into a perfectly thrown pitch. The ones that look easy.

Jack knew that a misjudgment of perhaps a quarter of an inch at the point of release—too high, too low, too wide, too narrow, too early, too late—translates into maybe a foot or even more by the time the baseball reaches the plate.

It has something in common with the action of a rower on his oar. If a coach wants to *lengthen* the stroke, making the blade hit the water earlier on the catch, he adjusts the pin that holds the "gate" on the rigger, perhaps bringing it a quarter inch closer to the boat. By the time that tiny fraction of distance at the fulcrum of the oar is transferred way down the shaft to the blade, eleven feet away, the sweep of the oar may have increased by several inches, producing a longer, earlier, and harder stroke. Rowers call it gearing.

So it is with a baseball pitch. The critical, tiny quarter inch is multiplied possibly forty times between the pitcher's hand and the plate. Which means every time a pitcher hurls the ball, he's on a knife edge, always trying to eliminate the quarter inch of error in his action. And he's doing this at high speed, under terrific mental pressure. His concentration needs to be total, because there is no other way to stay on the right side of the knife edge.

Right now Jack Faber was on the wrong side. And he knew it. He was afraid of the fastball, but the prospect of the slider unnerved him completely, because this pitch was essentially a fastball, moving with less velocity, with a sudden dramatic violent twist at the point of release. This fierce injection of spin is what causes the baseball to bite into the air during its trajectory, and dive downward and away, just before it reaches the plate.

Every pitcher knows the substantial amount of force that needs to be ripped into that baseball on the twist, right before release point. And the harder the ball is twisted the greater the drop-off in front of the hitter. A pitcher whose confidence is low may not have the daring to put everything into that twist. He'll play safe, "baby" the pitch, make sure it gets to the plate more or less straight and hopefully make its downward dive. The price for that timidity is invariably a slower, "fatter" pitch, with less drop-off, and the distinct possibility of being whacked. Hard. Just like it had been during his final St. Charles outings.

The slider requires its exponent to possess the courage of a gladiator, a pitcher who'll make that twist against all odds, with everything he has. A pitcher who will send it in, packing such a ferocious spin the stitches on the ball form a bright scarlet dot, bang in the center of the vortex, as it flies, transmitting a chilling signal to the hitter, direct from the Angel of Death.

Jack Faber used to be able to do that. Not always, but mostly, and he still knew perfectly well how to execute it. The issue was his state of mind, which dictated his willingness to give his basic mechanics free play. The tyranny of the off-speed pitch in the game of baseball is an ironclad testimony to Thomas Paine's observation more than two hundred years ago, "the harder the conflict, the more glorious the triumph."

Jack was not, at this moment, looking for glory. He just wanted a chance to send the ball dipping toward the hole in the tire without making a complete fool of himself.

He nodded once to his father and stood for a few moments staring once again at his target. Then he leaned back into his action and propelled himself forward, hard, getting that twist on the ball, hurling it toward the hole. It wasn't bad, but it wasn't much good either. Jack put some "bite" on the ball, but not enough, and it dropped well short, maybe fifty-six feet.

Ben tossed another baseball and said nothing. Jack knew more about this pitch than he did. There was nothing to say, and he watched his son wind up once more, guessing he would aim for more velocity in the delivery. He was wrong about that, and Jack just cut back the spin. The ball had no bite on it, floated in there, slowly, and hit the top of the tire. A halfway-decent hitter might have slammed it clean out of the park.

Ben tossed another baseball. Jack, now looking almost desultory in his approach, threw it in wearily. It never broke, never dived. It stayed right on the same trajectory, a dead flat plain, and thudded against the lowest part of the tire. For the second time in a half hour, Jack threw down his glove and stormed off the mound, this time muttering aloud to himself, "Why am I doing this? I just don't have it anymore."

And this time Ben did not go after him. He walked down to retrieve the balls and carried the bucket back into the barn. He realized the problem was worse than he had ever imagined, and he was relieved to see a diversion in the form of Jerry Segal's big blue-and-white Cherokee heading down the driveway in a cloud of dust.

Right behind it, there was a second vehicle, a white Toyota which Ben knew belonged to the dazzlingly pretty Angela Lansberg, Jack's dark-haired childhood sweetheart. The two of them had drifted apart in the past year since Angela had gone to college at the University of Virginia, but they were still in touch and Ben guessed that Angela was more conscious of the loss than Jack. *Hell, she's picked a hell of a day to revive the old flames, thought Ben. He'll probably throw her out of the house, mood he's in right now.*

Angela waved as she drove by and called out, "Hi, Mr. Faber. Is Jack here?"

"Yup. In the house—in a grumpy frame of mind. Tread carefully, honey."

Angela laughed with the bright assurance of a beautiful girl accustomed to dispelling gloom and despondency easily from male admirers, regardless of the circumstances. Meanwhile Jerry Segal parked his truck and walked over to Ben, grinning widely. Whatever the situation at the drilling rig, it surely hadn't worsened, because Jerry was apt to bring bad news wearing a face like a World Series loser.

"Hey, Ben," he said, holding out his hand. "Just stopped by to give you a little update."

Ben smiled and shook the hand of the man who held his destiny in his grasp. "Lay it on me," he said. "What's hot?"

"Well," Jerry replied, "we still have the geologists taking samples of the drill cuttings, logging the color and type, like sand, shale, and dolomite. So far all the marker beds giving indications on the way down are telling us we're geologically real high on the structure. Right now our objective is to find an anticline, or a structural high, to create a trap for the gas. And our geologist, the guy specially detailed to watch the cuttings getting washed up from the bottom of the hole is starting to see real good sand in the samples."

Ben blinked. "Is that good or bad?"

"That's not just good. That's excellent. We look like we're going from shale to beach sand, and that makes one of the best possible traps for oil or gas. Just yesterday afternoon we started to see the mud from the drilling fluid start to get bubbly. And goddammit, I took me a look down there—it was like a can of soda pop someone just shook up."

"No shit? Is that good?"

"Ben Faber, that ain't even very good. That's fan-fucking-tastic . . . I could see the gas bubbles breaking out on the surface, right there where the mud was rolling out to the shale shaker. We got a gas detector right there measurin' the percent background gas in the drilling fluid.

"I was so damned excited I whipped right over to the shed to check out the graph which prints out continuously, real steady, measurin' the quantity and quality of gas in the hole. And the graph wasn't steady no more. Goddammit, Ben, that gas detector was picking up methane, right in the middle of a major gas zone. And we were in there *penetratin'* it. Yessir. That little ol' graph was jumping up right off the chart."

"Holy shit!" said Ben. "That's sounds big."

"Big! It could be enormous. And I'm not playing this down no more. Nossir. Time I left last night, they'd decided the fluid in the hole was getting so light from the aerating, they were afraid the mud column wasn't heavy enough to control it. That's when they started mixing in barite to add extra weight, in case the whole fucking mud residue started to go into orbit."

"Barite? What the hell's that?"

"It's a mineral, barium sulfate . . . you pump it in there and it thickens everything up—holds the hydrostatic column of mud at a greater pressure than the fucking gas which is trying to flow all over you."

"Easy, Jerry, that's my natural-born gas you're insulting!"

"Well, the whole thing was getting a bit tense last night. They were circulating the fluid for several hours, piling in the barite, getting the hole under control. Jeez, there was some heavy gas inflow out there, and today they're getting ready to trip out the hole with the drill pipe and bit."

"You mean it's all over . . . you guys have done it . . . hit pay dirt?"

"Well, we've hit payload okay, we're just trying to find out how big. And this is a damned tricky process. I've been in natural gas fields where they already had miles and miles of pipeline laid to the well. Then they turned it on and discovered the goddamned gas was just one giant puff. Blew out and died, same week. The guys had just evaluated the data badly. Cost the company millions of dollars."

"Could that happen here?"

"We don't think so. Otherwise we wouldn't have spent so much time and trouble. We're running in a suite of logs right now to evaluate the potential of the payzone. We got a couple of logs calculating the water saturation, another two calculating the porosity of the zone, the percentage of rock with void space to hold the gas. Ben, this is looking very, very good . . . a good gas zone sticks out like a sore thumb in a good sandstone reservoir. And that's what we have right here. They're telling me the porosity log is already kicking left, high, and the neutron log is kicking right. There's heavy gas content down there, no doubt."

"It's all gibberish to me," said Ben. "You tellin' me I'm gettin' rich."

"Wouldn't put my life savings on that, Ben. But I might bet the ranch."

"Well, what happens next?"

"We're gettin' ready to lower the drill pipe back into the well and then isolate the pay zone with packers. When those packers get opened you can measure the influx of liquid from the formation, plus the pressures. It's the rate the pressure rebuilds that counts. We're looking for high permeability, rock that lets the fluid run through it. That's the reading that tells you, as near as dammit, the extent of the reservoir."

"And what happens to me if it's big?"

"You'll sell us a long lease on the land, plus all the mineral rights, for which you will be rewarded very well in cash and shares in the corporation."

"Where's the stock right now?"

"Around fifty-five dollars. Down from a high of sixty-eight. Up from forty-four last summer when the Ay-rabs were cooperating on oil prices, like they ain't doing now."

"Jesus. How many of those little fifty-five-dollar bastards do I get?"

"If this strike's anything like as rich as we think it is, probably a coupla million?"

"HOW MANY?!"

"Coupla million. A deep natural gas field like this is hugely valuable, probably run big factories, even small towns off it for thirty years. It'll generate wealth like you cannot imagine."

"Mother of God," said Ben. "Are you kidding me?"

"'Course I'm not kidding you. You wouldn't be the first landowner to make a hundred million off natural gas. Not by a long way. And we're damn busy drilling all over the Gulf Coast, on the land, in the swamps, out at sea, even abroad. That fifty-five-dollar, stock I'm talking here could probably double in the next coupla of years."

"What happens to the farm?"

"We'll turn it into a major pumping and distribution station. Miles and miles of pipeline taking all the energy out from under your fucking sugarcanes right to where industry and people want it. Natural gas, Ben. It's clean, less expensive than oil, environmentally friendly, and absolutely reliable. People love it for heat, cooking, everything. For me it's the single most valuable commodity in this country, and you're sitting on enough, probably, to light up the great State of Louisiana."

"Fuck me," said Ben.

"They'll be a few down-home bastards trying to do that when it gets known how rich you are." Jerry chuckled. "You'll need lawyers, and guys who understand business and investment. Someone hands you a hundred million bucks, you gotta put it to work, make sure it always earns you a coupla mil every week after taxes. Big money's good—gives you a warm feeling."

"Guess you'd know about that, rich son of a bitch!"

"Ben, I ain't in the league you're about to enter. But I nailed my colors to Louisiana Oil and Gas right outta college, and I been stockpiling the shares ever since, been buying equity and holding stock options down the years since they were only three dollars on the Amex. Corporation gives me a few thousand options every six months and I sure ain't complaining."

"You any idea what I been doing growing sugar for all my life?"

"Beats the shit outta me, Ben, Welcome to the sunny side of the street."

"You know, Jerry, I'm so used to failure and debt, and I'm so programmed to disappointment, I can't hardly take all this in. Can I ask you just one more time? Could this all go wrong?"

"Yup. It could. Right now we know we gotta serious-looking natural gas strike. We think it's millions and millions of cubic feet, which will probably last twenty or thirty years. The worst case would be a whole lot smaller than we think. Maybe enough for only two years. Valuable but not great."

"What would that mean to me?"

"Guess you'd collect maybe eight to ten million bucks."

"Worst case?"

"Worst case."

"Minimum?"

"Minimum."

"Mother of God," said Ben. "Am I rich, right now?"

"Hell, no," said Jerry, laughing. "Ten mil ain't rich. But you've got a nice little stack of fuck-you money."

"What's that? Fuck-you money."

"Means you can utter them precise words to any son of a bitch you feel like. Changes your perspective on life real quick."

Ben Faber chuckled. "Christ," he said. "Ten minutes ago I was al-most outta my mind with worry over Jack's pitching action—like it was the only thing in the world that was going to save the both of us from poverty."

"Well, that might have been true a month ago, old buddy. But it sure ain't true anymore. You want to get tight with good pitching ac-tion, go buy the Atlanta Braves or the Rangers."

"I might just do that," said Ben. "Funny, a half hour ago I couldn't have afforded a new Braves cap! But God moves in mysterious ways, eh?"

"You got that right, Ben," said Jerry, climbing back into the Cherokee. "Stand by for the next few days. We'll want you to come over to the office in New Orleans probably Thursday."

"If I can get a ride." Ben laughed. "Old Chevy's just about died on me."

"*Mister Faber,*" said Jerry. "For this journey we'll be sending the corporate helicopter to pick you up."

15

Ben Faber was about ready to walk back to the house, but he felt unaccountably weak at the knees, so he just sat down right out there on the mound and stared at the hole in the tire which Jack couldn't hit.

For the moment the prospect of untold millions of dollars flooded his mind almost entirely and his thoughts cascaded in all directions. *Talk to Jack . . . phone Natalie . . . coach Jack . . . murder Riazzi . . . buy a new house . . . burn the sugar . . . get a new car . . . get a new headstone for the grave . . . hire Ted Sando for Jack . . . throw a party . . . marry Natalie . . . buy the Braves.*

Ben Faber did not quite know where to start. But whatever, he was going to start where he always started, organizing Jack's baseball career. There was no way he would ever accept that Jack, at twenty-one, was finished.

He climbed to his feet, dusted himself off, and set off for the house, where he was startled to hear a strident phrase echoing out from the living room.

"SCREW BASEBALL! GET IT OUT OF YOUR LIFE! THERE'S BIGGER FISH FOR YOU TO FRY."

The voice was not even male. It was very definitely female, and it belonged to Miss Angela Lansberg, who was doing some significant yelling at Ben's only son. And Ben did not much like what he was hearing.

"What's them sacrilegious phrases I'm hearing in my own humble abode?" he said, striding through the door.

"Oh, that's just Miss Angela getting a little carried away, not for the first time in her life," said Jack, laughing. "You know how she's always been prone to outbursts of that type."

"Hell, this isn't an outburst," said Angela. "I'm here with serious information for both of you."

"That right?" said Ben, who knew Angela's father, Bradford Lansberg, was chief of a drilling crew for Louisiana Oil and Gas. Any information in the possession of this young lady was either from the University of Virginia or from Brad Lansberg.

She turned to Ben and smiled. She was spoiled, irreverent, and unpredictable. She was the sorority president, homecoming queen, and deliciously pliant, slender, and Southern, with long dark hair and dark eyes. She could have come from Spain, but that she didn't. Angela was from right here in Lockport, Louisiana, and she had adored Jack Faber since she was about eight years old. Angela was a girl who thrived on extremes, and she had some extreme news to impart.

"Why, Mr. Faber," she said, slightly coy and wide-eyed. "This whole town's talking about you. My daddy heard about it at the lawyer's office last night."

Holy shit, Riazzi's suing.

Ben's mind was filled with dread. "Now what'd Brad heard about me?"

" 'Bout the big strike, of course."

Jesus. The gas or Riazzi's fucking chin!

"What strike?"

"Why, the natural gas, Mr. Faber. Right here on your land. My daddy says it's one of the biggest reservoirs LOG's ever found. And I guess he ought to know. He brought the first drilling crew out here right at the beginning."

"Uh-huh. I sure remember that, Angela. But I didn't think they were certain how big this strike is. Least not quite yet."

"They might not be. But my daddy's damn sure. He's seen the drilling data. He says the geologists were astounded at the depth of the gas field. He says there won't be no need to drill anywhere else but right on this ground, and it's gonna last for decades. He says you might be a *billionaire* time they're all through."

"Well, money ain't never been our God," said Ben, fighting to stop himself laughing at the pious inanity of his sentence.

Jack shot lemonade straight down his nose, choking and laughing, trying to join the conversation. "No," he said, finally. "Dad's right. Money ain't never been our God. Nossir. Same way there's probably a few tribes of Pygmies up the Zambesi who ain't that crazy about on-line banking."

"This family's no stranger to money," said Ben seriously. "Except for just lately."

"Right on, Dad," said Jack. "Hell, we got a brand-new car in around 1890."

That more or less did it for the Fabers. All pretense at modesty fell right out of the window. They were both falling about laughing, calling out alternative intentions. *Buy the college . . . take out a contract on Riazzi . . . buy a couple of Porsches . . . give a mil to Tommy Thibodaux . . . buy a law firm for Tony Garcia when he fails his finals . . . buy the Chicago Symphony for his mom . . .*

Finally, Angela, who was not laughing, said, "Is this all gonna change things around here? Guess you'll have to leave the old place, and go live someplace else."

"We're not going far, honey," replied Ben. "We'll look for a place in the area, maybe a little bigger and better house, nothing too fancy. I know one thing about money . . . it changes everything it can . . . but some things ain't changeable . . . like the way you feel about old friends, family, and your regular way of life.

"Hell, me and Jack might want to travel some, take a look at the world, but we'll be coming right back home to Louisiana. No doubt in my mind. It's all according to where you belong. And we all belong right here. And goin' away to try to find something better among strangers ain't gonna work. Hell, I don't know what Tommy would do if I wasn't around to borrow all his money, his phone, and his trucks. He'd get depressed."

Angela smiled. She'd always liked Ben Faber, like most everyone else in Lockport. "There's an awful lot of truth in all that, Ben," she said. "I know that. But I was telling Jack that now y'all got rich and everything, he needs to find something a lot more serious than playing baseball.

"I just came right through that door, and found him all upset about his pitching. And only last week he told me on the phone he'd retired. And here we all are talking _billions_ of dollars, and he's not paying no never mind to any of that—just his stupid fastball."

"Slider," said Jack stubbornly.

"Sorry, just his stupid slider," said Angela.

"Well, there's an example for you," said Ben. "All the money in the world can't give you all your wishes. 'Specially those wishes real close to your heart."

"Guess not," she replied. "But I've never really known if Jack had any wishes _real_ close to his heart."

"Well, I have," he said, standing up and putting his powerful right arm around her shoulders.

"Well?" she said, smiling at him, and forming, to Ben, a very beautiful picture of softness, warmth, and loyalty.

"I got a few of those heart wishes," said Jack, hugging Angela. "And the first one's easy. I'd like to think we'd somehow end up living our lives together. And all the rest will probably fall into place what with all the new money and all.

"But there is just one thing more . . . I'd give up everything, all the money, every dollar of it . . . if I could ever pitch again."

"Where the hell's Jack Faber? That's what I want to know."

Russ Maddox, trying to start the lawn mower, looked mystified. Ted Sando, standing out on the mound and gazing at the infield, tossed a baseball absentmindedly in the air and observed, "Well, I don't know. But we didn't protect him, did we?"

"Not much point protecting the best college pitcher in the country when you know darn well he's gonna be grabbed by Team USA."

"Either that, or vanish in the first five minutes of the damn draft for more money than you and I'll ever see."

"Anyway, Jack's not in the lineup for Team USA. I was looking at the list in _Baseball Weekly_ this morning. They announced the twenty-nine, which they're cutting to twenty-two in three weeks. It said the players were already down there in good ol' Millington, Tennessee."

"Including a couple of our guys, right?"

"'Fraid so. And in my opinion we can forget all about the Tulane pitcher. They'll pick him for sure. But we might get that good lefty from Wake Forest."

"That damn Team USA is one gigantic annual pain in the ass, ain't it?"

"From where we stand, Russ, it's worse than that. You know, I think they look at guys we recruit to come here and then select 'em because they know we know a whole lot more'n they do."

"Wouldn't be surprised . . . where the hell are they going this summer?"

"On some kind of a swing round the Pacific fucking Ocean. I saw they were playing three times in Taiwan and the rest in Japan."

"That's heady stuff for a kid. You know, wearing the shirt with 'USA' on it, international air travel, playing for your country on the other side of the world."

"Yeah, and fat lotta good it does 'em. These kids never go to the Olympic Games, and there's no scouts in the Pacific watching 'em every night like there are here. Cape Marlin is the best career move a kid can make. But it's hard to tell 'em not to play for their country."

"Which brings me," said Russ, "right back to my original question. Where the hell's Jack Faber and why isn't he in the Team USA list?"

"Beats the hell outta me. Maybe he's injured."

"Can we get a look at the early rounds of the draft?"

"Yeah. It comes out tomorrow. First Monday in June, right? I'll check round one through twenty."

"Look, Jack Faber's a first-round draft pick, no ifs, ands, or buts. If he's not listed in the first five rounds, he's either dead or wounded."

"I'll find out."

The following morning, Russ Maddox already had the lawn mower under way when Ted's Chevy came racing into the parking lot. The pitching coach strode onto the infield, where the mower was cutting neat lines in the spring grass, and his news was astounding.

"Jack Faber's not in the draft. Not anywhere," he said, an edge of incredulity in his voice.

"What d'you mean, he's not in the draft?"

"Missing. AWOL. He's not in it."

"Then I guess I'd better say it again. *Where the hell's Jack Faber?*"

"We better call the school, right? I mean, shit, if we're gonna lose two pitchers to those Team USA bandits . . . Christ! I'd kill to get Jack back here . . . anyway, you have to make the call . . . head coach to head coach and all that."

Russ switched off the mower. "I'm doing that right now," he said, walking toward the field office. "Where the hell's my book? It's got the St. Charles number in it. What's the name of the coach? Joe Dwyer, wasn't it?"

"It was. But I think he went to the Cardinals. They got some new guy. Can't remember his name."

Russ dialed the number for St. Charles College in Louisiana's 504 area code and asked for the baseball office. The voice on the end of the line was gruff, impatient.

Russ introduced himself and said he had spoken before to Joe Dwyer, but had not yet met the new coach.

"That's me," said the voice. "Bruno Riazzi. I'm the coach here now. What can I do for you?"

"I want to inquire about one of your pitchers—Jack Faber?"

"Oh yeah, him," replied Bruno, inadvertently rubbing his chin. "He's still kinda on the roster. But he hasn't helped us at all this season. He's pretty well finished with the game, I think."

"Oh, really? He did a big job for us last summer. I kinda thought he might have gone in the early rounds of the draft."

"The draft! You must be kidding me? If *he's* drafted, there's gotta be nineteen guys right here in front of him."

"Bruno, you sure we're talking about the same Jack Faber? Big, athletic kid, screamer of a fastball, wicked slider?"

"Might have had 'em up there in the Northeast, Coach. Never had much down here. He ain't gonna be no good to you. Don't waste your time."

Russ Maddox was truly amazed, but could see no point pursuing this. He just said, "Okay, Bruno. Lemme know if you have any guys you'd recommend for next year?"

"I don't think Cape Marlin's any good for real players, Coach. Just ain't tough enough." At which point he just put down the phone.

"What a total asshole," muttered Russ, dialing again into the 504 area code, looking for a number for Ben Faber's farm.

Three minutes later he heard an old familiar voice on the line. "Hey, Russ. This is Ben Faber speaking. How you been, buddy? Got the new team ready for action?"

"Trying. Can't say much more. But I called about Jack. What's going on down there? I was sure he'd get snapped up by Team USA, and then get drafted real high. Where the hell is he?"

Ben hesitated. Then he said, "Jack's been having some problems. And I think it might be better if you spoke to him directly. I just don't want to talk for him, because I'm not sure where he stands right now. Here, take down this number—504-420-2937. You'll get him at the Lansbergs' house. He's there right now."

Russ thanked Ben, told him he hoped to see him real soon, and called the new number, and three miles from the Faber farm, the caller ID lit up to reveal an incoming communication from Cape Marlin.

"This Jack Faber?"

"Yup. Right here . . . hey, Coach . . . how are you?"

Russ moved the conversation quickly. "C'mon, Jack, Coach Riazzi tells me you're just about finished with baseball? That can't be right."

"It can. It is. I'm all washed up. Can't pitch worth a damn."

"What d'you mean, you can't pitch?"

"I just lost it right after I came back to school after the Cape. Couldn't find that fastball anymore, lost the slider, lost the curve."

"Now wait a minute. Ten months ago, at the age of twenty, you were probably the best college pitcher in the country. One of the best I'd ever seen. Now, at twenty-one, you don't know how to do it any-more? Is that what you're telling me?"

"Almost. I *know* how to do it. But I am not *able* to do it."

"Jack. Forgive me. But what the hell are you talking about?"

Despite himself, Jack laughed at the stunned reaction of Russ Maddox. "Well, it happened very fast. Took just a few weeks. I got worse and worse, and suddenly I was back in the bull pen. Not even relieving."

"Do you want to try and get it back?"

"Not possible. I can't even throw straight, never mind hard."

"Jack. I want you back. I'm about to lose one, maybe two start-ing pitchers to Team USA, and I want to sign you to come back to the Seawolves."

"Coach. You don't want me. Not the way I'm pitching. I'd just embarrass you and the rest of the guys."

"Listen, kid. I've been in this game all my life. And I've seen a hundred pitchers lose it, and then find it again. It's part of the game. All pitchers are neurotic. You're like actors. Slightest setback, they think they'll never be offered another part. You guys think you'll never strike anyone out for the rest of your lives . . ."

Jack laughed thinly. He liked Russ, and he respected him. But he knew the Seawolves chief had no idea of the depths to which he had descended. "Coach, for the last time, you do not want me. I'm no good to you or the team. I've lost it, and I can't get it back."

"Jack Faber. Bullshit. You haven't lost it. You just misplaced it, and I doubt that fuck-wit coach at St. Charles helped much."

Jack's heart skipped a beat. *Christ, he's spoken to Riazzi. God knows what he told him.* He thought the Chevaliers coach would have been nothing short of poisonous when talking about his pitching ability to an inquiring Cape Marlin coach.

"Well, I guess Bruno filled you in about me?"

"Well, he said I was wasting my time even bothering with you. And you're telling me the same . . . however, I'm not in the habit of listening either to senior or junior assholes. Jack, listen. Teddy and I want you back. Whatever you've lost, we'll find. I want you to leave tomorrow. There'll be an electronic ticket waiting for you at New Orleans International. Southwest. Around midday. I'll have Teddy pick you up."

Russ let that sink in for a few moments and then he said quietly, "Don't give up on yourself, Jack. That'd be a big mistake. I want you on the Seawolves team. I believe in you. So does Teddy. So get your ass in gear and get it up here. Hear me?"

"If you say so, Coach. I guess I'll be there. Just don't say I didn't give you fair warning."

"Go shove your goddamned warnings. Get your head up, Jack. You're the reigning pitching champion of the Cape Marlin League. Act like it. Meet me at the field tomorrow evening. You'll be staying with Ward and Ann Fallon again. We'll all be real glad to see you. Hurry up."

Russ replaced the phone. He looked up at Ted Sando and grinned. "This could be a lot of trouble, old pal. But he's coming."

Meanwhile, back at the home of Angela Lansberg, Jack had some explaining to do. He replaced the receiver and announced simply, "That was Coach Maddox, from the Seawolves. They want me back, and I'm going tomorrow morning."

Angela looked appalled. "But, Jack, I thought you'd retired . . . I thought we were going to spend the summer together . . . what about the gas strike and your duties to your father . . . you can't just leave him . . . and I don't want you to leave me . . ."

Jack stood up and walked toward the window, staring out at the flatlands, the blacktop surface of Route 1 shimmering in the heat as it made its long lonely run through the Southern swamps all the way down to Grand Isle on the Gulf. The sky, flecked with high clouds, was like molten brass.

"Angela, I've never really talked to you about my baseball. It's just been there since I was a kid, and I've always been able to do it better'n anyone else, so there didn't seem no need to go on and on about it. But a few months ago all that changed.

"I might as well tell you. I've never really told anyone else. But the new coach at school hated me on sight. Matter of fact, I think he hated me before that. But anyway, he set out to humiliate me in front of everyone, and in a very short time he ruined my confidence.

"When a pitcher loses that, he's done. Because a lot of times, standing out there on the mound, with a game hanging in the balance, you have to take risks, throw the ball right at the corners, knowing you might miss, and that the hitter might not swing at it. Well, Mr. Bruno Riazzi knocked all that right out of me. It got so I was just too scared to try. I was just trying not to screw it up. Then I decided to go right back to my old way, throwing the daring pitches . . . and I couldn't do it anymore. I've tried and tried . . . but I can't get it back . . ."

Angela walked over to his side and put her arms around him, and she whispered softly, "Then why are you going to Cape Marlin? You don't want to let yourself down, do you?"

"I'm going back because I have to go back. It's my only chance. There are two coaches up there who I'd trust with my life. And just there on that phone, the head coach told me we'd find it again. He really thinks I could pitch like I used to. I don't have any other option."

"But, Jack, you do." Angela was suddenly afraid of losing him, as she had almost done last summer. "There is this huge family business opening up for you right here. Even if it's only investment. Your degree is in business administration, and everything's being handed to you. You have to stay. My daddy says Ben is flying in to see the LOG president this week. I think you should round up a lawyer and go with him."

Jack pondered the sheer impossibility of trying to explain how he felt about throwing a baseball, knowing, as he surely did, that his desire to hurl it over the plate at 94 mph would never really die. In the face of awful setbacks, that desire might lie dormant. But it would never die. It could always be awakened, and it would always flourish again.

That desire, he knew, was impossible to extinguish. Here, in his darkest hour, it still dwelled within the soul of Jack Faber, and it would not need to be force-fed. It was settled, on a slowburn, simmering in some place even Jack could not locate. And it craved satisfaction.

Jack knew he would need courage, though he wondered if he had enough, so profoundly had the pain and the loss penetrated his mind. And he knew he was going back to the Northeast. But he was unable to explain all that to Angela, who stood looking quizzically at a young man who would ignore a brand-new family fortune in favor of a game which belonged in a schoolyard. At this particular moment, Angela had a soul sister in faraway Chicago, one Natalie Garcia.

"Angela," said Jack. "You just have to trust me. This is my chance, and it may be my only chance, not to mention my last. I have to go, because if I don't, I'll never forgive myself. And I might not forgive you either if you try to talk me out of it."

Angela shook her head, and eighteen hours later she was driving Jack and his father to New Orleans International Airport, listening to Ben issuing last-minute instructions. *Concentrate on your action . . . keep remembering the mechanics of the pitch . . . stay focused . . . work with Tony, if he's there . . . listen to Ted Sando . . . he's a purist. I like that . . . check your grip on the fastball . . . and remember, the slider takes a fast, hard twist at the release point . . . let it rip, Jackie, let it rip . . .*

Neither Ben nor Jack even mentioned the possibility of becoming maybe $100 million richer by next week. And Angela Lansberg found that, quite frankly, astounding.

Southwest Airlines' flight from New Orleans came howling in over the gray waters of Massachusetts Bay ten minutes late at Boston's Logan Airport. Ted Sando was having no truck with central parking and a long walk to the terminal, and he passed the time lapping the airport's complex one-way system, aiming to park himself right outside the big glass doors in front of the baggage hall. Bang on time. He was in touch on his cell phone with Southwest's automatic flight arrival recordings, and he knew he was awaiting a 16:24 arrival.

Five minutes taxiing, seven minutes to get off, eight minutes walk and wait for the baggage, two minutes to curbside. Twenty-two minutes total. Ted Sando loved calculations, and his Chevy would be outside the glass doors at 16:46.

Jack actually beat him by about a half minute, and stared around him on the terminal sidewalk, searching for his ride. He was still holding his bags when he spotted the Chevy, and Ted, weaving through the buses and cabs, snaking in from the far outside lane and pulling up right in front of him.

"Bags on the backseat, get in, and we're outta here." Ted Sando was all business, and he yelled instructions through the passenger window like a drill sergeant. "Good to see you, Jack . . . I got good news and bad news . . ."

"Gimme the good, Coach."

"We're gonna get you right back to where you were last year. We need you. And I know you can make it."

"Gimme the bad."

"Doughnut's arriving Thursday."

They both laughed, and Ted offered a high five, which Jack accepted, right in front of the slip road to the Ted Williams Tunnel, through which Coach Sando was clearly headed, illegally.

"We allowed through here?" asked Jack.

"Not really but I think it's about five-to-one against anyone bothering us in a busy rush hour like we have, just before five P.M. on a Tuesday."

"Oh, okay, Coach," replied Jack. "If we're going to jail, I just wanna get the story straight. Meantime I'll just consider the irony of the world's worst pitcher riding through a tunnel named for the world's best hitter."

"Do not speak in that way, Pitcher Faber," said Ted, unsmiling. "And remember the last real top pitcher in the Cape Marlin League, the one who collected the MVP Award, with a nine–oh record and a 1.68 ERA, was your very own self."

"Seems like a thousand years ago," said Jack.

"Well, it wasn't. It was ten months ago. Are you fit? Not hurting? No aches and pains?"

"I've never felt better. Not physically better, anyway. I still hurt pretty bad inside."

"Well, we're gonna cure all that," said Ted. "And in my view we look like having one hell of a team. We protected just about all the players, except the ones we knew we did not have a prayer of re-signing, like you, and then Scott Maloney and Aaron Smith, who were both offered contracts yesterday in the very early rounds. And Andy Crosby gave up the game when he finished college this semester. He's back running the marina."

"Did we get some halfway-decent replacements?"

"Sure we did. Russ wants to move Zac from first to third to replace Scott. And he's brought in a power man from the University of South Carolina—top hitter for the Gamecocks this year. Black guy, stands six feet two inches and weighs two hundred and forty pounds, name of Bo Hacker—that's Bo, as in Beauregard. His nickname's even better. He's called Boom-Boom, son of the Hilton Head Island Hotel golf pro.

"His dad told Russ the first time he let Boom-Boom swing a club, he hit a seven-iron about five hundred yards, and a putt nearly as far! Mr. Hacker decided right then and there his boy was always gonna have a problem with overhitting and made him take up baseball . . ."

Jack laughed, and asked, "What's he hitting in school?"

"Around .330."

"That ought to do it, right? He probably could step right into Scott's shoes in the lineup."

Ted nodded. "You sure don't sound like a guy who's retired, Jack. You sound like a guy getting ready for a big comeback."

"Hoping. But not too optimistic. Who else is coming to Seapuit?"

"Russ got a new hitter from Columbia, New York, Lou Gehrig's old school. He's called Steve Thompson, very fast between the bases, batted .392 and never hit a home run. He's a hell of an athlete. Ran the hundred-and-ten meters hurdles in thirteen-point-three seconds in the Intercollegiate. He's from Brooklyn, one of those families who sold out to Stargill for the new Ebbets Field. Guess he must have baseball in his blood, and he's got one reliable bat."

"Who does Columbia play?" Jack asked.

"Oh, Ivy League schools," said Ted. "You know, Yale and Harvard, Princeton, Dartmouth, Brown, and Penn. They got some pretty good ballplayers—Steve's dad's a captain on the Staten Island ferry."

"What's that?"

"You know, the ferry that runs people from Staten Island over to

Manhattan every morning, straight past the Statue of Liberty to the Battery. They must have heard of that down in the bayous."

"Not me. But I've heard of the Statue of Liberty."

"Congratulations, Jack. Have you ever seen it?"

"Never even seen New York, or Washington or anywhere much. I've been to New Orleans, though. And me and my dad drove around the outskirts of Atlanta one time. We got any new pitchers coming?"

"Yup, we got two. A guy from Santa Domingo in the Dominican Republic. Pedro Rodriguez. His family are friends of Pedro Martinez and his folks. Our Pedro's at Florida State, down there in Tallahassee. He had a hell of a spring season, went twelve–one for Florida, ERA of 2.17.

"He plays some tough competition in the ACC. Hey, that's gotta be brutal, facing Clemson, UNC, Virginia, Maryland . . . every weekend."

"Is Pedro big?" Jack wondered.

"Not really. He's about five feet ten inches, a hundred and ninety pounds. Hopefully he'll be a starter for us."

"'Specially if I carry on screwing things up."

"Do not speak in that way, Jack. You gotta get positive. You gotta assume you're on the way back."

"Okay, who else is coming?"

"We had to find another pitcher when Chris Cronin was suddenly snapped up by the Twins. Really, we went after a true closer, a huge guy from Georgia, six feet six inches, two hundred and sixty pounds. Covington Burrell. He's the son of a state police chief from Waynesboro way down in east Georgia. Apparently he's known as 'Cruiser.'"

Jack burst out laughing. "Cruiser! Because his dad's a police chief. Hey, that's cool. What's he got?"

"Well, he throws sidearm, right-handed. But he has an excellent eighty-eight to ninety mile-per-hour fastball. He's good for about thirty-five pitches, tops. Throws very hard for maybe two innings. He averaged two strikeouts an inning, and he led the SEC with twenty-one saves. There's one big strike against him, though."

"What's that?"

"He's Doughnut's best friend. They're arriving here together."

"Christ! Two of 'em."

"Can you imagine? Anyway, they've both had terrific seasons in the SEC, and you know that's the toughest conference in the country. Florida Gators, LSU Tigers, Arkansas Razorbacks, Tennessee Volunteers, Mississippi State, and all. You got to be real good to pitch down there."

"Tell me about it, Coach. You forgot the St. Charles Chevaliers. I used to be one, remember?"

"Yeah, come to think of it, I do remember. I remember a smoking fastball that scared every hitter in the Cape Marlin League half to death. I remember a curve that buckled knees, and I remember a slider that looked like it had just fallen off a goddamned cliff. And I remember a very tough kid who would pitch through pain, who refused to give in, who hated to lose. And who rallied the bull pen when we were in trouble. And I'm hoping to meet up with him again. Real soon."

"I hope so, Coach. I really hope so."

They rode in silence after that, heading south down the highway toward the bridge. Their ETA at the field was a little after seven o'-clock in the evening, but the traffic was terrible and it quickly became obvious they were not going to make it. So Ted called Russ Maddox and told him he would take Jack direct to his houseparents and the three of them would reconvene at the field at 8:30 sharp in the morning, when Jack would take up his old regular job as chief of ground staff.

Ward and Ann Fallon welcomed Jack like a prodigal son. They had been in touch with the McLures, and Tony Garcia was coming back, on Thursday, totally against the considerable will of his mother. Natalie had been persuaded by Ben that she was likely to do a lot more harm than good if she banned him from the game, whatever his law exams revealed.

They had excellent one-and-half-pound steamed lobsters from Maine for dinner. Ward Fallon whipped the little elastic bands off their claws and popped them, still kicking their tails, into the boiling water in the traditional Cape Marlin way. Fifteen minutes later, bright red, burning hot, and very dead, they emerged from the pot and Jack expertly prepared them for the table as he had always done the previous summer.

He wore rubber gloves, ripped off their long front antennae, then the claws. He broke the main pincers off, cracked them with a hammer, and popped the flesh straight out onto the plate. Then he broke the fins off the tail, twisted it right off the body, and used his middle finger to push out the biggest meat on the lobster, straight through the cavity and onto the plate. He drained excess water out of the main body, left the tumali, drained the plate, and handed it to Ann Fallon.

"Haven't lost that lightning touch with a crustacean, I'm glad to see," said Ann.

"No, ma'am," replied Jack. "Just wish I was as cool with my fast-ball."

"Russ Maddox told us you'd been very busy with exams and wanted your degree before you even considered a career in professional baseball."

Jack cottoned on in an instant. Russ and Ted did not want the community to know about his problems. For whatever reasons, they wanted to keep the reputation of the Lockport Flamethrower intact. And he trusted them, made his reply evasive, which was contrary to his nature, but plainly, in this case, necessary.

"I probably would have given it a shot, and then gone back to school if I'd failed. But my daddy wouldn't have it. Just refused to let me sign, turned down God knows how much money for me to go to the Brooklyn Bombers."

"Well, that's a relief," said Ward. "We're talking probably the richest and the worst franchise in either league. That Don Stargill, he went the right way about everything, leveling the ground, building a fabulous stadium right on the old Ebbets Field site. But by God he went the wrong way about building a Major League baseball team. All those big-name free agents he went for. You can have some guys on a team who are brilliant and loaded with money, and just past their best.

"But you need a nucleus of kids who are striving, fast, fit young guys who will run through a wall for you. Stargill didn't bother with them, and he's sure paying for it right now—the Bombers are losing game after game, and their farm system's lousy. I did hear he's about ready to sell the whole thing—but I think he'll probably hang in there, maybe go back into the market with hard cash. Those kind of guys always think they can buy anything . . ."

"Anyway, Dad wouldn't let me go," said Jack.

"That's because Dad knows what he's doing," added Ward. "How is the great man, by the way? We really hope to see something of him this season."

"He'll be here. No doubt—if I can just get my act together on the field."

"How long was your layoff?"

"A lot of weeks. Right now I need practice. Starting tomorrow, Ted's meeting me early."

"You need a ride?"

"No thanks, Mr. Fallon. I'll be running. I'm on a fitness program."

"That's good. Better get steamed into that lobster. Pure, packed white protein, build you up. Have some of this corn, and pass the salad. We're real glad to have you back, Jack."

The following morning Jack Faber set off for Cabot Field, a distance of around a mile. He wore his maroon track suit in a cool morning breeze, and moved at a fast pace for the short run. The village of Seapuit was quiet, and it was almost deserted beneath the huge towering oak trees which shade the sidewalk and most of the road all the way to the field.

A few people recognized him instantly—one of the girls from the village store, a man fixing his grass sprinklers, and a couple of passing gardeners calling out from their truck, "Hey, Jack, how you been? . . . Didn't know you were coming back, good to see you . . . Jack Faber, right? Go get 'em, buddy . . ."

Jesus. If they only knew.

It was strange how he felt so at home in the village. He had spent a total of only ten weeks here in his life. And yet he was welcomed like a returning hero, which to this baseball-mad population he most certainly was.

He ran on fast, pounding over the grass verge, driving forward, asking questions of his body and lungs, and receiving all of the right answers. He could see the deep-shaded turnoff to the field now, and he headed into the shadows, crossing the street. Out there before him was the parking lot, bathed in hot early sun. To the left was the long copse of pine trees among which the Seawolf players parked the few automobiles they had among them. He grinned to himself as he looked at the gap between the two tallest trees—the gap where the Dawgmobile had cooled its wheels throughout last season. The mere memory of Doughnut Davis always brought a smile to his lips.

He ran up through the empty forecourt to Cabot Field and stared out at the mound. The grass around it was cut but not manicured along the edges, and the dirt runways between the bases were rough and untended. There were, of course, no bags, no white lines. He'd have to fix all that.

Jack clipped open the tall, black wire gate to the infield and walked slowly over to the back of the mound. He hesitated for a moment and then he walked up the short dirt hill. He'd never lost a ball game up here, and he stared down to the plate, and he thought of his father, Ben, and how he too had stood on the mound at Luther Williams Field, in Macon, remembering far-lost glory.

He wondered if he too had entered the dream zone of the former pitcher, wishing it could all come back, knowing it never would. *There's only one thing sets me apart from Dad, and that's hope. I still hope it will come back. Dad knows it's over.*

Yet the memories crowded in upon him as if carried on the morning breeze. He felt the baseball in his hand, and he heard the howl of the crowd as he ripped that tailing fastball over the corner of the plate. And he heard the solitary yell of the umpire . . . *HEE-EEEE!* And if he concentrated hard, he could see Tony Garcia's big black catcher's glove way out in front of him. And he could hear the cry from the dugout of Coach Sando . . . *Throw it, Jack—throw it right now!* . . . The sound echoed in his mind.

No pitcher was ever prepared to try harder than Jack Faber. No pitcher.

Meantime he had not heard the arrival of Ted Sando's Chevy. And he had not noticed the big pitching coach leaning on the fence, with a somewhat amused smile, watching him standing alone, motionless on his old mound. And Jack turned quickly toward him, startled out of his daydream, and it was as if Teddy had read his thoughts.

"We'll get it back, big guy," he said softly. "We're gonna get it all back."

1 6

*T*ed Sando was a big man to be walking on eggshells. But he understood the fragile nature of his problem. One outburst of criticism, one insensitive remark, could very easily shatter what remained of Jack Faber's self-esteem.

He probably could risk the old familiar observations he had always made about Jack's work: *Keep your arm up on the breaking ball . . . shorten your stride a tad . . . you're a little long . . . elbow up . . . don't rush it now . . .* These were the tried and tested words of encouragement, uttered last season when Jack walked tall.

It was all different now, because Jack considered himself a midget among men who would once have scrambled just to hear his advice. Ted Sando was preparing to be very careful, concentrating only on the good pitches, ignoring the rubbish, forgetting the wayward, the slow, the high, and the wide, the fat, hanging curves, the slider that would not bite.

But first he needed to take a look, before even starting to build Jack up again, from the depths he now occupied.

Ted pulled on his glove and walked out onto the grass which was clipped down the left-field line toward the bull pen. There was no way they were going in there this morning.

He watched Jack walk off the mound and threw him a spare glove, and he watched the slow trepidation with which he pulled it on. Jack took off his tracksuit top and stood there just in his light warm-up shirt and sweatpants. "Okay, Coach," he said slowly. "Lemme feel the baseball."

Ted tossed it to him. Jack picked it up late and threw it back. There was approximately thirty feet between them. Ted threw again, watching carefully, trying to pick up in his mind a picture of the old Jack Faber, relaxed and fluid, every time he released the baseball. And already he sensed a stiffness in Jack's action, probably more of a tension than a stiffness. But it was there . . . "Just relax now. There's no one here. Just keep throwing the ball like always."

Ted edged back a little, increasing the distance between them to forty feet, and he threw the ball a little harder. Jack always caught it very easily, wherever he put it, but that infinitesimal suggestion of awkwardness was still there when the ball was returned.

Ted moved back some more and threw harder. Jack responded correctly, and after eight or nine minutes appeared to have found a rhythm. Ted went to fifty feet and began to put some real pressure on the ball, and Jack coped well, catching easily and throwing the ball back with equal weight behind it.

Now Ted could see something was wrong. He knew precisely what Jack Faber looked like throwing hard, even around 75 percent, as he was now. This, however, seemed different. The awkwardness had transformed into a rigidity to Jack's windup whenever he pulled his right arm back. And somehow the forward motion was rushed. At this speed Jack's aim seemed okay, and the ball was coming in straight, on the right side. They were only playing catch together, just warming up, but there was no doubt in the coach's mind, Jack was having to think about every throw.

This was not a natural motion. Jack Faber's lifelong affair with the baseball was on rocky ground. It was no longer second nature, and to recapture that silky-smooth delivery might be entirely dependent on the restorative skills of Ted Sando. The big lefty from Maine could already see the task was onerous, because Jack had lost his belief, and the very least of us need that.

"Jack, you feeling okay? Nothing hurts?"

"Yup. I'm fine."

"Okay. Let's go full-length for a few minutes. Just wanna watch you throw sixty feet, nice and loose. You look good, buddy, very steady, good easy motion." Both of them recognized the significant scale of the untruth.

The first six balls Jack sent in to Coach Sando revealed the obvious. He was trying to coax the baseball, forcing it, trying to aim it instead of throwing it, using the ball's own velocity.

"Slow down a little, Jack. Stick to your old fluid mechanics, keep your elbow up. Take something off it . . . just hit the spots for now."

Every pitcher knows that when a coach is saying "slow down," something is awry. And Jack allowed a look of irritation to pass over his face. Ted Sando noticed. *He thinks I'm just looking to criticize him,* he thought to himself. *What I really want to see is his rage, and frustration. That way I'll know he's deadly serious.*

He hurled the ball back to Jack, hard. And the pitcher caught it sharply. "Three more, buddy," he said. "Then we'll go and find Russ, maybe cut the grass a little."

Jack nodded and threw again to Ted, three times. Each ball came in at medium pace on the right, chest-high, where he aimed it. And each time Coach Sando could still see the tension that gripped Jack's body whenever he went into his windup.

They'd been throwing for twenty-five minutes. But Ted knew he had just stepped from one young lifetime to another.

Right then Russ Maddox came through the field gate and welcomed Jack back to Seapuit with warm enthusiasm. "Just take your time," he said. "Work with Teddy some more this afternoon, just hold it around seventy-five percent velocity, then we'll fit in a quiet bull-pen practice when Tony gets back tomorrow."

"Okay, Coach. I'm here to follow your instructions. Because I believe if anyone can get me back, it's you guys."

"You'll make it, Jack. I'm certain of that."

Russ Maddox was long on self-belief, and he was expert at handing it out to his players. And Jack was already feeling a lot better.

But the afternoon practice session with Ted Sando went no better. Jack listened carefully to the coach's comments. He could feel the curious awkwardness that Ted Sando could sense, and sometimes see. But it was life and death for Jack, and he tried everything to cure it. He told himself it was nothing less than nerves, and that he would ultimately get over them. But the longer he pitched the more permanent the condition became. He was like a tennis player who'd lost his backhand, a golfer whose touch on the green was gone, a fighter whose footwork had simply slowed down.

When he and Ted walked off the field that afternoon, Jack Faber was about ready to give up. And truthfully, Ted Sando's own brain was beginning to move in that same gloomy direction. And yet . . . and yet . . . Ted did not believe the problem was physical. He did not believe that somehow Jack had forgotten how to execute his art. So if he still knew *how to do it,* and he was in perfect physical shape *to actually do it,* how come he *could not do it?*

Clearly, Ted thought, it was rooted in Jack's mind. And he tried to think of a parallel, and there were many, but the best one concerned the immortal golfer Arnold Palmer, Ted's hero, golfer's hero. Arnie won four Masters between 1958 and 1964, which may seem like eight years but is in fact six years and three days. Between 1960 and 1963, he won a U.S. Open, and was twice runner-up. Between 1960 and 1962, he won two British Opens and was once runner-up, plus, during this short span of time, he won God knows how many other events.

Arnie was a howling comet, not a long-distance Boeing, like Jack, or Gary, or Faldo, or Tom Watson. But after 1964 he never won another major event. Not because he could no longer whack the ball a country mile, because he could. And not because he could no longer lay those long irons right up close, because he still could. What Arnie could no longer do was drop putts from all over the green, little pop-pop shots from twenty feet, ten feet, even four feet. And this was plainly not because he no longer had the strength, nor indeed that he had forgotten how to aim the ball straight for short distances.

This was in his mind. He called it the "gyps"—but somewhere, deep in the recesses of the psyche of one of the greatest golfers who ever lived, there was a sudden mental break, a tiny thought impulse that no longer told him, *Bang this baby straight in the hole, you can't miss,* but rather flickered and then suggested, *You can probably hole this, but it's a bit tricky.* Arnie no longer *believed* he could sink the big ones. At least, not like he used to.

That, in Ted Sando's opinion, was the root of the problem of 90 percent of all sports champions who go wrong. And he knew it was Jack Faber's. Worse, however, Jack was facing his demons all alone. He refused to talk about the issue. He would not reveal precisely what had happened to him down there in south Louisiana.

Thus the problem merely festered. And Ted Sando thought it would go on doing so, until Jack was ready to "talk it out," face the realities, and either smash them into shape, or quit. Right now Jack lived in some kind of a no-man's-land, where no one was speaking in a straightforward way. He was more or less restricted to "I can't." And Ted was afraid to lay some home truths on him, in case he caved in altogether. What Ted Sando wanted was a full, frank and fearless account of the predicament and inner workings of Jack Faber. And right now that was not even a possibility.

Both of them felt disconsolate as they left the field, but Jack was cheered up by the impending arrival this evening of Tony Garcia from Chicago and Ray Sweeney from Maine. Zac Colbert would be at Logan Airport at 9 P.M. and was being picked up by his houseparents. The Citadel guys were arriving tomorrow morning, and Kyle Davidson was coming in overnight from Los Angeles. Gino Rossi was driving up from New York. Doughnut in company with his buddy Cruiser was expected to steer the Dawgmobile into Seapuit from Georgia by lunchtime tomorrow.

Thus would arrive the nucleus of the new Seawolves roster. It was the biggest list of returning players Russ Maddox had ever welcomed home. And he treasured every one of them, even Doughnut, who had celebrated a surprisingly good spring season with the Bulldogs. He had successfully built some proper variations into his fastball and had somehow managed to find a couple of off-speed pitches. Well, nearly.

The fact was, the raging neurons that connected Doughnut's brain to his left arm were congenitally unable to resist the seething temptation to order a screamer, a 94 mph flame gun, straight at the plate, at all times, against all batters, in all circumstances. Doughnut could have thrown a great curve. In fact Doughnut *wanted* to throw a great curve. But an entirely different message kept elbowing its way onto his personal screen between the careful, planned windup and the release of the baseball: *LET 'EM HAVE IT, BABY . . . REAL SMOKE . . . RIGHT NOW . . . ONE HUNDRED MILES PER HOUR . . . THEY CAN'T HIT THAT . . . NOSSIR!*

All his life Doughnut Davis would have catchers contemplating the possibility of suicide as they stared up the hill at him, not knowing from one moment to another, what the hell was going to happen next.

Jack Faber began to laugh at the mere thought of the lanky Bulldog, but his own problems, as always, came crowding in upon him, and he jogged home in the late afternoon filled with misery, and an unnatural sense of loneliness, as if he was not a real part of the team, not a returning Cape League MVP, but an outsider, whose veneer of accomplishment was about to be shattered. And the expression on his face as he turned into the Fallons' driveway was not merely one of trepidation. It was a look of abstract terror for what the morrow would bring, when he finally stared down the sixty-foot six-inch space between the mound and the death mask of Tony Garcia.

The catcher from Northwestern arrived on the Cape at around six o'clock, checked into the McLures' house, and phoned Jack, who told him he was invited for dinner by prior arrangement and was to get his ass into gear forthwith.

When the two old buddies finally met outside the Fallons' front door, it was cause for celebration. Almost. Except that Tony knew something had gone drastically wrong with Jack's career. He'd heard a little from his mother, just snatches of her conversations with Ben, and Ted had called him shortly before he left Chicago, explaining a little, but not enough, of the situation.

In turn, Jack knew Tony had crashed and burned in his most recent prelaw exams, and only his father's intervention had persuaded Natalie to permit him to return to Cabot Field.

"Ben just about saved my ass," he said. "He told Mom I would never forgive her if she banned me from baseball. She let me come back, but boy, was she mad!"

"Will she come down here to watch you?"

"Are you kidding! Mrs. Garcia will probably never set foot in a ballfield again. She hated the game before. Right now she blames it for everything that's gone wrong with my academic career. And that's a lot of blame, trust me."

Jack laughed. "What did you do? Just give up hope?"

"Not exactly. But I only bothered with about half my workload for the junior-year law exam. I gambled that I'd be sure to get a few questions on the part I knew real well, so I'd stick to that and bag the rest till next semester. I figured I could do well enough to get through it."

"And?"

"No questions on the part I knew real well. Which left me to write about eight detailed answers on areas about which I didn't know diddly-squat."

"And what happened?"

"Well, from these slender indications of scholarship, the examining board concluded I was a fit and proper person to be flung out of the university on my ass."

"Holy shit! What saved you."

"A combo. My mom, my professor, and my baseball coach. She said it would never happen again, my professor said I was a near certainty in his opinion to become a Supreme Court judge, and the coach told 'em I was the best college catcher in North America."

"Not bad, right?"

"And not true either. The first two were really questionable, and the last one took into account my okay .271 average, but I threw a lot of guys out."

"Anyway you're here."

"Probably for my last hoorah. I have to get my schoolwork in order by Christmas, otherwise I'll have to give up baseball and work full-time the rest of the year for my degree. I guess if I got a huge offer in the draft, I'd take it, but I need that degree, and no one's going to pay me a ton of money if I'm not playing in the spring."

"You ever think of giving up the law and just concentrating on baseball?"

"I think about it every day of my life, but in the end I guess I could not do that to Mom, not after all she's given up for me. I have to get that degree, no matter what . . . anyway, how about you?"

Jack told him. Some. He also told him not to expect too much since he wasn't throwing real well.

And dinner was subdued for everyone, since both pitcher and catcher somehow knew Cape Marlin now represented a major turning point, for each of them.

By 1 P.M. the following afternoon, Jack, Tony, and Ray Sweeney were all at the field, leaning on the fence, chatting. Rick Adams and Bobby Madison were inside the team locker room getting changed, in company with Zac, Gino, and Kyle. The coaches were setting up the batting cage, and everyone was awaiting the arrival of Boom-Boom Hacker, whose reputation as a power hitter had preceded him and who was now crossing the bridge to Cape Marlin.

Steve Thompson was not expected until the next day, along with Pedro Rodriguez. The ETA of Doughnut and Cruiser was as unpredictable as everything else about the Georgia hurler, but rumor had it they were on the Cape, eating fried clams, and would hit the parking lot inside the hour. Zac Colbert had always carried a mobile phone, and he picked up Doughnut's first call from New Jersey. *"Making damn nearly a hundred miles per hour all the way, just like my fast-ball, right? Tell the guys to stand by . . . I'm gonna BE THERE! And I'm taking 'em all the way . . . just like last year . . . me and the Cruiser . . . YESSIR!"*

"Mother of God," said Zac. "Is this real? Or is he just another year younger?" And he shook his head briefly in amazement at the Dough-nut Davis time warp. He'd have shaken it some more had he been in the rear seat of the Dawgmobile, and seen the big man in the passenger seat raise his fist high and shout, *"YEEEE-HAH, DOUGHNUT, BABY . . . THEY'RE GONNA BE SAYING IT REAL SOON . . . ALL ABOUT US! HOW 'BOUT THEM TWO DAWGS!"*

The most recent message on Zac's cell phone read, "Eatin' clams right now, baby . . . Cabot Field two P.M. Clear the bull pen—we're comin' in." The caller was not identified, since Doughnut considered that the world, and indeed all human life, revolved entirely around him and his fastball.

Meanwhile the moment of truth loomed closer for Jack Faber. He and Kyle began warming up with Ted Sando and Tony Garcia, and Russ indicated he would accompany the pitchers to the bull pen.

Kyle Davidson went first. The six-foot 4-inch senior from Stan-ford had been drafted in the third round, but he had decided on an-other season in the Cape League. His father, an impressively wealthy senior partner in a Washington law firm, had told all callers to their sprawling Chevy Chase home that Kyle would not turn pro until he completed his degree, which did not please many of the callers.

Nonetheless, it did not discourage many of them either. The big be-spectacled hurler from Stanford was a rock-steady operator on the mound, impossible to shake out of his stride, thoroughly combative in his approach, with a tailing fastball that was near impossible to hit.

In the bull pen with Tony Garcia, he was much the same as last year, possibly a little stronger, but after just fifteen minutes it was clear he could very well claim the title of Strikeout King of the Cape League. The fastball was lethal, the curve unpredictable, the change-up deadly. And, better than the last half of the previous season, he was not hurting. The shoulder was good, the upper body strength improved, and no recurrence of the sharp twinges he had felt in his right knee. Mr. Reliable was all set to go.

And now Ted Sando called Jack Faber to the bull-pen pitcher's mound. He was well warmed up after ten minutes long-toss throwing with Zac Colbert, and now he walked up the dirt hill inside the cage and raised his left glove high for Tony to send him the ball.

Both coaches, Russ and Ted, stood discreetly behind Jack, and everyone watched Tony Garcia go into his crouch, full-length away from the pitcher now, and say softly, as he had done so many times before, "Okay, Jack . . . let's get nice and loose . . . let's find our rhythm . . . just fastballs, right? . . . Sixty to seventy-five percent . . . lemme have the inside corner first."

And Jack began to throw, sweating now, feeling that the entire world was watching him while he strove for the inside half of the plate. He felt strong, but the ball would not fly the way it once had. It had almost no "run" to it, no movement, no dip.

This was the first time Tony had caught Jack since the championship final last year. And there was a puzzled expression on his face. Finally he caught the tenth pitch and stood up. "Jack, you throwing all four-seam fastballs? Any two-seams?"

"Everything's two-seams. That's all I'm throwing."

Right then Tony Garcia knew his buddy was in big trouble. He'd caught a thousand pitches from the big right-hander, and he knew precisely what a two-seam fastball from Jack Faber ought to look like . . . even now he was still anticipating that lightning, dipping swerve of the ball as it streaked toward his glove. But there was no movement today. The ball came in flat and straight.

"Okay, pal," he said. "Let's go outside half."

Jack nodded, and sent in four fastballs, showing reasonable control, about two-thirds maximum velocity, to the outside edge of the plate. But again there was no movement, and then the fifth pitch got clean away and flew up and in, missing by almost two feet. Tony glanced at Jack and picked up a look of desolation on his face. For a split second he thought Jack might break down.

But he stayed cool and shouted, "Okay, Jack. Let's settle in here. Those first four looking good. C'mon, nice and relaxed up there, big fella . . ."

"Give me a minute, Tony."

"No problem," said the catcher, and moved toward the fence where Ted was now standing. "Ball's very flat, Coach. Real flat. It's as straight as a dart." Ted nodded and walked casually back to Russ, muttering, "Mechanics look okay, but there's sure as hell something not right."

Russ Maddox frowned.

Tony called out, "Okay, Jack. Let's see the slider." And he saw the pitcher visibly freeze. Last season he'd watched Jack react badly to a call for the slider. But not quite like this, because now he held his head low, communicating nothing if not despair.

Tony placed his glove on the outer edge, right-hand side of the plate. "Okay, babe," he said. "Let's go. Give 'em the ol' Faber snap, just like they're dropping off the table."

And Jack pitched four, none of them with any snap. Ted Sando walked in and Tony could not help himself. "No good, Coach," he said. "They all stayed right on the table."

And Ted shook his head, walked back to Russ, and told him, "You saw it. That's where his confidence is gone."

"You gotta get it back, Teddy. He's gotta find that confidence in all his pitches, especially his slider. Because if he doesn't have that, he's finished."

Ted Sando nodded and called out, "Okay, Jack. Five more. Two fastballs, a chang-up, and a coupla sliders mixed up."

And with marginal resolve, Jack threw again. None of the five pitches had any snap or swerve. And Ted walked in again, and tried to get into Jack's mind.

"Well, old buddy? What did you think of your first bull pen?"

"It sucked. And you know it."

"Well, why do you think it sucked?"

Jack hesitated. Then he blurted out, "Same reason I sucked all season. I don't have anything left. And it ain't comin' back."

"That's where you're wrong. And that's enough of that attitude."

The conversation might have been prolonged except for the squeal of a scarlet Cadillac convertible's tires on the blacktop parking lot accompanied by an atomic, stereo blast: *"BECAUSE WE'RE FROM THE COUNTRY—AND WE LIKE IT THAT WAY . . ."*

Both driver (Doughnut) and passenger (Cruiser) had their Bulldog caps raised high, and their arrival was well rehearsed. As the engine died, they yelled in precise unison, *"YEEEE-HAH! FIFTEEN HUN-DRED MILES, AND RIGHT ON TIME—NOT TOO BAD FOR A COUPLA DAWGS!"*

At which point they both dissolved into uncontrollable laughter, stunned at their own wit.

"Holy shit!" said Russ. "Two of 'em! Am I ready for this?"

Doughnut bounded out of the Dawgmobile, followed by his much bigger colleague. He walked straight to Russ, and announced, "I wanna pick this team up right where I left off last year. Get the fastball smoking, right, Coach? That's what you wanna see, right? The Davis fastball . . . one hundred miles per hour, right over the corner. YESSIR."

Before Russ could answer, Doughnut had hauled his six-foot six-inch buddy forward. "Right here I wanna introduce my teammate Mr. Covington Burrell from Waynesboro, east Georgia. He's a reliever by profession, hurls thunderbolts for about two innings. If he can't get 'em out, they can't be got out. Nossir. Coach, you can call him Cruiser, that's what most everyone calls him back in Georgia, 'cept for his history professor, who ain't never paid him no never mind on account the Cruiser don't know the difference between Henry Ford and Henry the Eighth, but he's reached ninety miles per hour—"

"SHUT UP, DOUGHNUT, WILLYA?" said Russ. "Just for a minute. Hey, Cruiser, welcome to the Seawolves. We got a big job waiting for you, and every report we have says you have the ability to make it happen."

"Real glad to meet you, Coach," replied Mr. Covington Burrell. "Heard a lot about you from Doughnut."

Russ grinned. "Most of it bad, I guess."

"Yeah, most of it was pretty bad," replied the Cruiser, ingenuously. "But that ain't gonna stop me and the Doughnut carrying this little outfit to glory. Nossir."

"Jesus, Coach," said Doughnut, interjecting. "You should have seen me and the Cruiser out there in the Bulldog uniform . . . one time against Tennessee we had 'em down seven–three—came out after seven and the Cruiser took 'em down with nineteen pitches! Nine called strikes in the eighth, nine strikes and a ball in the ninth. How 'bout that, Coach!"

At which point Doughnut moved onto one foot, raised his left knee high, and pumped his right arm furiously: *"WAY TO GO, COACH, RIGHT! BAM-BAM-BAM . . . GET 'EM OUTTA HERE . . . FASTBALL, RIGHT?"*

Even Russ laughed. But Doughnut, now in more serious mode, moved back onto both feet and declared, "Of course, he ain't as good as me, because he doesn't have my stamina or power. But he's an excellent reliever. If he just had my velocity on the off-speed pitches, he could probably follow me to the Majors."

"Doughnut," said Russ. "You don't have an off-speed pitch."

"Right, Coach, right. But that's what I'm working on right now. Good speed on the curves and change-up. That's what I'm aiming for."

"Doughnut," said Russ. "Have you ever thrown a curve or a change-up?"

"Not quite yet, Coach. But that's where I'm going. That's what I'm thinking. Soften 'em up a little with the ol' fastball, right? . . . then dazzle 'em with the off-speed . . . then back to the fastball . . . the way you like it, right, Coach? *BAM-BAM-BAM! YESSIR.*"

"Doughnut," said Russ wearily. "Will you get changed and report to Coach Sando in the bull pen—Tony's there. Take Cruiser. Show him the ropes."

"Before we go, Coach, there's one little routine you gotta see." And with that he and Cruiser went into a kind of crouch . . . low five . . . middle five . . . high five. Three sharp claps, and then the chorus, sung loud and off-key: *"GONNA MAKE A STRI-I-KEOUT FOR JESUS, AT THE HOME PLATE OF LIFE!"*

Neither player waited for the applause. They just bolted for the changing room.

"Fuck me," said Russ Maddox. "I guess the Bulldogs just landed."

Ten minutes later Cruiser took the mound, pitching sidearm to Tony Garcia. He threw rockets, the classic warm-up for a true closer. Jack and Doughnut stood watching with Ted Sando, watching Mr. Covington Burrell hurl some really nasty right-arm pitches across the plate to the right-hand outside corner.

"Jesus, he comes from behind the right-handed batter, doesn't he?" murmured Jack, to no one in particular.

When the Cruiser finished, and Doughnut introduced him to "the top Cape League pitcher last year, my good buddy Jack Faber," the two new teammates shook hands warmly.

"One thing, Cruise," said Jack. "Think about making that ball tail in on the righty's hands. Don't keep pitching to the outside like we do in college. You take that hard pitch to the inside half, you're gonna turn a lotta bats into firewood . . . You can nibble on the out-side—but you take my advice, you'll have 'em eating out of your hand."

Cruiser nodded gravely.

"Listen to him, buddy," said Doughnut. "Jack's the best college pitcher I ever saw. Even my own daddy says that, and he's some bi-ased."

Jack nodded and turned away, as if unable to cope with his own predicament, and without another word, set off on his regular train-ing run, pounding the outfield between the foul posts.

Coach Sando muttered, "He sure doesn't sound like a guy with no confidence." And then he thought, *Everyone knows he can pitch that stuff he's talking about, anytime he wants. Everyone except Jack Faber.*

By now Pedro Rodriguez had arrived from Florida State, and the moment he began pitching, it was plain he had modeled himself en-tirely on his hero and family friend, the Boston Red Sox ace Pedro Martinez, both of them from Santa Domingo.

The new Pedro pitched with a very loose arm action, and some-how the ball exploded out of his hand. He would have signed a pro-fessional contract as a youth, but he had made a solemn promise to his mother he would become the first-ever member of his family to have a college education. He was majoring in physical education, which wasn't very challenging, but Pedro possessed a superb fastball, and a truly brilliant command of his pitches. And those two assets would surely compensate him financially on the . . . well . . . home plate of life.

Tony wound up the practice, telling Coach Sando, "Right here we got a starter. Pedro can put the ball right where he wants it. I'd say he was around eighty-five, eighty-seven miles per hour today, but he's got a little more pop than that . . . you see how smooth he is?"

Pedro himself seemed pleased with his work. He flashed a wide Caribbean smile at the coach and said, "Okay, when's our day off?"

"What!" exclaimed Sando. "You just got here, for Christ's sake! What d'you mean, day off?"

"Gimme the dates we don't play, Coach, that's all."

"Well, we play forty-four times in fifty days, so there's not many."

"Can I get the dates?" Pedro persisted.

"Sure. They're not a state secret . . . I'm just a little surprised at your attitude. You're not on vacation, you know. You're gonna be a starting pitcher for the Seawolves. That's important, right?"

"Sure, Coach," said Pedro. "But my great friend Pedro Martinez has the best tickets in Fenway Park for me anytime I want to go see him pitch. He's sending a car down to pick me up, anytime I can make it."

And he beamed his great smile at Ted Sando and added, "You wanna come with me, see Pedro pitch, have supper with him afterward?"

"Jesus Christ," said Ted. "Wednesday. June nineteenth. If he's on the mound, count me in."

Meanwhile Doughnut was pitching to Tony, and he had never looked better. There were no off-speed pitches, but the fastballs were screaming in, more or less on target. Until the eighth pitch, that is, which rocketed four feet above Garcia's head and jammed in the wire fence.

"Thank God for that," said Tony. "I was beginning to think you'd lost your touch."

Doughnut glared at him. "I'm getting there, boy. Don't ever forget that. I'm getting there. Just wanna make sure you stay alert."

"Okay, fucking Georgia genius. Lemme have one up and away."

Doughnut hurled in a thunderbolt, straight at the dirt, kicked up two feet in front of the plate.

Tony blocked it, knocked the ball down, and stood up. "How about we try that one again? Just a little higher, maybe three feet, tailing outside, on the right side, as instructed."

Doughnut glared. Then he reared back and sent in a perfect tailing fastball at around 94 mph. Tony's glove whipped up across his mask, to his right, and the ball smacked into the leather.

"HOW 'BOUT THAT, COACH!" yelled Doughnut, wheeling around to face Ted Sando. *"YOU SEE THAT? YOU SEE THAT, COACH? I'M TELLING YOU . . . NO ONE HITS THAT PITCH. NO ONE. NOSSIR."*

"Outstanding," said Coach Sando. "Nothing less than outstanding. Stay focused now. Keep watching Tony's glove." And he tried to concentrate on the pitching of the Bulldog. But his eyes kept straying to the outfield, to the solitary figure of Jack Faber, running hard, alone, as ever, with his demons.

*   *   *

On Sunday afternoon, June 11, the new edition of the Seawolves began their defense of the Cape League Championship with their traditional opening game at Cabot Field against the Henley Mets. The little ground on the slopes above the ocean was packed with fans come to see a team with which they were extremely familiar— Adams, Madison, Rossi, Colbert, Sweeney, Garcia, the heroes of last season, all still in the lineup.

The pitcher, however, was new, because Russ Maddox had decided to start Pedro Rodriguez, with Doughnut ready to pitch in short or long relief. Jack Faber would start game two at Exeter. Kyle would face the Sentries at Cabot Field in game three.

As things turned out, the 'Wolves rolled to a big, easy lead, scoring nine runs on fifteen hits. Pedro shut the Mets out for seven strong innings before Doughnut came in to finish it. And, as always, he had his moments.

He sent down the first two batters at the top of the eighth and then swiftly loaded the bases with three consecutive walks. His next pitch was slammed back at him, and Doughnut snagged it on his right side, shoulder-high, six feet from the top of the mound. He grabbed the ball from his glove and hurled it at first base, dead straight, at close to 90 mph, approximately eight feet above the first baseman's head. The Mets runners at second and third both scored to make it 9–2. A spectator tossed the ball back into the park from the middle of a scrub-oak thicket.

Sando covered his eyes and shook his head. But Doughnut recovered and sent down three blazing fastballs, all called strikes, and he walked in with the loud applause of the Seapuit faithful in his ears. In the dugout, Doughnut was looking for his Georgia colleague.

"Hey! Cruise ! *HOW 'BOUT THAT?*"

"Doughnut, you were awesome, man. Came off that mound like a cat pouncing on that ball."

Sando just growled, "But the goddamned throw was like a stray cat. For fuck's sake, Doughnut. Two really stupid runs. You had him, then chucked it away. Goddammit."

But all he could hear, moving down the dugout, was the unmistakable voice of the Bulldog hurler: "I'm telling you, Cruise, I'm getting there. Fastball . . . they can't hit that. *NOSSIR!*"

The bottom of the eighth and top of the ninth were subdued. Both teams went down in order, and the score stayed at 9–2, Doughnut formally acknowledging the cheers of the crowd for his two called strikeouts and a pop-up fly ball to Rick Adams.

All the players went home early for dinner. They were traveling to the western shore of the Cape to the Maritime Academy the following day, but Russ did not think that the team there was much good. They traditionally had poor attendance, and it was a good place to give Jack a start. Kind of private. Not too much pressure.

However, two hours before they were due to report to the field to sort out the cars for the journey, Jack received a call from his father which was nothing short of staggering.

"Jack," said Ben. "Tomorrow morning I'm flying out of here in a helicopter to the main offices of Louisiana Oil and Gas. In return for any and all mineral rights on our land, they're transferring two million shares, which stand at fifty-six dollars each, into my name. In return for that, I've waived all bonuses in perpetuity. As of today, it's a done deal. I just have to sign my agreement. Son, that means you and I are worth about a hundred and twelve million dollars between us, right now. So get out there tonight and throw anything you darn feel like. Anyone gives you any grief, we'll buy their job, their team. Hell, we'll buy the darn league!"

Jack had to sit down. He knew, of course, that something like this had been coming. But now it was here, in reality. Ben and Jack were rich beyond dreams, and the consequences of that were huge. He knew that, and he tried to imagine what would happen to him, and whether that great fortune would finally mean the end of him as a pitcher, making him too rich to care any longer about baseball.

But when he spoke to his father, he spoke not of money. He spoke about the only thing that had ever really mattered. "Dad," he said. "Do you still think I could get back? Even though we're rich? I guess what I mean is, do you think I can get back to the way I was on the baseball mound?"

Ben Faber's heart was so full he was unable to find the words to answer. Jack's voice was a soulful cry of private anguish for his lost art, together with a simple betrayal of his undiminished love for the game he and his father had shared for so long.

Ben Faber had no need for illusion. He'd always had the wisdom to know that nothing lasts, except memories trapped in the evergreen outfield of the mind. The great and glorious American game was designed, after all, somehow to break your heart.

17

By midafternoon the 'Wolves were on their way to the windswept Cape Marlin side of Hawke's Bay, where the Maritime Academy was sited. Jack remembered that wind from last season, gusting and building throughout the early evening, even when the rest of the Cape sat sweltering in the normal dying twilight breeze.

He had pitched there only once, and was never comfortable on the mound. The wind often whipped up minor dust storms in the wide runway between second and third base, and the gusts from the sea seemed always to blow into the face of the pitcher, irritating him, making everything more difficult, whispering that tonight the force was with the hitters. In the present stacked deck of Jack's personal psyche, conditions at the academy would *never* be in his favor.

He warmed up for twenty minutes before game time and sat quietly with Kyle, watching the Seawolf hitters making early season swipes with their new wooden bats. In fact, Gino Rossi, the old stickball king of New York's Little Italy, whacked the second pitch he received hard down the third-base line. As a well-executed swing, it was nothing short of a complete fluke, but Gino came out of the blocks like a sprinter and beat the throw to first base.

While Rick Adams and Zac Colbert both managed to fly out to center, Rossi stole second. And up came Boom-Boom Hacker, the golf pro's son with the wide swing like Ted Williams. Second pitch, he nailed the baseball with a stupendous blow, and a low liner ripped through the grass, slashing its way past the Braves second baseman. Whatever else happened, Gino was in for the run, and the first baseman, set up for the cutoff behind the mound, dropped the ball as Boom-Boom came rounding the bag.

When the inning ended, a few minutes later, after Ray Sweeney was caught out by the right-field fence, the 'Wolves held a 1–0 lead. At which point, his stomach churning, his heart pounding, Jack Faber walked out to the mound for his first start since the championship game last year.

He stood behind the slope for a few minutes, squeezing the rosin bag in his right hand. Then he slowly climbed the little hill, which was a routine walk to work for most pitchers, but for Jack it was like scaling the face of Mount Rushmore.

Over the public-address system he now heard the words, *"And on the mound for the Seawolves tonight is last year's Cape League MVP, Jack Faber."*

"Oh, why the hell did they have to do that?" he muttered,

And he took his eight warm-up pitches in a gloomy frame of mind, knowing he was not up to this challenge, aware that he was still unable to put any movement on the ball, that he was afraid of throwing breaking balls, scared sideways that the hard twist of his wrist would somehow send the baseball into orbit. It was, of course, the endless nightmare of all pitchers, great and small.

He threw three hard fastballs, and five off-speed pitches. The velocity was fine, direction okay, movement poor. Tony Garcia knew this, and he prepared to watch his old friend submit to the wheel of fortune, trying to control a section of space, sixty-feet six-inches long, seventeen-inches wide, and three-feet high.

The leadoff Braves batter stepped up to the plate and Jack threw him a fastball almost a foot wide of the plate. The hitter left it, couldn't reach it. And Jack threw two more fastballs, both of which the batter fouled off. The umpire signaled a 1–2 count, and Jack hurled a fastball inside, but not tight enough, and the Exeter slugger lined it over the head of Rick Adams for a base hit.

The second Brave, another right-hander, came to the plate and completely ignored the first two pitches, high fastballs. Finally Jack fired one over the plate with a velocity of almost 88 mph for a called strike on the inside corner. It was a 2–1 count and the runner took off to steal on the next pitch. Bobby Madison moved into the bag, ready for that steal, and the hitter instinctively attacked Jack's next pitch, cracking the ball hard into the now bigger second-base gap.

The 'Wolves right fielder, Steve Thompson out of Columbia, came racing across to field the ball brilliantly off his left foot. He went straight into his crow hop and unleashed a rocket to third base. But it was just too late, and the Braves had runners on the corners with nobody out.

The next hitter stepped up, a big, burly, thoroughly bad-news slugger from Nebraska named Jed Rowley. He had not only hit .340 in the recent College World Series in his hometown of Omaha, he had finished second in the Big Twelve with seventeen home runs. And now he faced Jack Faber, warily, conscious of the pitcher's towering reputation last year.

The first two fastballs did not tempt Jed Rowley, They were both wide. Too wide, in the opinion of Tony Garcia. In fact, there was nothing about Jack's fastball he liked, and he rammed three fingers down his right thigh, signaling a slider, away. Jack's head was filled with alarm bells, and in the silence of the small Exeter crowd he turned to the dugout, and Ted called out, *"Confidence in yourself, son. Confidence."*

Jack pressed his index finger tight over the long part of the seam, his thumb directly underneath. He held the ball loosely with the rest of his hand, but he was apprehensive, timid, and he threw it with no snap. The ball floated in, breaking possibly three or four inches. Not enough. Rowley turned on it, crushed the ball right over the fence, deep into the woods. Exeter 3, Seawolves 1.

Tony Garcia immediately went to the mound, and his face was full of concern. He could see the frustration written all over Jack's face, and he told him, "Come on, buddy. You're okay. We'll get the runs back . . . just let's find the groove."

"I haven't had a groove since the last time I wore this uniform," Jack replied.

"Come on!" said Tony, who now stood there utterly perplexed at this terrible change in Jack's attitude. And he could only think of the Atlanta Braves' Mark Wohlers, who had surely been the best young pitcher in the country in the midnineties, and suddenly lost it right at the top of his game, ended up back in the Minors, and was then traded. He never found it again.

And then there was Rick Ankiel of the St. Louis Cardinals, the single-best pitching prospect in the country not so long ago. Rick suffered a traumatic collapse in his game and, like Mark, ended up in the Minors, often throwing pitches clean over the heads of both catcher and batter, straight to the backstop. No one could explain what had happened to either of them, but Tony Garcia was a catcher and he understood the hundredth of a second in which a pitcher can turn a perfect throw into a disaster.

He was consumed with sadness as he stared helplessly at Jack Faber. For all he knew, the pitcher was thinking the same thing he was, because it was now clear to both of them that Jack could not throw. And before the game was more than five minutes older, he had walked the next two hitters.

In Tony's opinion, this was becoming serious. The game was getting away from them, and on his very next pitch to the Braves catcher, the ball was slammed high into the gap in right field. Thompson, however, was on it, and he came hurtling toward center and made a sensational diving catch. He bounced straight up and hurled the ball into second base, doubling off the runner, who had hastily broken for third.

It was a freaky double play, but there was nothing freaky about the next sequence. Jack threw four straight balls to walk the next hitter, again putting runners on first and second. And the next Brave banged a hard gapper way out to the fence in right, and both runners scored, despite a terrific throw by Thompson to home plate.

Jack finally ended the inning when Ray Sweeney caught a long fly ball out in center field, but it was 5–1 Braves and the Seawolf coaches were not pleased.

Jack walked into the dugout with his head down. Ted came up to meet Garcia and asked him, "Where were those pitches?"

"Coach, when he's around the zone, the pitches are right down the damned chute. There's no action."

"Are you using all the pitches?"

"That three-run bomb was supposed to be a slider. It looked like a fucking beach ball."

Ted nodded, went back down the steps, and pulled Jack over. He had no time to say anything. Jack said it for him. "Coach, I don't have anything. I got nothing."

Ted Sando could not believe what he had seen out there, and he surely could not believe what he was hearing right now. And he snapped, "That's bullshit, Jack."

"I'm not trying to bullshit anybody. I've got nothing."

Ted was speechless and they all sat in silence as the big hitters in the Seawolves lineup proceeded to get nothing out of their second inning. It was as if the shattering pitching performance had cast gloom over the entire team, and the Seapuit faithful sat quietly in this particularly uncomfortable stadium, unable to believe their eyes. *What's going on out there? This is Jack Faber, right?*

Any other coach would probably have sent out a new pitcher for the bottom of the second, but Ted could not erase the memory of the peerless practitioner from last year. He just kept praying this nightmare would go away and that Jack would suddenly send in his howling fastball, tailing away over the corner, followed by that priceless dipping slider.

Jack walked back out to the mound. And his first pitch to the first batter was an inside fastball, two feet off target, which hit the batter on his upper arm, sending him to first. The next one was a soft change-up which the batter bunted nastily down the third base line and charged down the runway as the ball nestled in the chalk. He beat the throw, and there were two runners on in less than two minutes of the inning.

Sando instantly called *"TIME!"* and came out to the mound while Russ Maddox sent a pitcher down to the bullpen, Matt Donovan, newly arrived from Harvard.

Ted still had not given up. "Jack," he said. "You have to work your way out of this. But it's gotta be you that wants to. I can't give you that determination."

"Okay, Coach. I'll do what I can. But don't hold your breath."

And from that point, things went from bad to grotesque. Jack was hit twice in succession, both fastballs that dropped into left field. The new batter came up and in response to a call for a fastball low and away, Jack hurled in a fat-looking pitch that rode up and in on the hitter.

Tony signaled to the outside corner, and Jack threw one a foot wide. Again the hitter left it, and then stood back to watch Jack hurl a third fastball, straight into the dirt for a 3–0 count. The fourth pitch tailed up and away, and the umpire called out, *"BALL FOUR!"* And the bases were loaded.

Jack looked at the dugout in the unmistakable attitude of total surrender. And Ted said to Russ Maddox, "Right now we got a pitcher out there who wants nothing to do with this game."

"Yeah, we can't have this. Can't have a guy who doesn't want to compete for us. Get Donovan right away."

Ted called "*TIME!*" and walked to the mound. He held out his hand for the ball and Jack walked back to the dugout amid total silence.

Matt Donovan answered the signal and came loping out of the bull pen toward the mound. He took his warm up pitches and began work, but the situation could not be saved. Two more runs went in from the loaded bases, and the 'Wolves came out to bat at the top of the third, 7–1 down.

From there it was a grim battle for five more innings and no one could accuse the 'Wolves of lacking the heart for the battle. They scrapped and clawed for runs, while Matt Donovan did an unbelievable job of shutting the door on the Braves hitters.

The big Seawolf bangers, Sweeney, Colbert, and Boom-Boom, had six hits between them, Rick Adams stole two bases, and Steve Thompson stole three. When the dust cleared after the top of the eighth, the Braves still had it, but the score was 7–6, and the Wolves were in full cry.

Again the Braves came up to try to increase that slender lead, and now Ted Sando pulled the tired Donovan from the game, calling in the Cruiser to relieve for the first time. And the big man from east Georgia was everything Doughnut had declared him to be.

He sent down the first two Braves with six pitches, two called strikes and four fans. At the conclusion of this bombardment, an ecstatic Doughnut leaped to the top of the dugout steps, raised his right leg high, pumped his right arm like a locomotive piston, and yelled into the crowd: "*THAT'S MY BOY! THAT'S MY CRUISER! START THE SIRENS! THE CRUISER'S ON HIS WAY!*"

Out on the mound Covington Burrell heard the commotion and signaled back to Doughnut his own joy, moving onto one leg, pumping his arm, and yelling back: "*HERE'S A STRI-I-IKEOUT FOR JESUS AT THE HOME PLATE OF LIFE . . .*"

By this time the umpire had heard quite enough, and he bawled at the pitcher, "*PLAY BALL, WILLYA? THIS IS A BASEBALL GAME NOT A GODDAMNED REVIVAL MEETING!*"

The Cruiser nodded curtly, and sent in a fastball, tailing away over the corner of the plate for a strike. The batter hit the next one hard underneath and it shot about a hundred feet into the air, straight up. Tony Garcia edged back about two feet and caught it in his most leisurely, annoying fashion, one-handed, communicating to the opposition a very casual contempt. Garcia was great at that.

And the Braves went down for the eighth time, still holding the 7–6 lead, now only three outs away from victory. Right now the stakes were high, and the Seawolves began to line up, Gino Rossi running out to the plate, Rick Adams pulling on his gloves, Zac Colbert taking practice swings with the weighted bat.

The Braves pitcher opened the inning with a soft, off-target curveball, high and in. Rossi, who still had some pretty tough edges to him, leaned right in, took it on the upper arm, dropped the bat, and jogged to first base.

The Braves coach was out of his dugout like a bullet, running to the plate umpire, shouting, *"HE LEANED INTO THAT PITCH— GODDAMMIT, HE NEVER EVEN TRIED TO GET OUT OF THE WAY."*

The umpire was having none of it. "Get outta here, Coach," he said evenly. "He didn't have to get out of the way. He was waiting for the ball to break, and it never broke. That's all."

There was no emotion in the ump's voice, just the calm of measured judgment. And the Braves coach retreated, muttering, but not loudly. One on, nobody out.

Rick Adams came to the plate and swung hard at a junky knuckleball. To his amazement he whacked it on the top side of the baseball, and it spun awkwardly onto the dirt between second and third, one-hopping the shortstop off his chest. Rick took off, charging toward first base, and just beating out the throw.

This put runners on first and second, and they were two of the fastest men in the entire Cape League. The Braves pitcher was well aware of the situation, and three times he arrowed the ball to second, attempting to hold Rossi back from getting a big lead. But he was never even close to throwing Gino out, and when finally he did pitch to Colbert, he hurled a vicious fastball straight into the dirt, a foot in front of the plate.

The catcher blocked it, but the ball got away to his right. And the Seawolf fliers took off like Olympic sprinters. Rossi, going for his life, slid easily into third, and Adams, the two-hundred-meter star from The Citadel, beat out the catcher's throw to second without even coming off his feet. That put two Seawolves in scoring position, no one out, with a 1–0 count to Colbert.

The Braves coach came out to the mound but made no change, and retreated, leaving a frustrated and angry pitcher facing the distinct possibility of defeat. He reared back and launched an inside screamer at the edge of the plate, but the delivery was rushed and the ball was never going to tail in far enough. It just about bisected the plate, thigh-high, with nothing on it. Zac Colbert could not recall missing one of these since he left high school, and he slammed it straight out to the fence, where it hit the wire and rebounded two feet back onto the field.

Rossi waited to tag up, but Adams was already pounding toward third. As the ball hit the fence Rossi exploded down the final runway for home, with Adams now about six feet behind him, gaining with every stride, arms pumping, cleats churning up the dust as if he were crushing grapes.

The throw from the outfield was right on target to the cutoff man, who wheeled around and rifled a frozen rope straight into the catcher's mitt. The fielding was immaculate for a team under huge pressure to hold on to a one-run lead. But Rossi and Adams had already shaken hands by the time the ball got there, and the Braves lead was gone: 8–7 'Wolves.

There was still no one out, except for the Braves pitcher, who was summarily removed in favor of a big, lumbering closer named Kane from the University of Iowa. And he swiftly put a stop to the visiting team's onslaught. Ray Sweeney hit his first fastball straight at the second baseman, who caught it and doubled off Colbert at the bag. Then Bobby Madison popped up the second fastball to the shortstop.

Which left Cruiser Burrell to make the final three outs. And he went for it with all the inherent aggression that keeps the natural-born closer in business. His first pitch came tailing in about a foot from the hitter's wildly swinging bat. The second one tailed inside and snapped the bat in two, sending the barrel flying toward Cruiser's right ankle. Covington leaped high, snagged the soft one-hop ball as it came by, and threw instantly to first base for the out.

He sent down the second Brave with three straight called strikes, which sent Doughnut almost delirious with delight, and pumping his arm, he shouted, *"SOUND THE SIRENS . . . HERE COMES THE CRUISER!"*

The third Braves hitter was a very determined character from UCLA, and he stared hard at the 'Wolves reliever, took two strikes on the shoulder, and let rip at a dipping fastball, banged it straight back over the pitcher with undisguised venom. Cruiser's glove moved high, very high, well over eight feet above the mound, and everyone heard the clean catch, the unmissable sound of the ball smacking into the leather.

Cruiser raised his mighty right arm and spiked the ball hard into the mound with the force of a jackhammer. It stayed there like a white half-moon buried in the dirt. Without a second glance at anyone, Covington Burrell marched down the slope toward the dugout into a tumult of applause, with one voice raised high above the rest.

"THAT'S MY GUY, RIGHT! THAT'S MY CRUISER! HOW ABOUT THAT, COACH . . . ? HOW 'BOUT THAT FASTBALL! HEY! COACH . . . HOW 'BOUT THEM DAWGS!"

Doughnut, right arm still pumping, left leg still two feet above sea level, was as happy with vicarious glory as he would have been with personal glory. *"GEORGIA BOYS GETTIN' IT DONE, RIGHT, COACH? THAT'S WHAT IT'S ALL ABOUT . . . GETTIN' IT DONE."* Which added up to a lot of ecstasy for a guy who wasn't even playing.

At the opposite end of the scale, Jack Faber sat forlornly on his own at the end of the dugout. He did not feel like speaking to anyone, and no one felt much like sharing his personal gloom. For many pitchers, the team snatching victory from the open jaws of defeat might have alleviated the damage to pride and ego, after he'd given up, effectively, all seven runs. But for Jack, the triumph made it worse. In his mind it reduced him to the complete outsider. If he played, it was a disaster. But once he was removed, they could roll to victory without him. They didn't need him. He was just a liability.

He picked up his bag and made his way to Ted Sando's car, and waited for the coach to turn up for the drive home to Seapuit. He felt unable to face the upbeat mood of his teammates, preferring instead the stern lecture he would receive from his old mentor.

But Ted was very thoughtful. He drove the Chevy out of the parking lot and just said, "Team played pretty well, eh, Jack? And, by the way, Russ and I still want you to be a part of the team. Remember, neither Donovan, Cruiser, or Doughnut can hold a candle to you when you're straight. And the time's getting awful close when you have to tell me *precisely* what happened to you back at school last year."

"I've told you I lost it. Isn't that enough?"

"No. It's not. It's nothing like enough. I want to know everything. We gotta talk this out. I'm not a goddamned shrink, but you have to get all the hurt and stuff out of your system. Jack . . . you're a completely different person from last year. You're remote, separate, and obviously damaged. And you're damaged in some way I don't begin to understand. You act like a guy who's suffered some terrible injustice. And I don't know what's behind it."

"I told Russ not to bring me up here. I told him right on the phone when he called. The trouble is, no one listens to me."

"I think it's more like no one believes you. You just keep saying you're finished. But no one who knows anything about this game could accept that, not if they'd seen you pitch last year. That slider . . . Wow! That was some delivery. I never saw a kid could throw one better."

"Well, I can't throw it now."

"I accept that. But my question is, why? Why can't you throw it?"

"I don't know."

"You don't want to know. That's the trouble. Whatever happened to you was just too painful to face ever again. You've locked it all away. And until you open up and talk it out, it's gonna stay right there inside you, burning you up, eating away at you, making it impossible for you to come back."

"Maybe. But there's nothing much to tell. I just woke up one day and I couldn't pitch anymore. That's all."

"Yeah, right. That's all."

Ted Sando dropped Jack off at the Fallons' and made his way to the coaches' house, paid for by the 'Wolves organization. Russ sometimes stayed there, and the spare room was occupied by the junior coach Bill Matson. Tonight Russ had driven to his sister's home in Rhode Island, and Bill was out fraternizing with the players, which in Ted's opinion was not a good idea.

Anyway, the phone went shortly before 10 P.M. while Ted was watching television, the Boston Red Sox hammering the Blue Jays all over Fenway Park. When he answered he was mildly surprised to hear the deep Southern tones of Ben Faber on the line, just inquiring whether Jack had been any better tonight.

"Not really, Ben. He gave up five runs and we took him out with the bases loaded and that cost us two more runs."

"What inning?"

"Second. He couldn't get any movement or location on the ball, and that slider of his—well, I sure regret its death."

"I know it."

Ben, however, had not made the long-distance call to remonstrate. He had made it to update Ted Sando on the Faber fortunes, and to explain one or two matters which he thought might help Jack.

They chatted for almost an hour, and the coach was very thoughtful afterward. The Red Sox game was over, the Fenway victory intact, but he had a lot of thinking to do. And tomorrow he had a task to carry out, after the away game at Oceanside Field, home of their old nemesis, the Rock Harbor Mariners.

Ted's main concern was that somehow he was losing young Faber altogether. It was clear Jack had almost nothing to say, and that if he had one wish to be granted it would be to get the hell out of Seapuit and never come back. But Ted, like all true coaches, was concerned principally for the young ballplayers and what would benefit them most. And he felt that Jack's art was retrievable, though he was uncertain how to proceed.

The game the next night turned out to be a steady tightening of the screws by the Seawolves. The hitters jumped into a big early lead when successive base hits by Rossi, Adams, and Colbert loaded the bags and Boom-Boom Hacker grand-slammed the ball onto the beach before the game was fifteen minutes old. Kyle Davidson, pitching beautifully, held the Mariners scoreless for the next seven innings, during which time the 'Wolves managed one more run, a solo homer by Ray Sweeney.

Doughnut came in to finish off the home team, and hurled them out twice, with five strikeouts and a high fly to right field that Thompson caught easily. These masterpieces of the pitcher's art were in fact interspersed with three walks and one batter hit between the shoulder blades, but none of that fazed Doughnut. *NOSSIR.*

"YOU LIKED THAT, RIGHT, COACH . . . ? BIG FASTBALL LIKE THE CRUISER . . . BAM! RIGHT BY 'EM! THAT'S THE GEORGIA BOYS, RIGHT? LIKE MY DADDY SAYS, YOU

WANT VICTORY, GET YOURSELF SOME DAWGS! YESSIR!"

"Holy shit," said Russ.

Meantime, Ted was gathering up Jack Faber and heading out of the Oceanside Park for a little restaurant along the dunes at Nausset Beach. Its menu was limited, but it stayed open late, and always had plenty of seafood from the Truro fishing fleet.

Ted had reserved a corner table in the front screened porch, which looked out to the long Atlantic rollers, bright phosphorescent white in the night, as they crashed into the shallows. He told Jack to sit down and brought them each a tall frosted glass of cold beer. The lateness of the hour brought a waitress instantly into action and they both ordered a cup of clam chowder, with scrod, fries, and coleslaw to follow.

"Hey, Coach," said the miserable pitcher, brightening. "We never had a beer together before."

"You were too young last year, and generally I don't socialize with my pitching staff. It's bad for discipline. Gotta have a gap between the officers and the warriors."

Jack laughed, and he took a deep draft of beer, which tasted fabulous in the hot, muggy night. "I imagine I'm out here with you in order to be told where I'm going adrift and what to do in the future?"

"Wrong. I'm not doing any telling . . . I'm hoping *you* will . . . Hey, this beer tastes great, doesn't it? I'm getting another, want one?"

"Sure, Coach," said Jack, draining his glass. "Nothing like it when you're real thirsty."

They sat quietly watching the dark ocean, both taking generous swallows of their second tall drink. Ted ensured his glass was again empty by the time the waitress brought their food, and just as she was leaving, he said casually, "Better bring us another couple of beers, when you got a minute."

She smiled and nodded okay, and Jack could hardly believe his luck. When Ted began the conversation again, the pitcher was undeniably in a more garrulous mood than at any time since the previous season.

They were seriously into Drink Three when Ted finally said quietly, "Jack, I want you to tell me, chapter and verse, what happened to you when you went back to school last September?"

Jack took another swig of beer. "Well, you know Riazzi was new then, don't you?"

"Sure," said Ted. "Came in to replace Joe Dwyer, right?"

"Yeah. And for me that was like getting the fucking devil in place of Saint Peter."

"Why was it, Jack? I guessed as much. But you never told me why."

"Oh, he just started on me right from the first minute. Said I was late when I wasn't, just seemed to pick me out every time he saw me, said I was no good, never played for the team, only for myself. He just went out to humiliate me in front of everyone, even, one time, in front of my dad."

"Why you, though? That's what I don't get. Had he heard of you?"

"Christ. Everyone had heard of me in St. Charles. I was more famous than General de Fontainebleau."

"Who the fucking hell's General de Fontainebleau?" asked Ted.

At which point Jack blew cold beer down his nose, laughing at this display of irreverent ignorance.

"He's the French founder of the goddamned school," he said, mopping his face with a napkin. "He's some kind of hero from the Battle of Waterloo."

"Bullshit," said Ted. "There weren't any French heroes at Waterloo. Except for dead ones. Duke of Wellington kicked a whole lot of ass in that war. That fucker Napoleon left the game at the bottom of the seventh."

"Yeah, guess he did. Lost all his main weapons and took a lot of stick. Like me . . . anyway, Riazzi knew all about me. My picture was on the front of the fall yearbook, not to mention the local papers."

"You think he resented all the attention you were getting?"

"Dunno," said Jack. "But he sure hated me . . . no one ever hated me like that before . . . and I couldn't work out what I'd done . . ."

Jack drained his glass, trying to stop his mouth going dry. Ted sloshed some of his own beer into the empty glass and called for another pint. And then he noticed there were tears rolling down Jack Faber's cheeks, and he ignored them, and pressed on.

"Could you still pitch . . . even while he was hating you?"

"Some. But he kept yelling at me, telling me I was no good, never would be any good. In front of everyone. And I hadn't done anything wrong to anybody . . ."

"Was he criticizing your pitches, or just you as a person?"

Jack wiped his face, but he couldn't stop his tears anymore, and he just blurted out, *"That bastard. That godamned bastard . . ."*

Ted handed him a spare napkin and asked him again, "When did he start criticizing your pitches?"

"Well, he started on my fastball. I made a coupla mistakes and he bawled me out . . ."

"And after that were you too scared to let it rip?"

"Yeah. I was too scared. Every time I made a mistake he went out to humiliate me . . . and Coach, you can only take so much of that. You can only listen to it for so long. It would have affected anyone. Not just me. And I hadn't done anything wrong. I couldn't understand it . . ."

Ted gave him a few moments to compose himself, and then he asked, "How about your other pitches? How about the best slider I ever saw a college kid throw . . . ?"

"He tried to get me to change the mechanics on it. My best pitch . . . I just couldn't do it. But I did try, and it was a disaster . . . and then I went back to my old way, struck out a coupla of guys, and he went for me in the dugout, said I was uncoachable, had no future in the game. No one would ever want me."

"Jesus Christ," said Ted Sando. "I knew this was gonna be bad . . . but not this fucking bad. You better have this last beer. I'll get one myself . . ."

He walked up to the bar, contemplating the crass and willful destruction of a potentially brilliant career. And like Tony Garcia, he could only think of Mark Wohlers, and the brittle, fragile line a great pitcher must always negotiate—the treacherous frontier between daring and careless.

When he returned to the table, Jack had his head in his hands. For Ted the conversation had been perfect. The beer had done its work. Its effect had revealed all he needed to know about the state of mind into which Jack Faber had dissolved. He felt a cold fury toward Riazzi, but that was not productive. Since his conversation the previous night with Ben, Ted had checked out Coach Bruno very thoroughly.

He discovered an arrogant, semi-ignorant, opinionated bully, who was universally hated at Comiskey Park and had been optioned away at the earliest opportunity. Bruno kept bad company, low-life Chicago mobsters, and the story about his own teammates pounding him unconscious in the brawl against the Cleveland Indians was true.

It was also true they blamed the Tribe, who were collectively fined $50,000 by the commissioner for unsportsmanlike conduct.

The talk with Ted had done nothing to cheer Jack up. He'd just told the coach a lot of stuff he hadn't meant to tell anyone. And he'd revealed himself, the way Riazzi said he was. Timid, brittle, unable to take the setbacks of the game.

Ted had another swallow of beer. And then he said slowly, "Jack, you know why this asshole went for you like that?"

"No. And I don't guess I ever will."

"Well, I'll tell you . . . it was pure jealousy. His kind of flawed personality is often built upon his own obvious failure to make a career in the Bigs. He got to Comiskey late, and he couldn't hack it. He was full of resentment about his years in the Minors, years when he thought he should have been in the White Sox lineup.

"I've looked at his stats carefully. He had two terrific problems—a weakness throwing runners out at second. And he never could hit better than .242 in twenty-four at-bats with the Sox. His other weakness was an off-speed pitch. I got someone I know to read me the team coaching reports. Bruno was just a wild slugger, missed every time. The report said: "An inability to hit either a change-up, a curve, a knuckleball, or, especially, a slider will surely dog this player all his career."

"Jack, two weeks later he was gone. He was a very good catcher, with a strong but inaccurate throwing arm, and no subtlety whatsoever at the plate. It finished him. He went back to the Minors, ended up in Double A with all the same problems. Until he took up coaching and made a living frightening kids to death."

Jack nodded gravely. And Ted Sando continued. "Bruno arrived full of resentment. Can you imagine what he was like when they swiftly got rid of him? All that hatred, still inside him?"

"Guess so."

"Well, you know what guys like that hate most?"

"No. What?"

"Talent. Because they don't have enough of it. They have toughness, determination, guts, fitness, strength, a good eye for the ball. And they know nothing else. But they always have to take second place to real talent . . . and that, old buddy, was what he saw in you . . . a kid with a near-priceless gift . . . a kid who was going anywhere he wanted without much effort . . ."

"That's not me, Coach. I put in more hours throwing a baseball than anyone who ever lived."

"And that made you nearly perfect. And Bruno Riazzo was unable to deal with the perceived perfection. He assumed you never even needed to practice."

"Well, he was wrong."

"I know that. He didn't. So he set out to destroy this lightweight, who was blessed with a gift he never had. For him you were a Trust-Fund Kid of the Game. Never had to work for it."

"You mean he's some kind of psychopath."

"Yeah. I guess he is. But remember that White Sox coaching report I told you about—the bit about having trouble with off-speed pitches. It said, 'especially the slider.' And I think he's hated the practitioners of that pitch all of his life. But you, Jack Faber, were the first supreme practitioner of that pitch who he'd had power over. So he tried to make you change it, because he wanted it always to fail. Deep down, Mr. Bruno Riazzi has some very severe problems."

"Jesus Christ. I've been wiped out by a fucking nutcase."

"In a way you have," replied Ted pensively. "But I'd rather say slowed down by a fucking nutcase. Because I can now see the problem, and you've told me about it, and we've cleared the air. We both now know there was nothing wrong with you. There was something wrong with him. All we gotta do is get you back in there, throwing the ball how you want to throw it—make you lose the fear of screwing it up. Cast that bastard Riazzi right out of your mind."

For the first time in a very long while, Jack Faber cracked open that big wide grin of his. "Coach," he said, "you're one clever son of a bitch."

1 8

*J*ack Faber's first home was in shreds, and his other home was about to be flattened into the Louisiana swamps by bulldozers. The second one, the little sugar farm, did not matter, because it had always been shoddy and poor, and now he and Ben could get a better one, anytime.

The first one, however, represented darkness on the horizon. For all of his life, the game of baseball had been home to Jack, but somehow, in the aftermath of Coach Riazzi, Jack had left home. Worse yet, he had almost forgotten where home was, and that had left him lost and increasingly without hope.

He no longer felt the same when he entered a ballpark. The cherished game which had engulfed him since before his first double-figures birthday had retreated into a strange place of unspoken terrors. Yes, he had had a breakthrough with Ted the night before, but he still had to execute. He still had to do it.

Where was that old certainty inside him, the imagination that the sheer prospect of battle once inspired in him, the rapture of the strikeout, the vision of the perfect game, the simple possibility of glory? Right here was the epitome of that inbuilt American premium on enterprise and the individual. But for Jack, that had receded into grim unoccupied shadows.

He unclipped the gate onto the Cabot infield, and he stared at the plate, the symbolic diamond, toward which every hitter strives—and

Jack Faber pondered the game's most enduring purpose, to come home, to make it home . . . "That's all I want," he muttered. "Just to make it home."

He gazed out toward his own domain, the one he had once dominated, the pitcher's mound from which he was, in a sense, estranged. When he had pitched the other night, the mound at Exeter had represented a desert island from which there had been no escape. He remembered the feeling out there, of being unable to find his weapons, unable to summon the cavalry of his sliders. And he remembered feeling, when the pitches refused to cross the plate, that he would never get away from here, never walk back down the slope toward the dugout, never get back to the others.

And now he recaptured the same lifelong feeling right here, alone in the morning light in the infield. He just wanted to hurl the ball again, and somehow get back, to be with the others. Except he was no longer sure they wanted him. And if they didn't, then he surely was a man without a home. Because he knew no other.

Ted Sando arrived and detailed a bull-pen kid to start warming up with Jack, just long tosses. He'd join them in five minutes, but as they threw they could both see the coach leaning on the third-base-line fence, watching them from afar, assessing something, though neither of them knew what.

In fact, Ted had not recognized a whole lot of difference in Jack's throwing action from any other time this season. And he walked down and told him he wanted a good workout, to go to the bull-pen mound, and take thirty pitches at seventy percent to begin with, then thirty more at 100 percent.

At three-quarter speed Jack looked better, much better. But after thirty throws, when he stepped up to full velocity, Ted Sando could see he was still not unleashing his true power, not letting his weight finish forward.

He called out, "*STOP!*" And then, "Hey, Jack, you're holding back. Is that on purpose?"

"I'm doing what?"

"You're holding back. Not letting your weight get up over your front side. You're kind of praying the ball over the plate—I'm not seeing the authority in the throw. Think about it, concentrate on the weight transfer, hurl it all forward."

"I'm trying, Coach. Can you help me a little more with that?"

"Sure. I'm gonna stand behind you, and I'm gonna hold on to your shirt at the back. I want you to get to balance point and drive your hips and shoulders forward against my resistance. I'm gonna hang on tight to your shirt, and you gotta explode forward, try and break my grip. C'mon, baby . . . gimme a *big leg drive* . . . let's go."

Jack was bewildered. He had assumed his basic mechanics were the same. He was unaware he'd been holding back his drive. But he knew now. The three times he hurled his fastball at the catcher, the tension in his shirt told him they all lacked power.

The fourth time he let the ball rip with everything he had. It exploded out of his hand, and he felt the shirt wrench from Ted's grip as he plunged forward. The ball went screaming in, tailing across the outside of the plate, hard into the kid's catching mitt.

Jack saw him take it off, wincing, working his left hand and fingers, plainly stung by the brute force of the pitch.

"That's the drive I wanna see," said Coach Sando.

He let him throw six more, all very tough, as Jack Faber began to get back into the old rhythm, using his hips, pivoting his shoulders, maximizing his great strength.

"Okay, buddy. That'll do. Now I want you to throw some sliders for me. Don't wanna neglect your best pitch."

Ted saw the look of apprehension on Jack's face, like he imagined a matador might look entering the bullring without the muleta and sword.

He walked back up to the mound and began to throw, but he was somehow off balance; his own action somehow denied him the ability to snap the wrist with all of his force. And Ted moved up to stand behind, watched four more pitches, then walked forward to stand behind the catcher.

From there he could see more clearly, that Jack was opening up his front side too quickly, the left shoulder coming around left too far. Ted could see this was costing him power, and loading extra stress onto his right arm. In a sense, he was leaving it behind and then trying to whip it into place. To throw a slider, the right arm must come around with the whole of the upper body, pivoting like one complete unit; more simply explained, like the shoulders in a perfect golf putting motion.

Ted stopped Jack and pointed all of this out to him. Jack agreed with the principle, but was unaware he was not obeying it.

"Where do I start?" he said.

"I wanna see you drive your front side a fraction longer at your target. Then pivot right around, shoulders locked together—just make sure your hips rotate your upper body, not the other way around."

Jack nodded, and went back to the drawing board. He made the adjustment and threw four more. Immediately he looked better, at least his velocity was definitely better. But there was still no serious, sharp bite to the pitch.

Ted called the practice and said, "We'll go again in the morning. It's a day off, I know. But I really want to see that slider coming back."

That evening the 'Wolves played another old enemy, the St. Ives Red Sox, who were having all kinds of trouble with new kids arriving, especially two of their top pitchers. In a rampage that lasted only two hours and fifteen minutes, the Seapuit hitters fired in fourteen base hits, home runs from Zac Colbert and Ray Sweeney, and ended up 11–2 winners. Pedro Rodriguez pitched, relieved by the Cruiser, and Jack kept the chart.

He kept it assiduously, as he always did, but his mind was not in this game, which gave the team a 5–0 start. He was thinking about the following morning and the practice with Ted Sando. Somehow he understood this was a landmark. If he nailed down the slider, he knew he would play again. If he failed to do so, he might force them to send him home.

He drove back that night with Kyle, ate the big plate of chicken sandwiches Ann Fallon had left for him, swallowed about a half gallon of milk, and retired to his room overlooking Seapuit Bay.

The following morning he was at the field early, mowing the infield. When Ted showed up, he announced he was doing the catching himself, and they made their way back down to the bull pen with a bucket of baseballs.

Ted would look at the repertoire but he was mainly looking for the slider. Along the outer perimeter of the field there were two people walking dogs on the path between the fence and the woods. They were both local fans, and they both stopped to wave at the coach and last year's supreme pitcher. Little did either of them know they were within a few hundred yards of one of the great dramas of the season—the desperate attempt by Ted Sando somehow to pull Jacks' shattered career back from the abyss.

Ted moved back to the catcher's position and went into his

crouch, while Jack threw fifteen fastballs at 75 percent. This was really pleasing, the velocity was definitely back. Ted could see the fastball jumping out of his hand, and he knew that when he asked Jack to increase the speed, that would not be a problem.

He called for the change-up, and instantly saw it had good drag on it. It looked, of course, just like a fastball, but came spinning in around 12 mph slower, "dragging" out of his hand. This was not a bad pitch, not at all.

"Okay, Jack. Now we're gonna get serious."

"You might be," replied Jack. "I've been fucking serious all the time."

Ted grinned at the spark of confidence he was seeing. "Right, we're going to the slider now. And I want you to remember that finish, the way you've been turning that wrist too early."

"Well, that's what they tried to make me do . . . change it to a slurve . . . halfway between a slider and a curve . . . they *wanted* my wrist turned early, trying to get more of a break, trying to make it more reliable."

"Fuckwits," said Ted. "And we know who the leadoff fuckwit was, right?"

Jack Faber threw four sliders in succession. They weren't terrible but they were ineffective. Ted kept calling: *"Still a little early . . . come on, now. Think fastball . . . get that release point out in front, leave the snap a little longer."*

Jack threw again. Not perfect but better than anytime this year. He threw two more, neither of them an improvement, and Ted Sando decided to go to another tack, because he suspected, deep down, that Jack was a horse who might run for the whip.

A lifelong devotee of the racetrack, the coach knew some Thoroughbreds shy away from a whacking and could even stop trying altogether, some of them for life. Others respond to the urgency of the jockey's call. They tune in to the fury of the battle, and at the sting of the whip, they dig ever deeper. Jack, the coach hoped, might be the last kind.

And he looked up at the striving young pitcher and growled. "Are you deaf? Jack, for fuck's sake. Concentrate on getting that ball out in front of your eyes—make sure your arm is extended when you wind on that snap—right from the forearm, right through the wrist. Listen to me, do what I say, or are you fucking deaf?"

There was silence. Then Jack grinned and said, "Sorry, Coach, I didn't quite catch that? What did you say?"

It was a big moment for both of them. Ted knew he was talking to the old, usually fresh Jack Faber. Jack himself no longer felt threatened by his coach. And he reared back and hurled in the best slider he'd thrown since getting rid of the Mariners' .300 hitter Matt Burke in the league championship final last season.

The pitch was a dream, the wrist snap perfect, and the ball came flying in, before diving steeply, biting down toward the plate. Ted was ready and scooped it up. No hitter he had ever seen could have planted the wood on that particular baseball.

He looked up and said, "Thank Christ for that. I was afraid you were going deaf!" And he tossed the ball back to Jack, who was laughing, and then lazily went into his action and drilled in another slider, identical in every respect to the first.

"Can you do that anytime I ask you?" said Ted.

"I think so," replied Jack. "I think I can."

"Okay, that'll do. Watch for the team list on the changing-room door this afternoon. You're starting against the Sentries tomorrow night."

Jack gulped. "Who, me?" he said.

The fact that he was starting was a mild shock, but against the Sentries, in the cauldron of Andy McKillop Field, in front of a big hostile crowd, that was an earthshaker. Thus far the 'Wolves were on top in the League, 5–0, for ten points, but Lancaster was right behind with eight, 4–1. At their home field they were diabolically hard to defeat. You needed your best pitcher, no ifs, ands, or buts, especially for the early season starts when the Sentries were always so quickly into a stride.

For this game last season Kyle had started, and the outcome had been so tight, so important, Jack himself had been brought on in relief to finish it. But this was not last year. This was this year, and thus far, Jack had done nothing to suggest he was better than the 'Wolves' most junior pitcher. Nothing, except, somehow, to command the undying respect and belief of his two principal coaches.

Ted Sando said good-bye to Jack and went off to lunch with Russ Maddox at the Black Gull, a little lunch place on the town dock in Oyster Hills. They sat outside, watched the boats refueling at the busy marina, and Ted told him he planned to start Jack tomorrow night.

"Jack? You sure? Kyle's ready, isn't he? Don't you think we should just try and rebuild him for a few more days?"

"No. I don't. I think young Faber's about as ready as he's gonna be. I've been seeing big improvements. You know he's as rough and determined as a son of a bitch, we saw that last year. What he needs is a start, against a hot team in a hostile environment. Show him we believe, and tell him if he gets in trouble, he's gonna have to get out of it himself, stay there and work it out."

"Jesus, Ted. You wanna leave him in there, even if he's getting hit all over the place? No matter what he does?"

"That's exactly what I mean. Six innings minimum. He needs to learn how to be a bulldog all over again. Last year there was no one in the whole league tougher than Jack, including Kyle. Right now, after all he's gone through, I don't know if he's tougher than anyone. But I do know there's one place to find out."

"You're really saying he starts tomorrow and we just leave him out there at McKillop Field? Christ, we could lose it twenty to nothing."

"I know. But if we don't try, we get nothing. If he steps up to the challenge and comes through, you got Jack Faber back. And that Jack Faber's gonna win us probably eight games. Which might be a championship."

"You actually mean this is a balls-to-the-wall situation, right?"

"Russ, that's exactly what I mean. And I think he'll come through."

Russ Maddox took another huge bite of his lobster roll, munched luxuriously, and said, with his mouth still full of mayonnaise and succulent chunks of the local crustaceans, "Okay, Coach," he said. "Faber starts."

Meantime, back in south Louisiana, Ben Faber was supervising the packing up of his and Jack's personal possessions. Everything—and there wasn't much—was going into crates and being taken into storage. There were a few sentimental items, some of Jack's mother's things, and not much else. Much of the old, tired, furniture—beds, chairs, and sofas—would go under the bulldozers.

It would take his gigantic new portfolio of blue-chip oil-and-gas shares about an hour and a half to earn enough to replace the lot with superb reproductions and antiques. Ben had always thought he had an eye for a nice piece of furniture or a painting, and for the first time he would have the opportunity to give it a shot.

At 2 P.M. the phone went for the first time, and it was Jerry Segal to inform him they had issued a press release through the national news agencies that morning, announcing the huge natural gas strike in Lockport, and the stock had gone from $56 to $58.50 on the NYSE in the first two hours of trading. This had made Ben some $5 million richer right now than he was when he first awakened that morning.

"Mother of God," he said, crossing himself. "The hell with the expense, bulldoze another couple of sofas."

He was wearing his old Crawdaddies hat as he wandered through the house issuing instructions to the removal guys, who were packing, sweating, and cursing in the un-air-conditioned house. The temperature was around 102 degrees. Humidity: "Damned near total," in their opinion.

At 2:30 P.M. the phone went again, and this time it was Ted Sando calling from the Cape. "Hiya, Ben," he said, "I think we're making progress. Jack's starting tomorrow against the Sentries in Lancaster. Thought I'd give you the heads-up. You might wanna come."

"Hey, Teddy," he said. "Sounds like a good plan to me. Since I'm about to become homeless."

"You're what?"

"They're knocking the farmhouse down," he said. "I don't get the hell out, I'll fall into the frigging gas well."

Ted laughed. "You better get up here," he said. "We start tomorrow night, under lights, seven o'clock. Jack's pitching six for us, no matter what. It's a kind of make-or-break situation. And tell the truth, I think he'd like to know you're there."

"Thanks, Teddy. I appreciate that. Really I do. See you tomorrow."

Ben never even put the phone down. Just pressed the receiver button with his finger and dialed 411, for the number of the travel agent in Lockport. He blew an entire thirty cents having Directory Assistance put him straight through, and announced himself as "Ben Faber, local farmer made good," to young Kathy Pierson, who he knew worked there.

"And what can I do for you, Mr. Faber?" she said, giggling. "Just name it, we'll have an account opened for you."

"Okay, Kathy, can you fix me a coach ticket to Chicago O'Hare in the morning. Leaving around oh–eight hundred. Then two first-class tickets on United to Boston Logan leaving around twelve noon, one in my name, one in the name of Mrs. Natalie Garcia."

"Mr. Faber, those flights are awful full out of New Orleans to Chicago right now. Will you go first class if I can't get regular."

"Screw it," said Ben. "I'll go first class anyway."

"And how about when you get to Boston, anything more we can do for you?"

"Well, I need to get to a place called Lancaster, down past the Cape, but if there's time, I'd call into the Cape first."

"Okay, I'll have a limousine meet you at Logan and drive you, till you get to Lancaster. You want the driver to leave you there?"

"Well, I guess I'll need a car. I might be on the Cape for several weeks."

"Okay, what kind of car, new or old?"

"New . . . I guess."

"Big or little?"

"Big . . . I guess."

"Any ideas?"

"No, not really. I've never had much of a car."

"Look, Mr. Faber, the story in yesterday's paper said you had received in excess of a million shares for the gas field. CNBC just said the stock went up a coupla bucks this morning. You've got more money than you know what to do with. You want me to have a nice new car waiting for you in Lancaster."

"Well, thank you very much. That'd be great."

"Okay. Give me the address where you're going."

"Andy McKillop Field. The Lancaster Sentries baseball park."

"Okay, your driver will know all the details. The limo company will arrange all the insurance for three months. Don't worry about a thing. We'll have a car at the farm to collect you at oh-six-thirty tomorrow. Just don't worry about it."

"No, ma'am," said the brand-new multimillionaire to the nineteen-year-old daughter of his old buddy Hunter Pierson. And she smiled cutely into the phone, trying to add up what 5 percent of a brand-new Mercedes was going to mean to her father's little agency.

Ben, of course, had one minor loose end to fix. He had not spoken to Natalie for several days, certainly not told her about his new status in life. And now he picked up the telephone again and dialed her number in Chicago, hoping she was at home. He had her symphony schedule and he knew she was playing this evening, but not again until next week.

She answered immediately, wondered why Ben was calling in the middle of the day, and told him he had awakened her. They had played way out north of the city last night and she had not arrived home till 1 A.M. She'd done three piano lessons in the morning, starting at nine o'clock, and still couldn't pay the rent until next weekend.

"Then I guess with all that kind of pressure, you'll regard my request as kind of frivolous," said Ben.

"I just might at that—especially if it has to do with that awful game."

"Well, I can't deny the request and the game are loosely connected—kinda like the bassoon and the first violin in the orchestra."

Natalie smiled, and reminded him that the Chicago Symphony did not field a bassoon.

"Okay, you got me on a minor technicality." He chuckled. "But what I really want to know is, will you come to the Cape with me tomorrow morning, see the boys play in the evening?"

"Ben, are you out of your mind? I couldn't afford to get to the airport, never mind buy a ticket. Anyway, I can't. I have two lessons tomorrow afternoon, both in the city. Both for cash, two hours each; I can't afford to turn those down."

"How about if I buy you a return ticket and get you to the airport?"

"How? Unless you've suddenly found a lot of money."

"Well, I've got a bit," said Ben mysteriously, glad that she did not read the *Wall Street Journal* in which he had figured on the previous morning.

"Well, even if that was possible, I still couldn't, because of the lessons."

"How about you postpone them for a few days and I'll compensate you for the inconvenience? Couple of hundred dollars?"

"Ben, I can't take handouts, to go away for a few days, even with a man I like more than most others I've ever met."

"I guess that depends on how much you like him."

"You know how much. But I still can't come."

"Why not? I've already got your ticket."

"He could hear her giggling, very plainly. "You have! Why, Ben Faber, I'd have to say that's very presumptuous of you."

"Guess so. Will you come?"

"All right. If you really want me to. I'll postpone the lessons, but I will not take a cash handout."

"That's a bit of a relief really. I wasn't quite sure how I was going to manage my last offer," said Ben, cheerfully amusing himself. "But the tickets are all set. And there'll be a car outside your apartment at nine-thirty A.M. Come straight to the United check-in area for Boston. Our flight leaves at midday. I'll be there to meet you."

"Okay," said Natalie, not even bothering to ask where this car was coming from, who was paying, or where they were staying. "I have a few things to do now, so I better get off this line and start moving. You are a very disruptive person, and I still hate baseball."

Ben chuckled in that deep Southern voice of his. "So long, Natalie," he said. "See you tomorrow. Don't be late, now."

"I'm never late," she said. "Only broke. Tomorrow."

Ben fired in his next call to the Cape, where Ann Fallon was delighted to hear from him, and even more delighted to have him stay for a few days. Unlike Natalie, they did have the *Wall Street Journal* every day, and anyway Jack had briefed them on the situation. "You sure you don't want me to arrange something a bit more ritzy," she said playfully.

Ben guessed she knew, and just said, "You and Ward are about as ritzy as I'm gonna need, Ann. But just one thing—could you ever be kind enough to ask Paul and Nancy if Mrs. Garcia could stay for a few days. We're coming into Boston on the same flight."

"Well, well," said Ann Fallon. "Jack and Tony both told us something was developing. I'm surprised you still call her Mrs. Garcia!"

"Tell the truth, I've called her Natalie a few times in private," said Ben. "I'm just trying to throw y'all off the scent."

"Well, you're not succeeding, Ben Faber. I'm sure Nancy will be fine. See you at the game."

A lot of people think the Cape Marlin League does not get fully under way until the Seapuit Seawolves face the Sentries in the faded old waterfront mill town of Lancaster. Because there, baseball passions run high, and Walter Farrell's money leaves the locals with high expectations. Every year.

The 'Wolves-Sentries battles represent the fiercest rivalry in the League, like a college version of the old Yankees-Dodgers games. The Sentries, like the Dodgers once did, imagine themselves as the White Marauders from over the bridge. The Seawolves, aristocrats of the Western Division with their connections to American blue blood, regarded Lancaster as a bunch of blue-collar mercenaries, a bit too professional in attitude, a bit too ruthless in their interpretation of the rules both of the game and of the league.

They didn't like each other much. And their field names betray much of the inbuilt feelings. Andy McKillop Field was named for a local Scottish-born industrialist, descendant of a long line of slave-ship owners from the Clyde, a man who scorned polite society in favor of hard-edged trade-union leaders under whose auspices he made most of his fortune.

> Cabot Field . . . *This is the City of Boston,*
> *Home of the baked bean and scrod,*
> *Where the Lowells speak only to the Cabots,*
> *And the Cabots speak only to God.*

On the other side, the biography of the grandfather of the donor of Cabot Field to the ball club was actually entitled *Only to God*, in reference to the famous doggerel lines about "The City of Boston."

A Seawolf had much to live up to, playing in the image of the fabulously wealthy Boston Brahmins, whose ancestors settled North America.

And now here they were, the Seapuit Seawolves, face-to-face with their archenemy for the first time this season. And Jack Faber was warming up in the bull pen along the right-field line. Tony Garcia was catching him, watched by Ted Sando. Jack, assaulted by nerves, butterflies, the heebie-jeebies, and God knows what else, was trying to stay calm.

He finished throwing and his mouth was so dry he could hardly speak. There was a huge crowd in the stadium, possibly three thousand, which is a lot more than most college players are used to seeing at baseball games. Ted told Jack to get his warm-up jacket on despite the heat of the early evening. And to get a drink of water. He noticed Jack nearly drained the the cooler dry.

At that precise moment the limousine bearing Ben and Natalie swept into the crowded parking lot and headed straight into the open space reserved for directors. The driver let them out and led them to a gleaming midnight-blue Mercedes Benz S600, $125,000 on its Michelins.

"Just sign these papers, Mr. Faber . . . here's the keys, and it's all yours. Enjoy it."

"Guess I will at that," said Ben, who still did not look much like a multimillionaire in his jeans and white T-shirt. But he was slightly betrayed by the dark brown Gucci loafers he had bought at the airport, prior to pitching his best sneakers in the garbage.

The chauffeur moved the luggage from the limo to the trunk of the new Mercedes, which was parked in a specially designated spot next to the car of Mr. Farrell himself.

The flight had been late out of O'Hare and they just made the Seapuit section of the bleachers in time for the National Anthem, played on a CD at full decibel level by the band of the United Sates Marines.

They found themselves in the middle of a welcoming group of old friends, including the Fallons and the McLures. And as the applause from that rousing military rendition of the anthem died away, the sound of the Sentries' battle hymn echoed over the park, and the leathernecks of McKillop Field came out in rhythm to the strains of "Sweet Georgia Brown." The crowd went almost berserk at the sight of them.

In the dugout, Jack just muttered, "Oh, Christ," under his breath, wondering whether his father had made it, hoping he would not fall apart again.

And up to the plate ran Gino Rossi, full of confidence, New York cockiness, ready to bang the Lancaster pitcher clean over the fence if he got half a chance. The sight of Gino inspired the two hundred or so Seapuit faithful who had made the journey to see an always special game in a very unspecial place, and they spontaneously erupted into their chant of "*GEE-NO . . . GEE-NO . . . GEE-NO!*" Ben joined them. Natalie did not.

Unhappily the Sentries fielded an excellent pitcher from last year, the short, beefy, gum-chewing Aggie from Big Spring, West Texas, Split Candlewood, and he fanned the overeager Rossi with four pitches. Rick Adams landed the bat on three fastballs in succession, two foul-backs and a one-hopper straight to the first baseman. Zac

Colbert slammed the second pitch about ten thousand feet into the air to drop straight down into the second baseman's glove.

"Okay, Jack, old buddy, let's get out there and give 'em hell." Ted Sando sounded a whole helluva lot more confident than he was. But he was determined to carryout his experiment. "One more drink of water," he said. "Then go. And by the way, kiddo, I'm leaving you out there tonight. Six innings minimum. You get into trouble, you get out of it, all on your own. Russ and me are happy to lose this one just to see if you still have it, like we think you do."

The hair on the arms of Jack Faber literally stood on end. But he climbed to his feet and stepped out onto the field. Tony put his arm around his shoulders and said, "Okay, Jackie. This is it. Let's go nail these bastards right in their own cage. Fuck 'em, right?"

"Fuck 'em," Jack confirmed, but he felt none of the bravado those words implied. He reached the mound and began his warm-up throws. He wanted to feel confident—but he was haunted by the memory of his last dozen appearances. He ran through his mind the instructions of Ted Sando: *stay centered . . . watch Tony's glove . . . get your weight forward on the pivot . . . be confident in yourself.*

Garcia called for a fastball. And Jack, consumed with nerves, threw it too far outside and the hitter left it. Jack was determined to get this fastball straight, and he threw three more in succession, all of them outside, the first two by a long way, the third questionable. But the umpire called them all balls, and the first Sentry jogged up to first base.

Tony signaled not to worry and called for the same pitch, inside. Jack hurled it in hard, but it came in over the middle of the plate, and the hitter whacked it high into right field. Steve Thompson came arrowing in to make the catch while the runner on first went halfway, then retreated. One on. One out.

The third batter came up, and again Jack tried that fastball tailing to the outside. But again it had nothing on it, never tailed at all, came in straight, and the Sentry slugger swung right through the wheelhouse and caught it an almighty crack; sent it right over Rossi's head, all the way to the fence, about eight feet short of a home run. And the Sentry on first wheeled around the bases for a score of 1–0. The triple also put a man on third. Still only one out.

Jack had thrown only six pitches, and he was desperately trying to hold his nerve, trying to remember Ted's words. The fourth batter came to the plate, and Jack, now consumed with getting his bread-

and-butter fastball into shape, hurled in exactly the same pitch, and still it would not swerve.

The hitter anticipated it, saw it coming, and banged a hard ground ball to Rick Adams. Again the runner scored while Adams threw a pinpoint-accurate throw to Boom-Boom waiting at first base to make the out. That made it 2–0, with two outs.

Tony called for Jack to try the slider, since Dick Frazier, the Sentries coach, was surely aware of the substandard-fastball rut the 'Wolves' pitcher was in. But Jack shook him off and threw the fastball again to the fifth Lancaster hitter.

The only difference between this one and the rest was it came in a little higher, and the new batter whacked it hard, but caught it a tad too low, sending it high into center field and into Ray Sweeney's glove.

Even Ted was surprised at how swiftly the inning had gone. Two runs down and little sign of encouragement from the pitcher whom he had pledged to leave for six. "He doesn't improve we might be into a twelve–nothing score or worse by the stretch," he muttered. "Jesus Christ, I better tell him his dad's here."

They talked briefly, while the Seawolf hitters again drew a blank, and it seemed within moments that Jack was on his way to the mound again, walking out this time with Zac, who tried to rev him up. "Come on, Jack, you can get these guys. Just stay focused . . . you'll get 'em."

Jack concentrated with every ounce of discipline he had, and he removed the first hitter, who bounced a weak ground ball straight at Zac Colbert, who threw him out at first.

The second hitter came up, briefed by Frazier, that the Seawolf kid "will throw that fastball again—and it doesn't have anything on it."

And Jack threw it. Straight at the plate, willing it to the corners. But it didn't move in or out. It came straight in and the Sentries' right fielder smashed a scorching line drive over the leap of Zac Colbert, way down into the left-field corner for a stand-up double.

The hit was bad enough. But it had a terrible effect on Jack Faber. Instantly he was rattled, unable even to remember what it was like to fight back. He just didn't have the weapons to scrap with. It had been too long since he had used them. He caught the ball coming in from Rick Adams, and he turned away, his eyes tight shut, and he tried to tell himself, over and over, *No. No. You're okay. You're okay.*

But he wasn't. He was off balance, and he rushed his next delivery. The ball hit the batter hard in the triceps muscle at the back of his upper arm. Plainly it was an accident, but the hitter hurled his bat to the ground, glared at Jack, and jogged on down to first base. Two men on, first and second. One out.

Jack paced the mound, picked up the rosin bag, and flipped it in his hand. He walked back up the slope and stared hard at the two runners. But he did not see the clean-cut faces of the two Lancaster outfielders, he saw only the swollen, snarling face of Bruno Riazzi, and he heard again that voice screaming at him: *It's my way or nothing, you little bastard.*

Garcia could somehow sense his friend's torment, and he ran out to the mound. "C'mon, Jack. C'mon, man. Don't get too worried. Let's be good with our pitches . . . we'll roll up a double play, get 'em right outta here . . ."

Jack nodded, but he looked right past the catcher, as if he was in a trance. A few moments later he watched Tony go into his crouch, pushed his right foot up against the pitching rubber, and held his glove up against his chest. His right hand was holding the ball down by his hip.

Garcia signaled immediately for a leadoff change-up. Jack nodded and came to his set position. He stared once at the runner on second, then kicked into his delivery, and threw a 79 mph change-up, right down the middle of the plate. The batter was way out in front of it and took a monstrous swing, missing by a mile: 0–1.

And then, to Garcia's horror, Jack walked the batter with four straight balls, two tailing fastballs, up and in, a slider in the dirt, and another fastball that sailed over the ducking batter's head.

In separate places, in separate parts of this seething ballpark, Ted Sando, Russ Maddox, and Ben Faber covered their eyes, with a collective sigh of "Oh, my God" as poor Jack loaded the bases with only one out.

Sando called "TIME!" and walked out to the mound. There was no point, he knew, in berating his pitcher. Besides, he knew precisely what Jack was thinking. And he gripped his arm and hissed, "Get him out of your mind, Jack. Don't let that fucking nutcase get into your head. He's probably in a straitjacket by now. Come on, big fella, let's go now . . ."

Jack nodded, breathing deeply. "Okay, Coach."

The next batter was the returning Lancaster right fielder, Jake Quinn from Tennessee, an old enemy. And Jack led off with another fastball which went away, outside. Quinn left it: 1–0.

Then Jack sent in a slider, which traveled only fifty-nine feet, bounced off the dirt, and was brilliantly blocked by Garcia, saving a run, but leaving a 2–0 count.

No one understood the enormity of the situation more graphically than Jack. He'd thrown twice to Quinn, one too wide, one too short. And once more his thoughts cascaded: *Oh, my God . . . here we go again . . . none of my pitches work . . . my location's all off . . . I can't put the ball where I want it . . . I can't . . . I just can't . . .*

Jack knew one thing for certain. If he couldn't pitch to a precise spot, he would be hit, hard and often. If he could have done it, he would literally have begged to be taken off. Begged Sando, begged anyone who would listen. He just wanted to go home. To where?

But he had to pitch again. And he subconsciously knew he'd have to take something off the fastball in an attempt to get the direction right, just to throw a strike. That was as much as he dared hope for. In his mind, he could hear his own voice, very clearly: *I cannot, must not, dare not, walk this batter.* But there was another voice, more rasping, more cruel: *Forget it, Faber, you'll never be any good.*

Jack threw a fastball at the outside, 85 mph. But again left it too meaty, almost down the middle. And the Tennessee hitter sat back and fired the ball hard into the left-center gap. Ray Sweeney's anticipation was always terrific, and he picked this one up early, raced around the ball, and fielded it cleanly. He went directly into his crow hop and winged the ball at Bobby Madison at second, to stop the double; they succeeded too, held the runner to a long single.

But both runners were in, Quinn sliding hard, in anticipation of the throw: 4–0 Sentries. Still only one out, runners on first and third.

On the next pitch, the runner on first stole second, and right after that, the next Lancaster hitter cracked a sacrifice fly to left center, which Gino Rossi caught easily. He made a fabulous throw to the cutoff man, Zac Colbert, standing in the middle of the infield grass. But the fifth run was already in, and Zac knew it, so he tossed the ball to second base, where Bobby Madison caught it, and gave a quick fake to Rick Adams.

The runner spun around to get back, turned again to face Rick. Too late, Bobby bolted down the runway and tagged him for the third out. The last Sentry never even knew where Madison came from, it was so fast. And he had learned one of the many truisms in the game of baseball: Don't even bother to try to outwit the Sea-wolves from The Citadel. It can't be done. No one in the Cape League had ever done it.

It was still 5–0 Sentries, and Jack walked back to the dugout, growling to Sando, "I just don't have it. You've gotta get me outta here."

Ted was calm and he quietly pulled Jack over to talk to him alone in the corner of the dugout. "Jack," he said, "I've had a couple of long talks with your dad these last two days. And I guess you have to know sooner or later, two weeks ago Ben hit Bruno Riazzi with a punch to the jaw which knocked him out. Had to get to a hospital with a sus-pected fracture. Happened in Lockport, little bar called the Foxhole."

"Dad! Punched out Bruno Riazzi?"

"Apparently so. No contest."

"Jesus."

"Bruno's friend also came after your dad, but never laid a glove on him. Ben put him in hospital as well with two broken ribs."

"Holy shit!"

"You see, son, your dad believes in you." And right here Ted Sando thought long and hard. *Will I go to the whip again?* And he decided, yes. And then added, "Like I used to."

"You don't anymore, Coach? Not that I blame you."

Ted ignored the question and asked one of his own. "Jack, you know why your dad flattened Bruno Riazzi?"

"Well, not exactly."

"Because he said you would never have the balls to play this game."

"He did?"

And Ted stood up to walk away. But before he went, he said firmly, "And I'm afraid Bruno might have been right."

19

*J*ack Faber was stunned. And for a few moments he sat alone in the dugout, in stupefied silence, apparently wounded beyond repair at the words of his coach, friend, and mentor. Hurt was the overriding emotion he felt. And yet, from somewhere within, there was an anger, a rising fury, at the injustice and callousness of the world of baseball.

It seemed to Jack he had rolled with more punches than anyone since Ernie Terrell faced the lightning fists of the young Muhammad Ali over fifteen rounds forty years ago. He had that video, because Ben had collected all of Ali's fights on tape one year when the sugar market was good.

And now he too felt like the almost unprecedented human punch bag Terrell had been in Houston, twenty years before he was born. *More goddamned insults, more criticism, more abuse . . . who the hell do these people think they are?*

In place of the old familiar feelings of sadness and self-reproach, Jack Faber was seething. Months and months of unspoken rage and frustration came bubbling up to the surface, like the gas back home on the farm. It was all he could do to stop himself standing up and yelling "fuck you!" to the world in general, and Ted Sando in particular.

And he sat there, literally trembling with anger, running through a laundry list of his natural assets, trying to build a case for the downright impossibility of calling him all the things they had been calling him. *Jesus, I'm stronger than any of the other pitchers, I'm bigger, fitter, I'm fucking better . . . I KNOW how to do this . . . I've done it for years . . . I can throw a fastball as good as anyone in this league . . . I never saw anyone else up here could throw a slider to match my best . . . I mean, fuck it, what is it with these guys? I've had a couple of poor games . . . that doesn't make me a leper . . . Jesus Christ, who the fuck does Sando think he is, arrogant bastard . . . I bet no one ever told him he hadn't got the balls for the game . . . if they did he'd probably deck 'em . . . but I'm supposed to just sit here and take it, like that bum Terrell . . . well . . . well . . . FUCK IT!*

Right then, Split Candlewood sent down the third Seawolf hitter, in order, and Jack pulled down his cap, grabbed his glove, and walked out to the mound alone. He picked up the rosin bag and crushed it in his big farm-boy right hand, wishing it had been Ted Sando's throat.

He flung it down and walked up the slope, and glowered at the Lancaster leadoff hitter, a beefy slugger named Goose Austin from Kokomo, Indiana, Notre Dame's top hitter in the spring. Jack nodded at Garcia's call for a fastball, because he understood that at this moment, the hammer of Thor resided in his right arm.

Slowly he went into his windup and then unleashed the most lethal fastball he'd thrown for almost a year. Jack cast his cares aside. He was uninterested in where the baseball went, high or low, ball or strike. He just let it rip, in a tumult of violent, uncontrolled rage. The ball tailed in on the plate, four inches in from the outside corner, at 93 mph on the scouts' radar guns. The left-handed Goose Austin never swung, never moved, just stood there with his Louisville Slugger raised high above his shoulder as the ball lasered past him.

The umpire whipped both arms out to his left, dragged his right one back, as if firing a bazooka, and yelled, *"STRI-IIIKE."*

Tony Garcia shook his head and stared at the ball, which had cannoned into his glove, uncertain how it had gotten there. He looked at the mound in disbelief, and then he cracked his huge Latino smile, jumped up and down, and yelled, *"ATTABOY, JACKIE! WAY TO GO, BUDDY!"*

Everyone was smiling except for two people: the hitter and the pitcher. And Tony, not wanting to push the Seawolf luck, called for the slider. Jack glowered and shook him off, because he just wanted to throw harder and harder, and nothing was going to stop him. He took aim at Tony's glove and sent in a rocket, straight at the middle of the plate, this one clocking at 94 mph. Again the batter never even moved. *"STRIKE TWO!"*

Garcia whispered, "Jesus Christ," and signaled for another fastball, since he was going to get one anyway. He asked for it a little higher, and Jack nodded, grim-faced. He reared back and hurled it in, 95 mph, letter-high, smoke tailing behind it. Goose swung, way too late. There was no catching up with a pitch like that, and the swing became just part of his walk back to the dugout. And he trudged away, as if anxious to get the hell out of the way of that flamethrower on the mound.

Meantime, Jack turned to the dugout and gave Ted Sando a look of pure defiance.

But Ted sat expressionless, a stoic cast to his face.

"What the hell did you say to him?" asked Russ Maddox.

"I guess that's just between Jack and me," said Ted. "I just challenged him a little bit." To himself, he muttered, "Come on, kid, keep going. Lemme see that bulldog I used to know."

And out on the mound Jack went at it again. He hurled in three more missiles, simple, straight, called strikes, for the second out. And now the Seapuit crowd was up and cheering. Ben Faber was on his feet, trying not to weep with relief, but aware, even from this distance, of the look of pure hatred on Jack's face. He wondered what had happened between him and Sando; wondered what wiles of psychology the big lefty from Maine had worked on his only son.

The Sentries' third hitter, Boyd Berkowitz, a .300-hitting junior out of Mississippi, stepped up to the plate, and Jack threw his seventh fastball in succession at 93 mph plus, right by him. Then Garcia called for the change-up, and Jack nodded. But the batter had already made up his mind he was looking for yet another fastball, and he swung early, ended up so far in front of the ball he looked ridiculous.

And then came the crunch. Tony signaled for the slider. And he was signaling to a pitcher who did not even know the count, who was past caring what happened one way or another. Jack took his grip, in his old tried and trusted way, reared back, and with truly stupendous torque, snapped his wrist around on the release, full power surging down from his big muscled forearm. It should have hurt like hell, but it didn't. The pain somehow failed to penetrate the pent-up aggression, the rush of the adrenaline.

The ball swooped in at 83 mph. The batter could see the bright red dot in the vortex of the spinning baseball, and it appeared to be an incoming strike. He leaned back to give himself a chance, but the ball nose-dived toward his ankles. The hitter could not believe it, the staggering falloff as the bottom dropped right out of that ball. He swung wildly, missed by a foot, minimum.

Berkowitz had not even completed his hapless swing, the ump hadn't even called the strike, before one solitary figure in the stands leaped to his feet, his eyes shining, shouting at the top of his lungs, *"THAT'S THE ONE, JACKIE . . . THAT'S THE ONE. OH BOY! JACKIE, IS THAT EVER THE ONE!"*

The umpire finally yelled *"STRIKE THREE!"* amid the din of the wildly applauding crowd in the Seawolf section. The Sentries had gone down in order—one, two, three—in nine pitches, not one of which was touched by a bat.

But what exalted Ted Sando and Ben Faber was one pure and simply technical fact. No one could have hit that final pitch. No one. As comebacks go, Jack Faber's slider just made one.

He walked off the mound and on into the dugout. As he entered he muttered, "No balls, right? Bullshit!"

Sando said nothing, never even glanced around, just kept looking straight ahead, willing his pitcher to stay driven.

And that he did. In the next three innings Split Candlewood continued to shut out the 'Wolves, and Jack matched him pitch for pitch with four more strikeouts, surrendering only one base hit—just a flare over Adams's head.

But it was still 5–0 as the 'Wolves came up for the seventh, feeling unaccountably buoyant, feeding off their pitcher's supreme performance. They had never hit Candlewood hard, but they had hit him. And Garcia, batting ninth, led the inning with a walk. And then Rossi, crackling with New York bravado, suddenly whacked a fastball viciously over the second baseman's head, sending Garcia to third.

Rick Adams came up and smacked a one-hop ground ball scudding through the legs of the shortstop. It didn't look that important, but it was. It was a slice of luck, and it represented the big break the 'Wolves needed. Adams came flying into the base, and Tony Garcia scored. It was 5–1, with Rossi at second, Adams at first, no one out, and Colbert at the plate.

Candlewood, rattled by the shortstop's mistake, irritated by that cocky kid from New York at second, and always wary of the canny hard man of the 'Wolves' lineup, pitched to Zac very carefully, making sure he gave him nothing to hit. He hurled four tailing fastballs, low and away. Colbert left the lot, and the umpire called, *"Ball four."* Bases loaded. No one out. This was it for Seapuit, their big chance, and everyone knew it.

Dick Frazier came storming out of the Lancaster dugout, stopped to berate his catcher over his pitch selection, took out the tired Split Candlewood, and signaled for his reliever in the bull pen, the lanky, six-foot two-inch Charlie Thomas, from Huntingdon, West Virginia, one of the stars of Clemson University.

At the plate, like a hired gun, stood Mr. Beauregard Hacker, the hugely muscled South Carolina Gamecock—Boom-Boom to his friends—and the words of Ted Sando were fresh in his mind. *The guys say this pitcher takes a coupla outs to find his groove . . . so get after him, Boom-Boom, real early . . . try and hit one of his first three pitches while he's a bit tentative.*

Boom-Boom was ready. He took his stance and looked for an opening fastball probably at the plate. He got the fastball, but it was belt-high, and not fast enough. Boom-Boom saw it coming and opened his massive shoulders, and then he drove every last ounce of his 240 pounds weight, right into his swing, and he slammed that ball as hard as he had ever hit a baseball in his life. It was a towering drive, and it soared into the night air, almost a hundred feet above the white 410-foot marker on the fence, dropping into the far bleachers with a bang and a clatter.

The runners were long gone, but Boom-Boom rounded the bags at a stately pace, and he lifted a high five to the 'Wolves' third-base coach as he went. "Just a little ol' sand wedge, right?" said the golf pro's son, laughing, knowing his grand-slam homer had tied up the game 5–5 at the top of the seventh. Still no one out.

Charlie Thomas, however, was no one's pushover. He worked steadily, varying his pitches, and sending down Ray Sweeney with a called strike on a full count. He persuaded Bobby Madison to loft a soft fly ball to the third baseman, and Steve Thomas fanned on a curveball on a 2–2 count.

Jack Faber returned to the mound for the seventh time, and as he went, Ted Sando said brightly, "One more, Jack." And his pitcher never even looked at him. Just scowled his way across the infield muttering, "No balls, right. I'll show him no balls, arrogant fucker."

With renewed fury he hurled down five more successive strikes, none of them showing less than 93 mph on the radar guns. Then he let fly with a slider which damn nearly dived down at right angles to its own trajectory, for the second out. In the Lancaster dugout, Dick Frazier exclaimed, "*FUCK ME!* Who the hell told me this kid was finished? *FINISHED!* He looks like fucking Sandy Koufax."

The next hitter was Jake Quinn, who had banged Jack hard into the left-center gap in the third inning. And Jack, his anger subsiding, stood studying the Tennessee hitter for a few moments, before sending a very clear message, a fastball that swerved up under the hitter's chin. Quinn swayed back, but he was a tough college hitter, accustomed to playing at the highest level, and when he took his stance for the next pitch, he had not moved one centimeter farther away from the plate.

Jack threw again, a fastball, which Quinn fouled off, for a count of 1–1. Then he threw a screamer at the middle of the plate, and Quinn hit a long foul ball down the right-field line: 1–2.

Garcia called for the slider, and Jack hurled a good one. Quinn had no intention of swinging, and the ball broke downward just outside, to make it a 2–2 count.

"Gotta scrap my way through this," gritted Jack to himself. "Fuck Coach Sando. I'll show that faithless son of a bitch." And deep down he knew there was still thunder in his right arm, and he leaned back, his left leg kicking high, before launching a howitzer, which scorched in, tailing to the inside. Quinn swung, hit, and shattered the bat, the ball bounding toward third base. Zac Colbert angled in, picked it up without breaking stride, and threw it right into Boom-Boom's glove for the third out.

Jack came off the mound and walked in. "That's it, kid," said Coach Sando immediately. "You're all done."

"Get outta here," retorted the pitcher. "I'm not done. And you know it. I got two more left."

"No. You've thrown a hundred and one pitches tonight. That's enough. I'm trying to build your endurance. Not wreck your arm."

"But I'm good for it, Coach."

"No you're not. You don't have to prove anything else. You're back, goddammit."

Jack Faber sat down, suddenly weary, less angry but not calm. He felt as if a long journey had somehow ended, as if he had awakened from a very bad dream. The dugout suddenly seemed like home again, and Tony was sitting next to him, companionably, not speaking much except to murmur, "Jesus, Jack, did you see what Doughnut just did?"

And the two of them stared out to the bull pen, where the catcher was climbing the backstop trying to retrieve the ball which was jammed about seven feet above the ground. They could see the Cruiser standing there laughing.

"How 'bout them Dawgs?" said Jack.

And Tony slapped him on the back and asked, "Jack, was there ever a time you thought we'd never sit like this again, laughing at Doughnut?"

"Yeah. Guess I thought it was all up for me, in baseball."

"I always thought it wasn't. I always thought one day you'd get good and goddamned mad enough to bust your way back in."

Jack grinned. "Lotta fun, ain't it?"

And they settled down to watch Charlie Thomas put two Sea-wolves on base before sending down Rossi, Adams, and Colbert, in order, all caught in the outfield. Still 5–5.

Doughnut came in from the bull pen, jogging with long strides to-ward the mound. Tony Garcia stopped and had a quick word, and then waited for the Georgia hurler to settle in. And by some miracle, he pitched fast and steadily. He worked his way to a 2–2 count with all of the first three Sentry hitters, but sent each one of them down with his next pitch, the 92 mph fastball, swerving down and away. None of the Sentries put wood on any of the three strikeout pitches.

The 'Wolves came up for the ninth time, trying to break the tie. Everyone believed the momentum was with them over the last third of the game. They had already come back from the dead, and now big Ray Sweeney was at the plate, flexing his muscles, looking for a leadoff hit. He swung straight and hard twice, missed both times. Then he nailed a curveball that came down the middle. Ray caught it just a fraction high, and the ball shot into the grass just behind the mound, bounced low and hard, and threaded its way through a hole, to the right of the second baseman. It was a priceless "seeing eye" single.

Bobby Madison came up, all business, certain of his task, and advanced Ray on the second pitch with a sacrifice bunt, and was himself thrown out at first.

Steve Thompson was next, and he fouled two back, desperately trying to bring home the go-ahead run. But then Charlie Thomas threw that suspect, looping curve of his, and like Sweeney, Steve banged it, over the shortstop's head. The Sentries' center fielder came charging in to field the ball, by which time Ray was rounding third, running for his life. The ball came in to the catcher about two feet right, and that was all it took. Ray Sweeney scored; there was not even an attempt at the tag. The 'Wolves were in front for the first time, 6–5, top of the ninth, one out.

But that was all. On the very next pitch. Gino Rossi hit into an inning-ending double play, 4-6-3—second, short to first—and the game would swing on three last outs.

Cruiser Burrell's arm was still a little tender, so Doughnut Davis walked to the mound with a heavy responsibility, although no one would have known it by his attitude. "You got the right man, right here, Coach . . . let 'em have the ol' fastball . . . heat, Coach, heat . . . that wins ball games, right? Blow 'em right outta here. *YESSIR.*"

Ted Sando just said, "You got it, Doughnut. Stay focused now."

"I'm there, Coach. Right there." And with that he threw an opening fastball at 93 mph three feet below the press box and jammed it in the wire. One of the batboys climbed the fence to retrieve it.

Tony Garcia just stood there, shaking his head. He refrained from going immediately to the mound because he didn't think it would do any good. He just went into his crouch and hoped for the best. Doughnut pitched, and worked his way to a full count, before the leadoff hitter hit a ground ball to Madison, who threw him out at first.

Doughnut struck out the next hitter, but was whacked hard by the third man, way out to the fence, where Ray Sweeney ran thirty yards to make the catch for the final out. Seawolves 6, Sentries 5. It was a big win and it planted the 'Wolves firmly in first place in the Western Division.

Doughnut came in acknowledging the cheers, but Jack Faber sat quietly, declining to go out for the team handshakes. Ted Sando did not go out either. Instead he came through the dugout and sat next to Jack.

"You know I didn't mean it, don't you?" he said.

"Kind of," said Jack. "But I sure as hell thought you meant it when you said it."

"Jack. I didn't know another way. Someone had to make you good and mad. So I just said the worst thing I could think of."

"You sure as hell did."

"Well, did it work?"

"Guess so."

"You still mad?"

"A little."

"With me?"

"Nah. Just that Italian bastard at school."

"We still buddies?"

"Maybe . . . how d'ya like my slider?"

"Awesome. The best."

"We're still buddies."

Just then Ben came around the corner of the dugout and saw Jack and his coach sitting together. He held his arms out to hug his son. But first he said, "Thanks, Coach. Not many people will ever know what Jack and I owe to you."

"Wasn't anything."

"Well," interjected Jack, turning back to his father, "you flattened any more coaches this week?"

"Son of a bitch asked for it," said Ben. "I doubt even he would deny that."

"He might," said Ted. "Guys like that never understand how god-awful they really are; otherwise they'd change. I'm just glad he's the hell out of Jack's life . . . meanwhile we got another championship to win . . ."

"And from what I see, a good bunch of guys to make a run at it."

"Ben, if I'm any judge, this team's a little better than last year . . . The Boomer's just a tad more consistent at the plate than Scott was, and the Cruiser's a true closer, and he throws a little harder than Aaron Smith. Steve Thompson's faster than Andy Crosby, and Doughnut's become a halfway decent long reliever . . . and we got Jack back."

Right then Tony Garcia and his mother walked around the corner in front of the dugout. They were both smiling, Tony, for the pure and simple reason that the 'Wolves just wiped out the Sentries and Jack had held his own Natalie because Ben Faber was so unaccountably happy she just found it . . . well . . . contagious.

Also, she had not yet fathomed the source of Ben's sudden influx of cash. She knew it all had to do with the natural gas, and she knew there was certainly several hundred thousand dollars involved. If she'd known precisely how much, she probably would have died of shock.

Natalie had traveled a long way with Ben today, and she'd seen the sadness in his eyes, heard the resignation in his voice. The money, however much it was, had not alleviated his pain. Indeed, Natalie thought it might have brought about some deeper melancholy, or perhaps even a yearning for life as he once remembered it. And nothing changed all day; not until Jack blew three fastballs past Goose Austin.

At this point, Natalie noticed, a veil of darkness seemed to rise from the space Ben Faber occupied. He dug into his pocket for his old Crawdads cap, and pulled it down on his head for the first time. And he smiled as Natalie had not seen him smile since the championship games last season. Of course she had not seen him at all since then, but they'd spoken and he didn't sound like he was smiling much then. She'd heard the worry in his voice.

Now it was gone. Natalie did not know the difference between a slider and a knuckleball, but when Jack fanned Boyd Berkowitz, she heard Ben whisper, "The slider. Dear God, he's throwing it." And when the hitter swung and missed by miles, Ben was on his feet a full two seconds before even her own son. And Ben was shouting, waving, his eyes gleaming with joy.

Natalie had tried to put it all together, the grave and terrible concern Ben had carried with him for so long, about the quality of Jack's pitching. And now there some kind of lunatic redemption, just because Jack had uncoiled a bombardment of throws against the perfectly awful players in this perfectly awful town which all the Seapuit families seemed to detest.

It made some sense, but she would never fully comprehend the mystical doctrines of this befuddling game, and how, in just a few minutes, it had completely changed the yearlong mood of a man with whom she was trying not to fall in love.

Certainly the sudden arrival of a great amount of cash would alter things between them. But she had one bedrock belief upon which to lean: in the very early moments of their relationship, she had felt these stirrings of love for a kind, handsome, utterly penniless sugar farmer whose phone had been disconnected because he couldn't pay the bill. And she knew she would still feel them even if they cut off his phone again tomorrow.

Meantime they wandered out to the midnight-blue Mercedes. McKillop Field was rapidly becoming deserted, and the lights were turned way down, casting a high and ghostly illumination over the field. And Jack turned back just for a moment before they climbed the hill to the parking lot . . . "Just forgot something."

He had forgotten nothing, though. He unclipped the gate to the field, and he walked past the hissing infield sprinklers, and he stood once more on the raised dirt domain where he had helped win the game for the 'Wolves. He smelled the damp night sea air, and he gloried once more in his great strength, and he felt again the eternal promise of the pitcher's mound.

He just stood there, staring ahead to the diamond, feeling yesterday's regrets pass from him, drinking in the last remnants of the triumph he had found right here at McKillop Field, savoring the final moments of a game he would never forget. Just for a minute, before day was done.

Up the slope, with the last of the crowd, Ben turned back to seek out Jack. It was not difficult. He knew where he'd be. He saw his silhouette out there on the mound. But he said nothing, although he wondered whether Jack might one day bring a son back here to show him the place where he had once risen up from the dead to destroy the Lancaster Sentries on a warm June night. As Ben himself had once taken Jack back to Macon, Georgia.

Finally, they all boarded the Mercedes-Benz, Ben driving, Natalie next to him, the boys in the back. "I'll say one thing, Mr. Faber," said Tony. "As a family, you're real bad in the middle range. From the fifty-dollar Chevy to the most expensive car in the country. Jack's the same. Can't pitch at all at seven-fifteen. Best I ever caught at twenty minutes of eight. You guys are something."

Ben chuckled, and tentatively moved the smooth and silent S600 out onto the main street, the air conditioner running sweetly, the elegant rise and fall of Frédéric Chopin's most haunting nocturne, Opus 48, part two, in F sharp minor, playing softly on the CD player, the beautiful Natalie beside him. She had chosen the music in the airport store at O'Hare, and glancing at her, Ben guessed she was happy probably for the first time since he had known her. The Titan of the

Mound in the backseat, laughing in triumph with his best buddy, seemed also pretty pleased with his life. Generally speaking, Ben didn't feel too bad himself.

When they arrived back in Seapuit, the Fallons had invited everyone in for a late supper on the screened porch overlooking the bay. The housekeeper had a tall pot of delicious clam chowder simmering on the stove. There were gigantic roast beef sandwiches and glasses of red wine. Natalie managed one-half of a sandwich and one glass of wine, Ben ate a whole sandwich and two glasses of wine, and the boys devoured about a gallon of chowder between them, plus two whole sandwiches each, plus two glasses of wine, before spinning a coin for Natalie's spare half sandwich. Jack won. It was his night.

Ben drove Tony and Natalie back to the McLures' house shortly before midnight, and Tony carried his mother's suitcase inside and up to her usual room. The door was open and Paul McLure came out to say hello. He and Ben shook hands, and Natalie went inside, kissing Ben lightly on the cheek and reminding him to pick her up in the morning.

As a person currently of no fixed address, the ex–sugar farmer had decided to rent a house on the Cape for the season, and watch the baseball. He had, after all, not much else to do, except to count his colossal fortune. And here, as much as anywhere except Lockport, Ben felt very welcome.

He and Jack drove slowly home through the dark tree-lined streets of Seapuit. "Guess you're feeling pretty good?" said Ben. "And you ought to be. That was sensational pitching tonight."

"It was unbelievable," said Jack. "You know, I felt I couldn't miss. Whatever I threw was going right where I wanted it." After a pause, Jack added, "Thanks for coming. I'm glad you were here—all cozy again with Miss Natalie, right?"

"Easy, Jack. She's just here for a couple of days—I'm here till you guys win the championship again. I'm trying to rent a house this week."

"And I'm here to tell you that I'm Catfish Hunter if Mrs. Garcia isn't here to visit again on a very steady basis this summer. And it's not just Tony she's coming to see."

"C'mon, Jack. I really don't know her real well yet, and she still hates baseball. So I don't know how much more I'll see her. She's furious about Tony screwing up his exams. And she blames the game entirely."

"She might be furious. But she really liked you when you had a beat-up car, a debt to the bank, and no phone. Things are looking a whole lot better now."

"Yeah. But she doesn't know how much better. So don't tell Tony. Wouldn't want no Chicago beauties chasing me for my money!"

"There's a lotta guys wouldn't care why someone as pretty as Natalie was chasing 'em. Just so long as she was. Hell, Natalie looks like Penelope Cruz *hopes* to look like when she's thirty-nine."

"Who the hell's Penelope Cruz?"

"Major film star, one of the most beautiful women in the world. Had a big role in that movie about the Italian guy with the banjo—Captain Cappelletti, I think his name."

"The only Cappelletti I ever heard of was a running back for the Nittany Lions, John Cappelletti, Penn State."

"He didn't have a banjo, right?"

"Didn't need one. He had a Heisman Trophy. Anyway, listen, this is important. Always remember the beautiful Natalie and I were kinda close when we *both* had nothing. And that makes a lot of things different."

They pulled back into the Fallons' drive and parked the big Merc. It was a little after midnight, and both of them were sound asleep inside twenty minutes.

The following morning Jack was at the field while Ben drove around to pick up Natalie an hour later. She appeared looking sassy in a cream-colored dress, gossamer thin, slit at the front, her jet-black hair brushed to a sheen. She wore little makeup, and carried an expertly faked Gucci shoulder bag, the kind you can pick up from summer street vendors in Chicago for twenty-five dollars.

They spent the morning with two real-estate brokers, looking at two possible summer rentals, both along the south-running Seapuit shore, both priced at around $50,000 for ten weeks. Ben only wanted eight weeks, which cut no ice whatsoever. Either one was over fifty grand, no nonsense.

Ben was wavering at this monumental waste of cash, struggling as the very newly rich are apt to do at moments such as this. And so he stopped at the village store and picked up the *Wall Street Journal*, checked the stock price of Louisiana Oil and Gas, and saw it had jumped a buck and a half in yesterday's trading. This made him approximately $3 million richer than he thought he was this time yesterday.

"Mother of God," he muttered. And then settled for the more pricey $52,000 residence, a magnificent white clapboard house with a cedar-shingled roof, Doric columns, a narrow beach on the bay, and an eighty-four-foot long dock with two floats.

"Hey, I could put a powerboat on there, right?" he said to the real-estate broker. "Do a little fishing, chug around the bay. How about that?"

"What kind of boat, Mr. Faber?"

"Hell, I don't know much about Northeastern makes. What's that Boston Whaler like."

"Excellent boat. Tough, unsinkable, fast and comfortable. You want one?"

"Well, could I hire one?"

"No. you'd have to buy it this time of year."

"How much?"

"Twenty-three footer, maybe fifty-five thousand."

"Jesus."

The real-estate broker, who knew precisely who Ben Faber was, thanks to the Internet, grinned and said, "Come on now, Mr. Faber. Think like a rich man. Buy the boat, use it however and whenever you like, and at the end of a couple months, it's still yours, your money's still there. It'll last you ten years, probably fifteen. If you sold it, you'd probably get more than fifty-five thousand for it, damn things go up in price all the time."

Ben considered the fact that he was worth well over $100 million and plunged for the fifty-five grand. "Can you look after it for me?"

The real-estate man nodded. "That boat will be on your dock tomorrow afternoon. You want to keep it at the end of the summer, same boatyard where you bought it will service and store it for nine hundred till next year."

"Done," said Ben, and carefully wrote out a check to the real-estate office for $107,000. Of the $1 million in cash the corporation had placed in his account, only $760,000 was left. He'd better be careful, right?

When the deals were concluded Ben and Natalie drove back along the shore, and finally she asked him, "Ben, I have watched you spend probably a quarter of a million dollars in the last twenty-four hours. Could I ask just approximately how much money you have made from this natural gas strike?"

"Well, honey, if you read the *Wall Street Journal*, I guess you'da seen their estimate of around sixty million dollars."

"*SIXTY MILLION!*"

"That's what they thought."

"And was that right?"

"Half-right."

"God rest me," said Natalie Garcia.

They passed the rest of the day with a trip up to Nauset Beach, their old favorite; they bought sandwiches and a couple of cold beers, and sat on the long shore watching the waves pounding into the shallows. They left right after lunch for the ballfield, where they watched the 'Wolves win a tight one against the Cardiff Commodores, 3–2. Tony Garcia effectively won the game, doubling in Bobby Madison and the new backup catcher and designated hitter from Notre Dame, Griff Heeney.

And still Natalie was unable to share the joy of a hard game of baseball. When she looked at Tony she still could see only a young lawyer-in-training jeopardizing his career.

That night the four of them went out to dinner in Henley, and when Natalie had a second glass of wine, she steered the conversation deliberately to the academic goals of Tony Garcia. Tony, after two beers, was not argumentative, but he tried to explain to his mother how this game touched his soul, how it was not frivolous, how he expected big cash offers to sign pro during this summer.

Ben joined the discussion, in his quiet, measured way, and tried to explain the pure impossibility of asking probably the best college catcher in the country, certainly the best he had ever seen, to walk away from the one thing he had ever done better than anyone else.

"Ben," said Natalie. "I could see getting a prelaw degree and then trying baseball, like you said before, and going back to law school if it doesn't work in two years. But Tony's just crashed and burned for his degree. And he has to get that before he leaves college, so what's the point of discussing a career in this stupid game, because if he doesn't make it, he will have nothing to fall back on. He'll be a failed baseball player and a college dropout. Can't anyone see, he must go back to school to finish his degree course."

Even Ben did not have much of an argument to combat that, and he was forced to agree that Tony's academic disaster was not perfect.

The evening might have ended on a serious down note except that Jack was considering a two-year course at Harvard Business School if he decided not to sign pro forms. "I'm looking for another course in energy studies, oil-and-gas exploration and discovery," he said. "It's the biggest business, and in a way Dad and me are in it. I guess one of us better get a real handle on how it works."

Ben Faber smiled. For the past three years he and Jack had pinned their hopes on a big signing bonus from a Major League ball club to secure their future. It was curious how in just one week that had faded into total obscurity.

Natalie was beginning to feel a gulf between the Fabers and the Garcias. That great fortune stood between them, and she wondered if it would ultimately exile her and Tony from their friends from Louisiana. She imagined herself still struggling in a south Chicago tenement, Tony stuck in some Double-A club in the boondocks, while Ben and Jack lived in isolated splendor somewhere, with a grand summerhouse on Cape Marlin.

Tony did his best to cheer the group up, but there was no changing Natalie's mood. She felt, for no reason whatsoever, that her relationship with Ben was doomed and that Tony was bound for failure. Her somber, fatalistic view of the near future was born of a lifetime of struggle, of too much sorrow, too little reward.

It was all she could do to prevent herself crying, right there at the table, and when they left the restaurant, Ben sensed her mood, and put his great bearlike arm around her shoulders and whispered softly to her, "Don't you worry about a damn thing, Miss Natalie. I'm gonna take real good care of you. And that's a promise I can keep now."

He was just too late. Tears were already spilling out of her eyes, but she looked up at him, smiling through them, and said, "No handouts. I can't take money from you."

"Would you just relax?" he said. "I'm in command here." And he put on his deepest cowboy voice."Man's gotta do what a man's gotta do," he said. "You play the ol' sonatas and nocturnes, I'll take care of the big stuff."

And Natalie wanted to assert herself somehow. But it was not possible. She just clung onto Ben Faber's arm, unaware of how devastatingly beautiful she looked. On reflection, Ben regarded that modesty as her most enchanting attribute, but of course he'd never heard her play the "goddamned harp."

By the time they reached the car, Jack was in the driver's seat and Tony was sitting next to him. "Ballplayers in the front, lovers in the back," said Tony. "I'll just hit the ol' nocturnes on the machine right here, and we'll leave you guys to it. You want to go park somewhere?"

"Tony Garcia!" Natalie sounded more irate than she was. "Ben and I are mere friends. And if it's of any interest to you, we have never even kissed each other." She realized she was fudging a bit, to her embarrassment.

"I should think not," said Tony, with mock seriousness. "You've only spent about a half-dozen days together in your lives. However, Counselor Jack Faber and I consider that's just a matter of time . . . tell you the truth, there's a nice little spot to park right behind the ballfield—"

"Tony!" Natalie was trying not to laugh. But Ben and Jack were in hysterics.

"Admit it, Mom," said Tony. "You and Mr. Faber are an item."

"I'll admit no such thing," she said.

"Rubbish," he retorted. "You're an item. Anyone can see that."

Natalie did not answer. Ben did. "I sure hope so," he said quietly. "And I'd regard it as a downright honor if Miss Natalie even considered that a possibility in the future."

"The court regards that question as one which requires a straight yes or no," added Tony. "Mrs. Garcia, please answer the question."

"I didn't hear a question."

"May I seek the court's permission to rephrase it for the witness?" asked Tony.

"Certainly, Counselor," said Jack. "Kindly proceed."

"Okay, Mom," said Tony. "You fancy the hell out of Big Ben, or what?"

This was too much for all three male members of the court, who broke down laughing.

"I suppose for someone who's blown his exams, I might have expected a gorilla for an attorney," she replied. "And it's none of my dependent's business who I fancy the hell out of."

"Well, I'm blessed," said Tony, suddenly very legal again. "I find myself rephrasing—"

"Don't bother your little brain," said Natalie, suddenly laughing herself. "I would not be surprised if Ben and I became an item. He would, as you know, be my first boyfriend for a very long time. I also hope very much he'll be my last."

"*Right!*" yelled Tony. "*How 'bout that! I told you, Jackie, didn't I tell you six months ago? Right here we're witnessing, up close and personal, love's young dream—you're gonna be my goddamned step-brother*"

"Hey, you called that one," said Jack. "Called it before it got thrown."

In the backseat, both of them embarrassed by the prospect of amorous display in front of their sons, Ben and Natalie sat content-edly as always, except that the musician from Chicago clung to the farmer's hand as if she'd never let go. Even the wildly speculating baseball players in the front could not see that part.

20

atalie had to go home the following morning. And before she climbed into the limousine Ben had positively *made* her give him details of her battered bank account back home in Chicago . . . "just to make things a little easier for us, phone calls and stuff, tickets down here, cabs to the airport, call 'em joint expenses if you like . . . I just want to take a few of the little problems out of your life . . ."

Natalie agreed, finally, but still said, "No handouts, just a few expenses."

"Christ knows what she'll say when she see this," said Ben an hour later, cheerfully wiring $20,000 into her account, a hunk of cash he knew would be right there in Chicago before she'd even tuned up the ol' harp for tonight's symphony concert.

He wanted to go to the airport with her, but he had an appointment at the new house, just final documents, and Natalie felt he should be there to complete the rental. "I'll miss you," she told him. "But I'll be fine."

As she left, Ben had reminded her, "Logan Airport Friday lunchtime, July Fourth weekend. I'll be there. Call you tomorrow from my new residence."

And now she was gone and Ben faced ten days without her. But they turned out to be idyllic. He loved his new house, car, and boat in that order. Right behind the baseball. And the Seawolves were on a rampage, losing only three times in their first eighteen games.

After Natalie left, Ben saw Jack pitch twice more, one game a difficult one against the Henley Mets at JFK Field, which the 'Wolves won by 7–4, but which suddenly put Jack under a lot of pressure because the Mets began to hit the slider, and no one knew why.

They were holding a 7–1 lead in the sixth, with two outs, when Greg King, a big, burly catcher from Cal State–Fullerton suddenly slammed Jack's best slider clean over the fence for a three-run homer. Jack sat the last hitter down with a called strike, and then sent them down in order in the seventh. But King's big bang was worrying, because neither Jack nor Ted Sando could remember when *anyone* had hit that pitch as hard as King just did.

Doughnut came in to pitch the eighth, and Cruiser finished the game in the ninth. Jack had the win, having surrendered four earned runs on eight hits over his seven innings. There was little wrong with that, by anyone's standards, except that four of those hits had come off the slider.

And the subject preoccupied all three of the Faber-Garcia axis as they drove back to Ben's house for a late supper, prepared for them by his new twenty-five dollar-an-hour housekeeper, Mrs. Prentice.

Jack was upset and a bit mystified. Ben had been sitting too far away to shed much light on the problem, but Tony had a theory. "You know, Jack," he said. "There are times, when you think you don't have quite enough torque on that pitch, you tend to drop that right arm one slot on the slider."

He was referring to a tendency many pitchers have to release the ball with their elbow just too low, which softens the pitch, because the fingers are dropping to the side of the ball.

This method, dropping the right arm a fraction, will work because it eases the strain on the forearm of a tired pitcher. But it has one serious disadvantage. It decreases the disguise on the ball. Makes it harder to cover up the slider right through the release, which is, of course, one of the great beauties of the pitch. It's supposed to come in incognito.

"I thought I noticed you losing your action on the slider, about two innings previously," said Tony. "Nothing dramatic, maybe something only I would have noticed. But I was watching you, like always, and when that King guy whacked it, I knew it was the fourth time it had been hit, and I just flashed on your action in my mind. Jackie, I think you betrayed that pitch. I think King was waiting for it."

Ben, who was driving, nodded. Jack himself murmured, "You might be right. I was a bit tired. And I understand what you mean. I'm gonna talk to Coach Sando in the morning."

And that's what he did, and four days later when Jack pitched against the Wellfleet Athletics at Cabot Field, the problem seemed ironed out. Jack was not satisfied completely, but he got another win when the 'Wolves won it 9–5. He gave up only three earned runs in eight innings, scattering seven hits. But he had a season-high ten strikeouts. And no one hit the slider.

One day later Ben had a limousine take him to Logan to meet Natalie. He walked down to the gate, and she was among the first three people to emerge. He saw her first, and her appearance almost took his breath away, because she had plainly taken seriously his instruction "to get out there and spend three or four thousand bucks on yourself, for the first time in your life."

Natalie Garcia could have taken four strides off the cover of *Vogue* magazine. She was wearing a tailored Ralph Lauren linen suit with a jade-colored silk shirt. The cropped pants highlighted her long tanned legs and beige high-heel Gucci sandals. Real Gucci.

Ben Faber gawped as this vision ran toward him, and threw her arms around his neck. "I missed you, Ben," she said. "And thank you for everything."

"Who, me?" said Ben, hugging her. "C'mon, Natalie, just a few bucks."

She finally let go and looked up at him. "I just had the best time of my whole life," she said. "I spent three whole mornings wandering around my old haunts—you know, the outlets, cheapest clothes in Chicago. But this time I was in the designer outlets, 'specially the new Saks Fifth Avenue."

"Ma'am," said Ben, "you just moved into territory with which I'm not familiar."

"Oh, the outlets are wonderful. Drastic markdowns on fabulous clothes."

"That right?"

"You know, suits and things. See this suit I'm wearing? It's Ralph Lauren, it would cost sixteen hundred anywhere else . . . I got it for four hundred. The shirt was five hundred, marked down to seventy-nine. These shoes, Gucci, five hundred down to ninety-nine. I got another pair, in red."

"Christ, sounds like the sugar market, in fabric."

Natalie laughed, and she saw Ben looking at her beautiful new leather, buckle-front bag, which even he realized was expensive. "Donna Karan," she said. "Eight hundred. I got it for one-fifty."

"That *is* the sugar market." He chuckled.

Suddenly she broke away and pirouetted in front of him. "The belt," she said. "Hermès of Paris. The finest leather in the world, silver buckle, eight hundred dollars. I found it for one twenty-five."

She linked her arm through his and told him again how wonderful it all was. "Oh, Ben," she said. "I've never been so happy."

"How 'bout when Tony hit one over the fence in the opening game last season?"

"Oh, aside from that, of course," she replied in a voice seething with insincerity.

Ben grinned at her and said, "What else did you buy?"

She adored the way he was always interested in her, and what she did. "Well, I bought two fabulous summer dresses, a red-and-white print from Yves St. Laurent and a peach-colored Calvin Klein, priced around nineteen hundred each. I only paid six hundred for the two!

"Then I picked up a couple of cashmere cardigans from Pringle of Scotland, six hundred each, reduced to seventy-nine. I finished my little spree with an Armani raincoat, twelve hundred marked down to three hundred. Ben, I bought about ten thousand dollars' worth of clothes for twenty-one hundred."

"Does this mean we have to attend the bankruptcy hearings for Yves, Calvin, Ralph, and the rest?"

"No, don't be silly." Natalie laughed. "These are just end-of-season markdowns, clearing them out of the stores to make way for next season's new fashions, which everyone wants. The thing about these top designers is their clothes are classics. They look great anytime, any year."

"Then I'd say you must have a very clever eye, Miss Natalie. That's my judgment."

"Considering how little practice I've had . . . four years ago I bounced a check at Marshall Field by mistake . . . just trying to buy a pair of cheap jeans."

"Well, if my wishes come true, I think we can assume those days are slipping behind you now."

"You want to tell me your wishes, or shall we wait for a better place, somewhere romantic, for us?"

"You still thinking about that parking place behind the field Tony mentioned?"

"Not precisely." She giggled. "Not now that you have a big white mansion overlooking the water."

"Miss Natalie!" he said. "You're not proposing moving in with me, are you?"

"Not quite yet. Mostly because it would cause a national scandal in Seapuit, and might turn out to be a huge embarrassment for the boys."

"It would. That's why I checked you into the McLures' again with Tony."

"That'll be fine." But she put on a little-girl voice and added, "However, I do hope to be invited perhaps to your new house, some-time soon."

"Natalie, if you like that house, I'll buy it for you," he replied, and he was not smiling when he spoke, probably because he meant it.

"No handouts," she said, laughing again.

"Except for Calvin and those guys, right?"

"Right," she said. "Except for them."

By now they had reached the luggage area, and her suitcase was about five minutes away. "We driving down?" she asked.

"No, I sent the car down to the airport on the Cape to wait for us. We're going down in a little plane soon as your case arrives."

"A private plane?"

"Sure. Traffic to the Cape on July Fourth weekend is awful, miles of traffic trying to get over the bridges. These little planes go straight over 'em, and they don't cost much, 'bout five hundred and fifty dollars, forty-minute ride."

"Sounds like a lot to me."

"Guess so, coupla Calvin dresses' worth, right?"

"Well, what would the regular fare be for us?"

"Probably one-twenty each, one way."

"Well, that means we just blew three hundred bucks, right?"

"Yeah. Suppose we did . . . you know how long it takes my capital to make that three hundred in interest?"

"How long?"

"Around twelve minutes."

"Mother of God," said Natalie. "You're actually making a profit on the trip."

"Well, not till we're halfway there. Just down Massachusetts Bay, and we're making money again."

Like all farmers, Ben knew a lot about money. And he knew that high-yield energy companies like Louisiana Oil and Gas were going to make him 10 percent on his investment capital even in a recession. That worked out at $1 million a month, $250,000 a week. Every day he would earn something around $37,000. Every hour that would be $1,500. Twelve minutes to pay the extra for the private plane to the Cape.

Natalie just shook her head.

The twin-engine Beechcraft made the journey to the Cape in thirty-five minutes in front of a light northwest breeze. They drove first to the big house on the water, where Ben dismissed the chauffeur and put Natalie's luggage in the back of the Mercedes. They had a glass of iced tea on the screened porch and watched the juniors at the local yacht club locked in combat, racing a class of skiffs.

"My God, these kids are privileged," said Natalie. "Just imagine being able to do something like that at the age of ten or whatever they are. I never did one thing like that for Tony. Couldn't. But I guess kids like these just take it all for granted."

"Never known anything else, have they?" said Ben. "All they have to hope is the family cash holds out, and then their lives are going to be just fine. Otherwise they're gonna have to scrap and fight every yard of the way like the rest of us."

"Well, we've done our share of that."

"We have. But we're headed into fairer winds now, and the biggest thing we have to work on today is to select a restaurant for tonight. The guys don't have a game till tomorrow, then Jack pitches against the St. Ives Red Sox at home on Monday."

"If I know you, there's a restaurant already booked."

"Well, the place we're going doesn't take reservations, so I couldn't, but we're still going."

"Where is it?"

"Oh, down the Cape, out in the beach dunes at Dennis. It's called

Gina's-by-the-Sea. I went there once with Russ and Ted after we played at Nauset. It's a great old-fashioned bar, and the food's great. Italian, good wine list. Run by a sailor, real character called Ross. Our driver, Paul, who just brought us from the airport, works there part-time as a barman."

"Sounds fun."

"That's what it is. Fun and always crowded in the summer. But a lot of folks eat early around here; we'll be fine around nine o'clock. We'll have a driver."

"You're very extravagant these days. How much will that set you back?"

"About a hundred bucks."

"What's that? Ten minutes' interest?"

"Two."

"Go for it, Ben Faber. Go for it."

And so they passed a perfect couple of days, dining, riding around the islands in the new boat, looking after the boys, watching the 'Wolves win a close 5–4 home-field struggle with the Sentries, then lose 6–0 at Monomoy Stadium against the Rollers on Sunday.

On Saturday night, both boys had gone out to a beach party, and Ben and Natalie were alone at the house. They cooked a couple of steaks on the outside barbecue and ate them at the table on the long screened porch, slowly, just with a salad and a bottle of 1990 Bordeaux, Château Pichon-Longueville-Baron, shrewdly selected by Ben's new buddy Danny at the Seapuit liquor store. Ben, with that inbuilt French influence of south Louisiana, had always been a frustrated lover of good wine, but had rarely, if ever, been able to afford it, though one time, when the sugar was good, he had bought a case of Château Fontenil, which he made last for a year.

He reflected now that the case had cost less than the bottle he and Natalie were now drinking so many years later. He savored the deep, velvety wine, recognizing its aromas of crushed berries, with plum and currant undertones, and he swiftly ran the numbers, a lifelong habit . . . *two hundred a bottle, every night for a year, seventy thousand dollars, two days' interest on the capital. No problem.*

Natalie too appreciated the silky refinement of this particular glass of wine. "This, Ben," she said, "is delicious. I daren't even think what it cost."

"Not much." he replied. "We could go on drinking a bottle of this with dinner each night for quite a while."

"How long?"

"Oh, 'bout a thousand years."

Natalie laughed. But she noticed how the wonder of being suddenly very rich seemed to interpose itself everywhere. Even drinking a glass of wine, the sheer newness of the extravagance was always front and center. Still, it was a lot of fun.

After dinner they went back into the house and Ben went to the kitchen to see Mrs. Prentice, who was preparing coffee. And it was then that Natalie saw the piano, a black baby-grand Steinway, out beyond the main seaward room, in the corner of the small study, which was illuminated only by the picture lights on three superb nineteenth-century marine paintings, one of them a James Buttersworth.

She walked slowly toward the piano and opened the lid, running her fingers sideways, gently down the keys, as if stroking a great, sleeping bear. Then she sat at the bench seat and touched a few notes, glancing out at the moonlit water and thinking of the brilliant Beethoven.

She flexed her long fingers, and slowly she began to play the perfect notes of the fourteenth sonata, op. 27, part two, in C-sharp minor. At which moment Ben came back from the kitchen, and he could see her through the door to the softly lit study, her long hair falling about her shoulders, her face raised, eyes half-closed, as she played the most haunting notes of perhaps the most haunting sonata ever written for the piano.

Natalie looked up and smiled at him, but she did not stop playing, and Ben Faber just stood there, enraptured by the achingly beautiful sounds of the music. And his thoughts rose and fell as he watched her, dumbfounded at the sight before him, her beauty, her dignity, and her mastery of the Steinway.

And he thought of where she came from, and the thousands of hours she must have spent practicing, like a great ballet dancer, or a painter. And here she was in this room, with him alone, a virtuoso in her own right, at last in a proper setting to let him hear her, to show him a glimpse, for the first time, of the brilliance that had earned her a place, so young, in Sir Georg Solti's mighty Chicago Symphony, playing on a regular basis, three different instruments, the harp, the violin, and the piano, but still poverty-stricken.

Ben Faber was speechless, and he stood quietly while she finished the piece, and he clapped slowly at its conclusion, and then he walked toward her and took her in his arms, and kissed her for so long and so lovingly the tide could have retreated and returned without either of them noticing.

Eventually he whispered to her, "What was it called?"

"The *Moonlight Sonata*, silly," she said. "It's most people's favorite piano classic."

"Your people, Natalie. Not mine," he said, and for the first time he understood entirely the alien nature the world of baseball must have presented to such a musical scholar, indeed a virtuoso, of Natalie Garcia's stature. And he thanked God for Tony's fast left glove, which essentially had thrown them together.

But the hour grew late, and Natalie wanted to be back at the McLures' before her son, and the rising urgency of their relationship had to be put on hold, and Ben made it easy. He was a calm and reflective man, and he considered the rest of his life spread out before him in a relaxed and somewhat carefree carpet of fine, easy living.

He'd gone through forty-two years of the other kind, and generally speaking he liked the new kind better. And he knew that he and Natalie had time, and he was in no hurry. He took her home, and he kissed her once on the doorstep of the McLures' house, wrapping her safely in his arms.

Monday was Natalie's last day, and she wished she could spend the afternoon anywhere with Ben rather than at Cabot Field watching Tony catch Jack against the Red Sox. But they went to the game, and throughout that late afternoon she could only ruminate about how this great fortune of Ben's would ultimately stand between them. It would alter his perspective. It was already doing so. His tastes were changing, as they plainly must, and soon his friends would change. And perhaps one day, he might not be in any way interested in marrying a penniless musician from the Chicago tenements, with a college dropout for a son. If only Tony could go to law school. If only she could get something steady, establish herself, perhaps become a professor of music at Northwestern . . .

It was near impossible for Natalie Garcia to comprehend that Ben Faber was rapidly falling in love, simply with her, and that every day he admired and respected her more. It would be months before she would understand the dazzling effect her perfect rendition of the *Moonlight Sonata* had on him.

Because she had never met such a man as Ben Faber. Nor could she imagine the quiet, grounded souls of such men, forged on a life-long struggle with places like the flatlands of south Louisiana—with their merciless extremes of weather, the bountiful harvests of one year, and the blighted ones of the next. The memories always hung in their humid air. When men like Ben Faber made decisions, they were profoundly slow, long-considered, and devoid of embellishment. And those decisions carried with them a permanence that would not again be questioned.

And now she sat next to him, snuggled against him, hoping no one would notice. She was asking herself the same questions over and over . . . What could her son possibly be doing here, covered in dust, wearing that absurd mask, and a glove that ought to have belonged to Caliban? Would he never understand the damage he was inflicting upon everything she cared about? How could he not see the sheer useless-ness of this awful, plebeian game? And how it must, in the end, destroy both of their lives.

Out on the mound, Jack Faber was having one hell of a July Fourth. The 'Wolves had it 5–0 at the top of the ninth, with two out, no one on, and a count of 0–2 on the batter. The crowd stood in rapt fascination at the prospect of the first no-hitter seen at Cabot Field this year. Jack had given up three walks, but no one had hit the ball and reached first base.

So far he had equaled his season high of ten strikeouts, and Natalie had felt Ben's right arm vibrate every time one of them went in. She realized something important was happening, but Ben was lost in the tumult and the yelling. One section of the crowd was clapping rhythmically as Jack stood motionless on the mound. She stared out at him, this towering figure in his Seawolves hat. She saw Tony making contact, noticed Jack's curt little nod, and she felt, irrationally, that these two young men were on a wavelength out there she could never share.

Everyone was on their feet now as Jack stood one out from triumph. Ben held his breath as Tony hunkered down, positioning his glove high and outside. And Natalie saw Jack go into his windup, long and loose, his left leg raised high, and she saw him catapult forward, his right arm whipping over, releasing his 95 mph fastball.

She never saw the ball. Never saw it come screaming in, swerving over the outside edge of the plate. She would never understand the blind futility of the hitter's late swing, the way the bat slashed under the ball. She heard it smack into Tony's glove, and she saw her son's arm fly into the air as he pulled off his mask.

And she could see Tony's huge grin as he ran toward the mound, an expression of pure glee on his face. She saw the umpire ram both arms out to his left, and she saw him rip his right one back hard. But she never heard the call, never heard him bellow, *"STRIKE THREE!"* Because the noise from the crowd was about forty decibels too loud.

And above it all, she could see Ben, tears of joy streaming down his face, shouting over and over, *"THAT'S IT, JACKIE, THAT'S THE ONE!"* And she guessed, correctly, that was the sound Jack had been hearing all of his life, the sound which perhaps drove him forward.

She also had never known such unreserved jubilation in Ben's voice. And she knew for certain that the hundred million bucks, whatever it was, had never had such an effect on him. The money provoked in him a wry amusement. Whereas that last pitch of Jack's represented a brush with the Holy Grail.

The July Fourth no-hitter. The Fabers would never forget it, but, of course, Natalie could not understand the landmark. She was frankly surprised that anyone *ever* hit the ball, in *any* game, it was thrown so hard. And Jack threw it harder than everyone else, according to Tony, who she supposed must know. So why would anyone be surprised no one hit the stupid ball? So far as she was concerned, it was impossible anyway. So why all the fuss?

And why was Ben talking to people about another one of these pitchers? Who was it? Dave Righetti? Yankee Stadium against Boston? Another July Fourth no-hitter, twenty-five years ago? She imagined it must have been a significant parallel, though the full implications went by her like a tailing fastball. So she turned to Ben, and held his arm tightly, and told him she was quite sure Jack had done something wonderful, and anyway she loved all the Fabers she had ever met—just two—and to let her know later the deep technicalities of the no-hitter, which had thus far eluded her.

With eleven new strikeout notches on his gun, Jack felt his game was back in order. He and Ted had worked again on the slider for a while in the morning before the game, and its disguise from hitters was now as good as they could get it. In his first five games, Jack was 4–1, and as the season reached the halfway stage, the 'Wolves were way out on top of the Western Division with a record first half of 18–4.

The pitchers had done a stupendous job, and the team ERA was 2.19. Pedro lost one game and stood at 4–1; Kyle was 5–0, with Doughnut at 2–1. Cruiser was 1–0 in relief, and Matt Donovan was 2–1.

The hitters too had been on a rampage, averaging 7.4 runs per game, with an average of one home run every time they suited up. The local press had taken to describing a brand-new Seawolves Murderers' Row—Boom-Boom Hacker, Ray Sweeney, and Zac Colbert.

In the first half season, Boom-Boom slammed six baseballs over various fences. With twenty-seven RBIs, he had a batting average of .317.

Sweeney was right below him at .311, with four home runs, twenty-one RBIs, five doubles, and two triples. And Ray held a 1000 fielding percentage, no errors in twenty-two games, with forty-eight putouts, most of them near the fence, eight of them sensational. Two of these supreme catches were made as he thundered through the deep outfield, the ball coming in high, over the back of his head and into his glove.

As Russ Maddox observed, "The only outfielder I ever saw do that on a regular basis, either live or on film, was Willie Mays."

Zac Colbert was a huge boost to the team, urging them on, encouraging, harrying, and harassing. He reached the halfway point with an average of .301, with three home runs, eleven doubles, and twenty-five RBIs.

The Citadel cadets were immaculate. The shortstop Rick Adams was as good a setup man as Russ Maddox had ever coached. Rick was not a power hitter, but he had a superb eye and unbelievable discipline at the plate. He banged the ball into the gaps, earning himself a halfway batting average of .320, with twenty-six base hits and nine walks. His fielding percentage was .998, just one error in twenty-two starts.

Bobby Madison batted .278, but he was second in the league with twelve stolen bases. His teammates, the Olympic-class high-hurdler from Columbia, Steve Thompson, led the league with seventeen.

Gino Rossi was batting .291, with five doubles, two triples, and one home run. Tony Garcia, by now recognized as the best college catcher in the country, was watched each night by up to a dozen scouts. He hit .283 with three doubles and two home runs. If there were any doubters on Cape Marlin that this was the best team of college kids ever to play here, there weren't many of them.

The second half of the season was one continuous rampage, spread over a long hot month. Jack Faber pitched six more times, improving with every game. He finished the regular season 10–1. In his last six games he pitched two shutouts, one game with only one run scored against him, and two with two runs. The other one was at Rock Harbor against the Mariners, and the 'Wolves won it 6–4, and Jack had to dig deep.

At season's end, the Seawolves were well on top with a devastating record of 37–7, the best ever in the Cape League. The team made only fourteen errors among them, and that separated them from everyone else. The steel-trap, shortstop–second base combination of Rick Adams and Bobby Madison turned out better than anyone had ever imagined. They were a tribute to Russ Maddox's search for a combination from the same school, and they were the key cog in the defense. They were *every* Seawolf pitcher's best friends.

No one associated with the Cape League had ever seen a more flawless tandem. Rick and Bobby, the general's son and the steelworker's son, were a double-play machine. Baseball scouts were actively making comparisons with the great Alan Trammell and Lou Whitaker, the Detroit Tigers' legendary, near-telepathic shortstop–second baseman duo, who dominated the 1984 World Series when the Tigers beat the Padres 4–1.

Bat Markham, the Orioles scout, put Adams and Madison in the same class as Omar Vizquel and Roberto Alomar for the Cleveland Indians in the midnineties. "I'm not talking hitting ability, comparing college kids with Major League stars," he said. "I'm talking defensive infield brilliance, anticipation, fabulous glove, throw, and pure speed. I never saw Adams or Bobby miss anything, never saw either one of them in the wrong place, never saw a bad throw between them. And fast! Are those guys fast. I don't know what you have to do to be *better* than them. I just ain't seen it, that's all."

At the plate, Boom-Boom Hacker finished with thirteen home runs, and .318. Ray Sweeney was .313, with seven home runs, thirty-nine RBIs, and *still* a 1000 fielding percentage. Zac Colbert hit five home runs, nineteen doubles, forty-three RBIs, for .303.

The 'Wolves growled their way into the best-of-three divisional play-off and crushed the Cardiff Commodores two straight, with scores of 7–1 and 6–1.

In the championship final, against the Eastern Division champion Wellfleet Athletics, the 'Wolves' won 3–1 at Cabot Field and then 5–2 at North Fleet Stadium. Most people believed the championship would be wrapped up at the Seawolves' home field in the third game on Friday afternoon at 5 P.M., August 12, Jack Faber starting for the raging-hot favorites.

Natalie Garcia flew in from Chicago again, after a long weekend with the symphony, and then a two-day classical-music seminar at Northwestern University, at which she was a guest lecturer. Ben met her at the airport right after lunch, and again almost gasped at her appearance as she marched off the plane, in her Yves St. Laurent summer dress, the claret-colored Donna Karan bag slung over her shoulder, $300 Chanel sunglasses ($49 in the outlet) doubling as a hairband.

They hugged each other, closely but quickly. Because of the tight time frame, Ben had rented a helicopter to fly them directly to Seapuit, right down onto the wide clifftop lawn of his house.

Natalie had never even seen a helicopter up close, never mind traveled in one, and she sat incredulously up front with the pilot while Ben, veteran of one flight in his life, from Lockport to the offices of Louisiana Oil and Gas, sat reading, nonchalantly, *Baseball Weekly* in the backseat. They clattered down the shore of Massachusetts Bay, crossed the canal, and then swung almost due south, over the wooded country and long ponds, to the shore of Seapuit, touching down gently in front of the house. It took only thirty-five minutes, airport to screened porch.

"Twenty-four minutes," said Ben as they watched it take off.

"Oh really, I thought it took more than a half hour."

"I'm not talking flying time," said Ben, mock serious, deep-voiced. "I'm talking interest on capital, time lapsed, profit margins. We hit the black just south of Plymouth. I'm in big finance mode, and that's the way I like it."

Natalie squealed with laughter. "You are so silly," she said. "And I have so missed you . . ."

"Hell, I've called you twice a day for the last two weeks," he said, chuckling, and holding her tightly.

"Not enough," she said. "Not nearly enough."

It was almost 3:30 now, and Ben wanted to watch the batting practice before the final game, and he thought Natalie might like to see Tony hit. He was actually surprised, pleasantly, when she said she would like that very much.

And later, during the game, he was also happy when she began asking questions, about the catcher's tasks and the critical issue of his throw to a threatened second base. Natalie Garcia, mother of the Seawolves' wizard behind the plate, was actually quite surprised to learn that Tony assumed a loose command of the Seapuit defense every time he ran out onto the field; that it was he who decided the kind of pitch Jack would throw, unless Ted Sando had a strong conflicting opinion. And that it was Tony who had much to say about whether a pitcher, any pitcher, came out of the game; Tony, whose observations were considered, by the coaches, more than any other factor in the game.

She also wanted to know about Jack's pitches, when he threw the curve, or the slider, or the change-up. How fast was fast? How could Ben tell whether the pitch was outside just because of the position of Tony's glove?

It was strange, but Ben had sensed a change in Natalie. It was an increase in confidence, as if her virtuosity at the keyboard somehow made her equal with Jack's on the mound, Tony's behind the plate. She seemed less to feel the need to denigrate the game, even to despise it. It was as if the fine concert pianist she most certainly was, felt suddenly the freedom to be gracious to others, whose talents were obviously different but comparable.

Well, different, at least. Natalie would never regard the hurling of a schoolyard ball, no matter how hard or curved, as in any way comparable to the learning, understanding, and artistic execution of, for instance, Franz Liszt's Hungarian Rhapsody no. 11, at which she was an acknowledged expert.

Nonetheless, over the past five weeks, she had become inexplicably magnanimous about the great and glorious game, and seemed no longer to regard it as quite such a mortal threat to hers and Tony's existence.

Facing the Wellfleet Athletics, Seapuit had their bats swishing through empty space and their backs to the wall. The Wellfleet starter, Kurt Tillman from Coastal Carolina, went six innings, relying heavily on a blazing fastball, and he held the 'Wolves to one run, while Jack shut out the visitors completely.

Natalie wanted to know why no one could hit Tillman hard, and she simply could not see the venom in his fastball, or the deadly curve in his rare off-speed pitches. Kurt, a tough, broad-shouldered country boy with tree-trunk legs, did not have a slider but he had a change-up that drove everyone mad on the nine occasions he threw it.

Meantime, Jack kept pitching, hard and steady, giving his opponents nothing to hit, and varying his speeds just sufficiently to keep the Athletic hitters constantly off balance.

He stood them down in order at the top of the seventh, and after the stretch, Wellfleet sent Kurt Tillman to the mound once more. And right then, with his shoulder beginning to ache, he ran suddenly out of steam, and the 'Wolves were on him. Rossi, Adams, and Colbert loaded the bases, with straight base hits to the shallow outfield, and Boom-Boom banged the first two home with a blast to deep left field.

The Wellfleet coach came out and removed Tillman from the fray. The new pitcher was worse, and he was immediately hit hard to center field by Ray Sweeney. Two more runs went in for 5–0.

Bobby Madison banged a line-drive single up the middle, which sent Ray to third. And then the DH, Griff Heeney, from Notre Dame, slashed a one-hop base hit down the third-base line. The ball ricocheted off the infielder's chest and bounced six feet away, which kept Ray at third, but advanced Bobby to second. Bases loaded. No one out.

Steve Thompson was next up and he hit the first pitch hard into the right-field–center gap. Ray Sweeney scored, Bobby scored. Griff Heeney made third, Steve on first with a long single. It was 7–0, no one out, two on.

Again Wellfleet went to the bull pen, removing their first reliever and bringing in a freshman from Vanderbilt, a big Cape League rookie named Chuck Muldoon from Alabama.

Chuck took his eight warm-ups and settled down to pitch to Tony Garcia, who, generally speaking, had forgotten more about brand-new pitchers than young Muldoon would ever know.

Uncertain, Chuck opened with two curves, both of which dipped over the plate for called strikes. Then he made a strategic change and elected to hurl an 85 mph fastball, high and dead center. Tony Garcia saw it coming and absolutely detonated on that ball, slammed it straight over the scoreboard into the trees, sending Heeney and Thompson home and making a leisurely jog around the bases himself, looking up to wave to his mom, who, to his utter astonishment, waved back.

Jack came up once more to send the Athletics down, and Russ took him out, ordering Doughnut Davis into the fray for the ninth, to guard the safe 10–0 lead.

And instantly it was clear Doughnut was in erratic form. He walked the first two hitters and whacked the third man in the back with a high inside fastball which loaded the bases. He then whipped a tailing fastball four feet outside the plate, which Garcia somehow caught, almost standing on his head. And then the Georgia Bulldog threw a wild pitch into almost the same place except wider. Garcia missed it, and one run scored.

Ted Sando called *"TIME!"* and jogged out to the mound, cursing the fact they'd taken Jack out. "Come on, Doughnut . . . take a deep breath and relax, buddy . . . you got a nine-run lead, make them put the ball in play . . . slow it down, and watch Tony's glove. Get 'em the hell outta here, and let's go to the party."

"You got it, Coach. *YESSIR.* You got it."

And with that, he hurled in another screamer, too high, too straight, and the Wellfleet hitter banged it hard toward the fence. Ray Sweeney picked it up early, one hundred feet above the field. His eyes were glued on the falling ball, and he ran toward the fence, flying over the ground. Then he launched himself forward, making a breathtaking catch for the out. He rolled and bounced, flung the ball with all of his strength to the cutoff man, Rick Adams, who caught it and spun around, sending a sensational throw to Zac Colbert at third base, which held the runner at second. The score was 10–2, one out, a man on second.

Doughnut pitched again for a strike. Then another fastball for a swing and a miss. Then he sent in a soft curveball, and the hitter cracked a liner at Rick Adams. The officer cadet made a desperate leap into the air and snagged the ball, eleven feet off the ground, for the out.

The Wellfleet runner was twelve feet off the second-base bag, frantically trying to get back. He saw Rick's hard straight throw, and he could see Bobby Madison arrowing in to catch it. And he faced death with equanimity. The ball hit Bobby's glove for the double play in the split second before the Wellfleet man's outstretched fingers hit the bag.

The 10–3 victory made the Seapuit Seawolves champions of the Cape Marlin League for the second year in succession. The crowd rose for this team, standing up, clapping and cheering the most memorable season.

Doughnut came off the mound, acknowledging the applause as if he'd registered a no-hitter. He was raising his cap, tossing kisses to the crowd through his cap, pumping his right arm back and forth, leaping and bounding back to the dugout, calling out to Ted: *"Had it in my back pocket the entire time, Coach. Never even broke a sweat. Fastball. YESSIR. They can't touch that, right, Coach?"*

Teddy patted him on the back. He'd miss Doughnut, if only because cast-iron self-belief of that dimension was unlikely to manifest itself twice in anyone's lifetime.

And now the Wolves were piling out of the dugout, jumping and leaping into a wild celebratory heap. League officials were wheeling out the championship trophy for presentation, and Ward Fallon was on his cell phone to home, confirming that he celebration party was a go.

Rick Adams and Bobby Madison elected not to return to South Carolina in Major General Adams's military aircraft but to stay with their teammates. It would be the last time most of them would ever see one another.

Ray Sweeney was trying to find his father, who had promised to come down to the Cape from Maine to watch the game. He had actually turned up in a big lobster boat, *Sweeney Todd,* after a thirty-six-hour journey from North Haven across the Gulf of Maine, then east of Provincetown, through rough water off Monomoy Point, and across the Sound to Seapuit Bay.

Someone told Ray it was moored off the Oyster Company, but so far he hadn't located the skipper up in the bleachers.

Ben and Natalie came down to the field to congratulate the winning pitcher, the tireless catcher, and the home-run hero of the game. Tony Garcia was immediately named the league's MVP for "all-around excellence." And through the wildly applauding crowd in the parking lot came the aging convertible owned by the Massachusetts Senator Ted Kennedy, who was there to present the MVP trophy named in his honor, colloquially known among all college baseball stars as the Teddy.

Anyway, Tony had won the Teddy, and the press and local television swarmed forward to capture the moment as Senator Kennedy presented the catcher from Chicago with the gleaming silver cup. Thoroughly briefed as always, the senator told him, "This is the first time a catcher has won this for more than twenty years. And I'm sure you're going on to make a great name for yourself in the Major Leagues. Your coach tells me you're one of the hardest workers on this team, with cool judgment, a total grasp of the game, and when necessary, a ruthless streak—reminded me a little of myself, tell you the truth!"

This last remark predictably brought down the house, and the senator shook the hand of Tony Garcia and told him everyone down here on Cape Marlin was proud to have seen him play. "And what a moment when you hit the big home run this afternoon . . ."

"You've hit a few yourself, sir," replied Tony, unabashed to the end. "So I'm taking that as a major compliment!"

The senator patted him on the arm, a solid Irish gesture of friendship, and added, "We'll be watching for you—and don't forget to come back and see us when you're a big star." The crowd cheered, and Ben and Natalie clapped. And Senator Kennedy with all that natural down-home grace, suddenly spotted last year's winner in the throng of spectators, and he walked over to Jack Faber, remembering his name, never missing a beat, and said, "Hey, Jack, another great season for you too. Darn Seawolves got a lock on the trophy these days!"

"Seems like it, sir. But I got it after only twelve nights' work. Old Tony here had to work every night, played nearly forty games behind the plate. Never missed an out."

"Good to see a catcher get recognized," replied Ted Kennedy. "The heart of the team, right?"

"The heart of the team, sir," said Jack Faber.

2 1

It was the speech that did it. Russ Maddox climbed to his feet at the top table, right out there on the Fallons' lawn overlooking the bay, and as the full moon rose above the silvery water, he said: "This is the greatest college team I have ever seen. It may be the best college team there has ever been. In my view, the Seawolves could take on a couple of the Major League outfits and whip their asses."

A raucous, heartfelt cheer ripped up into the night air. Fists were raised, high fives were offered and executed, parents clapped, house-parents yelled, ballplayers raised their arms high. Doughnut and the Cruiser, both on their third beers, stood up on their chairs and bellowed, hideously out of tune, *"GONNA MAKE A STRIKEOUT FOR JESUS—AT THE HOME PLATE OF LIFE! HOW 'BOUT THEM DAWGS!"*

Everyone applauded, all sixty people, sitting six at a table, eating New York prime sirloin steaks, big fresh ears of exquisitely sweet local corn, and hot French baguettes. There was excellent wine, provided by Ben, and three big plastic garbage bins filled with ice, bottles of Rolling Rock beer, and sodas.

Russ Maddox had never received such a warm reception, and he continued his drift about the hard technical merits of his champion team. "We've had nights when big hits were not coming, and you guys dug deep, whacked the ball into the gaps, stole bases, scrapped for runs, scrapped for every yard. You guys were in one of the very rare teams which could still win, even when everything was going wrong.

"In defense, you gave nothing away. You broke your opponents' hearts. Coaches have told me guys literally dreaded coming to Cabot Field because there you had to *earn* every last hit, every run, every out. All season long the 'Wolves gave away nothing. Goddammit, I'm proud of every one of you."

Another burst of applause swept up into the night air, and when it died away, Russ Maddox congratulated the pitchers, naming them one by one, mentioning their highest moments, and making special reference to Jack Faber, "who overcame so much to give us, in the end, everything."

He mentioned each of the hitters, the big bangers, Boom-Boom, Ray, and Zac. And he mentioned the setup men, Gino, Rick, Bobby, Tony, Steve, and Griff. You could count on all of them. "In a tight corner, I always knew one of them, at least, would get on base, get a rally started.

"Our strength never varied. When we needed a hit, we got that hit. When we needed a strike, someone threw it. That's the essence of the game. The big play, when the chips are down."

Again the Seawolf family leaped to its feet, cheering and applauding the words of the coach. But Russ was not finished, and he moved into a very serious mode.

"I am reminded," he said, "of the words of Ty Cobb, who said, back in 1925, 'The great trouble with baseball today is that most of the players are in it for the money, and that's it. Not for the love of it, the excitement of it, the thrill of it.'

"Ty's words are about a million times more true today than they were back then. But the reason I am reminded of those words is because at this final gathering of the 'Wolves, there is very nearly a whole team of young men who are here because of their love of the game, the excitement of it, the thrill of it.

"And I mean by that, none of them is hell-bent on making a career out of professional baseball. And yet each and every one of them stood out there and fought for victory. They were calm, measured, and ferocious, like their ancestors two hundred and thirty years ago, not so far away at Bunker Hill. And I would like them to stand and remain standing when I call their names . . . in no special order . . .

"Ray Sweeney, the perfect outfielder, who, his dad tells me, will soon return to the family fishing business off the coast of his beloved Maine . . .

"Rick Adams and Bobby Madison, who will both answer a louder and more urgent call than that of the third-base coach—the sound of the bugles, as career officers in the army of the United States of America . . .

"Zac Colbert, our team leader, whose future lies in Oklahoma, running a vast ranch for a big man, who, like us, believes in him . . .

"Gino Rossi, another of our great outfielders, and our leadoff hitter—he's a city boy, and he learned baseball on some tough streets, and he's going back there to run a big Manhattan restaurant for his father . . .

"Jack Faber, our top starting pitcher, from Louisiana, whose family is now much bigger in the oil-and-gas business—I don't think Jack will sign a professional contract. His dad needs him more than some Single-A outfit in the boonies . . .

"Kyle Davidson, great pitcher, top economics student, son of a presidential adviser, a lawyer in Washington. Kyle has a shoulder more painful than he admits, and I think he has played the game this summer for the sheer joy of the contest—I don't look for him to sign a contract . . .

"And finally, our MVP, the incorrigible wit and embryo trial lawyer Tony Garcia. He wants to play ball, but his mom wants him to finish a law degree—she's very smart, very beautiful, very talented, and a lot too tough for him! Stand up, Tony, you're gonna be in school, trust me."

Tony stood with the rest of them. And Russ Maddox finished with a flourish. "Ladies and gentlemen," he said. "We also have some great kids who, for other reasons, find baseball their best shot for a professional career. I applaud them, I love them, and I wish them all the luck in the world. But the Seapuit Seawolves won this great championship because our bedrock was a wonderful group of guys who played their hearts out, not to impress the Major League scouts—just for the love of the game."

All of which would have been just fine. Except for one thing. There was a sportswriter from the *Cape Marlin Telegraph*, Tom Mangold, sitting with the houseparents of Steve Thompson. Tom was a regular at Cape League games, and had never been known to write a scurrilous word about any team.

But now his antennae were up, and after dinner he went to Russ Maddox and Ted Sando, both of whom knew him, and he asked, "Were you serious about the 'Wolves beating a Major League team?"

"Almost," said Russ, grinning. "There's a few teams in the Bigs with a lot of old guys on their staff . . . you can tell by the way they're mostly bottom of their divisions. But the issue is pitching, and if they're carrying a lot of late season injuries in the bull pen, sure we'd give 'em a run. There's a couple right now we'd beat . . . we'd be too fast, too young, too good—and we got guys who can pitch. Hard."

That evening Russ was feeling exuberant after a few glasses of wine, but the new dawn brought a blast of reality when he was greeted by the following headline in the *Telegraph,* which announced:

MY SEAWOLVES COULD WHIP THE PROS!
Coach Maddox Throws
Down the Gauntlet

"Christ!" said Russ. "This kind of stuff has brought down empires."

Essentially he ignored it. However, he did not know the news-distribution system that works in most provincial daily newspapers in the United States. The *Cape Marlin Telegraph*, for instance, shares stories with Associated Press, the wide-reaching international news agency.

Four hours before the *Telegraph* was off the press, AP had that story on the wire. And *The New York Times* ran it, on the fifth page of the Saturday sports section, just a short piece in a single column of four varied sports items, presented thus:

BASEBALL COACH CLAIMS COLLEGE
CHAMPS WOULD BEAT PROS

Cape Cod, MASS. Friday. The Seapuit Seawolves, with a 37–7 record, won the Cape Marlin Baseball League Championship last night, beating the Wellfleet Athletics by a score of 10–2. The Seawolves finished with the best record ever compiled in the nation's premier summer college league.

Their winning pitcher was Jack Faber, from St. Charles College, south Louisiana. The League's MVP and winner of the Senator Ted Kennedy Trophy was Seawolf catcher Tony Garcia of Northwestern, who hit a three-run homer on the way to victory over Wellfleet.

After the game, the Seawolves' coach, Russ Maddox of the University of Maine, said he believed his team could beat "a couple of the weaker Major League teams currently playing." He cited "substandard professional pitching, injuries, and players past their peak."

"They might find my guys too fast, too young, and too good," he said. "We have pitchers who can throw the ball hard. Our defense has been dynamite. This may be the best team of US college baseball stars ever to play the game."

And that was it. Nearly. Because on that particular night, New York was gripped by another baseball story that could surely have happened in no other city. It was the second lead on the front page of the main news section of the *New York Times*, it occupied the entire front page of the sports section, and it occupied the entire front page of the *Daily News*.

The *Times* headlines read:

DON STARGILL REFUNDS 15,000
BOMBER FANS TICKET CASH
19–0 Defeat by White Sox
sparks ultimate act of owner fury

The tabloid was more succinct. In an end-of-the-world typeface, set left, uppercase, the paper announced:

BROOKLYN BUMS
IN FREE SEATS!
"I wouldn't charge ANYONE
to watch this crap."
—Don Stargill

The facts were not in dispute. The Brooklyn Bombers had taken the most god-awful shellacking at the hands of the Chicago White

Sox. In the first seven innings the Bombers had given up eleven runs. Their three pitchers had scattered sixteen hits, and the defense had made four errors. And then, at the top of the ninth, Chicago had exploded on yet three more Brooklyn pitchers; hit two grand-slam home runs, both of them smashed high into the seats above center field.

It wasn't the worst thing that had ever happened in this ballfield. That honor went to the catastrophic 22–0 defeat inflicted on the Bombers the previous season by the Yankees.

But it was still diabolical, and Donald P. Stargill II was stunned and humiliated, since the whole of baseball knew he was shelling out weekly the highest annual payroll in the history of the game, $125 million, way more even than the Yankees.

And quite suddenly he had jumped up and stormed out of the owner's box, making straight for the game announcer's booth, seized the microphone, and literally yelled to the remaining faithful, *"FANS, THIS IS DON STARGILL, AND I WANT YOU TO KNOW I'M AS DISGUSTED WITH THIS AS YOU ARE . . ."*

A huge cheer went up, and the game stopped, mainly because the security guards swarmed onto the playing area, believing that a madman had taken control of the electronic communication system. Players on both teams looked around in amazement, especially the Bombers, whose defenses were also in disarray.

But Stargill was not finished. *"GODDAMMIT!"* he shouted, knowing his voice was bellowing right through the stadium. *"THIS IS A DISGRACE, AND I'M EMBARRASSED . . . I'M EMBARRASSED FOR EVERYONE HERE . . . AND THE LAST THING I'LL EVER DO IS TRY TO MAKE MONEY OFF IT . . . EVERY FAN IN THIS STADIUM IS GONNA GET A TWENTY-DOLLAR REFUND, RIGHT HERE AFTER THE GAME . . . AND I MEAN EVERYONE . . . I DON'T CARE HOW YOU GOT YOUR TICKET . . . I DON'T CARE IF YOU FOUND IT . . . THERE'S GONNA BE FIFTEEN THOUSAND TWENTY-DOLLAR BILLS WAITING AT THE TURNSTILES . . . ME? I'M GOING HOME RIGHT NOW . . . NINETEEN TO ZIP . . . JESUS CHRIST . . . CAN YOU IMAGINE? I'M DONE FOR THE NIGHT . . . OUTTA HERE . . . AND I'M COLLECTING MY TWENTY-DOLLAR BILL!"*

The biggest cheer of the Bombers' season echoed into the hot August night. The newspaper reporters surged to the executives' private entrance to meet the raging ball-club owner. They thronged the doorway, and they packed into a seething huddle around his limousine. Cameramen, columnists, television reporters, radio interviewers were on their cell phones, calling their offices, telling them to clear the decks. *"STARGILL'S FINALLY FLIPPED."*

There was bedlam in Brooklyn as the entire New York media piled reinforcements into the area. There were backup interviewers, backup cameras and microphones, feature writers, transmission staff all charging over the bridges toward the baseball stadium, where staff would shortly be manning the Refund of the Century, a $300,000 giveaway, no questions asked.

Back on the field of play, a calm settled over the diamond as spectators began to move down to the lower-level turnstiles. A private security truck, owned by the Bombers, was on its way two blocks to the Brooklyn and East River Bank, which was owned by Stargill, and which now had its night staff organizing the massive cash pickup.

In a sepulchral silence, after their thirty-five-minute assault on the Bombers' last-inning pitching, the White Sox jogged out into their defensive positions for the bottom of the ninth and sent their top closer to get rid of the Brooklyn team. He was a huge, long-haired giant named Al Cruz, who could throw a sensational 100 mph fastball about twenty-five times, flat out, before he fell in a heap, half-dead with exhaustion.

But he did not need the twenty-five to send the Bombers back to the locker room. He hurled three strikes in succession past the hideously out-of-form veteran catcher Pete McGuire, who was collecting $6 million a year for a batting average of .211 and a left knee no one in their right mind would value at more than around three bucks.

The power-hitting right fielder Don Hutchinson was next up, and he whacked the first two pitches in succession a hundred feet into the air, one fouled back down the right-field line, the other neatly into the glove of the White Sox shortstop.

The forty-one-year-old designated hitter Bert Muncie came in to end the agony, and wildly fanned three straight pitches, one low and in, two outside. Which essentially wrapped up what the tabloids would subsequently refer to as "Don Stargill's Night of Shame."

Meanwhile, down at the team executives' entrance, The Donald, as he was known, was giving vent to months of frustration. He was careless about what he said, uninterested in what the fifty or so journalists wrote, and determined only to inform the media what it was like "to pay these jerks a hundred and twenty-five million a year, for a team that can't beat anyone."

"*JESUS CHRIST!*" he yelled. "My old college team UCLA could beat these guys. I bet there's a half-dozen good college teams could whip these guys' asses. They're too slow, too old, and mostly too stupid!"

A battery of flashbulbs popped and the arc lights turned Bedford Avenue into a floodlit stadium in its own right, as the media questions came raining in, aimed at a man who was past caring what anyone thought, past caring if the Bombers lived or died, won or lost, past caring whether he bulldozed the stadium with the players in it, or outside on the sidewalk.

Generally speaking, it was like tossing a half ton of warm fillets of Dover sole to a couple of starving sharks.

"Mr. Stargill, a lot of people warned you about signing so many players who were past their peak, do you now regret that policy?"

"Are you prepared to sell the entire team and stadium?"

"Do you feel badly for the loyal Brooklyn Bombers fans?"

"Is it likely that you will not watch them play again?"

"Can we announce the Bombers are up for sale right now?"

"Do you regret ever having become involved in Major League Baseball?"

To each question Donald Stargill shouted: "*YES, ABSOLUTELY!*"

And then one of the baseball writers shouted, "*Mr. Stargill, what do you think has been the biggest factor in the team's failure to win—a lack of talent, a lack of team spirit, a lack of commitment, or a lack of fitness?*"

"*THE WHOLE FUCKING LOT!*" he roared. "*In case any of you are having trouble spelling or hearing, that's F-U-C-K-I-N-G L-O-T.*"

At this, another huge cheer went up, since there were now about two thousand spectators milling around, clutching their twenty-dollar bills. Some fathers with two or three children had eighty-dollars in their hands. A couple of private bus drivers, who had brought in coach loads of fans from Long Island, held as much as $700 for their passengers. And here they were, standing right there with the press, watching the owner of the Bombers unleashing this spectacular harangue against the team he believed had let him down, totally and utterly.

"Mr. Stargill, you do, of course, realize you are speaking on the record and this will all be reported both on the television and in the newspapers?"

"Of course I do. Only a goddamned journalist would think I made that much money by being stupid."

The crowd roared with laughter. *"WAY TO GO, DON BABY! YOU TELL IT LIKE IT IS . . ."*

"Mr. Stargill, you do realize the baseball commissioner may very well consider your actions and statements tonight as extremely detrimental to the game?"

"DETRIMENTAL!" bawled Donald Stargill. *"JESUS H. CHRIST! YOU DON'T THINK THIS GODDAMNED TEAM'S BEEN DETRIMENTAL TO ME?"*

"Well, I just thought the commissioner might issue some kind of censure, or even a fine, or maybe even ban you from the game."

"I just banned myself, or didn't you hear me?"

And then, as an afterthought he added, "The commissioner can stick his goddamned censures in the place where there is no sunshine. Unless he wants to come down here and pay the fucking one hundred and twenty-five million annual salary it costs to keep these incompetent assholes on the field. 'Dem Bums,' I believe, was the traditional title around here."

By now there were lines stretching all the way back through the stadium, but they were moving quickly, as the twenty-dollar bills were handed out. The Bombers' owner excused himself from the nonstop press conference and moved back among the fans, walking up to perfect strangers, shaking their hands, and saying, "I'm sorry. I'm Don Stargill. I'm just so sorry. They let us all down."

At this particular moment Donald P. Stargill II was possibly the most popular man in Brooklyn since Duke Snider returned home from St. Louis having shattered the Cardinals' stadium clock above the center-field seats with a home run.

The photographers followed him, trying to get pictures of the multibillionaire chatting to ordinary fans. And still the reporters fired questions at him.

"Do you regret not having a good farm system?"

"Is it true your lawyers are working on a complete shutdown, and that you'd let the Bombers corporation go into bankruptcy to avoid paying these players?"

"Do you regard these players as unsalable because of their huge salaries, and lack of success on the field?"

"I hear you never signed a contract making yourself personally and legally responsible for the debts of the Brooklyn Bombers? Is that true?

In the end, the Bombers' owner just retreated to his limousine, calling out as he went to the throng of journalists, "I just want to extricate myself from this mess. Baseball broke even Babe Ruth's heart. And I'm getting out before it breaks mine."

It was one hell of a story. And the only thing it absolutely obscured was the fact that Donald P. Stargill, in his as-yet-unbroken heart, *still* believed he could buy anything.

Back on Cape Marlin, the party above Seapuit Bay was winding down as midnight approached. Everyone was getting ready for the big evacuation of the next day, Sunday, August 14. They were all looking forward to going home, but there was profound sadness too, as young men who had fought it out together week after week on the ballfield, improving themselves, improving one another, mowing down the opposition, prepared to say good-bye for the last time.

For some of them there was comfort in the relative closeness of their homes, but for others the distance was probably insurmountable. No one thought they would see the mighty Zac Colbert again, or Ray Sweeney, or Jack, nor probably Tony, or Pedro. Certainly not the cadets, or the Cruiser. For most it was the first, serious adult farewell they had ever tackled, and there were a lot of openhanded slaps on the upper arm. *I'll miss you, man . . . don't forget, you're ever in my area . . . hey ! you nearly learned to play this game . . . bye, Zac, it's been a blast . . . bye, Pedro, great knowing you . . . bye, Ray . . . Bobby . . . Ricky . . . bye, guys . . . I'll miss you.*

And soon they would leave; by first light, Doughnut and Cruiser would be driving down the East Coast of the United States, headed for Savannah, Georgia, one thousand miles away. They would drop Rick Adams at Charleston, South Carolina, a hundred miles shy of their final destination, and Boom-Boom Hacker at nearby Hilton Head Island, arriving Monday afternoon. Chief Burrell would pick up his son in Savannah, in the real cruiser, around 5 P.M.

Ray Sweeney was driving north to Maine with Coach Maddox, who was aiming for Orono. Ray would disembark at Augusta, from where a friend would drive him down to Rockland, to the ferry for Vinalhaven Island, and home to Carver's Harbor, where the busy *Sweeney Todd* awaited him.

Gino Rossi and Steve Thompson were driving to New York together, midmorning. And at roughly the same time Kyle Davidson was setting off for Washington, D.C., eight hours away, straight down I-95.

Bobby Madison and Zac Colbert had very early flights out of Logan to Pittsburgh and Tulsa, Oklahoma. Pedro Rodriquez was leaving from Providence, Rhode Island, for Miami, and Tony Garcia, with Natalie, was leaving Boston for Chicago at 2 P.M.

Jack and Ben would drive them to the airport and then return to the Cape, since they had nowhere else to go for two weeks.

That Sunday in Seapuit thus dissolved into a blur of last-minute phone calls, disparate items of clothing and equipment restored to rightful owners, exchanges of addresses, uniforms returned, rushed sandwiches and sodas, revving automobiles, endless shouts of "Hurry, willya, we'll miss the flight." There were promises, and there was laughter, fabulous memories, and genuine sorrow at the breakup of a huge and thoroughly brilliant baseball family. There were tears from housemothers, and even more tears from local girl friends. Fans called around for final good-byes.

And then, it seemed quite suddenly, they were gone. And a warm sea breeze drifted over the desolate acres of Cabot Field. The bleachers were empty, and the locker room was bolted and barred until next season. Perhaps, in its darkness, there still lurked something of the heroes of that glorious summer. Used bats, old baseballs in the big white bucket, a hat, a glove, a pitching chart, a team list containing their names in the coach's hard, neat handwriting.

It was impossible to accept that they were somehow gone forever. But they were. And there was a shattering silence in the village of Seapuit.

* * *

Monday mornings were an outright chore for Jason Wright. At the age of twenty-six he was still in charge of the weekend newspapers in the Fifty-sixth Street offices of New York's second sports-radio channel, WFTD (AM 1200). Jason, who viewed his own journalistic talent somewhere between that of the late maestro Red Smith and the still-brilliant broadcaster Jack Whittaker, loathed the weekend newspapers.

They greeted him every Monday, at 7:30 A.M. They were piled on his desk like a cornerstone of the great Pyramids. There were thousands of pages of newsprint, filled, in Jason's opinion, with hundreds of articles, mostly consisting of complete, lightweight drivel. Worse yet, no one ever found a way to separate the parts he needed from the mountainous rubbish heap of show-business, cooking, and financial sections. Christ, he hated it.

It was fifteen minutes before eight o'clock and he had already sent for a messenger to "get these newspapers the hell off my desk." In fact he had dumped them on the floor, and now sat with a more manageable pile of news and sports sections from the *New York Times,* New York *Post,* the *Daily News, Newsday* (Long Island), the *Philadelphia Inquirer,* the *Boston Globe,* the *Hartford Courier,* and the *Washington Post.*

From what Jason could tell, Donald P. Stargill's performance would have eclipsed the Super Bowl. The story of the Great Refund was running coast to coast. Indeed, his own station was discussing nothing else, except for the regular ten-minute sports-news bulletins, which he was supposed to mastermind. After he had gutted the newspapers, that is.

Jason, a tall, flop-haired, gum-chewing graduate in journalism from the Universitry of Indiana, adored baseball and was entirely sympathetic to the emotional outburst by America's richest tycoon. He sat making notes from the story, chuckling and writing down carefully on his notepad such gems as, "I bet there's a half-dozen good college teams could whip these guys' asses . . . the team's for sale, stadium and all . . . I'm outta here . . . screw the commissioner . . . he can come down here himself if he feels like it, and pay these jerks their salary . . ."

Jason Wright, son of a local newspaper editor in Oklahoma, was also the fiancé of Jane Bertrand, a rising star of the New York City

Ballet. He did not see radio journalism as his final rung on the ladder of his ambition. And even though he might not have admitted it, he was always out there, seeking the big opportunity, watching for the chance to make a name for himself.

He had once read a book about England's most spectacular crime, the 1963 Great Train Robbery, when a gang stopped a London-bound express and relieved the freight car of over $5 million in used banknotes, a sensational amount then, probably $100 million in today's currency. Jason was fascinated by the story, which detailed how some of the bandits had gotten clean away, the most infamous of them, Ronnie Biggs, making it to Brazil, where he married and lived for thirty years.

But the part Jason always remembered was the chapter about the young English journalist Colin Betchworth, who actually located, more or less by accident in a London pub, the address and phone number in Rio of the world's most-wanted robber. He and "Biggsy" had talked on the transatlantic telephone and arranged to meet in Brazil to discuss the possibility of a book, which would be serialized for enormous sums of money in publications all over the world. Photographs of the fugitive "at home" would sell for thousands of pounds all over the English-speaking world and beyond.

Jason knew what he would have done. He would have seen this as his big chance, resigned from his newspaper, bought himself a high-class camera, taken a few lessons in photography, bought himself a ticket to Rio de Janeiro, and kept his mouth shut, tight, until he had formed an exclusive literary and photographic partnership with Ronnie Biggs.

In a sense, Jason Wright had been looking for *his* Great Train Robber ever since. And now, suddenly, as he combed through the *New York Times* sports section for follow-up news items, he found him. At least he thought he did. The name of Jason's robber was an amateur baseball coach named Russ Maddox, whose team had just won the Cape Marlin League Championship . . . *This may be the best college team there has ever been . . . take on a Major League team and whip their asses . . .*

The phrases were identical, those of Maddox and Stargill, and they meant the same thing—that the very best college teams could probably defeat overpaid, overweight, over-the-hill professional stars. And Jack ripped out page five of the Saturday sports section,

sliced it down the middle, and ran ten copies of the article which detailed the Seapuit Seawolves' victory. He was particularly interested
because he and Jane had spent a couple of weeks on Cape Marlin the
previous year and had been directed to a couple of Cape League
games by Bucky Crosby at the local boat marina.

Jason and Jane had actually gone to Bucky's his son Andy playing
right field for one of the teams, and it could have been the Seawolves.
But anyway, Jason had loved the games and loved the little ballfields
by the sea. He'd gone to Monomoy Stadium, home of the Nauset
Rollers, and to Oceanside Field, where the Rock Harbor Mariners
played, and he recalled being immensely impressed by the quality of
the baseball.

Of all the young New York broadcast journalists, completing
their Monday-morning chores, gutting the weekend newspapers,
there was no one to whom that little story about the 'Wolves was
more graphic, no one who could imagine the intensity of the Cape
League games with more insight. No one who could imagine better
the hotshot Cape League stars giving a Major League club a very difficult time.

The juxtaposition of the two baseball stories in Saturday's *Times*
fired Jason's eager imagination. There wasn't much of a story in it,
for a sports-radio station, except as a point of discussion. But what
if . . . ? Jason's mind raced. *What if Stargill could be persuaded to
put his team on the line in a big televised game against these brilliant
kids who play for fun?*

What if the nationally known Bums of Brooklyn could be made
to get out there and *prove* they were worth millions of dollars a
year? What if Stargill liked the idea? What about someone putting
up a $5 million prize, winner take all? What a promotion! And it just
might fire the imagination of the general public.

The question in Jason Wright's mind was, how do I insert myself
into the middle of this, with a chance of making some real money,
and maybe a brand-new career?

He was uncertain about that, uncertain whether he should even
mention it to his own boss, the sports editor of WFTD, uncertain to
whom he should speak. But the more he pondered, the more he believed he was onto something. The only thing he knew was he had
get the hell out of this office, one block down to the little park above
the East River at the Sutton Place end of East Fifty-seventh, where he

could sit quietly and . . . think. Think hard about his next move.

Three hours later he was sitting in a Fifth Avenue law firm drafting a letter which took one full page and umpteen *whereases* and *wheretofores,* to say: "If this idea should work, I will be entitled to one percent of all advertising revenues. If it doesn't work, you owe me nothing. I am available to assist in making it work, in any way you may wish."

At which point Jason Wright thanked Jane's attorney uncle, Thomas Bertrand, and set off into the great unknown. Twelve minutes later he was standing in the foyer of a Sixth Avenue high-rise, headquarters of CBA, the new television network sports giant. He was also informing the sports editor's secretary, on the internal telephone, that he had an appointment, and there must be some mistake. He had the legal letter the sports editor had asked for, and would she please pull herself together?

Eight minutes later he was led into one of the inner sanctums of the sports airwaves, and faced the formidable person of Art Mackay, the Boston Irish tyrant who ruled the entire domain with the verbal equivalent of a bullwhip.

"Listen, Jason," he grunted. "I can't remember what this is all about, but fill me in, and make it quick."

"You can't remember because we've never spoken to each other before," said Jason. "I had to bullshit my way in to see you. Which should tell you how good my idea is, because I realize you could have me thrown out of here in about three minutes, and I wouldn't like that."

Art Mackay lifted his bushy eyebrows. "Shit," he muttered. "It's not even lunchtime, and I've been conned already . . . but since you're here . . . enlighten me."

"Okay," replied Jason. "But first, I want you to read this legal letter, and hopefully agree to it . . ."

Art grabbed it, rudely, and scanned down the page. "All right, this says you got a big idea wants developing, and you don't get paid a dime if it doesn't happen, right?"

"Right. And if it does happen I will be paid one percent of the advertising revenue the television station earns from the project. You are my first port of call. I've so far spoken to no one."

Art Mackay still had the journalist's insatiable curiosity about a good story. And while this guy might be a nutcase, he didn't look like one, and he might just be onto something. Besides, the CBA sports boss was becoming intrigued by this self-assured young devil who had single-handedly stormed the garrison of the network. Art was a very powerful executive, who essentially answered to no one, and he didn't give a damn about one percent of anything.

"Here," he said, taking out his pen and scrawling his initials on the letter. "Take this, put it in your fucking pocket, and start talking."

Jason said he assumed Mr. Mackay was well up to scratch on the Donald Stargill story.

"You assume correctly, young man."

"Well, you will remember this quote from him," he said, handing over another sheet of paper, upon which he had written the sentence about whipping the asses of the Major League professionals.

"Got it," said Art.

"Well, take a look at this story, which appeared in the same edition of the *New York Times* on Saturday."

Jason handed over another piece of paper, and Art Mackay read the three paragraphs about the Seawolves carefully, noting the fighting words of the faraway Russ Maddox. He nodded and looked up. "Bit of a coincidence right there," he said. "Well spotted."

He read it through again, and then said, "What do you have in mind—some kind of a forum where experts discuss the merits of old pros against young tigers? Because if you do, it's quite nice and we could probably build it with a few inflammatory viewpoints. But I'm not seeing anything on a major scale."

"No? Then I wonder if you're the right man for me," said Jason thoughtfully.

It had been a while since anyone had dared to speak to Art Mackay like that, and he was more amused than anything else. "You plainly believe you're several jumps ahead of me," he said, wryly. "Quite a lot of people have thought that before. But not all of 'em have been right. Kindly explain, before I get impatient."

"Sir," said Jason, holding back his burgeoning excitement. "I'm suggesting we stage the fucking game, right there in Ebbets Field, the best team of amateur college players there's ever been against the highest-paid Major League baseball team in history."

Art Mackay got it. "You could be talking prime time," he said.

"Sir, in the one-week buildup to this game, you're gonna get several big TV 'specials' on these kids. You're gonna build them into household names in just a few days. You're gonna have the entire college system of the United States up and rooting for 'em. You're gonna get audiences in places you never even knew existed, and if I know anything about this country, it's gonna be gung ho for the amateurs all the way. For the kids, who do it for the thrills, for the love of the game, not for money . . . and Mr. Mackay, if they should win, it'll be in front of one of the biggest, happiest television audiences ever. It's America going right back to the roots of sport. Victory. Just for the love of the game."

Right now Art Mackay *really* got it.

"Okay, in principle I'm with you. Now, have you thought how we get it, and own it?"

"I have. CBA puts up a five-million-dollar winner-take-all prize. If the Bombers win, Stargill gets it. If the kids win, the Seawolves ball club will have enough probably to buy their ground and set up an endowment for their future. With the five million comes the exclusive television rights . . . for the purpose of this game, you will become the promoter, renting Ebbets Field for the night. That'll get the Major League blanket coverage contract out of your life. You'll pay just a regular agreed-upon fee. I doubt Stargill will be obstructive, not if he agrees in principle."

"Sounds sensible . . . hold on a minute . . ." Art hit a button and growled, "Send Pete and Charlie in here right now."

"Have you spoken to Stargill?"

"Only very briefly," lied Jason. "He wants more details. By tonight."

"How about the Seawolves?"

"I haven't approached them yet."

"Where are they?"

"Dunno, sir. But I'll find 'em."

Pete and Charlie came hurriedly through the door, and their smiling boss briefed them.

Pete Morris, the sports-news editor and producer, said simply, "I love it. I absolutely fucking love it. This is real down-home stuff. Everyone's sick to death of the money these guys make. It's fucking obscene. This . . . oh, boy! . . . It's just beautiful."

"See that, Jason?" said Art. "That's just an everyday sports fan, and he's gonna be *willing* those kids to whip the Bombers' asses . . . are we agreed, guys, we're gonna give this a shot?"

"Agreed." They were agreed all right. They were champing at the bit, never mind agreed.

"Who's in charge?" asked Pete Morris.

"You are," said Art. "Keep me posted, and hire Jason what's his name here. Get him down to see Stargill. That's the key. And give him an office. I'll call an executive meeting soon as Stargill comes through. And remember, keep this damn tight. Operate like the military, on a need-to-know basis only."

Fifteen minutes later Jason Wright was through to the Manhattan headquarters of Microlink Incorporated. And a secretary was telling him the chairman would not be available all day, since he was tied up in meetings and was currently lunching in the boardroom with his directors.

"I'm sorry to have bothered you," he said, banging down the telephone and making for the elevator.

It took him only six more minutes to arrive by cab at Rockefeller Plaza, where the Internet czar made his stronghold. It was a busy entrance hall, and Jason, as an assistant radio broadcaster, knew it well. He walked through with a group of young executives, scanned the directory on the main wall, and went up to the nineteenth floor.

He told the receptionist he was an executive of the CBA television network and he needed to see Donald Stargill on a matter of extreme urgency. Right now. For a minimum of a half hour.

Mr. Stargill was unused to such requests. And he might have said, "Tell him to shove off." But today he did not. The uproar over the Refund was dying down, and he was just beginning to miss the frenzy of attention. He ordered the receptionist to seat the CBA man in a conference room, to bring him some coffee, and request he wait for fifteen minutes.

And, right on time, Donald P. Stargill showed up, sat down and told Jason Wright to start talking, fast. Jason was getting used to this kind of treatment and he outlined the project, stressing the huge promotional impact of working with a television giant like CBA.

Stargill was thoughtful. "What precisely do I get out of this?" he demanded. And Jason was ready.

"For a start, you get five million dollars because your guys are bound to win. Then you get another five million as your share of the TV rights, then you get another hunk of change, probably a million bucks for the rental of the stadium. But above all, you get a chance to lay on a great extravaganza for the Brooklyn fans. CBA's boss, Art Mackay, will be the promoter of record, and he's planning to sell inexpensive tickets, maybe ten bucks. Little kids get in free, college kids associated with the players also get in free. Brooklyn Bomber season-ticket holders get their regular seats.

"Your players are free, because you gotta pay 'em anyway. And the Seawolves are free because they're amateurs. But the main thing is you will look like a great sportsman—a guy who spoke his mind and then set out not only to prove what he said was true, but to prove he meant it. That's a straight-up guy, Mr. Stargill. Christ, if we pull this off, you could run for president."

Stargill was thoughtful. "Will I get airtime?" he asked. "So I can state my views about baseball in the Majors and the way it's going— and I know I'm the biggest culprit. It starts with me, and I want it to change. I've developed a real hatred of the free-agent system, which turns big-name players into hired guns, guys who will play for anyone . . . I deeply regret the loss of the old loyalties . . . I have a genuine feeling that the franchises should be more equal, that the ball clubs should have a salary cap, maybe sixty million dollars for the season. Just so the little guys don't lose their top players to the biggest outfits in the biggest cities, to teams that just have more money, not necessarily merit. All those issues? I need airtime."

"You got it."

"One other thing. How about the NCAA? We gonna get an objection of any kind?"

"Not unless we pay the kids, which we won't. And anyway there's been several precedents, usually at spring training. College teams have occasionally warmed up the pros. Nothing matters unless someone finds the kids got paid. That's the only time the roof falls in."

"Okay, kid. Let's get it on. Tell Art Mackay and his henchmen to meet me at '21' for dinner, say eight P.M. I'll be there, but right now I'm out of time. Book a table, my name . . . see you later."

And with that, he was gone, leaving Jason Wright, former newspaper cuttings man at a local radio station, essentially in charge. Plainly he had been fired from WFTD for going AWOL in the middle of the day. But he seemed to be earning a crust as the apparent acting chairman of CBA. Dealmaker, confidant of Art Mackay.

"Holy shit," muttered Jason.

22

Jason Wright missed the dinner at "21," which he considered to be unfortunate. But while Stargill, Art Mackay, Pete Morris, and a lawyer were dining beneath the famous array of toys on the ceiling of the clubby West Fifty-second Street power-scene restaurant, Jason was headed northeast on the CBA corporate jet, bound for Cape Marlin. He had already drawn a complete blank on the telephone trying to locate the Seawolves.

There was no reply from Cabot Field, and no other listing in the phone book. The Cape Marlin League appeared to have no offices or headquarters anywhere, and the Seapuit post office was closed. The general store knew nothing, except that baseball was finished, and there was "some writer guy down near Point Arabella has something to do with it." Offhand, the store owner couldn't remember his name.

Jason wondered if he was wasting his time on the phone, and he was also facing the chilling realization that the Seawolf players had all left the Cape after the season, and were now scattered to all four corners of the nation. He had money, he had power, and he had backup. He'd just mislaid one-half of the players' lineup.

The Learjet aircraft touched down at Henley Airport a little after 9 P.M., and Jason's limousine was waiting. They went straight to Seapuit, which was dark on this Monday night, and located the one and only little restaurant in the area. No one in the bar could remember the names of any of the committee members, but the barman himself came up with Dick Topolski, a local dentist. "He's the president—I think," he said.

He was nearly right. And shortly before 10 P.M. Jason knocked on the door of Dick and Jane Topolski's house, apologized profusely for calling so late, and tried to communicate the urgency of the situation.

He was immediately asked in and offered coffee or a drink, and then for the third time that day he outlined in detail the grand design of the Brooklyn Bombers–Seapuit Seawolves extravaganza. Five million bucks on the line, winner take all.

"I saw the original story in the *Cape Marlin Telegraph* on Saturday," said Dick. "I though Russ had gone a little over-the-top. But I never guessed it would end up like this."

"Well, Mr. Topolski, what do you think? Can it happen?"

"I doubt it. First of all, the Seawolves no longer exist. The team disbands every year after the season, and they all go home, then back to college. Secondly, I'm not the president of the Seapuit Athletic Association, and that's who you should be talking to . . . I'm the general manager, and at this stage in the year, I do not have access to one single player."

Jason looked crestfallen. But Dick Topolski was still in the game. "Listen," he said. "Someone shows up here from a major television corporation offering us the chance of five million dollars to secure the future of this franchise forever, we have to pay attention. Our president is Mrs. Martha Jamieson and I'm gonna E-mail her right now and tell her to expect you at her house at eight-thirty tomorrow morning . . . where you staying?"

"Probably in that limousine waiting outside. I haven't had time to arrange anything . . ."

"Okay, Jason, you can stay here. We've had ballplayers in and out of the house all summer, staying, leaving, coming back. You'll slot right in . . . got a bag?"

"Yup. Lemme get it . . . will I tell the car to pick me up here at say eight-fifteen in the morning?"

"Perfect . . . why don't we all have a glass of brandy before we go to bed, and see if we can't come up with a plan . . . Five million dollars. Jesus. That'd solve a lot of problems around here."

"Okay, Dick, sounds great. I just have to make a call to New York. I'll use the phone in the car. Be right back . . ."

Jason headed back out into the hot, muggy night air and climbed into the limousine, where he found the driver sitting patiently, running the air-conditioning. He picked up the phone and dialed 1-212-582-7200.

"Good evening, thank you for calling '21'—how may we help?"

Moments later the house telephone was brought to the table still occupied by Art Mackay and Donald Stargill, and the TV sports chief was on the line. "Hey, Jason, what's hot?"

"We have a major snag, sir. The Seawolf team has disbanded and scattered all over the United States. I just need to know, will CBA take responsibility for reassembling the team, bringing the players to New York, booking hotels and transport, then getting them home? There'll probably be fourteen guys and three coaches, plus four officials, you know, the general manager and an assistant, a trainer, and probably their president."

"Jason, I'm afraid that's gonna be a bridge too far. We're putting up five million dollars, and the teams that are playing for that money have got to get their own asses to the ballfield in Brooklyn in order to win it . . . I don't have the staff to tackle that kind of a logistics problem . . . it sounds like a nightmare anyway, these kids trying to make journeys from thousands of miles away.

"I don't want to be negative, but I'm not competent, nor willing, to undertake the task of running the fucking game, putting together a team, and organizing it. No, Jason, the Seapuit Seawolves want that five million, they gotta put their team on the field. I'll make 'em rich and famous. I don't run their ball club."

"Okay, sir. I understand. But even if I could get the players together again, and somehow get them to Brooklyn, there would still be the question of expenses. If they lose, which they probably will, Seapuit would go bankrupt financing the team in New York . . ."

"Sorry, I'm not getting involved with those details."

"Well, would Mr. Stargill consider covering their costs, if the Bombers win?"

"Hell, I'll ask him . . . wait . . ."

Moments later Jason heard the voice of Donald Stargill. "Listen, Jason, I got a lot on the line here. There's a team of young tigers coming to New York specially to whip my guys' asses. No mercy. I'm damned if I'm paying their expenses to give them that privilege."

"Sounds a bit tightfisted from someone as rich as you . . ."

"So it may. But if the Seapuit organization wants that five mil, and everything that will inevitably go with it, they gotta find their own way to my ballpark. I'm not financing them, because then it just seems like a stunt—you know, like appearance money. That always takes the edge off any sporting competition. My guys will have everything on the line—reputations, and future, maybe even the future of pro ball in Brooklyn. You tell the Seapuit guys to get that team here, otherwise all bets are off."

Jason Wright, in that instant, felt the project was doomed, and he returned to the Topolski living room deflated, and very pessimistic. They all went to bed, and Dick was unable to offer any form of encouragement.

The following morning Jason presented himself at the home of Martha Jamieson, and for the fourth time presented details of the grandest scheme in the history of amateur baseball. Only in conclusion did he mention the financial snag of possibly $40,000, which it might cost to underwrite the operation, with three nights in New York hotels, air travel, meals, and local transport.

"All that, and we still have to win," said Martha. "Even if it was possible to reassemble the guys, which I very much doubt, the downside's too risky for us. Even if the upside is sensational, which it plainly is, I could not commit this organization to bankruptcy. We only live from season to season, on a nonprofit, voluntary basis. When we add up our income, it usually pays all our bills. We never have anything left. Certainly not forty thousand dollars."

"Mrs. Jamieson, do you realize, that if the guys *nearly* beat the Bombers, you might sell a zillion Seawolf baseball caps to kids all over the country? If you did beat them, you *would* sell a zillion Seawolf caps to kids all over the country. How about that?"

"I suppose we might. But we don't know how to do that. And even with the possibility of such riches, I still could not commit us to drop forty thousand dollars helping a bunch of professional sharks get rich."

"Yes, but the kids might win."

"More likely," said Mrs. Jamieson, "the kids will lose. And I'll be left holding the coffin of the Seawolves. You know, I understand Mr. Stargill refusing to pay for us. But it does seem unreasonable that the TV company will not underwrite our expenses."

"Martha, there's a hidden agenda there. All TV networks are petrified of upsetting the NCAA. Putting up a straightforward, cards-on-the-table prize to a nonprofit organization like yourselves is one thing. Picking up tabs, booking hotels, paying expenses is entirely another. Even you guys would have to be careful there, treating these amateurs as if they were professional sportsmen. That, as you know, is a goddamned minefield. Those guys could throw them right out of college ball a year before the draft."

"I do know. And we're always careful. Quite frankly, I think it was all a lovely idea, which will ultimately flounder on financial nit-picking."

"I'm gonna give it just one last shot," said Jason. "I'm going to talk to that coach of yours, see what he says. And I am gonna try to talk to a player, see what he says. Who's nearest?"

"Well, we have our center fielder in Maine, offshore on a lobster boat out of Vinalhaven. And we have two players in New York City. The leadoff hitter, Gino Rossi, lives in Little Italy, where his father owns a restaurant. The right fielder, Steve Thompson, lives in Brooklyn with his parents. I can give you addresses and phone numbers for all of them. You'll find Coach Maddox at the University of Maine in Orono."

"You think I'm wasting my time, don't you?"

"'Fraid so. But you're having fun."

"Nearly," said Jason, smiling through his crushing disappointment. He took down the addresses, thanked Mrs. Jamieson, and headed back to the car.

They made the end of the short driveway, and the limo was about to pull out into the street, when Martha Jamieson came running out of the house shouting, "Stop! Stop!"

The driver saw her and came to a halt, winding down the windows.

"Jason," she said. "I forgot to tell you. There's one player still in town. He's our top pitcher, Jack Faber, and you'll find him with his father at a big white house on Ocean Drive, number forty-one, just outside the village, heading south down the bay."

Again Jason Wright thanked her and told the driver to head for number 41. Ten minutes later he was sitting with Ben and Jack, on the screened porch, explaining for the fifth time the incredible opportunity there would be if the Seawolves could be regrouped and on parade at Ebbets Field sometime between this Tuesday morning,

August 16, and Saturday next week, August 27, when the demands of college would begin to claim the players.

Ben listened wide-eyed until Jason finally revealed the problem—the $40,000 expenses which the 'Wolves would be stuck with should they lose. The representative of CBA added that he believed there would be tremendous promotional and merchandising opportunities if the 'Wolves could somehow find a way to play the game.

"Okay, let's get into this," said Ben. "We can finance it, so we need a date. Can't round up the team if we can't tell 'em when they have to leave home, and when they play."

"Mr. Faber," said Jason, "I've already spent time with your general manager and your president, and they both say there is no money to do this. And no one's going to give it to the Seapuit Athletic Association and risk falling foul of the NCAA and the ten thousand rules they have to protect their players' amateur status."

"We don't need a backer," said Ben. "I'll pick up the tab myself. If it can be done, it will be done. So let's get a date."

"Yessir," said Jason incredulously. "I'll get Art Mackay on the line . . . wait here while I go to the car . . ."

Jason flew out of the door, dived into the backseat, and picked up the phone, going through to the sports chief's private line. "Art, baby," he shouted, casting all forms of formality to the winds. "I think we got it . . . but I need a date. Do you have a provisional?"

"Hey, Jason, 'baby,'" said Art, chuckling. "There is only one date that really works for everyone, and that's Friday night, August twenty-sixth, seven P.M. start, under lights. It suits us well, gives us ten days to get moving on material to promote the kids. The Bombers had it down as a travel day, for the game against the Braves on Saturday evening. Stargill says they can stay in New York, play the 'Wolves Friday night, and he'll have the charter jet take 'em to Atlanta ten A.M. Saturday morning."

"Sounds good. But I can't hang around. I'm with the guy who's giving them the expense money. Talk to you later."

"That's my boy," said Art Mackay as he put down the phone.

Jason charged back into the house. "It's Friday, August twenty-sixth, seven P.M.," he yelled. "Ebbets Field . . . what do we do now?"

"We get Martha and Topolski here fast," said Ben. "Then we phone a few other board members for a general agreement. But that's not a problem. Mrs. Jamieson is the best president we've had for several years. If she wants to play this game for five million dollars, that game will get played."

Jack came in and said, "Soon as Martha gets here, let's draft an E-mail and circulate it. Meantime I'll try and call Coach Maddox and Ted, let 'em in on the secret."

Ben used a cell phone to summon Martha. She called Dick Topolski, who called his assistant GM. All three of them were at Ben's house inside twenty minutes. They wrote the E-mail and outlined the project, taking care to clarify the fact that Martha Jamieson was in favor and that the game against the Brooklyn Bombers would go ahead unless someone had a vehement objection. This would, as Martha phrased it, "be heard but not necessarily acted upon."

"It'll go ahead if we can raise a team," said Ben wryly. "We better just wait till Jack gets ahold of the coaches."

This took another twenty minutes, but the news from Maine was good. Both Russ and Ted had almost died of excitement. If the kids would come back, the coaches would parade them at Ebbets Field at the appointed time. *Are you kidding!*

Meantime, Ted called Ray Sweeney in Vinalhaven, Ben called Natalie and then spoke in length to Tony Garcia. Jack called Zac Colbert, and by 10:30 that morning, the Seawolves had their catcher, their center fielder, their third baseman, and leading pitcher in place. Then Ben called Kyle Davidson, Jack got on the line to Savannah, and Doughnut's father Bo Davis promised to get his son and the Cruiser organized.

Martha called The Citadel and spoke to the school president, who cleared the cadets to play. Then Dick Topolski contacted Rick Adams in his room. Rick called Bobby Madison in Pittsburgh, and Bobby called his other main buddy, Boom-Boom Hacker, who was trying to arrange a golf foursome at Hilton Head for the two Citadel players and Mr. Davis.

Pedro Rodriguez had gone back to the Dominican Republic, which made things difficult because his family had no telephone. But Gino Rossi said Pedro lived right next to a restaurant he and his father had visited in Santo Domingo last January.

"Pedro can take a call there, Mr. Faber," Gino told Ben. "He told me. It's called the Docksider. He even gave me the number. They have to take a message to his house. Then he can phone back. You want me to make the call? I'll do it."

By 2 P.M. the Seawolves were rolling. The batting lineup was in place—Gino, Rick, Zac, Boom-Boom, Ray, Bobby, Steve Thompson, Tony, and Griff Heeney. They had the pitchers they needed—Pedro, Jack, Kyle, Doughnut, and Cruiser. Coaches and officials were all present and accounted for.

This was the opportunity of a lifetime and every player knew it. It was fantastic exposure for those who wanted professional careers, and it represented a shot at immortality for those who played just for the love of the game. It was nothing short of a miracle for those who had to run the team and raise the money every year. Victory for the 'Wolves in Ebbets Field would change their financial world for five million different reasons.

Jason went back to Martha's house with Jack to print up the Seawolves' lineup, along with addresses and phone numbers. The TV network would begin a series of features on these young gods of the amateur game. Jason called Art Mackay with the hardening news, and the CBA sports desk was onto their affiliate in Bangor, Maine, dispatching them instantly up the road to Orono to interview Russ Maddox, whose enthusiastic words had begun all of this.

Ben Faber pulled out a large map of the USA and decided the big Eastern contingent would have to travel step-by-step. And it would have to be a chartered private aircraft. Two of them. So far as Ben could see, there was no way they could risk one of the kids missing a flight and going to the wrong place. To eliminate that possibility, they'd need private jets, with on-board telephones, all the way from Florida to Maine and back to New York.

For the East Coast they'd require a private Gulfstream III to pick up Pedro at 5:30 A.M. in Miami, and then head straight up to Savannah for Doughnut, Cruiser, and Boom-Boom. From there, they'd make a hundred-mile flight to Charleston for Rick Adams; then to Washington, to collect Kyle, before striking west for their demon second baseman, Bobby Madison, in Pittsburgh.

It would be a long eight-hundred-mile flight across Pennsylvania and on to Bangor to pick up Ted, Russ, and Ray. They'd refuel and fly straight down to La Guardia Airport, New York. Gino and Steve would meet them at one of the New York hotels, and there'd be a team dinner, with the following day devoted to practice and strategy.

Jack and Ben needed to be at the oil company in Louisiana next week, and they would leave the same day as the others, Wednesday,

August 24, in a smaller Learjet, at first light, from New Orleans International, seven hundred miles up to Tulsa to collect Zac Colbert; then another long eight-hundred-mile run to Chicago, to collect Natalie and Tony, before swinging southeast to Fort Wayne, Indiana, for the DH from Notre Dame, Griff Heeney.

The 750 miles from Fort Wayne into New York would make it a 2,500-mile eight-hour haul, with a refuel at O'Hare. They should be in La Guardia by 4 P.M. The costs would almost treble with the private jets, but Ben thought any other course of action was just too risky.

It was midafternoon when he called called Universal Jet Aviation in Boca Raton, Florida, and calculated the cost of a Gulfstream III: Miami–Savannah–Charleston–Washington–Pittsburgh–Bangor, Maine–New York—three hours and thirty minutes for the principal Miami–Maine journey; seven hours with the four stops, then one and a half hours to New York. Seating capacity fourteen. At $4,500 per hour. Total: $38,250. One way. They could fly back commercial.

The Learjet 55 was $2,100 an hour; capacity: eight people. The New Orleans–Tulsa–Chicago–Fort Wayne–La Guardia flight would be seven hours: $14,700. Total cost for the private jets: $52,950.

"'Bout a day an a half's interest," muttered Ben. "Shit, it's a lotta laughs having cash!"

That night, on CBA's ten-o'clock sports news, the entire ten minutes was the "sensational" story about the Brooklyn Bombers and the Seapuit Seawolves. The most expensive team in the Majors had accepted a $5 million winner-take-all challenge from the Seapuit Seawolves, reputed to be the greatest college team ever to play the game in North America.

The newscaster, aided by his blond female assistant, ran through the stars of the Seawolves team, citing the Louisiana Flamethrower, Jack Faber, then the league's MVP, the best college catcher in the country, Tony Garcia of Northwestern. He mentioned the lobster fisherman in the outfield, the finest center fielder in the United States, Ray Sweeney. He talked of the other leading pitcher, Kyle, son of President Reagan's former adviser Buck Davidson. He was very big on Boom-Boom because of the televisual backdrop of Hilton Head Island's superb golf course. And the rancher Zac Colbert. And mentioned the "next Pedro Martinez," Pedro Rodriguez from the same Caribbean island town . . . all of the kids, which the network would feature in the coming nine days before the battle at Ebbets Field.

"There is no doubt, this is a significant milestone in U.S. baseball history," he intoned. "As a nation, we have long been uneasy about the vast multimillion-dollar salaries being paid to the practitioners of the national pastime. Are they worth it? Are they *that* much better than talented college kids?

"Ladies and gentlemen, Friday night, next week, we're all going to find out, and the ramifications of this game will be long remembered . . . that's all from us at Stadium Newscenter . . . from Tracey and me, have a great evening."

At which point all hell broke loose. The story was exclusive, and while everyone knew about the uproar last Friday night in Brooklyn, no one knew about the Seapuit Seawolves, who they were, or what they had done to deserve this apparently unprecedented treatment by a national television network and the richest Major League franchise in the country.

CBA had been darned clever with their coverage, holding back on a Donald Stargill interview, not revealing Russ Maddox on the screen, just sending out enough of a message to provoke every other broadcasting corporation in America to join the stampede for news about the best college team ever, before they finally faced the Bombers in a $5 million showdown in Brooklyn.

In fact, the print media were in much more of a panic than the broadcasters, as the hour drew closer to 11 P.M. The ticking time clocks at newspaper sports desks all over America, up to and beyond midnight, represented the scribes' prime time, the hours when the morning sports sections were "put to bed." Those editors and reporters knew about extra time, extra innings, and rain delays, because those lousy little demons represented lateness and resultant chaos. Right now, 10:12 P.M., they were facing lateness.

A thousand daily newpaper computers slammed into the Internet to check out the Seawolves. *Who the hell are these guys? What've they won? Cape Marlin, where the fucking hell's that? How come their goddamned players come from all over the goddamned country? Jesus, who are these players? How come we got the starting pitcher from Stanford in the same team as the catcher from Northwestern and the leadoff hitter from Seton Hall? Will someone just tell me what the fuck is going on with this Seawolf shit?*

Answers were slow in coming. But slowly it was becoming apparent to the practitioners of American sports journalism that the Cape

Marlin League was the number-one summer baseball arena for college players in the entire country and had been for more than fifty years. The Seawolves had just won it, with the best record ever, and their team was chock-full of guys who could really play the game.

The 'Wolves' Web site did not mention the speech of the coach, because it had been made at a private party and was, anyway, more or less exclusive to the *Cape Marlin Telegraph*. And now the newspapers turned to the *New York Times*, as usual, and ran down the story which had reported the quotations from Russ Maddox.

They besieged the phone system at the University of Maine, where the switchboard was closed. They raided the local Directory Assistance for the number of the Black Bears coach. They woke up Ray Sweeney's father, which did not please him since he was going out before the tide at 4:30 in the morning to the cold, granite-bottomed lobster grounds of eastern Maine. There was a total of 286 phone calls dialed into the dark and deserted field office of the Seapuit Seawolves.

The press never found the Seawolves officials, never found Ben and Jack, or Tony Garcia, or Zac, or the cadets. They got ahold of Gino Rossi and they found Kyle Davidson's dad just before midnight. But basically they came up with little more than had been revealed on the CBA sports news at 10 P.M.

The lack of new knowledge, the apparent secrecy, the obvious truth that *someone* was keeping a very tight grip on this story seemed to inflame the journalists to greater efforts. Editors and layout men were expansive in their assessment of the story's worth. Headlines were huge, discretion moderate. Hype was the watchword. Tons and tons of hype.

STARGILL'S REFUND SPARKS SHOWDOWN FOR THE BOMBERS

BOMBERS TO PLAY COLLEGE KIDS IN $5 MILLION SHOOT-OUT

STARGILL SENDS IN THE CLOWNS—AGAINST A KIDS' TEAM

BOMBERS TOLD TO PLAY THE KIDS—STARGILL'S THREAT

The newspapers had reacted precisely as Art Mackay had known they would. And by 11 A.M. the following morning, there were over eighty journalists, print and broadcast, thronging the press room and its environs at Ebbets Field.

At 11:30 A.M. sharp, the Bombers first baseman, Greg "Legs" Diamond, thirty-nine-year-old veteran of twenty Major League seasons with the Red Sox and Braves, presented a legally drawn petition to Don Stargill, informing him that no member of the Brooklyn Bombers would take the field against the Seapuit Seawolves, on the grounds of the potential for personal humiliation, potential loss of earnings, potential loss of professional reputation, and a probable assault on each man's human rights and entitlement to happiness. It was signed by every member of the Bombers dugout, including the manager, the pitching coach, the hitting coach, the trainer, and the batboy.

"Fuck 'em," growled Stargill as he read it. And the great street-fighting industrialist who had started off in these same streets of Brooklyn, bellowed to his long-suffering secretary, Miss Matts, *"MATTIE! WHO'S THE RINGLEADER OF THIS GODDAMNED MOB? SEND THAT SON OF A BITCH IN HERE RIGHT NOW, AND TELL HIM TO BRING HIS GODDAMNED LAWYER, SINCE I MAY AS WELL TEAR HIS ASS OFF AS WELL!"*

Meanwhile, down in the press area, two other Bombers strolled by, the thirty-eight-year-old center fielder Buckskin Moseley, and the DH Bert Muncie, who had spent nineteen seasons with the Cubs. Deliberately they called out, "Don't even waste your time hanging around here, guys. There ain't gonna be no game against these fucking Seawolves. Because we ain't playing it. No way."

The reporter from the *New York Daily News* moved fast, sidled up to the ballplayers, and hissed, "You guys told this to Stargill? Is this an official players' petition?"

"You got it, Tex. Drawn up by the lawyers. We ain't putting everything on the line against a group of amateurs. Hell, we got everything to lose, nothing to gain. Stargill can forget this shit. He won't get one player out there."

The *Daily News* man hurtled into a doorway and grabbed his phone, dictated the story direct to the afternoon sports desk. Within minutes they were resetting a front-page headline:

PLAY THE SEAWOLVES? NO WAY.
BOMBERS THREATEN WALKOUT

Meantime, Greg Diamond was with his lawyer, facing the wrath of Stargill.

After hearing the objections, the team owner said, "Listen to me, you fourth-rate assholes. I got a contract right here which states freely and clearly you'll play the game of baseball for me whenever the fuck and wherever the fuck I happen to stipulate. In return for this, Diamond, you are paid eighteen million dollars a year . . . that's one of the largest contracts in Major League history . . . and it's to operate my center field. It works out at seven hundred and fifty thousand a week.

"You, Lowenstein, negotiated this contract on behalf of Mr. Diamond on the basis of his sixty-eight home runs two years ago with the Red Sox. Since then, he's hit nine home runs for the Bombers. I ought to sue your ass under the Honesty in Advertising Act. And now you say you're not going to play *one extra game for me? Three hours for me?* You wanna know where you're going to be at one minute past seven on Friday night next week, Diamond? Right out there on center field is where you're gonna be."

"I'm afraid that kind of bombast is not going to work here," said Jules Lowenstein smoothly. "Because none of the players here will play the game. It's not just Greg. It's everyone, and I'm afraid you will have to call this game off."

"They've all got contracts," snarled Stargill. "And those contracts state they must play where this ball club stipulates. It doesn't say anything about a one-night strike because they don't like their opponents. I have the right to make you play for Brooklyn anytime, and there's nothing you can do about it. You're playing the Seawolves; now get out."

"One moment, Mr. Stargill. I think you will find it does state the games must be those of the Major League Baseball Commission."

"Bullshit, Lowenstein. I know it doesn't because these guys have to go and play for the Triple-A team anytime we say so. That's how the contract was written. I wrote most of it myself . . .

"Anyway, let me clarify something else for you. If these jerks refuse to play, I give you my word I will take the following action: I'll close the ball club, bankrupt—that means no one gets paid. Then I'll calculate my losses on the Seawolves game and I'll sue every one of you for compensation, for deliberately taking the ball club into bankruptcy, when we're losing forty million dollars a year.

"And it won't be a hardship. I could hire ten midtown law firms twenty-four/seven, for a hundred years, and not even miss the legal fees, not even know I'd spent 'em. Don't be even more fucking stupid than most lawyers are, Mr. Lowenstein. Tell 'em they're wasting their time, as you well know they are."

The two men left in silence, but Stargill pursued them to his office door, yelling down the corridor, "DIAMOND! If that asshole you're walking with tells you to go on defying me, remember he'll send you a large bill at the end of it. Do what I say and all that's gonna happen is you get paid your preposterous salary, again, and again, and again. *THINK ABOUT IT, ASS . . . HOLE.*"

Greg Diamond had already thought about it. "Fuck this," he said. "I'm playing."

"Good idea," said Jules. "That's what I'd do, if I happened to be employed by a fucking mega-rich lunatic."

Art Mackay could hardly believe his luck. The story about the players' strike at Ebbets Field dominated the afternoon papers in every city in the United States. And it dominated the early evening news programs on televisions and car radios in every corner of the nation.

All day long, players had been interviewed on the air. Camera crews were still mobbed around the Brooklyn ballpark. Pete McGuire, who twelve seasons ago had inspired the Montreal Expos to make him first pick of the entire college draft, came on air with his .211 batting average and snarled: "Listen, these guys are pros, they've spent years building their reputations, lifetimes, and we don't care how much money Stargill has, we're not about to be humiliated. Not by a group of hotshot kids who have everything to gain and nothing to lose. Shit happens in that type of game."

PLAYERS DEFIANT IN BROOKLYN BOMBERS STANDOFF

Even young D. J. Mahoney, the twenty-three-year-old second baseman who had signed the largest contract in Bomber history right out of the first-round draft, was heavily involved in the twenty-four-hour strike. At 3 P.M. he stood before the great curved-brick facade of Ebbets Field and declared, "Baseball has been my life. My lawyer tells me not to get involved in no losing shit against kids, and I ain't doing it. All my teammates are together on this. We ain't playing kids. Nossir."

Mahoney's numbers in the Minor Leagues had not represented a natural passport to a coast-to-coast speech on national television. Indeed, he was on the team only because of the huge amount of money the Bombers had invested in him. He'd made eighteen errors in the field this season and was batting .229. Nonetheless, he felt entitled to air the views of the Brooklyn Bombers dugout.

"I mean, jeez," he declared. "Like some of these kids are fast, man. And they're gonna be swarming out there, running down everything. I'm not gettin' paid enough to risk my career this publicly."

But surely you do that every night, whichever team you play?

"Yeah. But these guys are just amateurs. And we'd show up real bad if we got beat. Pros play other pros, not kids who ain't even left school yet."

How much are you paid each season with the Bombers?

"Hey, I ain't going there, right? My lawyer has told me to stick to the facts. And that's what I'm trying to do over here. We ain't playing, and that's all I'm talking about."

"BOMBERS FEAR A MAULING FROM THE 'WOLVES"
—Second Baseman Mahoney

Meantime, high in the ivory tower of CBA sports television, Art Mackay had in his hand a copy of the agreement signed by the entire roster of players at 7 P.M. that evening. It confirmed that they *would* play the game. Stargill had wrung that piece of paper out of Jules Lowenstein practically at gunpoint. Actually it was gunpoint. Financial gunpoint. Because Stargill had met everyone in the big clubhouse room, in company with five lawyers and a document declaring the Brooklyn Bombers officially bankrupt. His words were delivered in the subtle tones of a jackhammer.

"You guys see this legal document here?"

Everyone nodded.

"That legal document says this ball club is bust, in need of a cash transfusion of twenty million dollars just to keep going to the end of the season."

He paused to let his words sink in. Then he rasped, "You know what stops this ball club going bankrupt? . . . I stop it."

He paused again. "If I say I will not put another dime in, we shut the doors tonight. We cut off the phones, and we cut off the electricity, but not before I put my signature on this document I have here. And that ends it. Did you ever hear the phrase 'The Lord giveth, and the Lord also taketh away'? That's me, and I'm about to taketh away, because I don't happen to give a fuck whether you play ball again. You've knocked the enthusiasm out of me, nearly, with your goddamned sloppy performances and your huge salaries. If I bankrupt this ball club, none of you will get paid another dime, because you'll just become another creditor. The club has no assets; you rent this stadium from one of my property corporations."

He paused again. And then continued: "And yet, gentlemen, redemption may be just around the corner. That, by the way, means a way out." And he produced another document, attached to two blank pages, which he waved theatrically. "This document is to be signed by all of you. It will confirm you will each feel truly honored to play the Seapuit Seawolves right here at Ebbets next Friday night. Anyone doesn't sign, he's benched till his contract runs out, and meantime I will sue each and every nonsigner for deliberately and willfully jeopardizing the narrow future of this potentially bankrupt ball club.

"Anyone thinks they could beat me? Just try it. I'll lawyer you all to death, I'll hang you guys out to dry with legal fees for years and years. I won't even know I'm doing it, but you guys will never sleep soundly again.

"NOW GET UP HERE, AND SIGN THIS FUCKING THING RIGHT NOW . . . BEFORE I GET ANGRY . . . LOWENSTEIN! . . . TELL 'EM . . . TELL 'EM THEY HAVE ZERO OPTIONS, EXCEPT TO DO AS I SAY!"

Jules climbed to his feet and said simply, "I think that under these difficult circumstances, it would be prudent to follow the instructions just issued by the team owner."

The players formed an orderly line, and each in turn signed the document. It took three minutes. The "strike" was over. But no one outside of this clubhouse would know that, not until Don Stargill and Art Mackay were ready to release the information. No player would be permitted to leave Ebbets Field until after the ten-o'clock news was over. That was the unanimous all-station network broadcast which would announce that the game against the 'Wolves was off, featuring strike leader D. J. Mahoney on camera.

And now it was 10:15, and back at CBA they were ready. Art Mackay ordered a dramatic interruption of an interview with Joe Paterno, and on screen in big type, with thunder and lightning in the background, accompanied by crashing Wagnerian music, came the words:

NEWSFLASH EXCLUSIVE

And a voice right out of a 1950s detective comic book intoned:

We are truly sorry for the interruption, but right now CBA brings you exclusive news, broken in the last three minutes.

The screen cleared and the regular newscaster came on. In a voice normally associated with the death of a president or the declaration of war, he said:

Within the past few minutes, the CBA news team has learned that the threatened strike by the Brooklyn Bombers players against owner Donald P. Stargill has been called off.

The ball club has just announced the that Bombers game against the champion college team the Seapuit Seawolves of Cape Marlin will go ahead as planned at Ebbets Field on Friday next week, August twenty-sixth. The game will get under way at seven P.M.

Negotiations are believed to have gone on for several hours throughout the evening, after a strike petition, signed by all the players, was presented to Mr. Stargill. The entire Bombers lineup had flatly refused to go out and face the amateurs.

A spokesman for the ball club has stated: "Mr. Stargill is profoundly grateful to his players for their understanding in this matter. He realizes what a huge risk to their reputations this is, and wishes them every success against probably the best U.S. college team there has ever been."

The Bombers second baseman, D. J. Mahoney, was quoted a few moments ago outside Ebbets Field saying: "We did not want this. No one wanted it. All we know is we have to win at all costs to protect our reputations."

And then onto the screen came a live picture of Seapuit's two pitchers from the University of Georgia, Mr. Doughnut Davis and Mr.

Cruiser Burrell. An offscreen interviewer was talking to Doughnut and as the pitcher spoke, the camera presented his face in close-up:

"Ain't no one gonna beat the 'Wolves this season," he said. "Man, we're too fast, we hit hit too hard, and we're too smart. Me? I'm first reliever, and I'm going to be in there. FASTBALL, RIGHT? AIN'T NO ONE CAN HIT THAT. NOSSIR."

The screen switched back to the studio, where the newscaster concluded, "Boy! That's gonna be some baseball game. Tickets will be hard to find, but the game will played right here, live on CBA sports, where the action never stops."

As commercials, for a televised baseball game go, that was a masterpiece. And as the news hit the airwaves, the production of every newspaper in the country came to a shuddering halt. They were all running stories that declared the Bomber-Seawolves battle was off, after a threatened strike by the players. And now they had to change every aspect of those stories. And they were late, and a fierce instinct of pure urgency took hold of every journalist trying to piece it all together.

But the newspaper industry is accustomed to running on blind panic, and night staff all over the country were up to it. Anyone not aware of the late-night CBA newsflash now read the full story in the morning papers. And with each headline it seemed the drama heightened.

BOMBERS FORCED TO PLAY THE SEAWOLVES
OWNER STARGILL LAYS DOWN THE LAW

BOMBERS CLIMB DOWN AFTER STARGILL CALLS THEIR BLUFF

STARGILL SCUTTLES BOMBERS' STRIKE THREAT

Generally speaking, this was playing out precisely the way Art Mackay had planned. CBA would be asking $3 million per minute for advertising space during the game. And his publicity plan was not finished yet, not by a long way.

They would run six selected pieces, one every night from the coming Saturday through Thursday, the night before the game. They would begin in Chicago, at the home of the Chicago Symphony, interviewing the beautiful harpist whose son played behind the plate for the Seawolves.

From there they would go to Jack and Ben Faber, standing out by the old swinging tractor tire at the family farm, now being ravaged by the natural gas drilling. *This humble dirt lot, deep in the Mississippi Delta, where the best college pitcher in the country learned his craft, coached by his dad* . . .

Then Ray Sweeney, on board the *Sweeney Todd*, out between the islands, down east, hauling the lobster traps out of the freezing North Atlantic. *Arms of steel, honed out here all his life, in the family fishing business, Maine's greatest center fielder.*

From there the filmmakers went to The Citadel and met the 'Wolves shortstop and second baseman, and they posed them both in full uniform with the ramparts of the eighteenth-century military college in the background. *Rick Adams and Bobby Madison—The Citadel's watchwords-honor, integrity, loyalty, and patriotism—are safe in the hands of these two Seawolves.*

Then they went to Spavinaw, Oklahoma, where they located the vast cattle ranch northeast of Tulsa. *This is Zac Colbert, the Seawolves third baseman, who may bring back to this little Midwestern town the glory it once knew as the birthplace of Mickey Mantle.*

Last stop was Hilton Head Island Hotel Golf Club. And they posed Boom-Boom Hacker with his dad, out on the first tee. *The Seawolves power-hitting first baseman was brought up right here on one of the loveliest golf courses in America. But he never took up the game seriously, he went for baseball* . . . at which point Boom-Boom tossed a brand new Titleist into the air and slammed it into orbit with his Louisville Slugger.

All week, the CBA publicity machine ground out the colorful stories that would send the ratings skyward while Americans sought the answer to the increasingly posed question: Can the overpaid pros defeat the kids who play just for the love of the game?

Not in all the annals of modern sports had there been a poser of quite this level of fascination, certainly not since the 1970s, when they wondered first, if the ladies' world champion Billie Jean King could beat the ex–Wimbledon men's singles champion Bobby Riggs . . . and then if the giant filly could beat the colt—the unbeaten Ruffian against the Kentucky Derby winner Foolish Pleasure, a ten-furlong match race at Belmont Park, New York, June 1975.

Most experts thought any Wimbledon men's champion could beat any woman, no matter the age difference; most experts thought a good colt would always beat a good filly. And right now, in their hearts, most experts thought the pros would eat the kids alive.

The scribes had but one restraining influence on their daily speculations—the sure knowledge that deliberate mismatches are apt to create a very nervous favorite and a particularly ambitious underdog.

And all through the week Art Mackay had his inventive afterburners wide open—as he placed the fifteen-minute feature spots on the Seawolf stars—bang in the middle of prime-time viewing. And he judiciously repeated them twice during the day.

Every night he slanted the news to add tension, controversy, and heat to the battle, tapping his partnership with Donald Stargill for the exclusive angle which would cause everyone to follow up, afraid they might be left in the broiling wake of CBA sports.

Owner Donald Stargill claimed last night that the future of professional baseball in Brooklyn hung on the result of Saturday's game against the college stars from Cape Marlin.

"I made my outburst against the team at our lowest moment," he said, live on-screen. "I felt then, and I feel now, that my players have not given enough, either to me or to the loyal fans of Brooklyn. They're costing me millions a week, and if they go out there and get beat by the kids, goddammit I'm done. I'm closing the doors. No more good money after bad."

And again the print media stampeded to catch up, trying to find Stargill, even calling the CBA sports desk, an unheard of point of surrender in the cutthroat business of packaging and presenting sports news.

STARGILL ULTIMATUM:
"Beat the kids or I'll
shut down the Bombers"

Art Mackay was not just excellent. Art Mackay, like the Seawolves, may have been the best there ever was. And right now he had the entire country eating out of his hand. He had masterminded a Good Guys vs. Bad Guys showdown, High Noon at Ebbets Field.

And there was not a household anywhere unaware of the group of wonderful young American college guys who were going out there to play the arrogant, overpaid, over-the-hill, cowardly Bombers. And most of those households cared passionately about who would win.

In turn, Art was less partisan. But he did care passionately about the thirty-two minutes of prime-time advertising, almost $100 million income, which would be crammed into the four-hour Friday-night television spectacular he and Jason Wright had created.

23

Ben Faber's private jets landed within one hour of each other at La Guardia Airport, alongside Grand Central Parkway, New York, on Wednesday afternoon. Awaiting them was a brand-new air-conditioned luxury bus, spaciously fitted with just thirty-two seats and painted in full maroon-and-white livery. In massive letters, beautifully scrolled along each side of the bus, was one word, twelve feet long, SEAWOLVES. There were no rear windows, and the entire aft section consisted of a huge photograph of a crouching catcher, staring at the oncoming traffic, mask down, glove just outside the plate, two fingers rammed down the inside of his right thigh. Scrawled across the red dirt in front of the plate was the legend FAST-BALL. UP AND AWAY! GO SEAWOLVES!

There was, it seemed, no limit to the ambitions of Art Mackay's publicity department. But then, for $100 million, there wouldn't be, would there?

Both Gino Rossi and Steve Thompson had come out to the airport from the city to meet the sixteen new arrivals. Martha Jamieson, with Dick and Jane Topolski, had traveled to New York by car from the Cape, and were already ensconced in the Drake Swissair Hotel, which occupies the northwest corner of East Fifty-sixth Street at Park Avenue.

Each member of the twenty-strong Seawolf party had a private room at around $400 a night. Martha would settle the account with a check drawn on the normally flimsy Seapuit Athletic Association bank account, currently standing at a near-unprecedented balance, thanks to Ben Faber and about two hundred billion square feet of natural gas, sloshing around in some distant Louisiana swamp.

The bus was out of the airport by 4:45 in the afternoon and made its way deliberately into the worst of the rush hour, crawling south down the FDR Drive, cutting off west along East Fifty-fifth and then turning south in heavy traffic down Fifth Avenue all the way to Thirty-fourth Street. The bus was cheered and applauded along every yard of this carefully orchestrated publicity run. They swung back north up Sixth Avenue and almost caused a mob scene at the Forty-second Street intersection, where a huge crowd gathered at the stop sign, cheering and chanting, over and over, *"GO SEAWOLVES! . . . GO SEAWOLVES . . . GO SEAWOLVES!"*

Inside the bus, the players were stunned. Zac, Jack, Griff, Tony, and Cruiser had never even been to New York and they gazed in awe at the towering high-rise office blocks, at the yellow cavalry charge of the city's cabs, and the massed throng of New Yorkers fighting their way to the train stations and buses.

When they reached the hotel, they were absolutely unprepared for the pandemonium that greeted their arrival. Outside, under the red awning, a uniformed doorman was engulfed by more than eighty journalists, cameramen, technicians, and soundmen. CBA alone had a team of twelve people, six of them manning three big handheld television cameras.

When the bus door opened, the first Seawolves at the top of the steps were almost blinded by the flashbulbs and lights. Zac Colbert with Ray Sweeney just stood there while the interviewers consulted photographs for identification and yelled questions: *"Are you the rancher from Oklahoma? . . . Hey, that's the lobsterman . . . Where's the harpist? . . . What happened to the army officers? . . . Where's that Georgia boy with the fastball?*

"Hey, Russ, you got the guys ready? Over here, Natalie, how about a smile? Mr. Faber, is it true you're the richest man in Louisiana? Steve, you going for the Olympic high hurdles or staying in baseball? Hey, Gino, are they all headed down to your dad's place for dinner? What's the name of the restaurant? Doughnut, over here, buddy, gimme that fastball quote, willya? Hey, Ted—Teddy Sando, are your pitchers ready? How many will you use?"

All pretense of order and organization was cast to the wind in the mindless scrimmage for information. Four New York cops moved in to prevent the uproar moving into the hotel itself. Ted Sando appointed himself the official muscle, along with Ray and Zac, and they formed a human shield in order to steer the others into the foyer, where Martha Jamieson had organized mass registration procedures to be completed by each member of the group in the privacy of their rooms, assisted by two desk clerks. All four hotel elevators were placed at the disposal of the Seawolves for fifteen minutes in order to lift them out of the madhouse that used to be a lobby.

Ben and Jack had a suite on the sixteenth floor, with large adjoining bedrooms for Tony and Natalie. The Drake management had managed to accommodate the entire Seawolf party on that one level. And for the moment all phone calls were being funneled through the Topolskis' room, where Dick would try to stonewall the endless requests for photos and interviews.

That evening, every television news station—local, national, and intergalactic—carried the arrival of the 'Wolves in the Big Apple as a main news item. CBA led off with it, and featured a previously recorded interview with Russ Maddox in Maine, during which he said, "This may come down to pitching. And I'm fielding five damn good ones. The Bombers have probably the worst bull pen in the Majors—too many has-beens, too many injuries, not enough heart. And remember, my guys will lay everything right on the line to make a play. They've been doing it all year. We'll beat 'em, you know, I'd bet on it."

This, of course, sent the news media into a collective dance of death because CBA, again, did not air it until ten o'clock. Front-page stories were rewritten, headlines altered, the general gist being:

SEAWOLF CHIEF COACH SAYS,
"WE'LL SHUT DOWN THE BOMBERS"

Not to mention, in the New York *Post*:

"SEAWOLF PITCHERS TOO STRONG—
IT'S THE DEATH KNELL FOR PRO-BALL IN BROOKLYN."
—Coach Maddox

It had all started off as something of a caper. Right now it was much more like a war. And the Bombers were worried, growing unnerved by the dire threats which apparently lurked behind every headline.

And right up to late afternoon on game day, the media pursued this story. They tracked down spokesman from both teams, they badgered the Bombers relentlessly, on the road and in Brooklyn, and they swarmed after the 'Wolves wherever they went, mobbing the practice ground loaned to them by Columbia University.

And nothing much happened that was in any way new, even though you would not have realized this watching the CBA sportscasts, which made every Seawolf bulletin sound like the Gettysburg Address.

In the hours leading up to the game, the only real story took place in the Sutton Place home of Don Stargill, where his twenty-four-year-old wife, Zelda, thirty-two years his junior and bride of eighteen months, had a simple request: "Would you allow Sandy to start this game, darling? I have told him I was sure you wouldn't mind, not now when we're selling the ball club and everything."

Sandy was more formally known as Alesandro Salazar, a six-foot two-inch, darkly handsome Venezuelan who had once been a society hairdresser in his native San Joaquin, but had converted at the age of twenty-one to starting pitcher for the local professional ball club in the Valencia League. He spoke hardly a word of English.

Mrs. Donald P. Stargill had plainly fallen in love with him during a trip to the island with her sister, and actually brought him back to New York, direct to Sutton Place, in the astonishing belief that with this "discovery," she had somehow saved the Bombers from further humiliation in the Major Leagues.

Stargill had been livid—first, because his new wife had arrived home with a gigolo with whom she might very well have slept. And second, because there was no place on the Bombers roster for any more pitchers, certainly not one who had never thrown a ball in the US of A.

Zelda, however, looked like Zsa Zsa Gabor looked in the 1940s, and she had a very effective little box of tricks of her own. And, in the grand, king-size, four-poster bed on the third floor, she swiftly and skillfully convinced Donald that Sandy Salazar deserved his chance. On the mound that is, not in the four-poster.

She might have been nearly right if they'd been talking about a Triple-A team, but she was not right about the Bombers. Sandy could pitch pretty well at a certain level. But he had a mideighties fastball, an inconsistent change-up, and a just-adequate curve. But he was not Major League material, and he never would be. Donald should have gotten him the hell out of there, but Zelda would not hear of it and she begged and pleaded, and Donald was under her spell. Sandy stayed, at a salary of $450,000 a year. Stargill could cheerfully have murdered him. And now this sex goddess to whom he was deliciously married wanted him on the team against the Seawolves.

He was nearly certain the Bombers veteran manager, Spooky Anderton, would have a heart attack if he even mentioned the name of his wife's pet pitcher. So he decided to go on the offensive, writing a provocative memorandum to the team boss pointing out the grotesque inadequacy of the Bombers bull pen, the shuddering effect of going into the record books for conceding two grand slams against the White Sox in one inning. "Your pitchers don't do it for us," he wrote. "I want Salazar in for the first two innings, let's see what he's got. If it doesn't work, take him out. The kid deserves a shot."

Anderton glared at the note. "That's according to Zelda, not Donald," he muttered, and made his way up to the owner's office, where he stated the obvious. "Kid's not ready, sir. Not even close."

Don Stargill stared right back at the lean, dark-haired, unshaven former Yankees pitching coach and said quietly, "When I send a note to my manager in the dying days of this ball club, I do not regard it as a subject for debate. I said Salazar starts. That means, Salazar starts. So long, Spooky, get him ready."

Spooky padded out of the office, moving softly on his cushioned trainers. He shook his head a couple of times and kept going down to the locker room, still shaking his head. CBA announced the change to the Bombers starting lineup on the 6 P.M. bulletin, one hour before game time. Ted Sando heard it and left the bull pen, made a phone call to South Dakota, to an ex–Maine pitcher now coaching the Bombers Triple-A team, the Rapid City Rednecks. By 6:15, like Spooky Anderton, Ted knew the Bombers were in deep trouble.

Two hours previously the Seawolves had arrived at the ballpark in the superb battle bus. The great sprawling forecourt of Ebbets Field was crammed with television crews striving for items for their early evening bulletin. The afternoon newspapers were done for the day, the morning newspaper staffs were not yet in the stadium, and CBA was preparing for an advertising bonanza.

The 'Wolves' bus drove right up to the players' entrance and the team disembarked, one by one, and headed for the visitors' locker room, accompanied by Russ and Ted, plus Dick Topolski, his assistant, and the trainer. There were two other coaches in the party who had come down from Maine by car to help out at first and third base.

Jack Faber, Kyle Davidson, and Pedro all walked out to the field immediately, trying to familiarize themselves with the battleground. The place felt vast in its present deserted state, but the well-defined distances of the original Ebbets Field were geometrically in place. The center-field fence stood 416 feet from home plate, the famous right field was 301 feet, topped by a 38-foot fence.

Jack walked onto the mound and stood there, as if measuring with his eye that all was in place, the 60-foot 6-inch distance between the pitcher's rubber and home plate, the four 90-foot base paths, the 127-foot, 3 3/8-inch distance from first base to third, from home plate to second.

He looked at the field boxes he would face tonight and tried to count the rows, to where he knew his father and Natalie would be seated, as if seeking comfort in their presence. There would be other friends from the Cape here too. Martha Jamieson and Jane Topolski, with Jason Wright, would watch the game with Ben and Natalie from the same private field box right behind home plate. One hundred other special seats had been sent to Seapuit board members and major contributors to the team.

But tonight's circumstances were unique. And no pitcher could avoid the feeling of isolation that goes with the territory. And for Jack, the nervousness was already setting in. His mouth was dry, and he felt butterflies in his stomach. He could eat nothing. The most he could face would be a glass of orange juice, or perhaps just water. He wondered if everyone else felt the same.

The stadium would pack in a crowd of forty-two thousand tonight. And the din from them would probably make it impossible to hear a shout from the dugout, or even from Tony Garcia. The single biggest added attraction was the 329-strong Notre Dame Marching Band, resplendent in the their blue, white, and gold uniforms.

They were here in honor of Griff Heeney, the Seawolves' DH, and at
the request of Art Mackay, who screened a lot of Fighting Irish football games and felt that the most famous sound in all of college
sports should pervade the stadium, the city, and electronically, the
nation.

Huge television screens had been erected around the area. The big
streets which surrounded Ebbets were all effectively owned by
Stargill, and tonight they were closed to traffic, except for automobiles headed for the Ebbets parking tower.

It had been only two weeks since the 'Wolves had last played
competitively together, though it now seemed like a lifetime. In practice on Thursday afternoon they had been sharp, and so far as Russ
could see, their fitness had held. His principal task was to keep them
calm, but as the stadium began to fill, it was clear there were some
extremely nervous ballplayers in the Seawolves' lineup. Tony Garcia
and Doughnut were not included among the nerve-racked.

Outside on the forecourt the mighty marching band of the Fighting Irish was in tight formation, blasting out music and casting a carnival atmosphere over the entire evening. A massed crowd of
baseball fans stood and watched, and the Goodyear Blimp cruised
overhead beaming pictures across a nation in which more than 60
percent of all the televisions were tuned for the forthcoming showdown between the Bombers and the 'Wolves.

Forty minutes before game time a black stretch limousine pulled
up at the main entrance, and the television crews surged forward.
Ben Faber stepped out first, followed by Natalie, dressed head to toe
by Pierre Cardin. She looked nothing less than spectacular and she
clutched Ben's arm as they made their way forward.

One of the cameramen yelled, *"It's the harpist from the Chicago
Symphony! Stand back, I gotta get these shots."*

The director of music from the Notre Dame band heard the
shout and, without missing a beat, snapped, *"This is the one—
Beethoven . . . three . . . four . . . five . . ."* And the mighty line-up of
musicians thundered into the composer's Fifth Symphony in honor
of Natalie, the catcher's mom . . . *DAH-DAH DAH DAAAAH . . .
DAH-DAH DAH DAAAAH . . .* the majestic sounds soared over
Brooklyn, sixty trumpets, forty saxophones, forty clarinets, and a
twenty-six-strong drum line. No one in the crowd had ever heard
anything like it.

Natalie laughed and hung on to Ben, who turned and kissed her. It was a deeply unprivate moment, since the television ratings had now hit 30 million sets with approximately 120 million people watching the buildup to the game, coast to coast on CBA.

"We don't get a whole lot of privacy, you may have noticed," said Ben. "This is one of the rare times we have been separated from Jack and Tony, and you've replaced them with the biggest band in the world and a TV audience of zillions."

"What do you mean, *I've* replaced them . . . you think *I* shipped this army of buglers in from the Midwest!"

"All I know, honey, is right now they're playing our song . . ." Which made Natalie laugh all over again, and the crescendo of the overture followed them both all the way to their VIP seats.

The field box was empty when they arrived, and there were souvenir programs on each seat. Automatically Natalie searched for a picture of Tony while Ben scanned through the pages looking for Jack. And then, quite suddenly, Natalie said, "Can I ask you a question?"

"Sure," he said. "Go right ahead."

"Do you love me, Ben? I mean really love me?"

"Only since the first minute I met you."

"No. I'm serious. And I'm talking about serious love, because I have a feeling tonight is a big turning point for all of us . . . look around here . . . this is unbelievable . . . and it's because of you . . . and I'm so proud of you and what you are . . . I'm just so proud of you . . ."

Ben was uncertain what he was supposed to say to that, so he came back with a question of his own. "Well," he said. "do *you* love *me*?"

"I tried to learn about baseball, didn't I? And for me that's a sacrifice beyond price . . . but I have to think about things, you know, what's going to happen to us . . . will I just go home to my apartment and carry on as before . . . just seeing you sometimes, when we can? I've been thinking a lot these past two days, and I just need to know if you really care about me, and what happens to me?"

Exactly then, Martha and Jane arrived . . . "Hell, you picked a real quiet place to have this little heart-to-heart, I'll say that, Miss Natalie," whispered Ben. But then suddenly there were people everywhere, houseparents walking by, trying to locate seats, well-wishers who had made the journey from Cape Marlin, regular Seawolf fans.

Ben found a white space in his program, took out a pen, and wrote carefully, "You know what I think. Now you have to answer my question—sometime soon. Your ever-loving, devoted natural gas tycoon, Ben." Natalie always laughed at him. Always would.

By now the marching band was inside the stadium on its way to a big block of seats out beyond center field. The players were milling around the dugouts, and the Bombers were waving at the crowd, slick, confident, and aggressive.

In the Seapuit dugout, Ted Sando was holding court, getting his players charged up. He was back and forth to the bull pen, where Pedro and Kyle were throwing. But his message to the hitters was urgent. "Their starting pitcher is no good. His fastball's nothing you haven't seen before, and it's his best pitch. You guys have gotta go after him right from the get-go. You've got to hit him, because he's not gonna last.

"Gino, the minute you get up there, *go go go*. Base hits, guys. Zac, Ray, and Boom-Boom, you can bang this joker all over the field. We can win this fucking thing in the first coupla innings. Sandy Salazar's his name, and I want you guys to end his fucking career."

Everyone could see Ted was on the edge of his nerves. But that was because he truly believed the 'Wolves could win this—and he did not want "any goddamned mistakes."

At five minutes to seven o'clock the Brooklyn Bombers took the field, led out by their catcher, Pete McGuire, his left knee heavily wrapped beneath his uniform. They fanned out into their field positions, and the announcer made his first call of the evening *"And on the mound for the Bombers tonight, from Venezuela, Alesandro Salazar.*

"And the leadoff hitter for the Seawolves . . . from Little Italy and Seton Hall, New York's very own Gino Rossi . . ."—at which point a stupendous burst of applause broke out, from two sources—every member of Gino's high school, and three hundred patrons of his father's famous restaurant, Tiberio's, near the junction of Mulberry and Houston, a half block from where "Crazy" Joey Gallo was gunned down on the sidewalk in 1973. From another section there came a transplanted chant direct from Cabot Field: *"GEE-NO . . . GEE-NO . . . GEE-NO!"* And a great baritone roar burst forth from the Italians, and they joined in, and then everyone joined in: *"GEE-NO . . . GEE-NO . . . GEE-NO!"*

"*OKAY, PLAY BALL!*" yelled the plate umpire, above the din. And McGuire went into his crouch, signaled for a fastball, and Salazar hurled in the first pitch of the long-awaited game. And immediately the 'Wolves could see Salazar had a slightly weird action, very deliberate, but he had a kind of spin on the end of his kick, and he seemed to be looking up to the sky.

Nonetheless he sent in a straight pitch, at the plate, around 88 mph. Gino watched it, and let it go. *Strike one.* The second pitch was a big, round, looping curve, which dropped in, on the outside corner of the plate, for strike two.

And then, with the game just a couple of minutes old, Alesandro made his first mistake. He sent that exact same pitch ballooning in again, but slower, only 71 mph, and Gino recognized it. He stayed back then flicked the bat head out at the ball and dropped a crisp single just over the second baseman's head.

Gino took off, hurtling down the runway to first base, and the Notre Dame band, at the top of their lungs and drumsticks, struck up the theme from *The Godfather*, and the crowd went absolutely wild. For one tiny corner of time, half the population of North America was talking about Gino Rossi.

To the plate came Rick Adams, announced over the sound system as "a future general in the army of the United States." Rick took his stance, a hard disciplined stance, and he glared down at Alesandro as if daring him to throw at the plate.

Salazar let fly with a low split-finger for a ball. Adams never moved. The second pitch was a fastball, but in the split second when the pitcher raised his leg, Rossi took off for second. On his third stride, he glanced left at the batter, and he saw Rick hit a hard ground ball just behind him, into the hole that had been the second baseman's ground but was now unoccupied, because D. J. Mahoney was racing in to cover the bag, trying to stop Gino's steal.

But Adams had executed the perfect hit-and-run, and he was sprinting, flat out, down the base path to first. Rossi, driving for second, now glanced up to third and saw Coach Brad Colton waving him on, circling his arm, and he never broke stride, stormed around the second-base bag, and kept running.

The Bombers' thirty-eight-year-old right fielder Don Hutchinson, once known to have the strongest arm from the outfield in the entire

Major Leagues, hurled a bullet into third. Rico Fiore caught the throw on one hop, and he swept the tag in on the diving Rossi's out-stretched arm as he clawed in desperation for the outside corner of the base.

Dust flared everywhere as Rossi came in, and the umpire took two jog steps forward, almost on one knee, peering at the bag, trying to get closer to the play. And his arms were outstretched, as he bel-lowed, *"SAFE!"* The roar from the crowd could have been heard in Staten Island. But this was not over.

Fiore was outraged, and he raised his arms and banged them down to his sides. He stamped his feet and turned to the umpire, nose to nose, protesting the call. At which point Adams, the two-hundred-meter sprinter, rocketed off first base, running for his life.

Mahoney, at second, screamed for the ball. But Fiore was beside himself in his rage with the umpire. In fact, he was still beside him-self as Adams came charging into second, standing up, right there on second base, without even a throw attempt.

Fiore spun around, and saw the damage. And in a blinding rage he spiked the ball hard into the dirt, still sounding off at the umpire. And now the Bombers manager, Spook Anderton, came running out of the dugout to argue the call, but his main purpose was to stop Fiore from being thrown out of the game.

The umpire answered them both plainly. "The tag was on the upper arm, while the hand was on the bag. I was very close, six feet from the play. The runner was safe." It was a miracle anyone heard a word he said, because there were near-riot conditions in the bleach-ers. The place was on its feet, the aisles jammed, all the inbuilt anxi-eties of this game surging into reality.

The white anchor of hope had dug and held, and with Trojan gusto, the giant band from South Bend, Indiana, struck up a devas-tating rendition of the hymn of the United States Marine Corps, es-pecially for the future general on second base. *". . . FROM THE HALLS OF MONTEZUMA TO THE SHORES OF TRIPOLI . . ."* Two on, no one out.

Colbert was up. Big Zac Colbert, who hit nineteen doubles and had forty-three RBIs in the regular season. This had to be a chance for the Seawolves.

Salazar pitched again, two fastballs, both of which Zac fouled back before popping up a towering fly ball into the infield. Salazar thinks it's bang overhead and he yells, *"Arriba! Arriba!"* which the shortstop, Joe Roberts, a seven-time All-Star, and four-time Gold Glove winner, was pretty sure meant, *"Mine! Mine!"*

However, the ball was farther back than Salazar thought, and Joe raced in on a near-collision course with Mahoney. They both hesitated at the pitcher's call, and then rumbled forward again. The ball dropped dead between them, eight feet behind the mound.

Mahoney picked up the ball and looked at Rossi on third, at Adams at second, Colbert at first. All safe. And then he looked at Roberts, protesting, "I thought you had it, man!"

"I thought the pitcher had it. I don't speak fucking Spanish," yelled the shortstop. And he turned to Salazar and told him, "Olé! Shithead. If the ball's in the fucking airo, get the fuck out of the wayo!"

In the bedlam of the crowd's jeers, he could see Spook Anderton pacing the dugout, crinkling his hat in rage. Bases loaded. No one out. Boom-Boom Hacker moving to the plate.

On the mound Salazar was pacing around, muttering in Spanish, trying to compose himself, trying to work out what he had done wrong. He reared back and grooved a fastball in at only 87 mph, right at the middle of the plate. Boom-Boom, all charged up by Ted Sando, hammered that ball hard down the third-base line.

Fiore dived for it, reaching right across his body with the glove on the backhand. Everyone in the stadium was sure he had it. And five years ago he would have had it. Zac Colbert would have had it. But thirty-seven-years old is too old for balls hit that hard, and it whistled past his gaping glove.

Rossi scored. Adams, running home right behind him, scored. Colbert reached third. Boom-Boom made second, no trouble: 2–0 'Wolves, runners at second and third, no one out.

The CBA commentator almost died of excitement. *"They said they could do it, and by God they're doing it! The Seawolves take the lead!"* And all over the country, fists tightened as big Ray Sweeney came out to the plate.

Salazar immediately went behind in the count, 2–0, and Ray hit his third pitch, a hard, one-hop ground ball which the Bombers' first baseman Greg Diamond snagged. He stared down at Colbert, daring him to try. But Zac never moved, and Greg made three steps to the bag for the out.

Bobby Madison was next up, and he faced an Alesandro Salazar already getting rattled. He hit Bobby high on the arm with his first pitch. The Citadel cadet never ever winced, just headed up the runway to load the bases for the second time.

The Bombers pitching coach, Slinger Simmonds, an ex–sidearm reliever for the Detroit Tigers, came running out of the dugout to calm down the frantic Salazar.

This was not easy, and it was several minutes before Steve Thompson came up to the plate and banged a short fly ball to left field. But it was quite not deep enough, and the Bombers left fielder Steve Gallant, a thirteen-year Major League veteran with Texas and Baltimore, loped in to take the catch for the second out. Zac Colbert took a few steps, bluffing, but he wasn't leaving third base unless there was a real good reason to do so.

And this brought up Tony Garcia, and he came to the plate bursting with aggression, fired up, ready to run through a brick wall. The catcher, misjudging his man, decided to try to rile the kid, his opposite number in the Seawolf field.

"Hey, kid," said McGuire. "How much would that sexy little mother of yours charge me a for few music lessons? You know, maybe a little more?"

Garcia's mouth was, if anything, faster than his glove. "Zip it, penis breath," he snapped. "I hear your dick's as limp as your left knee." That even got a chuckle out of the umpire.

Salazar pitched two fastballs, one a strike over the outside, the other up and in, close to Tony's chin, right into that zone in which the hitter has a hundredth of a second to overcome fear, the fear that is never absent in this game, with its history of terrible injuries.

That fastball was a message from the catcher, who had called it. Garcia knew that. And McGuire watched with satisfaction as this fucking little upstart swayed back, buckling his knees.

Pete McGuire grinned and said, "Hey, kid, buckling the knees a little, eh?"

"At least I have knees, asshole."

McGuire called for a fastball on the outside, and Salazar pitched again, sending it in at 86 mph but too far in the middle. Tony picked it up on the release, zooming in toward the plate. At 2–0 he had the green light, and he unleashed on that pitch, took a huge swing, and cracked the ball straight back to Salazar. If he had not ducked, the ball would have decapitated him.

The pitcher fell back, and the ball rocketed up the middle. Zac took off from third at the crack of the bat and made home easily. Boom-Boom took off from second, running hard. Waved on at third, he came bearing down on the plate.

The Bombers center fielder Buckskin Moseley, a veteran in his late thirties with a lifetime .998 fielding percentage, ran in to grab the ball on its third hop; he unleashed a missile to his catcher.

McGuire stepped forward to block home plate and take the ball. But it had barely touched the leather when Boom-Boom came pounding over the dirt like a freight train, and he lowered his shoulder and put a hit on McGuire that Dick Butkus would have approved. McGuire's feet were airborne when Boom-Boom charged in, and he was hammered backward into the ground, dropped the ball, thought he was dead.

"*SAFE!*" bawled the umpire, his arms outstretched. And within a half second Spook Anderton was out of the dugout, roaring at the top of his voice, "*INTERFERENCE—GODDAMMIT!*" Not that anyone could hear him, because the stadium noise was deafening as the 'Wolves took a 4–0 lead.

Spook went nose to nose with the umpire, the faceless figure of judgment, and as the thunder of the crowd began slightly to decrease, Joe Catano from the Bronx delivered his infallible verdict. "Spook," he said, "the ball arrived at exactly the same time as the runner. It was a clean play." And he turned his back on the infuriated Bombers manager, and the crowd roared its approval, and the band struck up with "*Nothing could be finer than to be in Carolina . . .*" in honor of Boom-Boom Hacker.

With Bobby Madison on third and Tony Garcia on second, Griff Heeney, the designated hitter from Notre Dame, came to the plate. It was the moment every one of the 329 musicians had waited for, and the familiar sounds of the college fight song, with its reminders of a thousand football games, echoed up into the night and then slowly died away. And the stadium was hushed as Heeney took his stance, fouled back two, and then slammed into an inside curve from Salazar.

The ball flew high and far, but Griff had not caught it quite perfectly, and it tumbled out of the sky, directly into Steve Gallant's glove in left field. Which ended a brilliant first inning for the visitors from Cape Marlin.

Meanwhile, in the Bombers dugout there was havoc as Donald Stargill himself made an appearance specifically to rail at the players. *"Where's the pride?"* he yelled. *"Will someone just tell me, where's the fucking pride?"*

Pride? Right now there wasn't even shame. The Bombers were in total chaos, angry at the score, uncertain how it had happened, why it had happened. To a man, they did not want to be here. But the future of the ball club was on the line, their jobs, their lifestyles. Goddammit, Bert Muncie had a wife, four kids, two girlfriends, and eleven automobiles to support. And no one else was going to pay him like Stargill.

For Bert, history hung in the balance. He was chasing three thousand hits-sixty-one away—and he was nursing a .293 lifetime average. He had promised to go into the Hall of Fame as a Bomber, despite his nineteen seasons with the Cubs. And now this, nine innings from death.

Bert looked on disconsolately as Pedro Rodriguez jogged out to the mound and took his warm-up pitches. For the first time the crowd was silent as everyone anticipated the moment of truth. Would the vastly experienced Bomber hitters bang the college pitcher all over the field?

Up in the commentary box the CBA team was speaking to the nation in quiet voices. *"Rodriguez is a close friend of Pedro Martinez . . . down there in Santo Domingo they swear by him, like he's the Second Coming . . . he went twelve–one at Florida State in the spring. ERA of 2.78. The kid can pitch."*

Pedro was ready, and the leadoff hitter for the Bombers was at the plate—the left-handed Steve Gallant, who led the Majors for eight seasons in stolen bases, averaging sixty-four. Right now the thirty-five-year-old Gallant was trying to hold a lifetime batting average of .317. But he was hitting only .261 this year, and he'd had four operations on his knee.

Pedro pitched a fastball, then a curve, and Steve fouled them both back. Tony Garcia signaled for another fastball, holding his glove a little higher, telling his pitcher to "climb the ladder," tempting the hitter to chase it. Pedro hurled it in, tailing at 91 mph, high over the outside corner. Gallant went after it, swung hard, and missed by around six inches. *"STRUCK HIM OUT!"* screamed the commentator. *"THE KID STRUCK OUT STEVE GALLANT!"* and the stadium literally shook with the roar from the crowd.

Joe Roberts, eleven-year veteran shortstop with the Minnesota Twins, was waiting on deck, trying to "get centered." Joe was hitting only .247 this season with a career high of sixteen errors, and for the past twenty-four hours he had been determined to make this a good night personally. And he came to the plate determined and focused.

Pedro threw a fastball and Joe jumped all over it, for a ground-ball base hit which scudded straight between Colbert and Rick Adams. The first baseman Greg "Legs" Diamond was up next, and on an 0–2 count, he banged a low, hard drive at Adams. The ball ricocheted up off the dirt, and the Citadel cadet dove outstretched to his left to snag it on that first hop. He fell backward, almost behind second base, and still flat on the ground, reached into his glove and flipped the ball straight to Bobby Madison, who was now standing on the bag.

Bobby caught it bare-handed, wheeled around, and hurled a bullet to first base, where Boom-Boom took it in his outstretched glove, beating the flying Legs Diamond by a half stride for the six-four-three double play. And again the stadium erupted, and the CBA color commentator, his voice shaking with emotion, could only shout, *"They're doing it . . . this is actually happening! The Bombers first inning finished in three minutes."*

Once more Gino Rossi headed for the plate to face the erratic inefficiency of Alesandro Salazar. Spook's hands were tied. Stargill wanted him in for two innings and that could not be change. The entire stadium was up and chanting *"GEE-NO . . . GEE-NO . . . GEE-NO!"* And the United States of America watched in glee as the Seawolves prepared for their second-inning assault.

The first pitch came in slowly, and the quick-witted Rossi instantly converted his bat angle into a bunt, dragging the ball down the third-base line and taking off like a greyhound for first. Rico Fiore, a six-time All-Star third baseman in his time, came off the bag like a thirty-seven-year-old, too slow, and no longer agile enough to get down on the ball. He grabbed it bare-handed and threw it right across his body to first base. It looked great, but it wasn't quick enough, and the flying Gino Rossi beat it.

Rick Adams was up next, and Salazar, unnerved by the owner in the dugout, yelling, unnerved by the bunt, sent in a hanging split-finger at only 79 mph. Adams stepped right into it, and hammered a single over the shortstop's head. The 'Wolves had men on first and second with no one out.

Zac Colbert, however, was gone after one pitch. He took a mighty cut at a curveball and popped it up in foul ground near first base, where Diamond caught it. Boom-Boom, flushed with success, fared no better, took three tremendous swipes at successive pitches, and missed them all. Two on, two out.

In the dugout Sando was pacing. "Come on, Ray baby . . . they're going to take this joker out . . . we haven't long . . . get up there and hit him, for Christ's sake hit him . . ."

Ray flexed his massive fisherman's forearms and took his stance. The first pitch came in low and inside, and Ray fouled it back. The next one was a real bad curve. Ray slashed at it with all his strength, and the ball screamed back past his shoulder clean into the Bombers dugout, smacked against the back wall, sending Donald P. Stargill diving to the ground for cover, trying to avoid the ricochet.

Spook rushed over to help him to his feet, but Stargill was in a towering rage, ranting and raving about the "worst night of my fucking life," his "mad wife," and "gigolo pitcher." And *WHAT THE FUCK IS GOING ON HERE!*

Salazar was aware of the uproar in the dugout, and his next pitch was worse than the last, an inside fastball at only 88 mph. Alesandro was trying to get the ball in on Ray's hands, but he left it right over the heart of the plate. The steel-armed Ray Sweeney turned and swung, and everyone in the stadium heard the crack as the ball soared out over the outfield, into the upper deck, about ten feet short of Duke Snider's 1951 homer against the New York Giants.

Rossi came racing in again, Adams right behind him. It was 7–0 and there was nothing short of pandemonium in the stands as the band burst into a tribute to Ray Sweeney with the University of Maine's anthem:

> *FILL THE STEINS TO DEAR OLD MAINE,*
> *SHOUT TILL THE RAFTERS RING!*

The game was becoming a massacre, and it was likely to stay that way until someone took Alesandro off the mound. Up in the owner's box, high above home plate, Zelda Stargill wept uncontrollably. And in the dugout Spook Anderton finally cracked, and he confronted Stargill angrily. "He's not ready, sir. I told you he's not ready. I know you own the fucking team, but we got professional reputations to protect. One more out, and he's gone. Either that or we're all gone."

Donald Stargill nodded. He had seen enough. And he watched in trepidation as Bobby Madison came up to the plate, took one on the shoulder, and then hammered what looked like a sure triple, deep through the right-center gap, the ball rolling to the fence.

Don Hutchinson ran it down in the gap and arrowed in a long throw to Mahoney, the cutoff man, who in turn flung it hard to third, where Rico tagged out Bobby, no ifs, ands, or buts. Again the crowd held its breath because it was a huge hit, out or no out. And it was surely the swan song of the pitcher from San Joaquin. He would leave the game having given up seven runs in two innings, more or less as Ted Sando had thought he might.

Back to the mound came Pedro Rodriguez, confident now, convinced the pros were not supermen. They could still hit, however, and Rico Fiore got ahold of Pedro's fastball but hit it right to Bobby Madison, who gunned him down at first. Pete McGuire hit one too, a deep fly ball to Ray Sweeney.

It was now up to Don Hutchinson, who in his day had earned three batting titles in nineteen seasons with the Angels, Mariners, and the White Sox. For the Bombers he was batting .297, which made him the team's top hitter. And now he grooved down into his lefty stance and instantly pulled an inside fastball down the right-field line for a stand-up double. Steve Thompson used all of his speed to track the ball down, stop it from being a triple. Madison raced out to take up position as cutoff man while Adams covered the base. Hutchinson, with two outs, held at second.

Bert Muncie, too old to play in the field anymore, came in to DH and hit a hard line drive off Pedro's curve, straight up the middle. Hutchinson took off on contact and charged to third, rounded the base, and kept going.

Sweeney ran in to field the ball and put a great throw into Boom-Boom, who had bolted across from first base to stand cut-off right behind the pitcher's mound. The run was plainly going in, and Bert, certain Boom-Boom would throw to home plate, rounded first and headed for second.

Boom-Boom saw he could not throw Hutchinson out, and he

whipped around and flung the ball to Madison for the tag at second. Muncie slammed on the brakes thirty feet short of the bag, turned back, and ran, with Bobby charging down the runway, chasing after him, and catching him, the ball held high in his right hand. The crowd went berserk, because Rick Adams had bounded across to first base like a panther, and now his left glove was held high, and he snapped crisply, *"NOW, BOBBY!"*

Young Bobby Madison, for the umpteenth time in his life, found Rick Adams's glove accurate to a hundredth of an inch. The perfectly turned-out officer cadet from Charleston accepted the surrender of the stubble-faced Bert Muncie, tagging him out without further resistance.

Seven hundred and sixty-three miles south of Brooklyn, in the great hall of the military academy of South Carolina, the entire Citadel faculty membership of 220 scholars, three major generals, one brigadier general, and seven army colonels, sat watching a giant television screen. As the ball landed in Cadet Rick Adams's glove, they leaped to their feet with a rebel roar like Stonewall's men in the Valley.

It was a roar that echoed across the campus, and everyone stood to attention, glued to the screen, watching Bert Muncie trudge back to the dugout, listening to Notre Dame's army of musicians thundering out the U.S. Marine Corps' battle hymn, especially for Bobby and Rick, two of their own.

24

With the score at 7–1, the Bombers sent in their new pitcher, Bob Higgins, thirty-seven-year-old winner of three Cy Young Awards with the Orioles, with four twenty-win seasons to his credit. In days long gone, Bob could throw 95–98 mph fastballs, but now he relied on a dazzling array of split-fingered fastballs, and screwballs to get batters out. He'd averaged only ten wins per season these past three years with the Bombers.

But he was still a force, and the old master sent down Thompson, Garcia, and Heeney with lazy ground-outs, mis-hit off the split-fingers, the ball tumbling in and then being driven into the ground.

Pedro was coming out after three, and he came to the mound for the last time and proceeded to throw with all his heart. He had given up two hits, and now he pitched with everything he had, fired out three in a row—Mahoney on a ground ball to Colbert, who threw him out at first, and then Moseley and Gallant, who both hit towering fly balls to the warning track, caught by Sweeney and then Rossi. It was still 7–1 after three, and the atmosphere was tightening, frustration building in the Bomber dugout.

Back came the Seawolves at the top of the fourth, only for Bob Higgins to bedevil them again. He made his first strikeout of the game when Rossi went down swinging. Adams was very resistant and worked the count to 3–2 before he got right underneath a side-spinning screwball and sliced it up to the shortstop.

"*I—I—I—I GOT IT!*" yelled Joe Roberts, anxious to avoid a second foul-up. And then Zac Colbert, overanxious, frustrated, though not as badly as the Bombers, swung three times, hard, and missed three times, to end the inning.

And this brought Kyle Davidson to the mound, but even while he was taking his warm-up pitches, Ted Sando could see immediate signs of uneasiness. He walked over to Russ Maddox and muttered, "He doesn't look himself, does he? Something's wrong."

Russ could not really answer that. But it was soon apparent that the words of the big lefty from Maine were prophetic. Kyle sent in two high fastballs, both ignored, for a 2–0 count, and then Joe Roberts ripped the third pitch, a clean line drive single to left.

Greg Diamond was next up, and the first pitch he saw was a curve. In the dugout Ted knew the absence of Kyle's blazing fastball so early in the inning signaled something serious. Greg whacked the curve, a monstrous drive, straight over the fence in left center, for two runs. It was 7–3, bottom of the fourth, no one out, and a few Bomber fans cheered.

But the big band stayed silent, and it was clear that Brooklyn was on a hiding to nothing. Almost no one in the immediate environs, or in the vast country at large, actually *wanted* them to win. Except for a few iron-souled local masochists who were able to tolerate the endless nightly defeats in one of the finest ballparks in the United States.

Kyle then walked Rico Fiore. And in the dugout, Maddox snapped, "Teddy, get Doughnut loose." The pitcher from Georgia, sensing the immediacy of the problem, headed quickly to the bull pen with the reserve catcher. Ted went to the mound and asked the big Stanford pitcher, "Something's wrong?"

And for the first time Kyle admitted his shoulder was killing him.

"Jesus, you should have told me."

"Coach, I'm pitching against a Major League team, in a Major League stadium. I couldn't let my family down—you know, not even give it a shot."

"Kyle, you're a brave kid, and I admire you, but you can't stand out here pitching with a badly injured shoulder. That's no good for anyone. I'm taking you out."

Kyle, the quiet-spoken veteran of so many winning battles on Cape Marlin, the toughest and most reliable of pitchers, handed the baseball to the Seawolves pitching coach for the last time. He walked back, his head down, clutching his throbbing shoulder. There was only a smattering of applause, because no one knew how badly he hurt, and how hard he had tried to pitch through the pain. Up in the stands in a VIP box, Buck Davidson knew, and the longtime presidential stalwart of the cold war had to walk back into the restaurant because he did not want anyone to see him this upset.

Doughnut was loose before he went to the bull pen, and now he was ready, yessir. He came loping out to the mound amid rolling applause, thanks to his television appearances. The stadium communications team had been waiting for this, and the rasping beauty of the voice of Ray Charles rang soulfully through the stadium. *"GEORGIA . . . GEORGIA . . . THE WHOLE DAY THROUGH . . . JUST AN OL' SWEET SONG KEEPS GEORGIA ON MY MIND . . ."*

Mr. Bo Davis sprang to his feet and whipped off his Bulldog cap, holding it over his heart, as if Ray were singing the National Anthem. "Right here, boy, we're talking heritage," he said to Chief Burrell, sitting next to him. "That's the great State of Georgia Ray's singing about. For me and my boy. HOW 'BOUT THEM DAWGS!" Bo Davis was almost as big a character as Doughnut. Almost.

And out on the mound, the Bulldog was up on one leg, pumping his arm, hat in the air, loving the atmosphere. And as the applause died and the music faded, he started his warm-up, hurling in his eight to Tony. The situation was critical, he knew that. There was no one out and Pete McGuire was at plate, listening to the outrageous Garcia telling him he once got a parking ticket on his baby carriage while his dad was watching Pete hit for the Expos at Wrigley.

Joe Catano pulled down his mask so McGuire would not see him laughing, but he still told Tony to shut up.

The night air was still now as Doughnut went into his windup. Then he unzipped a blazing fastball, 95 mph, straight down the pipe, right bang at the middle of the plate. Even McGuire, in the autumn of his career, could hit a fastball like that, and he was waiting, slammed it as hard as any baseball was ever hit, high into the upper deck, amid a shattering silence. As usual, Doughnut was attempting to rely on speed alone.

The two-run homer that scored Rico Fiore was the icy barometer of the difference between an amateur and a pro. McGuire came running in, growling at Garcia, "Way to pop 'em, right, kid. And I got another pop right here for your mom—heh-heh-heh!"

"Go shit in your hat," said Tony inelegantly, pulling off his mask and jogging out to the mound, where he found Doughnut distraught at the 7–5 score and at being hit that hard, first pitch.

The Georgia lefty was almost in a state of humiliation. But not quite. "Lucky swing, right? The guy just got lucky . . . he couldn't do that again . . ."

"Not till the next inning," said Tony. "Doughnut, any of these bastards could do it. McGuire's not even that good anymore. But listen, you gotta relax . . . you just cannot throw the ball straight past these guys. And if you keep trying, we're in for a long night. You must try to hit the spots . . . watch my glove."

But Doughnut was agitated. That was obvious. "Yeah. Yeah. Right," he said. "Hit the spots. Yeah."

Tony jogged back, went back into his crouch, and watched, dumbstruck, as Doughnut threw exactly the same pitch, a smoking 95 mph fastball dead at the plate. And this time, the big outfielder Don Hutchinson was waiting. And he smacked the ball into his own territory, right-center, for a stand-up double.

Again Tony pulled off his mask, signaling to Doughnut, raising his hands up and down in front of him. *Slow it down, man . . . you gotta slow it down.*

Finally Doughnut got it. He sent in an excellent fastball on the corner of the plate, which old Bert Muncie chased and fouled back. Then he sent in a tailing fastball, and a curve which broke across the plate. Bert was outta there on three pitches. One out, one on.

The next hitter, D. J. Mahoney, hit a clean catch to Zac Colbert at third, and then Doughnut threw a really nasty pitch, an inside fastball to the Kirby Puckett look-alike, Buckskin Moseley. The ball rode in on his hands, breaking the bat and rebounding into the infield. Bobby Madison charged the ball and winged it to Boom-Boom, easily beating out the once-speedy Buckskin to end the catastrophic fourth inning: 7–5 'Wolves.

Hacker, Sweeney, and Madison came up in order at the top of the fifth, and went down in order, still befuddled by the crafty Bob Higgins. It took almost fifteen minutes, but no one placed wood on the ball, and the patient former Oriole was grinning as he walked in. Right now the Bombers believed they had this game in the bag.

And there was a lot of joshing in their dugout as Doughnut made his way back to the mound. *"Just get on the bases, guys . . . no big hits till we got two on . . . then someone bang this fucking nutcase from Georgia . . ."*

Garcia called for the fastball, low and away, then another, a little higher. Steve Gallant swung and missed twice. Doughnut pumped his arm, and the crowd roared. The ump signaled the 0–2 count. Gallant could not make up his mind whether the next pitch would bisect the plate or not. So Doughnut made it up for him, and hurled his best pitch all night, 96 mph, smoking over the outside corner. Gallant never moved. Strike three. One out.

The Bulldog was throwing very hard, and Joe Roberts had trouble with the first two pitches; both swerved away from the plate, and he fouled them both off. The next fastball was perfect location, high and away. Roberts went down swinging. Two out.

Doughnut was growing in confidence, and he stared down at Rico Fiore, a man in the twilight of a great career, a man who, in thirteen Major League seasons with the Marlins, Devil Rays, and Bombers, had hit 417 home runs. He was hitting a career low of .271, but he was still dangerous.

Doughnut decided to do whatever the hell Garcia wanted. And he threw a great first pitch to Fiore, 95 mph, knee-high, tailing away. The Bombers third baseman swung and just clipped it foul. Garcia raised his glove, asking Doughnut to "climb the ladder," as pitchers say, throwing the next one just a little higher. Tony thought he could tempt the hot-tempered Fiore to swing twice more, and he was right about the first one. Fiore swung again, and for the second time fouled Doughnut off.

Tony went into his crouch, raised his glove again, narrowly outside the plate, confident Fiore would now go after the next pitch. But what the catcher could not hear was a small, still voice in Doughnut's mind telling him to send a 96 mph guided missile "straight past this ugly ol' bastard," right now. *YESSIR.*

It was the voice that had guided Doughnut all his life. The voice that had got him into more trouble on various pitching mounds than any other aspect of his game. But Doughnut was pumped. He'd just thrown six pitches, and struck out two Major League hitters.

And here he was, on the mound at Ebbets Field, the spiritual home of his lifelong Dodgers hero, Sandy Koufax. Right now Doughnut believed he *was* Sandy Koufax, and he shook Garcia off. Then he reared back and unleashed a 96 mph fastball, straight as a

gun barrel, straight at the heart of the plate, precisely into the forbid-
den territory, from which Garcia had banned him.

Rico Fiore pulverized it. He swung the bat right through the ball
and caught it a stupendous bang. It was the shot heard around the
world. Or at least the shot heard around the USA. The ball flew high
and far, out toward center field, swooping out of the sky into the
middle of the Notre Dame band. One quick-thinking, blue, white,
and gold trumpeter, sounded the mournful notes of "Taps" while the
ball was still rattling around the drum line. With the Bombers up and
out of the dugout cheering, the military funeral call might have
sounded like the death march for the Seawolves. But the trumpeter
missed the high F totally, which spoiled the effect, and all the Italians
jeered.

Rico rounded the bases, bringing the fifth-inning score now to
7–6 Seawolves, two out and no one on, with the tying run in the
form of Pete McGuire ambling to the plate.

Doughnut was devastated, sorry, in a sense broken. Because he no
longer knew what to do, except to follow his instincts, which was at
best a flawed policy. In the dugout, Ted grabbed Russ and said,
"Buddy, we gotta get him outta here. I'm damn sure he's not the answer right now."

Russ said, "We'll go to Cruiser—right away. He's loose and he
gets ready in about four minutes . . . we gotta stop the bleeding."

Ted Sando sent Covington Burrell to the bull pen, with the reserve
catcher, and then called "*TIME!*" and headed to the mound. Garcia
was already there, talking to Doughnut, who was not answering.

"Did he shake you off, Tony?"

"He did, and then he threw the one fucking pitch I damn near
begged him to forget. Straight at the fucking plate . . . I cannot believe this . . . I just cannot believe this . . ." If anything, Tony Garcia
was more upset than Doughnut.

Ted turned to Doughnut and said, "Sorry, kid. I'm taking you
out . . ."

"No . . . don't. I can do this . . ."

"Doughnut, we can't wait for you. This isn't Exeter or Oceanside
. . . this is Ebbets Field, New York, and you just gave up three runs
on homers because you will not take instruction . . . sorry, old pal. I
love ya, man. But I can't afford you right now."

Doughnut handed over the ball and walked in. Bo Davis was

shattered, and most of the crowd felt the same. The 'Wolves had hit Salazar, but not a real Major League pitcher. And now they were hanging on, trying to protect a slender lead of only one run.

Cruiser Burrell, all six feet six inches of him, came jogging in from the bull pen on an easy stride. He looked just what he was, the best relief pitcher in the Southeastern Conference, a big-time closer on his way to the Majors. He took his eight warm-ups, throwing hard at Tony's glove, sidearm, right-handed, 90 mph plus.

The crowd watched him throw, and a new frisson of excitement swept through the stadium as Pete McGuire stepped into the batter's box to face the coming onslaught. Pete was nervous, and he was right to be so. The Cruiser hurled two smoking fastballs straight past him, one outside, one inside. Then he sent in a curveball, away. Pete swung and missed, for the third out. "Siddown, asshole," growled Garcia under his breath.

But the 'Wolves still could not deal with Bob Higgins, who sent down Thompson, Garcia, and Heeney in order, all swinging. All missing. And again Cruiser came to the mound at the bottom of the sixth, with the left-handed Hutchinson at the plate.

Garcia called for a fastball over the outside corner, a difficult throw right-hander to lefty, but it was the Cruiser's best pitch and he ripped it in there, leaving the ball away, left to right at 91 mph. Hutchy never swung and the umpire called it a strike. Garcia told him to do it again, and still Hutch never swung. But he unloaded on the next pitch, a looping curve, missed it by about a foot, and headed for the dugout.

The next hitter was Bert Muncie, and Cruiser suddenly had trouble with his range. He mixed up three balls with two foul-backs, and then sent Bert down with a 92 mph rocket, thigh-high, inside, for a called strike.

D. J. Mahoney was next and he demonstrated that split-second edge that separates a very good hitter from an average one. D. J. did not quite have it. Six times he fouled back the Cruiser, until the huge Bulldog blazed one past him on the outside for the called strikeout. It had taken sixteen ferociously hard pitches to turn back the Bombers. And Cruiser's arm was already aching. And it was still 7–6 'Wolves.

Ted Sando's plan had always been to use five pitchers, with Pedro throwing the first three and Jack Faber the last three. It was unorthodox, but he had long been worried about Kyle's shoulder and Doughnut's erratic approach to the game. However, he knew they were both, at their best, effective. And his ace was Jack Faber, who was always ready to pitch nine if he had to, and he would improve steadily with his first fifty pitches. Especially if his slider was working.

Now, with all of his worst fears realized, Ted had to face the fact that Kyle and Doughnut had given up five runs between them in one and two-thirds innings, three of them homers. Now he was counting on Jack Faber to go out there and hold the Bombers at bay for three more innings. It had to be Jack now, because he was not the type of pitcher to be treated as a closer. He would need three to reach his best in the ninth, and Ted was praying Jack was ready to roll.

Right now he was in the bull pen warming up, throwing half speed, Griff Heeney catching him. At the plate was Gino Rossi, and the New York crowd was in full cry, despite the obvious fact that the Seawolves were hitless in their last four innings.

There is an urgency about the seventh inning in baseball. The game is two-thirds over, and the screws are tightening. The team in the lead wants another two or three runs. The team that is losing is desperate to tie it up. Close games cause emotions to heighten. They're no longer charging down the backstretch, where anything can happen, they're no longer jockeying for position. They're straightening up for the stretch run, and the battle is suddenly defined, the competitive balance is already skewed in favor of one of the contestants.

And here at Ebbets Field, the Seawolves still had it. And although the Bombers had whacked the injured Kyle and the eccentric Doughnut, they had been ineffective against Pedro, and got nothing off the Cruiser. Now they would face Seapuit's best pitcher, the big kid from way down in south Louisiana, a former Cape Marlin League MVP. It was by no means certain the Bombers would find two more runs. Not certain at all.

Before they even had another shot at offense, Bob Higgins had to remove the top of the Seawolves order. As ever, he would try to weave a lifetime of cunning into each of his pitches, floating them away from the slashing bats of Rossi, Adams, and Colbert, all of whom were smart, determined, and frustrated.

The band played "O Sole Mio" loudly as Rossi came up to the plate, and again the crowd burst into their thunderous chant of "GEE-NO . . . GEE-NO . . . GEE-NO!"

Rossi had a strategy. Higgins threw one pitch, a slow tumbling screwball Rossi thought he could hit, but he never threw it until he was ahead in the count. Thus Gino took two split-fingered fastballs on the shoulder for an 0–2 count. And right on time, the screwball followed it, slow and awkward but right where Rossi hoped it would be. He caught it a tremendous whack, deep into the left-field corner, for a stand-up double.

Adams came to the plate, left two off-speed pitches over the corner, and then fired a one hop ground ball past Fiore and made first base. Rossi made third, but held when Gallant fielded the ball very fast. The 'Wolves had runners on the corners, no one out.

The band played the overture from Rodgers and Hammerstein's *Oklahoma!* as Zac Colbert came to bat. He went down swinging, but Adams stole second. Bob Higgins blew Boom-Boom away with two called strikes, and then a split-finger outside caused yet another swing and miss. Two on, in scoring position. Two gone.

But Ray Sweeney could not move the runners around. He hit a high pop-up just behind Mahoney at second, and Joe Roberts ran in to take the catch, stranding Rossi and Adams on base.

Ben and Natalie had watched most of the game in companionable conversation, their mood rising and falling with the ebb and flow of the contest. But now the chips were down. The Seawolves had only two more at-bats. The Bombers had three. That's a minimum of nine Major League hitters, all with one avowed intention—to knock one of Jack Faber's pitches over the wall.

The seventh-inning stretch came and went. And suddenly the Seapuit players were out of the dugout, running into position. And jogging out behind them was the unmistakable figure of Jack, his cap down, glove held loosely in his hand. The stadium announcer called, *"And on the mound for the Seawolves now, from St. Charles College, South Louisiana, Jack Faber."*

Ben could feel Natalie's grip tighten on his arm. This was a major national event, and the entire thing hung on the ability of Ben's son to throw the ball. Most of the Seapuit supporters knew of his early season travails, and everyone felt for him. But no one felt for him like Ben Faber.

Natalie could feel the tension in the ex–sugar farmer's arm, and she thought she could feel his heart beating. Jack took four warm-ups and then Tony ran out to speak to him. They saw Tony bang him lightly on the shoulder and jog back to his station before Jack pitched four more fastballs.

And up to the plate came Buckskin Moseley, a man who had lived for the big occasion at the height of his career, but was now in decline. Ben silently prayed Jack would strike Buckskin out, and build his confidence. He alone could see how nervous his son was, and he watched Jack walk off the mound, pick up the rosin bag, then he walked back up the slope to pitch the bottom of the seventh.

You'll never cut it in the majors, Faber. You'll be all washed up by the time you leave here. The ghost of Bruno Riazzi shot into Jack's mind. However hard he tried, he could not cast it out. He just kept on churning over the words of the coach who had almost destroyed him. He knew it was crazy, but the sweating, jowly face of Riazzi would not go away as Jack prepared to pitch to the pros. He understood the face of Riazzi represented only the face of doubt, but how could he possibly not have doubt, when the only Major Leaguer he'd ever been coached by said he did not have the guts for it? That he would never get good hitters out.

Garcia signaled for a fastball, and Buckskin took his stance. Ben Faber's heart stopped dead in his chest, and Jack wound back and ripped a strike right over the outside corner: 0–1. Immediately Tony called for the slider, and Jack threw it, but it did not break very well and Buckskin banged it hard up the middle for a single.

Jack cursed. He turned away, walked back down to the rosin bag. He could see the leadoff hitter Steve Gallant at the plate. And tried to get Riazzi out of his mind, walked back to the pitching rubber, got his sign, and went into the set. He hurled a fastball high. Ball one. Already he could feel his stomach tightening. He tried to break into a new rhythm, and threw the change-up. Low. Ball two. Tony signaled for a fastball to the outside of the plate. But it went in high and just too far outside. It was 3–0.

Jack knew he had to straighten up and get the ball over the plate when Tony signaled. But his fourth pitch was high and inside, and Steven Gallant walked. Two on, and the stadium was quiet, and in the silence Jack heard Ted shout, "*MY TIME!*" Joe Catano threw up his hand and also yelled "*TIME!*" And Ted Sando was on his way to the mound. Natalie could feel a soft tremor right through Ben Faber's body.

Ted's purpose was just to calm down his pitcher. But Jack was so nervous he could hardly speak. There was a rising noise from the crowd as Legs Diamond, who won the Major League Triple Crown with .349 batting average, fifty-eight home-runs, and 157 RBIs in his fourth season in the Bigs, stepped up to the plate. Now his task was clear—to hit this kid hard if possible, but to get Buckskin home to square it up, no matter what. If the pitch was right, maybe he would deliver the deathblow to the Seawolves by driving one over the wall.

Legs waited for the pitch, assessed it, and immediately squared around to sacrifice-bunt. But he popped the fastball into the air and Jack came off the mound, fast, dived forward, and took the catch. The Stadium erupted. The runners held. And Legs headed for the dugout.

The explosion of applause made Jack feel better. A lot better. The crowd was still with them. And he reared back, sending in a superb fastball to Rico Fiore, a strike across the inside corner.

Jack went to his sinking fastball, and Fiore hit it onto the ground straight back to the pitcher. Jack grabbed it and fired the ball to Bobby Madison, who hurled a frozen rope to Boom-Boom at first for the double play.

The Bombers went to the bull pen, taking out Bob Higgins and now bringing in the thirty-six-year-old Red Rollins, five times winner of the Rolaids Fireman Award as the best closer in the Major Leagues. In his early career he could throw at 97–99 mph, and that power had brought him within forty-eight of Lee Smith's all-time save record, most of them with the Royals. But Red had had "Tommy John surgery" on his right elbow, and he threw at only 89–91 mph these days, but he was still a serious force.

So serious he struck out Bobby, then Steve Thompson, then Tony Garcia with only thirteen pitches. Which brought Jack back to the mound after only twelve minutes.

Bottom of the eighth, and Pete McGuire was next up. He was angry, focused, and determined to win. Jack threw him a fastball on the inside, and Pete went after it, caught it a terrific crack, right to the warning track in center field, where Ray Sweeney caught it. Six more feet on that ball, and there would have been a tied game.

Don Hutchinson came to the plate and Jack threw him back-to-back strikes, a fastball and a change-up. But Hutch nailed the third pitch, straight down the third-base line. Zac Colbert took one step and lunged. Everyone thought he had it, but the ball flew off the outstretched glove, and into left field. Hutch rounded first with a single.

Bert Muncie came up, and Jack threw the slider, much harder, and it dipped down for a called strike on the outside corner. Then he let him have a fastball, which Bert fouled off into the left field fans. The third pitch was another slider, outside. Bert swung and missed. Strike three. The Bombers had two out, one on.

Mahoney took his stance, and Jack hurled a dipping fastball. The batter missed and Hutchinson took off to steal second, but Garcia gunned him down with a bullet straight into Bobby Madison's glove for the third out. It was *still* 7–6 Seawolves.

And here they came again, for the perhaps the last time, the ninth inning. And at the plate was Griff Heeney, the designated hitter from Notre Dame. And Rollins decided to go right after him with two fastballs down the heart of the plate.

Griff missed them both, but he did not miss the next one. He anticipated it over the plate, then blasted it high out toward that big blue 38-foot-high fence in right field, 301 feet from the plate.

"THAT COULD BE OUTTA HERE! THAT BALL'S GOING . . . IT'S CLOSE . . . NO! IT'S HIT THE TOP OF THE FENCE, FALLING BACK INTO THE BALLPARK!"

And Hutchinson was on it. The ball fell, and bounced once, and the Bombers' top hitter snagged it, hurled it to the cutoff man Mahoney, who winged it to Joe Roberts, and he held Heeney at second.

The Notre Dame Marching Band, playing from the heart, for one of their own, thundered into the anthem of the Fighting Irish. The drum line sounded like a sonic boom. And the crowd cheered, and Brooklyn was on its feet inside and outside the stadium, where the giant television screens showed the 'Wolves had a man on and no one out, in the ninth.

And Ebbets Field was swelling to a crescendo of riotous noise which would not be stilled. The band was late finishing its most famous piece, and the deafening chant of *GEE-NO . . . GEE-NO . . . GEE-NO!* filled the night as Rossi stepped up to try to get Griff Heeney home.

But Rollins was cautious and the young Italian-American from Seton Hall was on the edge of his nerves. The legendary closer knew what to do—three fastballs, two on the outside, both away, one up and in. Gino went after them all, missed them all. Red Rollins proceeded to strike out Rick Adams on a 3–2 count, and Zac Colbert banged his second pitch high and far to center field, where Buckskin Moseley was waiting.

The 'Wolves were all done for the night in regular innings, and as the commentator reminded the nation, *"Right now they're still holding on, seven runs to six, and it's all up to young Jack Faber, and he wants three more outs against Buckskin Moseley, and then the top of the Bombers' hitting lineup, Gallant and Roberts."*

In the private field boxes, Natalie Garcia felt there was no one else in the stadium seats except her and Ben. She kept asking about the counts, checking on the outs, trying to see when the umpire called a ball or a strike. She had never taken this much interest in a baseball game in her life. And she clung to Ben as Jack came loping out to the mound, amid truly momentous applause. He represented the last hope for victory for the millions of real sports fans of the United States. Every newspaper had announced that the Seawolves had five pitchers. Every last person in the stadium knew that Jack was the fifth. Every true fan, with a love of the underdog, said a prayer for Jack Faber.

And now he stood on the mound, his heart pounding, his life passing before him as it is supposed to in the instant before death. He fought to stay focused, and he forced a picture into his mind of the old tire hanging out by the barn, and he thought of his dad, and he fingered the little silver Saint Christopher his mother had given him when he was twelve.

You'll never cut it in the Majors . . . too timid . . . brittle . . . predictable . . . no guts.

Jack took off his cap and ran his fingers through his mop of hair, as if trying to shake out from his mind the haunting words of Bruno Riazzi.

Buckskin was at the plate, and Jack knew the little center fielder had banged his slider up the middle for a single back in the seventh. He was much more confident now, but behind it all there was still the chill, the dread of what would happen if he gave up a run, or worse yet, two, in this, the final inning of the biggest game of his life.

Garcia signaled for a fastball, up and away. But Buckskin did it again, swinging fast, and lining the ball for a base hit, first pitch. Jack clenched his fist in anger, but betrayed nothing, and went back to the rosin bag, in readiness to throw to the leadoff hitter Steve Gallant.

Once more he climbed the little hill to the Ebbets Field mound, took his time, and threw one strike with a fastball, and then two balls, with another fastball and the slider, which was, he knew . . . well . . . a little timid. The count was 2–1, and Gallant ripped into the fourth pitch, banging the ball out to Rick Adams, who took the well-hit grounder hard off his chest, but still flipped it expertly to Bobby Madison for the out at second.

Joe Roberts, the third batter, betraying the tension in the Bombers dugout, literally ran to the plate. The recriminations were already starting. Spook Anderton held the pitchers blameless after Salazar, but he found it astounding that no one had hit anything worthwhile since Burrell had come in just before the end of the fifth . . . *"AND NOW IT'S THE FUCKING NINTH AND WE GOT ONE OUT AND THE GODDAMNED BALLCLUB'S CLOSING . . . THERE'S GOTTA BE ONE OF YOU CAN HIT THE FUCKING BALL OVER THE WALL AND WIN THIS THING . . . COME ON, JOE—LET'S GO!"*

Jack stared down at the Bombers shortstop, a seven-time All-Star. Tony signaled for a fastball, up and in, and the canny veteran of eleven years with the Minnesota Twins leaned right into it and let the ball hit him on the upper arm. It hurt, but Joe believed it a small sacrifice to retain the gigantic salary he was paid for a .247 average. And there was a smile on his face as he jogged to first.

Jack knew what Roberts had done and the crowd sensed it was a pretty suspect tactic, and a version of bedlam broke out, rumbling around the stadium.

The two commentators said that he probably could have gotten out of the way of the pitch—but, more importantly, Jake Imeson said, *"That was a very critical play . . . the Bombers have runners on first and second with one out, and the old homerun king Greg Diamond's on his way to the plate . . . he hits young Faber hard, the ballgame's over . . . and I know he's way past his best . . . but the last thing any hitter loses is his power . . . it's his timing that goes. And right now Greg's facing a college kid. Right now I'd say you gotta like the Bombers . . ."*

Garcia called for the slider, and Jack threw it. But again he held back on it, afraid now in this charged atmosphere to let it rip, and the hell with the expense. Greg drove it deep into left field, where Gino Rossi caught it sharply at the base of the fence. But both runners tagged up and advanced to second and third. Two out.

At this precise moment, with Jack one out from victory and the situation fraught with peril, Ben Faber leaned across and whispered to Natalie, "Do you think you love me enough to marry me?"

Natalie turned and smiled, but her reply was lost in the bedlam of Ebbets Field as Jack hurled a high fastball to Rico Fiore, and the umpire yelled, *"BALL ONE!"*

She held Ben's hand and asked him, "Will Jack throw a strike now?"

"I sure as hell hope so."

"So do I, and this is still one hell of a spot to propose to a girl."

Ben chuckled, and Jack hurled a fastball on the outside. And Rico left it. Ball two. And every heart in the Seapuit dugout was gripped with fear on the 2–0 count.

Tony signaled for another, and Jack tailed in a 92 mph fastball, going away, which Fiore greeted with a monster swing, and a mis-hit foul-back. The 'Wolves exhaled for the first time in two minutes.

It was 2–1 and Jack went to his change-up, but he hurled it in too low and again Rico left it. Ball three. A 3–1 count.

Once more Garcia called for a fastball, and again Rico Fiore almost hit the sweet spot. But for the second time he fouled it off, hooking the baseball deep into left field, thirty-eight rows back. There was a full count, 3–2, two on, two out, and a six-time All-Star at the plate, hanging on to a career batting average of .313.

Jack and Tony turned to the dugout simultaneously, and saw Ted Sando, signaling to the catcher. Garcia nodded, and Jack turned away in horror. Sando wanted the slider, the pitch he had not really thrown well all night; the one pitch which might get whacked hard unless it was perfect, the pitch his father had taught him back in Lockport, out there by the old tire.

"Jesus Christ," muttered Jack, and he stared into the field boxes, trying to find Ben, but too many people were standing. All sense of order was disintegrating. And up in the commentary box, Jake Imeson's voice was rising in the excitement. *"Right here we're gonna watch the pitch which may shut down professional baseball in Brooklyn for good. Stargill has said it, and most people believe him. The Bombers lose to these kids, it's all up at Ebbets.*

"Jack Faber throws another ball, the bases are loaded with Pete McGuire batting next . . . but if he strikes out Fiore, we will have witnessed here tonight something to touch the heart of every American sports fan—an affirmation of this great nation, who we are, and what we can achieve . . . as so often in the past, baseball will have marked our times . . . catching the American mood and rid-

ing it . . . goddammit, these kids are flexing the muscles of the United States . . ."

Down in the field boxes, for the first time in his life, Ben Faber felt he couldn't watch, but he stared transfixed at the isolated figure of his son, willing him to throw the slider, just the way he'd taught him. The big snap, right on the release . . . *Give it everything, Jackie, make sure you give it everything.*

Natalie was literally trembling, and she leaned forward, her hands clasped tight together. Suddenly she asked, "Does Tony have to catch this . . . I mean if Jack throws it past the hitter, what happens if Tony misses it?"

"Tony has to catch it," said Ben. "Otherwise the ball will bounce to the backstop and one run will score for certain, maybe two."

"Oh, my God," said Natalie.

Jack held the ball softly in his glove, raised it to his right shoulder, and felt his fingers on the red-stitched seam. He stared at Tony as the catcher went into his crouch, his right foot sliding just wide of the plate, before he rammed three fingers low and hard against his right thigh. The slider.

Jack nodded imperceptibly. And the roar from the crowd was almost frightening, the Notre Dame Marching Band was up and playing, regardless. In the Bombers dugout, Spook wanted to protest having his third baseman trying to hit in a "fucking disco." He picked up the telephone to Don Stargill's box and demanded the band be stopped.

"You want me to walk over and tell 'em to stop in the middle of this, you must be fucking crazy," snapped the Don. "Just tell Fiore to hit the goddamned ball and shut up."

By now the band was hammering out, for whatever reason, "The Battle Hymn of the Republic," and everyone cheered, the explosion of sound rising up from the open stadium into the skies over Manhattan.

Fiore stared at Jack, probing for a weakness, sure in his mind the kid's tailing fastball was on its way in at probably 92 mph plus.

And now Jack tightened his grip on the ball, deep in his glove His index and middle fingers locked hard onto the horseshoe, against the seam, while his thumb found the other horseshoe directly underneath. The batter could not possibly have perceived the change in his grip.

Jack turned slowly back toward the dugout, and in the overpowering din he could see Ted Sando yelling soundlessly, pumping his right arm. Jack did not need to hear him. He knew what he was saying *"THROW IT, JACK, FOR CHRIST'S SAKE THROW IT!"*

He began his windup, turning slowly back on his right foot, his left leg high and raised. It was old familiar lazy action, same one he adopted for the fastball. His left knee came right across his body now, his right arm pulled way back, and his were eyes glued to Tony's glove sixty feet and six inches away.

He turned his body, summoned his every last shred of strength, and hurled his arm forward. One-hundredth of a second later, he converted the fastball into the slider, snapping his wrist around clockwise, harder than he had ever dared snap it in his life, inches in front of his right eye.

The ferocity of the motion sent him forward, and his left foot crashed into his own hammered-out footprint. He kept his balance, and his fingers brushed the red dust, and he looked up to see the ball flying in at 80 mph, heading for the bat of Rico Fiore.

Rico had picked up the bloodred dot in the vortex of the ball, and he knew the ball was spinning hard. It was no fastball. And he was standing way too far back. In another tiny fraction of a second he knew his fate. Jack Faber's slider dipped down and away, viciously from its trajectory, bang against the outside corner of the plate.

Fiore swung hard. Jack closed his eyes, dreading the sound of the bang. But there was no bang; the only sounds were from the helpless swish of Rico's bat through the empty air, the whoop of Tony Garcia as he lunged forward and scooped the ball out of the air, and the bellow of Joe Catano, his right arm dragging theatrically back into his body. *"STRIKE THREE!"*

And in that instant the slim and beautiful figure of Natalie Garcia leaped from her seat, her eyes shining, her right fist clenched, held high above her head, and she was calling out *"YESSS! . . . YESSS! . . . YESSS! THAT'S THE ONE, JACKIE. THAT'S THE ONE!"*

At which point pandemonium broke out. The stadium announcer shouted formally that the Seapuit Seawolves had beaten the Brooklyn Bombers by a score of 7–6.

And Jake Imeson was beside himself, shouting wildly into the CBA microphone, *"WILL YOU STAND UP, AMERICA? . . . WILL YOU STAND UP, AMERICA? . . . THESE BOYS HAVE DONE IT*

. . . THEY HAVE DEFEATED THE BROOKLYN BOMBERS BY A SCORE OF SEVEN TO SIX RIGHT HERE IN EBBETS FIELD TONIGHT . . . AND BY GOD! THEY PLAYED THE GAME OF THEIR LIVES . . . WILL YOU STAND UP, AMERICA? . . ."

And Natalie Garcia threw herself into the arms of Ben Faber, saying over and over, "I love you, Ben. I love you. I love you. I love you."

EPILOGUE

*J*ack Faber never played baseball again, having reached what he judged to be his own lifetime pinnacle in the game. He went to Harvard Business School and gained degrees in business administration and energy studies. He and his father founded an investment fund, specializing in world oil-and-gas exploration and discovery. He later married his childhood sweetheart, Angela Landsberg.

Tony Garcia never played again either. He went back to school and completed his law degree, before accepting a partnership in his stepfather's New Orleans–based Faber Corporation.

Dr. Natalie Faber obtained her doctorate in music at the University of Tulane. She is chairman of the board of governors of the Saenger Theatre on Canal Street, New Orleans's premier venue for symphony concerts.

The family still summers in the same big white house Ben rented and then bought, right there on the shores of Seapuit Bay on Cape Marlin, one mile from Cabot Field.

Down Baseball's
Endless Highway

Don Stargill closed down the Brooklyn Bombers, as threatened. The superb Ebbets Field was purchased by the National Football League's New York Jets, marking their celebrated return to home turf after years of exile in the New Jersey Meadowlands.

Russ Maddox and Ted Sando opened a successful baseball training center on the Cape, continued coaching the Seawolves, and in time became members of the team's board of directors.

Rick Adams and Bobby Madison both retired from baseball and were commissioned into the United States Army. Both made major before the age of thirty.

Zac Colbert retired from the game and returned to Oklahoma to run the vast ranch he would one day inherit.

Ray Sweeney returned to Maine and took over the family lobster business. He worked all the hours God made, out on those deep, lonely waters. Owned three big modern fishing boats before he was twenty-eight.

DOUGHNUT DAVIS was drafted by the Diamondbacks but remained an erratic genius for three years, making AA but no further. He dropped out of baseball to run his father's car business in Savannah . . . renamed it UGA Autos. Doughnut's trademark was a big white crinkly bulldog, giving a knowing wink . . . HOW 'BOUT THEM DAWGS?

KYLE DAVIDSON's suspect shoulder haunted him for four years in the Minnesota Twins' Minor League teams. He retired and went to law school, eventually joining a partnership headed by the eminent San Francisco attorney Bill Peavey Jr.

BOOM-BOOM HACKER made it big, all the way to the Bronx, as the New York Yankees' first baseman.

CRUISER BURRELL also made it, regular closer at Fenway Park for the Boston Red Sox. He was also for years a regular visitor to Cabot Field.

BRUNO RIAZZI lasted one more year at St. Charles College before finally, in a drunken rage, attacking and injuring two of his pitchers with a baseball bat. He was committed to an institution for the criminally insane.

ACKNOWLEDGMENTS

*M*y adviser on all of the finer points of the game was Ted Novio, the towering ex-pitching coach at the University of Maine, and of the Cotuit Kettleers in the Cape Cod baseball league. Ted sat next to me throughout the many months it took to write *Slider*, planning the plays, recounting the potential outcomes, and reliving a thousand moments of high drama at Lowell Park.

Throughout the book, Ted was conveying what he would have said to college pitchers, how he would have corrected them, and what he would have expected of them. Thus, the character of Coach Ted Sando, in the book, runs very close to that of Ted Novio: full of humor, fire, fury, and a genuine understanding of the young and complicated.

We did not start the book intending that. It just evolved, replete with all the tensions of the coach–pitcher relationship in the heat of the contest. Ted's into his thirties now, still a massive presence on any mound, a wonderful teacher, and the chief coach at Mike Coutts's Frozen Ropes Baseball Training Center in Franklin, Massachusetts.

Coach Coutts was also unfailingly helpful to both of us, offering, whenever asked, opinions and insights that were gained in a lifetime in baseball, especially during his years at the University of Maine, and then during his five years as chief coach to the Cotuit team in the Cape League. In five seasons, Mike won two championships on the Cape, and he came achingly close to winning two others.

I am obliged to admit that a true story lies at the heart of *Slider*, perhaps not quite so dramatic as I have made it, but nonetheless a real and extremely emotional set of circumstances, which put a wonderful young pitcher on the razor's edge until he was helped to safety by Mike and Ted, subsequently to take his place as a Major League hurler.

I also owe thanks to my great friend Bill Koch, winner of the 1992 America's Cup, who introduced me to the mysteries of natural gas exploration in the State of Louisiana, where he once inaugurated an entire business on behalf of his gigantic family corporation.

Bill's own energy business is in West Palm Beach, Florida, and his top executive, Bud Cherry, another old friend, took an entire afternoon to write out for me precisely what happens when a natural gas field comes rumbling toward the surface. To Bud I offer my thanks.

I am grateful also for the patience of the eminent Massachusetts attorney and sportsman, Tony Tilton, who sat for many hours deciding whether the final game of the Seapuit Seawolves was *a)* possible, *b)* feasible, and *c)* legal.

In the end, after a few nips and tucks, he decided *Slider* was sound, in body and mind, which was a relief.

I have used fictitious names for all my college teams, and they play in the Cape Marlin League. Everyone, of course, realized I have based the story on various disconnected events in the Cape Cod League, in particular upon those of my own ball club, the Cotuit Kettleers. The decision to use only fictional names was made strictly to protect the innocent!

—Patrick Robinson
CAPE COD, FEBRUARY 2002